STONE IS NOT FOREVER

STONE IS NOT FOREVER

MICHAEL ANDOSCIA

CITIOFBOOKS, INC.
3736 Eubank NE Suite A1
Albuquerque, NM 87111-3579
www.citiofbooks.com
Hotline: 1 (877) 389-2759
Fax: 1 (505) 930-7244

Ordering Information:
Quantity sales. Special discounts are available on quantity purchases by corporations, associations, and others. For details, contact the publisher at the address above.

Printed in the United States of America.

ISBN-13:Softcover   979-8-89391-204-3
           eBook   979-8-89391-205-0
Library of Congress Control Number: 2024914330

TABLE OF CONTENTS

DEDICATED

To my beautiful and loving wife, Dr. Jennifer Andoscia and my wonderful children, Tekoa and Ainsley.

Part I

La Miseria

Maria-Angelina Mastradelfiori
Nato 15 Gennaio 1884—Morto 12 Giugno 1916
Riposi in Pace

The name on the tombstone blared at him, an indictment, as he brushed the vines away from its cold face. It was a whim that brought him to this hill; a whim that he was in the village at all. Now there he was, standing on that hill where he last stood...well...a long time ago, an eternity. He pushed his eyes closed trying to force the memories of this hill from his mind, down his throat, into his bowels where they would hurt his guts but touch not his heart. When he could hold his eyes closed no longer, when his sockets became sore from the effort, he allowed his wet lids to part. He stared at the stone, reading the name, Maria-Angelina, Maria-Angelina. He read it over and over praying that he was reading it wrong, that it was another Maria-Angelina, not his Maria-Angelina, his *Pratolina*.

With his good hand he caressed the chilly, gray face of the stone, and ran his fingers over the smooth, carved letters. Maria-Angelina. She was only thirty- two. Again, he closed his eyes. He did not want to think about her. He did not want to see her, so beautiful, even in his mind. He did not want her to touch his heart—not now. He only wanted to feel the cold of the stone, letters carved by a skillful hand. He wanted to be lost like his heart, his hope. 'But please Lord don't let me think about her. I can't do this right now. I can't be in pain. Please

Lord, you've taken so much from me. Now you've taken her. Don't take any more.'

It was nineteen-eighteen. The war to end all wars was grinding to a bloody end. Dom was tired. He was tired of fighting one war after another, wars with different names, different enemies, and different weapons. Not only was he tired, but he was also alone. For the first time in his life, he was truly alone. At this moment it was just him and the stone. There was nothing left of him but this tombstone, the cold on his fingertips as he closed his eyes and traced the letters over and over, begging the Lord to save him from the memories that would only bring him greater sadness. He begged the Lord to save him from the memories that kept his soul alive after months in the trenches of France and Italy; the memories that held his mind together among all the filth and the ruined humanity that surrounded him. 'Please Lord, no more. No more sacrifices.'

"*Parlo Italiano*?" A voice pulled at him from behind. A woman's voice, soft, but solid. The voice of a woman who had seen the worst and did not let it defeat her.

"*Si.*"

"*Buono.*" She continued in Italian. "I saw the uniform. Most Americans don't speak Italian."

Dom nodded and tried to smile, but the effort was too much.

The woman sat beside him on the dusty ground. She was in her mid-thirties and pretty of face, but her body bore the burden of many babies and many late nights. Such was life for women in this *paesera*. They were firm of body and then the baby making started and then...and then they were just as beautiful as they were when they were young. Yes, just as beautiful, but different. And this woman was beautiful, though her beauty would not photograph well.

"She spent much time on this hill, looking over the village. It was a very special place to her." The woman sighed. "I really don't know why, but I guess we all have our special places, don't we?"

Dom did not respond. He did not have a special place.

"And she was so pretty, too. I think every man in fifty kilometers was in love with her, but she wouldn't have any of them. Couldn't have any of them, really. But that was fine with her. Her heart was somewhere else."

It was then that Dom looked up, looked at her in earnest. He looked into her eyes and noticed the far awayness to them. She had deep, brown eyes under heavy, black brows. "Did you know her well?"

She was startled by the ease of his dialect. "You speak very well. You're from around here."

"Did you know her?" Was Dom's only reply, urgent, yearning. He did not want to talk about himself. He was not interested in himself. "What happened? Please tell me." The tears that refused to fall from his eyes crackled in his throat. "How did she die?"

The woman shook her head and pursed her lips. "It doesn't really matter. She got sick. One way to die is just as good as another. She just got sick and died. All the medicine went to the front to fight the Austrians. That's what was important. Not poor *Pratolina*. Not a drop of medicine for *Pratolina* so long as the Austrians were on this side of the Alps." She looked into Dom's eyes, wet and black like oily coal. "Everyone called her *Pratolina*. I don't know why."

Dom nodded. "Tell me about her. I really must know. Please tell me about her."

She shrugged and raised her palms. Dom's desperation was clear. She realized just how important her story could be. Those oily black eyes that lost their fire but still held the remnants of a lifetime of burning were all she needed to understand. When she realized who he was, her skin became cold, not from fear, but from the immensity of her position. She knew who he was, but he was not ready to tell her, and she had to respect that. She knew the men of this area could not be pushed lest they fall apart, run away, never to return.

"I guess I know more about her than anyone else."

Please. His eyes begged. There was so much pain, too much pain for her to deal with. Thankfully, he turned his face and stared once again at the stone, sparing her from the pain of his gaze. His eyes closed with tight creases and his dark face became red at the cheeks.

"I don't know when this started, but it seems she was in love..."

CHAPTER 1

There was something about the sound of metal on stone that intrigued Dom. Tapping, steadily tapping the chisel along the stone, gently striking the chisel head with the hammer, applying just the right pressure to remove just the right amount of stone from the face. The sound of the hammer tapping, the chisel scraping along the face of the rock was all Dom needed to concentrate.

Perhaps concentration was not the word. One would think that he was concentrating as he tapped along the face of the stone, but a closer look into those black eyes revealed something different, beyond the temporal, the mundane. It was the tapping, but Dom was beyond the tapping, part of the tapping, part of the stone. He knew that stone. He knew where it would fracture, how much would fall, how it would feel before he rubbed his fingers along its plane. He was an artist, and he was happy, and all about him was satisfaction.

That satisfaction glistened in his father's own eyes. He stopped spinning the grindstone, taking the opportunity to ponder his growing son, to stare at the beauty of his oldest surviving boy. Enrico Rossa sat straight and proud on his stool, running his thumb along the hot metal of the newly sharpened carving knife and admired the form of the boy before him, the boy...no...the man. For Enrico realized, albeit with reluctance, that he shared his home with a man, tall and strong.

Though he gleaned immense pride from this, so too came worry. As his son grew into a man it would not be long before he would have to face the treacherous terrain of manhood, a world in which his honor would be tested every day, and his soul would be under incessant attack. Soon his son, so filled with fire, would face the suffocating winds of manhood, the tearless sorrows, sleeplessness, foolish pride, and false honor.

But for now, Enrico enjoyed his son. He reveled in working with his boy, teaching him the Rossa trade, generations old. The Rossa's had always worked in stone. Rossa blood and sinew and sweat baptized stone works throughout Campania. Cathedrals in Naples, Caserta, Salerno and even Rome herself bore the immortal fruit of the Rossa blades. Enrico's mind wandered along all the walls built, columns erected, the Rossa legacy, a legacy to be handed down to Dominico, perhaps to Paolo when he got a little older, but certainly to Dominico.

For Dominico inherited his grandfather's grace with stone. Enrico's father would make love to the stone until it became exactly what he wanted it to be. 'Papa was always more than a stone carver. He was a sculptor, an artist. And so too is Dominic.' Enrico pondered this truth every day in the last few years as his son's talent blossomed. Here was Dom, seventeen years old, and had already surpassed his father's thirty years' experience with stone. Enrico never did make love to the stone. He could speak on the ethic of his own father's work, the philosophy of stone, but he was like a priest who never truly received his calling, never really saw the light. But Dominico! Dominico was something special. Dominico was destined to leave his mark and the Rossa name would shine brighter than it had in twenty years.

Or perhaps not. Enrico felt the change coming. The century had just turned and with it the entire atmosphere of the world. The very air he breathed seemed stiff and unyielding. He fought off that terrible feeling that his was the last generation of Rossas to work in stone. And such an ignoble fall indeed, for Enrico never did see the light; he never did make love to the stone. He never would.

"*Figlio*," He whispered easily to his son, careful not to disturb him, timing the interruption so as not to shake Dominico's steady hand.

"Just a little more, Papa. I'm almost done." Dom replied, a tiny ball of sweat hanging from the end of his strong, jutting nose.

Enrico smiled. His boy was arched over the emerging form of an angel. Her face turned to the sky, giving thanks for being freed from her marble prison. One day soon she would peer down on the city of Naples from atop a new library, a project consigned by the king. He tapped, gently on the stone, muscles gliding under his glistening skin. Dominico's bare back and thick arms were a reddish brown, a dark cedar painted by the summer son, for the boy refused to wear a shirt while working. Working with stone since he was eight years old had hardened his body. Like Enrico, Dom's body had become like the stone with which he worked. Though now the elder could feel his own muscles loosening, the hardness eroding away under the weight of time. Manhood, so fresh and new for Dominico, was becoming burdensome for Enrico. Soon his back would be bent, and his shoulders rounded and his body unable to sustain the relentless weight of manhood.

"*Figlio. Dominico.* Come now, you are losing your light. You'll make a mistake."

Dom, still arched gracefully over the angel, turned to his father. A broad, straight smile softened the features that only moments before were rigid with intensity. It was a confident smile, bright white teeth highlighting his black smiling eyes. Enrico laughed, reading the smile like a sign. 'Sometimes I really am a fool.'

"Dominico, you are better than I've ever been, but even you can make a mistake. Especially when you have no light. We'll get back to it tomorrow."

Dom stood and the setting sun danced along his chest, painted it gold and red. 'How easy he stands.' Enrico thought, feeling the stiffness and pain in his own back as he lifted his weight from the stool.

On legs stiff from stillness, he walked over to the angel and examined the work. This was unnecessary. There would be no criticism of the work, nothing that Enrico could add to expand upon Dominico's skill. His rough hands brushed along the sculpted wing feathers. They were perfect in every detail though they would be so high that no one would notice such quality work. Dominico could stop and claim he had finished, but he wouldn't. There was still something in Dom's mind that was yet to be transferred to the stone. The task was not finished until Dom's vision was realized.

"You've done well. Your grandfather would be proud."

The smile on the young man's face widened. He did not need the praise of his father. He knew how good he was. Regardless, there was something about his father's praise that held so much meaning. His heart drummed just a little bit harder. His soul burned just a little hotter to hear Papa say, 'you've done well.' The invocation of his grandfather was the ultimate praise. *Nono* was Papa's idol, his ideal.

"You've really learned the philosophy of the stone." Enrico stared into his son's eyes. "Stone is forever. Your grandfather and your grandfather's grandfather and his grandfather before him, they are all forever. Look all around Campania and you will see them."

Something had come over Enrico. The love and pride flowing and flowering inside of him needed to find expression. No. It was pride mixed with something else. It was pride tinged with fear. There was fear in Enrico's heart as he admired his son, body and soul. It was the fear endemic with being a man, being a father, being a tradesman, being Campanian. This fear needed expression, but Enrico could not be afraid. Men were not afraid. Twisted irony of manhood, so full of fear yet so full of stubborn, foolish pride.

"Be like stone, Dominic. Your body can only be flesh, but your mind and your heart must be like stone. So much lies ahead of you, *figlio*, you must be like stone."

Dom nodded and stared into his father's eyes. The boy's smile drifted away, for the fear that his father could not express made its way into Dominico's heart. He did not understand it. He could not define it. Yet, it was there, and it was indelible. 'Stone is forever.' Dom thought. 'Be like stone.' The mind of the new man so malleable, so fresh. This must be forever. This must be like stone.

Enrico smiled and shook his head. He clapped his son on the shoulder with his big, dry hands. The sweat of Dominico's back soothed Enrico's parched skin. "*Figlio*, one more thing. Wear your shirt from now on. We are in the middle of town."

"Papa," Dom smiled, "it's too hot for a shirt. It's July. And I like the sun on me. No one has complained."

"'No one has complained, he says.'" Enrico shouted jovially. "Those girls keep hanging around across from the work-yard there'll be some complaints, by Joseph. I'm sure they have chores they're supposed to be doing."

Dom's smile grew, his face ruddy and hot.

Enrico's eyes widened, "Oh, I see, I see," he said, waving his finger at his son. "*Le ragazze! Le ragazze!*" He grabbed his son's chin and shook his face. "You just keep your mind on your work. You're too young to be fooling with girls."

"But Papa," Dom smiled wider, "I'm almost eighteen. How old do I have to be?"

"Forty-five."

Dom winced. "Papa, you're only forty-three."

"That's right. That's right. And until I'm old enough you don't even think about it." He tapped his son's face three times with the palm of his hand; they both smiled. "Now let's go get cleaned up. Mama'll be calling us soon."

"*Signore* Rossa! *Signore* Rossa!" Dom heard hooves pounding along the hard, dirt road. The horse, brown and wet complained as the rider tugged the reigns, its forelegs springing twice in protest. There was no need for Dom to respond. He was not yet referred to as '*Signore*.' 'Someday,' he thought, 'a rider will come in and say *signore* and he will be talking to me.' Dom simply pumped the water from the well and splashed it over his hot back and chest. It was cold, refreshing after a day's exposure to the intense summer sun.

Enrico approached the rider, whom Dom recognized as *Signore* DeVallo from Salerno. *Signore* DeVallo often rode into the surrounding *paesere* with important news. Dom watched, splashing himself with water, as his father spoke to the messenger. Judging from the lathered horse this news was significant.

Yet Enrico did not look concerned. As *Signore* DeVallo seemed feverish, Enrico only shrugged and shook his head. This caused DeVallo to become even more emphatic. He waved his hands, punctuating his sentences by thrusting the back of his hand toward Enrico, then toward God. He continued to hold the reins, so his movements agitated his steed. This created the illusion that even the horse was upset by some dire, human event. Finally, Enrico nodded, and *Signore* DeVallo calmed down.

"*Grazie, grazie mille*." Enrico stroked the horse's brown, wet hip, then pat DeVallo three times on the knee.

"Papa?" Dom dried his shoulders as his father approached.

"Bah! Nonsense!" Enrico said irritably, throwing his hands up then slapping his thighs. "Umberto was assassinated yesterday. We might want to hold off on those angels."

"Someone killed the King?" Dominic was surprised by his father's attitude. He seemed more concerned with the loss of a commission than for the death of the nation's sovereign. It was not uncommon for Dom to hear his father refer to the King by his common name '*Umberto*,' Humbert.

"It doesn't really matter. This kind of stuff doesn't really matter at all. You'll learn." Enrico rarely discussed his politics with the children. This was a threshold moment.

"Do they know who did it?"

"They suspect some *Anarchico*. They always suspect Anarchists. That would make sense, wouldn't it? But in the end, it won't really matter. Talk to your grandfather. He'll tell you. He'll tell you who really makes the rules. He'll tell you that it really doesn't matter who's in charge, nothing ever really changes for men like you and me. We still spend our lives working until our bodies break counting our blessings if we can put enough food on the table for our families. Then we grow old and die, and it doesn't really matter if we die in a kingdom or a republic. And all DeVallo can think about is our alliances, but hear me, in Germany and Austria there are people just like you and me who will work, grow old and die and it won't really matter to them either. DeVallo thinks he brought me news. He brought me only more of the same."

Enrico scrubbed his face, speaking at the same time. His words became garbled in the flow of water across his lips.

"So, who's the next king?" was the only response that Dom could make to his father's polemic.

Enrico stopped cold before splashing more water on his face. His incredulous eyes bore into his son. "You weren't paying attention," he said, his voice cold and indignant.

Dom felt shame in the face of his father. He could taste his ignorance, the shallow depth of his new manhood. He could not speak. When it came to stone, he was his father's equal, even his superior in some respects. When it came to politics, to the ways of the world, Dom felt like a child. He longed to return to the stone where he could feel the exhilaration of manhood.

His father stood, a half-smile on his face. "Never mind, *Figlio*. You have time." He put his hand on his boy's shoulder.

"If all there were to life was girls and stone all would be good. But those who make the rules won't let that happen. Never! So, people rise and fight and die and assassinate kings and just when they think they are changing it all, they've only helped it to remain the same. All they're doing is thinning the herd." Enrico shook his head. "But you never mind my ranting. I've inherited your grandfather's bitterness. You'll learn soon enough. But you don't need to know now. No, by Joseph, you don't need to know now. There's so much more you need to learn first."

There was something underneath the bitterness, however. Dom lacked the experience to know what it was. He did not understand passion. But he would. He knew he would, and he was excited. The relief he felt that his father did not hold his ignorance against him was overwhelmed with the excitement that he could share in his politics. This, too, was to be short lived.

"Papa! Don Alfredo!" He pointed along the road leading into town. Three riders sauntered toward the work yard.

"Of course! *Un bel niente*!" Enrico stood, drying his hands as they approached.

Don Alfredo Belan was the wealthiest man in the area, and the voice of the *paesera*. He was the first and the last word in the town. All who lived in the village lived on Don Alfredo's land. He was the *Padrone*. Nothing was done without Don Alfredo's permission. His pale gray eyes were the eyes of the law, his heartbeat the lifeblood of the town. The way he rode affirmed his power, easy, swaying, the world waiting for him to ride through.

Halting his pale, gray steed before the gate of the Rossa work-yard Don Alfredo stared with haughty impatience at Enrico. The carelessness of his gaze reflected the impunity of his position. Dom and his father approached the fence. Enrico fastened a plaster smile on his face.

"Don Alfredo, bless me, your honor, it truly is a pleasure." Enrico pushed a congenial façade through his teeth as he kissed the man's gloved hand.

Once again shame washed into Dominico's soul as he watched his father supplicate himself to another man. He felt the weight of manhood in his heart, the complexity of it. There was his father, hardened by a lifetime of work, his body broad and strong playing the part of a good-man to a pasty-soft fop. Don Alfredo was ten years Enrico's senior, but his face was soft and white like his shirt—made from real oriental silk. He looked like a man who had never bled, never sweated, never despaired, his body lacking the color vouched by the sun and the wind and the rain.

Enrico was a stark contrast. His body was carved and hardened by the exertions of labor, tempered by the elements of life. Yet Don Alfredo could sit in judgment of Enrico. He could sit in judgment of and wave the back of his feminine hand at men, real men who could break him between their fingers if they so desired. He could wave such men off as if they were flies buzzing around his ears.

Dom could see the years of manhood pressed harshly into the wrinkles of his father's face, into the corners of his eyes, his mouth, into the grooves along his cheeks, and the lines across his forehead. He noticed, for the first time, the preponderant gray streaks in his father's hair, once coal black—once thick and full, now thin and receding. His father's left shoulder drooped slightly, the result of a dislocation he suffered while working. He knew of the pain in his father's back. Enrico never mentioned it, but he grimaced when he stood. Dom realized, for the first time that his father walked with a slight limp, he knew not why. Yes, his father's body was battered, yet it stood. It was a testament to the stone that was his father's soul.

It was this stone that Dom saw sinking. His father's soul shrunk under Don Alfredo's gaze. This feminine man before him held such power. He resembled the soft ladies in the gilded carriages, not the true men of the village. Enrico's manhood folded before this lady/man and Dom felt ashamed. A part of him retreated from his father at that moment—retreated in shame and anger. Only moments before Dom felt a kinship with his father, a kinship that he had yearned for his whole life. That kinship lasted mere minutes, for at that moment Dom wanted to run. He wanted to hide from the shame of being his father's son. He wanted to hide from his own shame. 'This will never be me!'

"*Signore* Rossa." Don Alfredo whined. "I was recently informed that the ground under my west wall is eroding. I believe you were responsible for the construction of this wall. Therefore, you are responsible for the erosion."

Don Alfredo did not speak in the usual, Campanian dialect, but a flawless, feminine kind of speech, a contrast to the course dialect that Dom spoke—course, yet…better, stronger, more passionate.

"I beg your pardon, Don Alfredo, but I told you that you would have erosion there. That's how you told me to build it."

Don Alfredo removed his gloves with a gentle gesture, revealing long, white, flawless fingers. Dom looked at his own hands, broad, brown, and dry. His cuticles were gone. The pads of his hands were rough and callused. He then noticed his father's hands, wiping the nervous sweat from his forehead. His father's hands were thick and swollen, palms like old shoe leather, knuckles wrinkled and cracked. He stared at his father's hands and looked into his own future.

Don Alfredo waved his silky hands, his fingers limp and flitting. "Never mind, never mind. None of this matters. I'm expecting this problem to be remedied immediately, and without cost. And to compensate for the inconvenience that you've cost me you can replace the cracked cobbles along my entrance."

Enrico bowed his head. "Of course, Don Alfredo. We'll start in the morning, first light. I apologize, Don Alfredo."

"Yes, yes!" The man on the horse waved his hand again and huffed the hot, July air. He put the spurs to his horse and trotted easily down the road, the two others following behind like obedient dogs.

Enrico watched the men ride away. With their increasing distance his back straightened, and his soul resurfaced in his narrowed, angry eyes. He glared at the horsemen, wishing his very gaze could pierce their soft backs, break their useless spines. Anger, fire. What was the use?

He shook his head and turned to his son.

"See, Dominico. Nothing ever really changes."

CHAPTER 2

Enrico was silent as he climbed the stairs from the workshop that led to the cottage above. It was a loud, heavy silence that pushed its way into Dom as he followed. Dom needed to be away. He needed to be away from his father. He needed to be away from the village. The silence was burning him, making his shoulders heavy, his round arms weak, his knees unsure. He'd never been present when his father talked to Don Alfredo. It was good that he never witnessed such dishonorable interactions. He wished his father had turned to him this time and said, "go help your mother," as he'd done many times before.

Seeing his father brought low, talked to in such a way as if he were some irritant that needed to be scratched with haughty words and contemptuousness worse than nails, worse than a blade. Indeed, it was better to be cut than debased by another man. Better to sustain physical ruin than injury to soul. 'This will never be me!' He swore. 'This will never be me!' But in his heart, he knew this was not true. It would be him. His future might as well have been carved into stone by his own strong, graceful hand. 'Be like stone,' was his father's words.

He looked up at his father climbing the creaking stairs. He was so much less than stone Dominico's eyes.

Enrico could feel his son's critical eyes on him. He knew that his place, secure within his son's personal pantheon, was forever lost. He was kicked out of Eden, never to return. He wished he had sent his son away, sent him to help his mother. Dom did not have to learn this lesson yet. He could spend more time seeing his father as a man of courage. But he had to learn it eventually. Oh, Dom would learn. He would understand. His soul would be scarred and marred by a thousand sabers piercing his dignity, slicing his honor. Enrico's greatest sadness was the knowledge that his son would one day be brought low. He too would have to forfeit his pride in the face of another— another of greater wealth, thus greater power. 'Be like stone.'

"Be like stone." He turned to Dominic, staring down at him from his position on the dry, rotted stairs. Enrico resented what he lost in his son at that moment. More viscerally, he resented what he knew would bring his son to understand.

Dom nodded but could not force himself to smile.

He did not understand. He could not understand. Don Alfredo owned the land. He therefore owned the people on it. There was a time when this was law. Now, in a unified kingdom full of speeches about land reform and property rights, the law was reduced to mere fact of life. Nothing had changed. The old rules remained just as they were a hundred years before, and a hundred years before that and a hundred years before that.

In fact, it could be argued that things were now worse than in the days of the *padrone* who owned the land by law. At least the feudal lords had a sense of responsibility for those who served them. But men like Don Alfredo...they were a different breed. Their cruelty was capricious. They knew no honor but their own wealth, no faith but that which they could buy. They created men with their largesse. They crushed men without rhyme or reason.

"Papa!" Paolo ran from the corner where he played with a small wooden top. The ten-year-old boy hugged his father, pressing his head into Enrico's sweaty, rounding stomach. Enrico stroked his boy's curly, brown hair.

"That's a good boy," he said. Dom smiled at his brother, wishing he could return to the happy ignorance that he saw in his young brother's eyes.

"Enrico," Sara called to him as she handed a bowl of lentils to Paolo and pointed at the table outside. Summer in Campania was outside. The heat made being indoors intolerable. Paolo grumbled but obeyed his mother. "*Signora* Patrillo has some cheese. She brought it over. We will be eating with the Patrillos tonight. It's been so long since we've had cheese here."

Enrico nodded and kissed his wife on the forehead. This was his signal that he needed to be quiet. She understood and kissed him on the cheek. She would not complain about not having cheese. That was the last thing her husband needed on his mind, whatever was troubling him.

"Hortensia went with *Signora* Patrillo to bring some chairs over."

"Where's *Nonno*?" Enrico asked, his voice low, just one step removed from the silence that cursed Dom since the talk with Don Alfredo.

"Your father's outside already. I think he's cleaning the statue."

Enrico left.

Dom felt stifled in the intense heat of the kitchen. The cottage baked from without under the July sun, and baked from within by the old, black stove. The dust in the air created a surreal mist that made everything look artificial and dirty. His mother's hair was wet and flat from sweat, her blouse stained with the salt of her body. Fatigue showed in her wide, black eyes, but still she forced a smile. Her oldest son had inherited her coal black eyes. That always made her smile. "My Dominico. Come." She opened her arms.

Dom hugged her. Her salty, wet clothes clung to his forearms. She was hot—unnaturally hot. "Hello Mama."

From behind, another set of arms grasped around both of them. Dom turned and returned a hug for Anna, his little sister, kissing her gently on the head. Dom was her favorite. She loved her brother, loved mussing his hair and running. He would chase her, pick her up, and twirl her around. Her long, black hair would fan around, and she would scream with joy.

She loved him so much. More than anyone else, Dom looked forward to hugs from Anna.

"Anna, stop bothering your brother." Mamma called out. "Is the bread ready."

"Yes, Mamma," she said, mussing Dom's hair. She giggled, as she knew her brother could not chase her in the house. "I brought it out to cool." Bread was made once a week in a clay oven behind the *casa*.

She turned to her brother, looking up into his adoring eyes. "I made you fresh bread today, *Fratello mio*."

"You're my favorite sister." He smiled.

"Of course, she is!" Hortensia's voice hissed from outside. "She doesn't make you work. Come get some of these chairs from little Bipo here."

Hortensia carried two chairs, one under each long, brown arm. Behind her was little Bipo, struggling to pull two more chairs. Bipo was *Signore* Patrillo's youngest son. Dom was not sure of his real name, nor how he got his nickname. But Bipo, despite his age and his diminutive size refused to be outdone by a girl.

"Here, Bipo, let me get those." Dom jumped.

"No, no. I can do it." Bipo protested.

"Well, let me get one. I'll feel bad if you don't let me help." Dom cupped one chair under the backrest. It was surprisingly heavy. Bipo allowed it, not wishing to make anyone feel bad.

Enrico was sitting at the table already. He was speaking to his father who had just finished cleaning the small icon of

San Giuseppe and was placing him perfectly in the center of the table. This was *Nonno*'s ritual before every meal. "*San Giuseppe* presides over our good fortune." Enrico informed him of King Humbert's assassination. *Nonno's* reflected Enrico's ambivalence at the news.

"What about the angels?" He asked.

"I don't know. I told Dom to stop working on them for now. I really don't know. There may not even be a library now."

"That's how it goes." Replied the elder Enrico Rossa. He stooped haltingly over the table to adjust the icon a bit. His hands shook from the pain this caused, but there was no complaint, no grimace or concern crossed his aged face. Every minute of his sixty-five years was carved into his body as if from a dull blade. His face was drawn and wrinkled. What was once bronze skin was now pale, almost gray. A body once robust and graceful in youth shook with strain as he lowered himself into a seat.

"Here's a chair with a backrest, *Nonno*." Dom ran to his grandfather's side. Small stools surrounded the Rossa table. The Patrillos were carpenters and wood workers, however, and their furniture was considerably more comfortable than that of a stone worker.

"You're a good boy, Dominico." Creaked the old man as he allowed Dom to place the chair under him. The elder looked up and patted Dom on the side of the face. His eyes were set deep into his shrinking skull, but they were still sharp and quick as if nothing went unnoticed. 'Be like stone,' Dom thought.

"Are you teaching him how to do business?" The elder turned to Enrico.

"Yes, Papa." Enrico bowed his head. "We had a talk with Don Alfredo today."

The elder Enrico bowed his own head, understanding the ominous meaning to that statement. "He's the son of pig and a dog." Dom's grandfather spat. "His father was the same. He was the reason for my back. And he sat and laughed as I lay there. Laughed like I was an animal."

Dom had heard this story many times. His grandfather was raising a column in the Belan *palazzo*. Alfredo, just a boy at the time, tinkered with the winch, causing the top section of a column to fall, knocking over the scaffolding on which the elder Enrico stood. Dom heard that his grandfather was confined to bed for almost four months, unable to move. He never really recovered. His back pained him for the rest of his life. This pain increased as he got older until just two and a half years ago when it became debilitating. He was no longer able to do the physical labor necessary for working with stone. He took part as best he could, but his days as a stone worker were over. It was sad how quickly and easily he was robbed of a glory so richly deserved of his skilled hands. Dom watched his father stretch his own back. He, too, suffered from an injury, though it did not seem to bother him much.

"Now you hear me." *Nonno* turned to Dom, his shriveled, pale finger arched gracefully in the air. "Your Papa is going to teach you the business. What happened with Don Alfredo was business."

The Patrillos and Rossas were coming together around the table as the last of the food was placed.

"Your Papa has a family to feed and shelter. He must be reverent to that rodent whether he likes it or not. You don't hold that against him."

"Papa!" Enrico interrupted, "He has time. He'll learn. But now it's dinnertime. Let's not discuss business at the table."

"*Va bene.*" The eldest Rossa sat with eminence at his family's table. Despite his age and disability, he was still the spiritual head of the family. Enrico had, long ago, taken over the responsibilities of the business. He was the one who put food on the table. The soul of the family still rest with the old, crippled man with the penetrating eyes.

Dom clasped his hands as his grandfather led the family in prayer before the statue of *San Giuseppe.* After the prayer *Nonno* stood and grabbed a loaf of bread, still warm, and placed it before him. In the thick crust he cut a small cross then kissed the blade of the knife before cutting a piece from the bread. This piece he placed before the statue, his hands shaking as he stretched to the center of the table. Enrico supported his father with a gentle hand on his flank, guiding him back to his seat. The families could now eat.

Signore Patrillo cut a slice of cheese, Dom noticed that it was a very thin slice, and placed it on top of the bread before the statue. Enrico and his father nodded their appreciation. *"Grazie."*

It was not unusual for more than one family to eat together. Normally, combining resources made for a more satisfying repast. It was not necessarily more food for everyone, but it was normally tastier. As it happened, the Patrillos were able to get their hands on some cheese. This cheese was eaten with the bread, and spread upon the lentils, heavy with garlic and red wine vinegar. The vinegar was the Rossa's contribution to the meal, as the Patrillos had long since run out of wine as well as vinegar.

What wine the Rossa's had was watered down to last a little longer. Enrico poured it with great solemnity before placing it before each person at the table.

Dom's mouth watered as the cheese came around to him. It had been a long time since his tongue had been graced by cheese. He smelled it, admired the texture of it, the yellowness of it. Ah, wonderful cheese. He placed the knife blade on the yellow block and looked around for disapproving looks. He could not take more than his share. As a boy he could be excused for such extravagance, but he was a man now and could no longer afford to make such a mistake.

During the meal Dom's grandfather regaled the families with tales of his great ancestor and namesake, Enrico Rossa, who served with Robert Guiscard on his campaigns through Capulia and Sicily. He even accompanied the Norman into Byzantium. He was there by Robert's side as the army marched into Rome itself to liberate Pope Gregorio from the evil king, ironically also named Enrico. Grandfather's stories were full of bravado and men of honor and courage who fought and died bravely in the name of God.

Dom loved to hear these stories. He knew little about history. Listening to his grandfather provided a much-needed manna for his curious and fecund mind. He imagined himself riding off with the Norman Knights-Errant. He especially loved *Nonno's* tales of the Knights Templar and their famous deeds. Sometimes his grandfather told more contemporary stories about building cathedrals and palaces in Naples and Rome. Yet even these stories had the same tempo and adventurous flavor to them.

And humor. There was always humor, always deep, rich laughter. Laughter that came from the soul. Souls so dulled with the mundane grayness of everyday life that they sucked up the color of laughter like dye spilled on fabric. The families fed upon laughter, the spiritual necessity of laughter, just as their bodies fed upon the physical necessity of food.

Dom learned that a meal was not just a means of meeting a physical need, to nourish the body and fill the quaking gut. The meal was total nourishment, nourishment of the body, mind, and spirit. The food may be sparse and bland, but this was only a third of the meal. The rest was the stories, the laughter and the people around him sharing a repast for the soul.

The food eaten, Anna and the women cleared the table. The flies were becoming thick as the meal progressed. Enrico poured some more wine for the men who remained seated at the table. The sun had descended two hours earlier and the evening became cool, the air fresh. The stars were brilliant in the velvety, moonless sky. The candles cast a yellow aura on those around the table. *San Giuseppe* was shrouded in gold Godly light.

"Paolo." Enrico called the attention of his youngest son who was desperate to remain with the men. "You go help Mama, then go to bed. You will be helping me and Dom tomorrow so you will have to get up early."

Paolo grunted, "Yes, Papa." He walked away, his head bowed, and his lips pursed.

"Hey!" cried Enrico. "You come here." His voice was stern, commanding. Paolo approached. Enrico grabbed the young boy's face and squeezed his cheeks harshly between his thick, rough fingers. He stared deep into the boy's eyes, his own narrowed and cutting. "What have I told you about pouting, huh?"

Paolo was silent.

"You will answer me!" Enrico demanded, shaking the young boy's smooth face between his rough fingers.

"Men don't pout." Paolo's words were distorted through a compressed mouth.

Enrico let go of his face, lifting the boy's chin with his strong index finger. "Look at me." His voice was softer yet maintained its firm nature. "Look at me. You don't ever pout or hang your head like that. You mind me. Do you understand? You'll be able to sit at the table someday."

"Yes, Papa." Paolo replied, his voice crackled. Dom knew that Paolo would cry later that night. He understood. He had gone through the same thing himself.

"Now go help your mother, then go to bed." Enrico patted his boy's bottom as he walked away. "That's a good boy."

"So, tell me about that Don Alfredo." The elder Enrico's rasping voice broke the silence as they watched Paolo walk away.

"His wall is eroding, just like we said it would."

"The west slope, downhill?"

Enrico nodded. "He did not say, but it must be. That's the only place."

Dom sat silently. He'd been allowed to sit at the table with his grandfather and his father since he was sixteen. He never said a word unless spoken to. He listened and tried to soak in as much knowledge as he could. At first it seemed that he was being ignored. He was given the right to sit at the table with the men, but his existence was never acknowledged. Lately, however, his father and his grandfather solicited his input. They asked him questions, little questions at first, but with time they became increasingly technical.

"*Mastro* Rossa," *Signore* Patrillo leaned back in his chair. The Rossa's were recognized as masters of their trade. "If I can be of service..."

Enrico raised his hands and shook his head, "*Grazie, grazie.* No. I'm afraid we can't pay you..."

"Can't pay me." Patrillo waved his hands. "I haven't paid you for the stone you made for my little Mina, may she rest in peace." *Signore* Patrillo made the sign of the cross and sent a kiss skyward to heaven, to his youngest girl who never knew more than two weeks of life. She lived long enough time to be baptized as she burned with fever. "Really, *Mastro*, it would be my honor. I want to help."

Enrico looked at his father. The elder shrugged. "*Va bene.* I don't know the extent of the erosion, but we might need help with some supports. I always wanted to put a drain there to take care of the runoff. If we use cement, would you mind building the cast?"

"No, no. That would be my honor."

Dom watched *Signore* Patrillo. 'My honor.' It always returned to that. Honor, pride. *Signore* Patrillo owed a debt to Dom's father that he could not pay with money, but he could pay with sweat and labor. Dom wondered, 'was this the measure of a man?' Sweat and labor?

In the end, honor was always expressed with sweat and labor, often blood and pain. Dom was learning the rules of manhood; he learned that though *Signore* Patrillo owed the Rossas a debt, Enrico would never ask for the payment. It was left to the other man's honor to pay. A man pays his debts and is glad to do it. This is the definition of honor.

"Well, what do you think, Dominico?" Enrico placed his sturdy arms on the table and stared at his son.

"Pardon?" blood rushed to Dom's face. He was paying more attention to the rules of the game than he was to what was being played out before him.

"How do you think we should approach this?" Enrico asked more precisely, a hint of agitation in his voice.

Dom's mind raced. This was a test, sudden and severe. He had to pass. He had to prove himself. He could not be shamed in the face of his father—not twice in one day.

"Um...Ah...Well...We really don't even know what the damage is. I mean...we haven't seen it. I guess we should go to the *palazzo* and see what the problem is, then come up with what we are going to do about it."

"No." Enrico shook his head. "Don Alfredo is going to want to see us working at once. We're going to want to start taking down that section of the wall when we get there if only to pacify him. Then we'll start from scratch."

"But this time we'll put the drain in that you wanted." Dom responded, very much out of character, but he could not allow himself to be wrong. He had to be right about something.

Enrico scratched his chin, his stubble scraping rhythmically under his leathery fingers. "Yes," He nodded. "Let's plan that drain tonight and figure out what we'll need. Let's get down to the workshop, Dominico, and come up with a design. We can also get the tools together."

"I'll come with you." *Nonno* thumped the table with the palm of his hand. Enrico assented, understanding his father's need, his father's honor, to contribute what little he could to the family trade—to be like stone.

CHAPTER 3

The night was clear, and cool as compared to the stuffiness of *la casa Rossa.* The thick walls held the torridity of day on top of the heat emanating from the iron stove. The *casa* was small and dark, crowded with stone cutting tools, cooking implements, and various paraphernalia collected over generations. True rooms did not exist within the walls. The children slept on pallets in the same room as the stove. Hortensia and Anna shared a pallet closest to the stove while Dom and Paolo did the same at the far end. A long curtain hanging from the gray rafters separated the boys and the girls. In the morning, the pallets were put up and the curtain taken down. The men would split from the women, and each would perform their appointed chores.

Enrico and Sara shared the only other room, separated by a thin, wooden wall erected when Enrico was born. It was a gift from the Patrillo family to the elder Enrico and his young wife upon the birth of their first son. Yet Enrico was not the first son. The elder Rossa had been married previously. He had a daughter from his first wife. Then a son was to be born, but mother and son did not survive the labor. The boy had died inside of her womb and brought her with him upon his gloomy, bloody birth. Such was life in Campania, ruthless and hard. Campania was for the survivors. Yet now it was becoming increasingly difficult to be among such select few. This was especially true for the poor, the peasants. Death had a special preference for the poor.

A painting of *Nonno* hung on the far wall, across from the window. One would not know it was the Rossa patriarch from the look of the faded young man who stared with stern countenance from the wall. This painting, the frame chipped and battered, stood as a reminder of greater times, days that the elder Rossa was the last to see. This was a time when the Rossa's were known all over southern Italy. It seemed nothing was built in stone that was not graced by a Rossa hand. The senior Enrico could afford a beautiful blue suit. He could afford to hire an artist from Naples to paint his portrait while wearing that suit. Every evening there was meat on the table, and a horse, new tools when he needed them. The artist adeptly captured the confidence in the young man's eyes. Time, a more adept artist, captured the fading of youth as the once sharp colors paled in the hot son of the *Mezzogiorno*.

So too, glory had faded. Enrico's son had little access to new tools. He became an expert at repairing and maintaining his own tools, choosing those that 'would do,' at the moment. He could not remember the last time he had tasted meat, or even salt. He craved salt. Or perhaps he just craved. He craved for something...something more. He craved a flavor to life that was unfairly denied him.

And Dom. What would Dom inherit? A dying trade in a dying world that he would have to face with dull and worn tools. Soon his senses would dull in this pale and flavorless village. His hopes would fade in the harsh sun. Youth, beauty, hope, pride. They all seemed to fade in *Il Mezzogiorno*, like old paint, once bright and full of promise, full of color, now dull and uninspiring.

Dom could not sleep in the heat of the house. Paolo's body so close to his own worsened the sweaty discomfort. He envied his younger brother's ability to sleep under even the most adverse conditions. Dominic recalled many sultry nights, bathed in sweat, in which his brother breathed deeply in the cool comfort of sleep. How did he do that? What was his secret? Dom had forgotten that this was his own gift just a few years ago, when he was a child, when he was not yet introduced to the weight of manhood. His body was now tight and trembling, as if his nerves would not allow the surcease of sleep. The pangs of manhood, so new, so important, how could he sleep in the heat of this?

So, Dom his father's habit. He climbed out of bed and sat by the open window relishing what little breeze caressed his face. There he occupied his mind with thoughts that he could control—man thoughts. He thought about marriage. Who would be his wife? Would his parents choose a pretty girl, one with a white smile and long black hair? Perhaps he would marry the Patrillo girl. The eldest girl had just turned fifteen. Clara Patrillo spent dinnertime barely eating, trying desperately not to look at him. Yes, she was pretty enough, her face a little plain, but her smile was white and her hair long and black, elegant hands not yet parched from the extremes of women's work.

He thought about his own work. Upholding the family tradition was of the utmost importance, and it lay with him to fulfill this obligation. This was his burden as the eldest son. Pass on the Rossa name; pass on the Rossa legacy. Though this was a burden, he loved the status. He loved the importance of it. He loved becoming a man, being looked at as a man.

Mostly, he loved working in stone, carving and scraping and smoothing the stone to the desired shape. He loved to see the character of the stone become alive under his hands, the fulfillment of his vision under the weight of his muscles, baptized with his sweat. He loved to turn around at the end of the day and see a wall where one did not exist under the dawn sun. A twisting, serpentine wall, well built, had its own essence, its own life as it rolled with the contours of the hills.

Yet Dom knew that there was so much more than working the stone in upholding the Rossa legacy. This afternoon he gained a glimpse of the darker side of being a man and a Rossa. There was an ugliness to manhood that Dom did not expect. This ugliness twisted and distorted his own father, body and soul. Dom did not understand the depth of dark abyss, but it was there.

It was then that he heard his parents talking behind the thin wall that was their only vanity. He heard the footsteps on the ancient, wood floor and could picture his father pacing, head in his hands. His mother sat on the bed, a real bed ages old.

"Enrico, come to bed. You need your rest for tomorrow."

"Rest! Rest! There is no rest!" Though he spoke in a whisper he seemed to shout. "I told that rat's bastard that there would be erosion. I told him that we could build a drain, but he wouldn't have it. He wouldn't pay the extra expense. Now we'll have to put it in for free and this is my fault. God knows how long it will take. What will we live on until then?"

"We'll get by Enrico. Come to bed and rest."

"We'll get by. Isn't there more than getting by? We're always getting by. We used to work for princes and dukes and generals of the army. There used to be meat on the table. Now look at us! And it'll only get worse. The work for stone carvers is almost gone. So, we learn to build walls like common laborers. Now there's almost no need to build walls anymore. Everyone is leaving. There are no more princes or dukes, only *padrone* who steal food from our mouths."

"Enrico, please. You'll be half asleep tomorrow. We'll be all right."

"I can't even marry my own daughter. She'll be a spinster, I guess! We have no dowry for her, who will take her? Am I to marry her to some peasant? She'll be a peasant wife, all dirty and living underground!"

"Please. Let the Good Lord provide." Sara stood up and placed a comforting hand upon her husband's hard, brown arm. He was hot, burning from the inside. Then she smiled. "The Patrillo girl is almost of age. Clara. Perhaps the Patrillos have a dowry for her. She and Dominico would be a good match and carpenters in the family might help business. We can then use that dowry for Hortensia."

Enrico stopped pacing. A solution. He heard a solution for one of his many problems, and his fatigued mind grasped at it. "I did see her walking with her mother in the marketplace last week. They must be ready to marry her. They must have a dowry."

On the other side of the wall Dom's face flushed. He was to be married. His heart raced. He was to be a husband, a father, like his own father. Without shame he pressed his ear to the wall.

"Yes, my husband. I spoke with Sophia this afternoon. There is a dowry. Talk to *Signore* Patrillo. We can work something out."

Enrico nodded, "Yes. Tomorrow. I will see Patrillo tomorrow after I return from the *Palazzo*. Yes. After we talk about the wall, we'll discuss Dominico and Clara." Enrico sat on the bed, rubbing his temples in furious circular motions. "Yes, that is good, that is good." He laid back. Sara stroked his hair until she fell asleep. But Enrico never slept.

Dom was awake when his father stepped out of the bedroom. The sky was turning a deep blue just before sunrise.

The air was too dry for reds and yellows. Dom dressed by the pallet and looked at his father. He could not repress a smile, his face scarlet, almost red enough to be seen in the gloom of the *casa*.

"*Figlio*. You are in good spirits this morning." Enrico tried to smile, but he was not looking forward to the day. His head ached, his eyes heavy from sleeplessness.

"Yes, papa." Dom replied then bent down and gently rocked Paolo. "Paolo, get up. We must go."

Paolo stirred and stretched, moaning loudly, his glassy eyes gazing upon a new day.

"*Ragazzo*." Enrico tapped the pallet with his foot. "I want you to go find Georgio. Let him know we'll need his help. Go now."

"Yes papa." Paolo lifted himself from the pallet and stretched the sleep from his muscles.

"Hortensia." Enrico thumped the curtain. "Some bread."

A long, bronze arm raised and untied the curtain from the rafter. Hortensia folded the cloth from the end. "Anna, get Papa some bread. And that jar of olio."

Anna was already sifting the ashes as Sara filled the bin with kindling, preparing the stove for that evening's dinner. She reached into the breadbox and pulled out a crusty, brown loaf, still warm from the night before. She handed it to Enrico with a wide smile. Anna arrived with the olio. "Here, Papa."

"Thank you, *Ragazza Mia*. You are a good girl." Anna blushed and lifted her tiny shoulders with pride.

"Papa," Dom called. "I'll get Bruzzo ready. I already sorted the tools."

Enrico nodded, "Very good. Here." He handed his son a piece of bread dipped in olio.

Dom nodded with an unusually broad smile and turned for the door to the shop. He braced himself. It happened every morning before he walked out of the house. Anna stopped what she was doing, ran across the room and locked her arms around Dominic's waist, pressing her tiny, red head into his stomach. Dom hugged her and stroked her unkempt, morning hair. "I'll see you tonight, *Sorella Mia*. Will you make me something special."

"I will, Dominico, I will." She smiled and ran back to the stove, pulling the ashbin and dumping the ashes out the window.

Dominico bit into the bread, the garlic was heavy in the olio. He savored the bite as he walked into the shop.

Bruzzo was an old mule whose will was as strong as his body. Dom learned long ago that he needed to be stroked gently in the morning or the day's work would not get done. For some reason Dom seemed to be the only person who could persuade the animal to move in the early hours and keep him moving throughout the day. As Dom approached, Bruzzo stomped his left foot three times, shook his head, and stared defiantly at the young man. But he did not bray, and Dom interpreted this as a good sign.

"Here, Bruzzo. Here you go old man." Dom held out a piece of bread to the old, gray mule. Its soft lips pulled the bread from Dom's hand and its mouth clapped and chomped loudly.

Dom hugged the animal's big, ugly head and scratched him under the chin for a few minutes. "Now, Bruzzo, we have some work to do today. It's very important work," Dom whispered into the mule's flinching ear. He fanned the flies from around the noble creature's face. "Today we go to Don Alfredo's *palazzo* so you must be at your best behavior." Dom continued to caress the animal along its neck and shoulders. Its hair was dry and course, almost sharp to the touch. "Do you understand?"

Bruzzo nodded in exaggerated circles but made no noise. All four feet stayed on the ground. He enjoyed the garlicky taste of the olio as much as Dom.

"That's a good boy." Dom placed the leather satchel full of tools over the mules curved and bony back. He was careful not to let it strike the animal's flanks too hard. Bruzzo was temperamental and did not like to be misused. "There you go."

Dom then picked up a leather strand with three chimes tied to it. "That's right, we have a long walk." He placed the chimes around Bruzzo's neck. The chimes calmed the animal on long walks, especially when Bruzzo was expected to pull a wagon loaded with mortar and brick.

"Can I lead Bruzzo today, *Fratello*?" Dom turned and noticed Paolo standing in the work-yard with Georgio. Georgio was a peasant boy whose family wanted to apprentice him to Enrico. He was to learn a trade and help save his family from inevitable starvation, but there was not enough work to do, and Enrico could not accept the apprenticeship. Georgio was a hard worker and a surprisingly smart boy for his station. Enrico felt that he would make a fine brick or stone layer, but no stone carver. Even at that, he would be successful if only there were enough work. When there was work, however, Enrico called on the young boy to help. He taught Georgio what he could, then sent him home with some food. When possible, he paid the boy with cash, but money was hard to come by.

Dom was wary of trusting his young brother with the responsibility of leading the old mule. Paulo was too young and light of step. He had no patience. Bruzzo was old and cantankerous. He did not like to be rushed. If he felt that he was being pulled along, or walked too fast, he would sit where he stopped and no amount of pulling or whipping could entice him to move. Dom knew just the right pace to keep Bruzzo satisfied.

"I don't know." Dom looked at Paolo through the corner of his eyes.

"Please, Dominico. I'm big enough."

"All right. But you don't walk faster than I walk."

"I won't, Dominico."

"And you watch your step. The roads are full of ruts."

"I will Dominico."

"And if he sits down, you're getting him up, or you're carrying the tools the rest of the way."

"All right, Dominico.

The road was dry and dusty. Only the *piazza* was cobbled with red, cracked brick. What few roads there were in the village were packed dirt worn into the earth by two thousand years of feet and hoofs and carriage wheels. Of late, there was little traffic. The roads became dry and cracked in the summer sun. The cracks were often so wide that a person's foot could fit easily. Many horses and mules had to be put to rest after breaking an ankle in the wide cracks.

Paolo did a fine job leading Bruzzo to the *palazzo*. He was proud that his brother trusted him. When Enrico noticed Paolo holding the reigns he stared at Dominico. "I told him he could." Dom assured his father, who shrugged, handing his youngest son a piece of bread.

The walk to the *palazzo* was long and ominous. Even Georgio, always happy and energetic considering his station, was captured in the morose pall of the day. Dom's earlier glee hardened as he walked along the arid earth. His youthful vigor drained from him like the moisture of his skin in the noon sun. He did not say a word.

The only member of the party immune to the dolorous atmosphere was Paolo. His only feeling was pride in being trusted to lead Bruzzo. This became an irritant to the rest of the party, especially Dom, who was the target of his brother's ill-timed good humor.

"I think I'm doing well in leading Bruzzo. Don't you, brother? Can I lead Bruzzo again, tomorrow? Bruzzo likes me. I can tell he likes me just like he likes you Dominico. Do you think he likes me, Dominico? Maybe I can help you get Bruzzo ready tomorrow. Would you like that, brother...?"

Dom and Enrico listened in silence. Paolo's voice became an incessant fly swirling around their ears,but it was not his fault. He was a boy, and not subject to the stern realities of men. Indeed, Dom reasoned it was his own fault for letting the boy lead the mule. He did his best to answer Paolo's questions with short, curt answers and ignored the rest.

They approached the southwest corner of the Belan estate and stopped the mule.

"There it is." Enrico pointed. "Look, right at the corner, just as I thought."

"It's not as bad as I thought it would be." Dom commented.

"It will get worse if we don't fix it right. Paolo."

"Yes, Papa."

"Take a chisel and separate the mortar at those seams on the top shelf, there, there, and there. We're going to redo that whole section. Dominico, lift your brother up onto the wall."

The Rossa's set to work. Georgio emptied the wagon while Paolo separated the mortar from the shelves. Enrico and Dom, using hammers, broke the façade and revealed the bricks inside. It was going to take a lot of work, but Enrico was determined to get that wall down by the end of the day. However, this would not be the only wall to come down on this day. Dom did not realize at that time, but he was at a crossroads and the walls that contained his heart would not be standing when the sun set.

CHAPTER 4

Hammer striking stone, a sharp, trembling rhythm, a heartbeat resolute though faltering. Fatigued arms lift the hammers, heavy, awkward, shoulders strain, round and knotted arms glisten wet and sanguineous. Then the dance of the swing, a slow-motion study in muscular perfection. The hammer strikes the stone, violent and harsh. The arm shakes, smooth and gliding muscles become sharp and angular, resenting the sudden and irresistible halt of their grace. The head of the hammers striking the thick stone of the wall, shaking and shocking the bronzed bodies of the men who wield them like some sick interruption of an otherwise sensual dance. Again, the process starts, the pull, the arch, the violent strike the end of the dance.

Enrico and his son kept a perfect rhythm despite their fatigue, one striking the stone after the other. Shards and dust rose, cracks spreading along the surface of the wall. One strike, cold clank, then another, then another sharp, coughing, hacking sound. Then the break—one could see a section of the wall give, loose itself and shake sickly against its innate solidity.

Dom stepped back as a large section of brick and mortar fell flat in a great slab, a deadening thud, like a giant falling dead. Dust floated from the parched ground in a wan yellow cloud about the men's feet. For a moment, the hammers were still, and the dancers tended their aching muscles.

"Paolo, Georgio. Separate these bricks. Keep the ones that are not broken. We'll be using them again. The ones that are broken, put in a pile over there. When you're done use the chisels to separate the mortar."

"Yes, Papa."

Enrico and Dom eyed their work, stared at what was left and then focused their attention on the rising yellow sun. "I'll have this section down by sundown. We need to keep working. We'll go to the other side while the boys pick this up."

Dom understood his father's desire to be done with this job. This was not simply a matter of repairing a wall. This was a matter of the soul, a blight to his work, his pride. It was a sickness best pushed through as quickly as possible. His father's virus showed in his ruddy face.

Sweat seeped from his brow, his fever, the wrinkles that circumscribed his cheeks were deeper, longer. Enrico was old, sad, in pain. This task would be his ruin. He knew it. There was nothing else, nothing more to do but to push through and finish the job. Finish with the wall, the drain. Finish with the *Padrone.* Then rebuild with what remained. Rebuild. The hammer striking the stone, harsh sound, sharp and violent, slowly chipping away. Rebuild. The hammer striking the stone, the soul, chips falling into the dust weakening the structure, the whole. It would fall. Soon it would fall to the dust, never to be the same.

How small the half-naked humanity striking at the stone, their hammers so much like twigs compared to the great structure surrounding the *palazzo*. How fragile the flesh against the stone. How relentless the clanking sound of the hammers' relentless striking and chipping, fractures no wider than hair, then another and another, a dozen more, a hundred more. Chips falling to the dust. Then a brick comes loose--one insignificant brick. Then another. Then the fall, floating yellow dust. Another hole in the mighty wall. Another weak point in the structure. One more sadness.

The unforgiving sun rose slowly, over the *Mezzogiorno*. The sky, once blue with the promise of morning, became pale with the unrestrained heat of noon until it seemed almost white, burning everything it touched. Even Enrico removed his shirt, brown skin beginning to show the spotting and soiling of age contrasted sharply beside Dom's smooth bronze. Sweat glazed their skin, matted their black hair streaked into their burning eyes. Yet they worked on, striking the stone, squinting as chips of rock stung their faces. The sun knew no mercy, no rest, glaring down upon the earth, upon Campania, upon the Rossas. The still air, not so much as a single breeze, weighed against their wet, burning skin.

They stopped for water that they carried with them in canvas flasks. It was cool and tempting. Dom had to fight the urge to slake himself completely, to empty the flask into his dry and gritty throat and experience a moment of contentment. But he was only halfway through the day. There was more sunlight left, and sections of the wall still stood.

Of course, it stood. Enrico stared at his handy work. It was built to stand, built by Rossas. It was strong and thick. Even relentless Campanian weather could not mar the Rossa wall. Weak and withered, the earth may erode from beneath causing it to fall, yet the earth would give way before the wall. 'Be like stone.'

Be like stone. Though the earth beneath you might be washed away, be like stone. Enrico ginger fingers probed the wall. Mortar, dried and cracked, traumatized, crumbled to his touch. Mortar is not stone. Be like stone, for stone is forever.

Dom could no longer bear to look at the damnable wall. It had become his entire existence. It was all he could see. His vision narrowed on the tiny spot on which his hammer must fall. His aim was true and strong, the rock gave way to his focus, his will. Yet all he could see was the next tiny spot. There were no trees, no white sky, no sun. Only rock and mortar, dust and heat. Cracks and chips, falling stone and swirling dust were his only reality.

Finally, Dom diverted his focus. He scanned the trees that grew beside the estate grounds. Cool, green grass grew under the trees' thick canopy. It was the grass that broke the young man's focus. It was a rich forest green. How perfect the scene before him, rows of verdant trees lined the wall jutting up from an emerald river of grass.

Then a graceful, golden foot appeared from behind one of the trees. One small, graceful foot stepped into the grass—one irrepressible light, a gentle breeze. A dark-haired nymph in a blue, flowery dress, stepped into the grass, into his sight. She would soon, with equal grace, step into his life. Unaware that she was being observed, she stooped, reaching for something on the ground. Her tiny tan fingers plucked at something. *Pratoline*. Small daisies growing in the dappled shade of the trees.

Dom closed his eyes, pressed his lids together. He wiped away the sweat from his lids. When he opened his eyes, she was standing, caressing the flowers with her fingertips. She held the flowers to her breast and stooped to pick some more. Her motions fluid, a cool breeze in a tiny field of daisies. Dom's skin became cool, healed by the breezy oread as she placed the white flowers into the curls of her long black hair.

Her hair hung just below her shoulder blades brushing the elegant curve of her back. Dom had only ever seen his sisters with their hair down. She brushed it back. Dom's skin became cooler, yet he blushed. Her neck was long and brown, curving slightly under a perfect, round chin. He forgot about the wall. The sun and the dust were dim and distant. Only she remained. Only the presence of this breezy oread meant everything to him. She was beautiful. Her golden-brown neck, her long black hair, her graceful bare feet. He felt like he was standing next to her though he was fifty meters away.

"Hey, *figlio*. Let's get started."

His father, in his ignorance, had shaken Dom from the bliss he found. Enrico could not see the Grass Nymph from where he stood around the corner. "Yes, Papa." Dom tried desperately to keep her in the corner of his eye as he picked up his dusty hammer. Not watching where he was going, he tripped over some fallen brick. He turned, flushed scarlet, to see if his father saw his misstep.

"Are you all right, Dominico." Enrico offered a sly smile. He could see Dom blush. Once he knew his son was unhurt, Enrico derived some satisfaction from this rare moment clumsiness on the part of his son. It was his first laugh of the day.

"Yes, Papa." Dom picked up the hammer then glanced back at the stand of trees. She was gone. The heat returned to his bare skin.

As the sun descended, Enrico and Dom dug the base rock from the crusty ground. The corner of the wall was gone, a large, surreal gap, a cancerous sore in the polished and precise structure. Enrico felt the cancer in his soul, in his empty stomach, as he lifted a piece of slate and carried it to its corresponding pile.

Dom's stomach growled, empty as well, but the work had to be done. Hunger was not unusual for the Rossas. The skin, tight on their bodies, was quite obviously not of the idle class, *gli Galantuomini,* soft with luxury and satiety. Dom continued to dig, to work through his hunger.

Along the road a peasant walked sullenly, his head down, chin tucked into his gray and mangy beard. An old, swaybacked donkey limped behind him, its legs thin and marred with cankers. The animal shook like old parchment with every step.

Dom's shovel cut into the earth. He pried another slab that his father lifted from the ground with his dried, cracked hands. It was then that he turned to see the estate. He had never seen the *palazzo* grounds before. They were always hidden behind the forbidding wall. Now, through the gaping hole he and his father broke he had access to another world. It may have been a different universe.

He tried not to look into this other world, the *latifundi.* He did not belong there. There was no sense looking into a forbidden world, for such leads to coveting, to desire for a life that's not your own. But he had to see. He had to know a world he could never have. Once he looked, his amazement could not be quenched. Grass. The entire area was carpeted with dark, thick grass. Trees lined the property in neat rows. These trees would bare olives and nuts and figs later on in the year. They were tended and pampered by groundskeepers, *gli giornalieri.*

Following the rows of trees deeper into the estate, Dom gasped as he gazed at the front of the *palazzo.* It was a palace of great standing and elegance. Its grandeur was no surprise to Dominico. What slackened Dom's jaw was the fountain. A large, marble fountain stood tall at the steps of the *palazzo*. Clear water flowed in ceaseless streams from stone ewers held by stone women, falling crisply into stone leaves until reaching the stone pool.

One might think that Dominico would be enthralled by the quality of the statues, the precision and artistry of the sculptor. No. Not this time. It was the water. The clear, cool water seemed to come from nowhere. During the summer season the best those who lived on the other side of the walls could look forward to was pale-yellow water coaxed desperately from the well. The water he and his father had been drinking was a reddish brown and full of grit. It had been boiled and was safe to drink, but here was perfectly clear flowing water being used as a decoration.

There was no sense thinking about it, for it was not his world.

He looked back at the rows of trees and that's when the breeze caressed his torso, neck, and face. He did not recognize her at first. Her hair was pulled back and wrapped neatly on her head, no longer decorated with the *pratoline*. She was no longer bare foot, but constrained, guarded—no longer graceful, but erect and rigid. Dominic did not recognize her, but he felt her, felt her breeze, her light. She was no longer the Grass Nymph, yet her presence remained the same.

Stiff and wary, she walked next to a young man Dom recognized as *il Piccolo Alfredo,* Don Alfredo's son. He was dressed in a black suit and tie, walking with his hands clasped behind his back. It was strange how men who never created, never worked with their hands, walked with their hands behind their backs as if they would have nothing to do with them—as if even swinging their hands as they walked was the mark of the inferior, working class.

Behind the couple, following at about ten meters, were two older women and a passel of children. The children were running and laughing zigzagging through the trees. One of the women was the dark-haired girl's mother, Dom knew, the other was likely an aunt. Neither woman looked old enough to be a grandmother. *Il Piccolo Alfredo* was courting Dom's oread with the long black hair, taking her for a walk along the estate that he would someday inherit. He was letting her know without overtly telling her, that he would be a good husband. Through him she would enjoy a life of comfort that no other man in the village could provide. He, and only he, could bring her into this world of grass and trees and crystal-clear water flowing from fountains. The mother and aunt followed the couple to ensure that the girl remained 'marriageable' and that no improprieties, or even rumor of impropriety, could attach itself to the girl and detract from her pristine value.

Enrico stopped to get a sip of water. When he noticed that he and his sons were in the presence of women he picked up their shirts and threw them to his sons and Georgio, putting on his own. His movement caught the eye of the girl with the long black hair. She looked over at them, then her eyes rested on Dom as he wiped the sweat from his chest and back with the shirt before donning it. Dom could feel her looking at him, feel the breeze of her gaze. She was too far away to really see her eyes. She could have been looking at anything, a bird, a dog, anything, but she was looking at him—her gaze touched Dom's body, which lost its integrity, its stone-like quality.

She then turned to look at her suitor as he pointed out some trees. Her lissome neck now stiff and unnatural. She smiled and nodded. Dom could not hear her polite sigh in response to Alfredo's boasting.

Enrico handed his son the flask of water. It was noticeably light. There was not much left to drink. "Take the last of it, *figlio*. We'll be going home soon."

Dom gulped the last of the gritty water. It was wet and cool, and he could feel it fall down his throat and into his gut. Its coolness dissipated inside of him as his body sucked the water like dry ground in a gentle rain.

He pierced the ground with his shovel again, pulling up another piece of slate. However, he only looked at the ground when he needed to place the blade before stepping on it and pushing it into the earth. The rest of the time he kept his eyes on the girl with the long, supple neck, whom he had named 'Pratolina'—Daisy. She and the younger Alfredo were approaching. Soon they would be close enough for him to truly see her. Of course, then he would have to be most careful. He could not look at her for the sake of propriety, but he must look at her for the sake of his heart.

The only distraction was the guards at the gate as the peasant approached. The gate opened and the dirty old man and his mule were allowed to enter. A foreman on horseback galloped to Alfredo and pointed to the gate. The couple could not see the gate from where they were in the trees, but Alfredo must have been informed of the visitor. He reached for Pratolina's hand and cupped it within his own, begging her pardon, as he must take momentary leave of her. She acquiesced politely, understanding his position. As Alfredo walked away the mother and aunt stood with her. The children continued running and laughing through the trees.

The old *contadino* limped to Alfredo as he stood like an imposing statue at the end of the column of trees. Enrico and Dom stopped their work and watched the proceedings not only out of curiosity, but out of concern. Interaction between a *contadino* and a *padrone*, even a future *padrone*, did not bode well.

"Signore Belan," the peasant bowed his head, looking only at the young man's shoes. "I've come to satisfy my debt to the *padrone*." His voice was faint, trembling with his dirty, gray chin.

Pratolina held her hand up to her mother who was urging her to leave. Men's business was not for the scrutiny of women. But Pratolina wished to see what was to happen, and her will was strong. She watched Alfredo and the peasant with probing curiosity.

"So, you've raised the money, old man." Alfredo smiled. "Where is it? In the satchel?"

The old man shook his head. "I have no money. There were no crops. The locust got to what did not burn up in the sun when the river dried. I have no money, but *le Padrone* insists on payment…"

"Get to the point, *vecchio topo*." Alfredo huffed.

"Please, *Signore* Belan. Accept *mio asino*. She is all I have. There is no more."

Alfredo laughed, looked up at his foreman who smiled without humor. "This old bag of gristle. What am I to do with this old thing? If it lives through the summer, we could feed it to the dogs. That's about it." Alfredo turned to Pratolina, shrugged, and offered a mocking gesture. Pratolina's stoic expression did not change. Alfredo continued, "No, you must come up with the money."

The peasant closed his eyes. His brows were thick and white, furrowed over his crooked, pockmarked nose. Tears welled and then streamed from under his dingy, wrinkled lids. "She's all I have…she's all I have."

Alfredo walked over to the animal, hands clasped firmly behind his back. He did not want to get too close as the flies that circled the animal offended him, and the odor of livestock was beyond his ken. He walked completely around the trembling, old donkey until he stood in front of the peasant again.

"Three *lire*." He said, "And the *Padrone* is not going to be happy."

"Three *lire*!" The peasant fell to his knees. He reached for Alfredo with desperate, shaking hands—hands stained permanently from a life in dirt, soil, and manure. Alfredo, by reflex, stepped back and the peasant fell forward, unable to catch himself. "I owe the *Padrone* ten. I owe ten. What am I to do? This is all I have. There is no more."

"That's not my problem. You complain. You should be paying me to take this thing off your hands. Three *lire*. No more. You'll have to come up with the other seven. Now go before I change my mind."

"Please, *signore*, please!" The peasant cried, tears streaking his soiled face. "She's all I have. There is no more. Please, *Signore*!"

Alfredo turned to his foreman, hands still behind his back. "Get this cur out of my sight."

The foremen trotted his horse to the peasant and clasped him around his frayed collar.

"PLEASE, *SIGNORE*, PLEASE! I BEG YOU! SHE'S ALL I HAVE." The foreman dragged the peasant. The tattered canvas that covered his feet, protected them from the hard, hot road, were torn from him. The peasant was dragged out the gate and dropped like a sack in the middle of the road. His heals bled.

The peasant stood and tried to enter the gate as it was being closed, only to be struck and pushed by one of the guards. He fell backward, landing flat on his back, the wind forced from his lungs. It was minutes before he moved.

Dom stared at the old man. He dared not approach, but his heart went out to him. He turned to look through the hole in the wall and stepped backward as if pushed by an unseen force. Pratolina was staring at him. Her eyes, wide and brown, locked on his. She was confused, looking at Dom as if he could explain what they had both witnessed. But there was no explanation. That was the way it was on this side of the wall. Be like stone. Dom could only look at her and shake his head. He wanted to communicate something more meaningful, but he did not know what. Why was that important? There was no reason. It just was. He wanted to say something to her through his eyes. Even though he did not know what he wanted to say, somehow, he knew she would understand. He lifted his eyes in her direction, filled with one last, unspeakable message, but his view of her was blocked by the younger Alfredo as he approached the Rossa work site.

"So, what have we here?" Alfredo stepped up to Enrico, a malignant look in his eye. "It looks like you've made quite a mess of things."

Enrico shook his head. "We're going to put in a drain to stop the erosion, *Signore* Belan. As your father requested. We had to take this part of the wall out."

Alfredo nodded, an exaggerated frown on his face. "And just how do you propose keeping the curs out?"

"I beg your pardon, *Signore* Belan," Enrico shook his head, his round, knotted shoulders jutting up.

"The curs, the curs. Those mangy pests that walk around the town eating feces. How do you plan on keeping them out? If they get in, they'll defecate all over the place and may very well ruin my mastiffs. I have no intention of having to drown a litter of mutts just because you had to put a hole in our wall." Alfredo's tone rose in mocking condescension. Dom could feel his blood becoming hot, but he stood silently as his father was brought low once again. "So, I ask you one more time, you piece of trash. HOW ARE YOU GOING TO KEEP THE CURS OUT!" Alfredo's face almost touched Enrico's. His eyes wide with anger.

"I...I...I did not give that any thought. We...I guess we could build a fence, but we are losing our light. We won't have time. I need to get some wood..."

Alfredo pushed Enrico. Too solid to fall, solid like stone, Enrico took one step back to appease the young tyrant.

Alfredo held up his hand as if soiled from Enrico's sweat, the water of his life. "Enough! One of you will just have to stay here tonight and keep the curs out."

Enrico's eyes narrowed. His lips quivered with repressed anger. He stepped forward.

"I'll do it, Papa." Dom intervened. He could tell that his father was having difficulty controlling his anger. Losing one's anger with the son of the *Padrone* would have ruinous consequences. "I can stay."

Enrico shook his head. "*Figlio*, no. You need your rest."

"Not as much as you and Paolo, and little Georgio. Really, Papa, I haven't really been sleeping anyway. It's too hot. It's OK."

"Well, I'm sure you two will figure it out." Alfredo yawned waving his hands in his father's feminine fashion. "But let me tell you this. If one cur comes into the estate, the *Padrone* will not be pleased! He really loves his mastiffs." He walked away, wiping Enrico's sweat from his delicate hand.

"It's all right, Papa. Go home. I'll be all right." Dom turned and looked at Pratolina once again. Despite her mother's protestations, she had moved closer and could hear what transpired. Dom could see her. He could see the sadness in her eyes. He could see the depth of spirit that they betrayed as she returned his gaze, looked into his own eyes. She apologized to him with her eyes as Alfredo took her by the hand and led her down another row.

The older women followed at the prescribed distance as the couple disappeared into the branches. The children ran amok between the trees.

CHAPTER 5

"*Fratello!*" Dom looked up from his lap where he sat and contemplated in front of the fallen wall. Anna was running toward him, her little legs pumping. Her red hair bounced loosely behind her a great, white smile upon her face.

She held a lantern in her right hand to light her way. A cooking pot dangled from her left, the silver sheen long since dull and dented. Between the handle and the cover of the pot were two pieces of bread, wrapped with a tattered, clothe napkin. She ran stiff and tall to keep from spilling the contents of the pot. She was mostly successful.

Dom could smell the garlicky contents as she approached, and his mouth watered. His stomach pulled at him from inside, growling anticipation. He stood as he waited for his sister to reach him, his arms out for an embrace.

He was not disappointed. Anna was careful to put the pot on the ground. One did not take chances with food. Once the pot was secured, she sprang like a cat into her loving brother's arms, her legs wrapped around his waist, she kissed his cheek.

She clung to him with a strength that betrayed her ten years of age.

"I've missed you, *Fratello*." She kissed him on the other cheek.

"Come now," Dom smiled. "Cut it out. I've been swinging a hammer all day." He took her under the arms and pried her from him, holding her out in front of him. She was so light. It seemed to him that a girl her age should be heavier, but he refused to let bad thoughts enter his mind. Not about Anna

"I've missed you, too." He smiled and placed her gently on the ground.

"Papa was going to send Paolo with your food, but I asked him if I could come. Paolo was very tired." Anna twisted back and forth, her hands behind her back, her chin tucked coyly into her shoulder.

"I'm glad you did. You are my favorite sister."

"I brought your food. Mama said I must make sure you eat it all. Mama said you'll need your strength for tomorrow." Anna brought the pot to him. A lentil soup steamed from inside as Dom opened the lid. He dipped a piece of bread in the soup and ate the soggy end.

"I brought you a clean shirt." Anna reached behind her where the shirt was folded and tied to her apron. "I cleaned all of your shirts today."

"*Grazie mille*." Dom took the shirt from her but put it aside. "I'll put it on when I'm done eating. I don't want to spill anything on it. You've eaten, haven't you?"

"Yes. Mama made me eat before I could come. I didn't want to wait, but Mama made me."

Dom loved the attention he received from his sister. She loved him so very much. He could feel it warming his soul. Anna walked around him, looking into the estate exposed through the wall. She saw the grass, the trees, the fountain, but seemed only partially interested. Mama told her not to talk to her brother too much while he was eating, so she endeavored to keep herself busy. Mama said that making him talk so much would give Dom a tummy ache. Anna did not want to give her big brother a tummy ache. Indeed, she strove only to make him happy.

Dom accepted her silence, but ate quickly, knowing that it was difficult for his little sister to ignore him. In fact, Dom did not want to be ignored. He loved Anna. She was his favorite person in the world. Her spindly little body and big blue eyes. Blue eyes were such a rarity in this region. Her smile made him happy. He felt warm and cheerful inside.

As he swiped the last of the soup from the pot with the last piece of bread Anna came and sat beside him, hugging his big chest, listening to his heart beat strong under his ribs. "Why do you have to stay here, Dominico? Why can't you come home?"

Dom smiled, 'why indeed,' he thought. He shrugged. "I have to keep the dogs out."

"Why?"

Dom laughed. "I don't know. I guess Don Alfredo doesn't want them messing up his property." But Dom knew. He knew that it was the *Padrone's* way of bringing them low, sapping the pride from the Rossa heart. However, *il Piccolo Alfredo* was using a flawed strategy. Dom took pride in the fact that he could care for his family by keeping watch. He would remain awake the whole night, not daring to sleep, not daring to allow a blight to his honor and the honor of his family. No, the Don himself could not have his pride—be like stone.

Anna closed her eyes, concentrated on her brother's heartbeat--her favorite heartbeat. "Dominico?"

"Yes."

"Are you a man now?"

Taken aback, Dom did not really know how to respond. Only a child would ask such a question. How beautiful that she should ask so crisply what is normally so vague and little understood. Dom struggled to answer. He ran his fingers through her soft, red hair. "Yes," was his only response, but it seemed inadequate. There was so much more that Dom did not understand. He felt the need to explain but lacked know-how.

"Papa said you're a man now." Anna sighed.

Dom swallowed hard. His sister could hear his heartbeat quicken, pounding harder.

"I guess."

"Does that mean you can't play with me anymore." Her voice was faint now, so far away. Her eyes became wet, but she would not cry. She could not cry.

Dom tightened his arms around her. "No, no, *sorellina.*" He whispered to her. "I can still play with you. But there might be times when I can't because I have responsibilities. I don't know...it's complicated." Complicated indeed. He did not want to stop playing with his little sister. "But I'll play with you whenever I can."

"Will you be able to play with me when you marry Clara Patrillo?"

"Who told you that?"

"Will you be able to play with me?"

Dom did not know what to say. He did not know what it meant to be a husband or a father. The truth was, he did not know if he would be able to play with Anna once married. He never thought about it. When he overheard his parent's conversation that night he was caught up in the wonders of his new status as a man. He never considered the sacrifices. Nothing comes for free, especially in Campania. Anna could never understand this. She did not need to know about sacrifice right now. She did not need to know what it was to be a man.

"I'll always be able to play with you, for as long as you want me too." He said and smiled, but his words came out too slow.

Anna's arms tightened around him. 'She knows.' Dom realized. 'She knows that that was not really true, and she just told me that it was okay.' His little sister always surprised him. She possessed a depth that Dom could not fathom. He could not understand the connection between Anna and himself. It was just so much a part of his life.

"Hey, *Sorellina*. You must go now. It's very dark. Mama will not want you out in the dark much past your bedtime."

"I don't want to go, Dominico." Her big blue eyes pleaded. "You're going to be all alone, and I won't be able to sleep at all. Please don't make me go, Dominico. I want to keep you company. Please don't make me go."

Dom shook his head. "No, Anna. You must go. You know Mama'll be mad if you're out too late. Give me a kiss then run along. *Va bene?*"

"*Va bene.*" Anna pouted. A long, dramatic sigh of discontent preceded the words.

Dom could not help but laugh. He wrapped his sore arms around his tiny sister and kissed her, squeezing her until she squealed. "I'll see you tomorrow as soon as I get home. Don't you worry."

Anna returned the kiss then stood. She meandered down the road. A short distance away she turned to her brother. Those big blue eyes pleading with him, projecting their sadness into his soul.

Dom had to swallow hard but nodded and urged her to continue. "Go ahead. I'll see you when I get home. I promise."

When his sister left Dom climbed the wall to sit up top. He wanted to investigate the *latifundo* more, to gaze upon its wonders. Indeed, he wished for the cooling breeze that preoccupied his mind. He hoped to glimpse his barefoot oread with the flowers in her long, black hair. He imagined that she would walk like a sensual dance through the trees and appear to him.

Instead, he noticed the arbors.

The arbors were barren and gray from exposure to the elements. They were like skeletons that once held up a body of lush, green grapevines. The Belan's had made their money in wine. In fact, the town existed because of the grapes, the wine, the wealth of *il Mezzogiorno*. Some decaying winepresses could still be found around the *paesera*. Presses once stained red with grapes, smelling sharp of wine and vinegar, now rusted stiff, the wooden slats gray and corroding.

A parasite killed off the last of the grapevines a few years back, throwing the entire area into economic turmoil. Even the impregnable *latifundo* was not immune to the blight. Dom wondered how this affected the *Padrone*. What did this mean for his wealth? Was this why he was being so harsh about the payment of old debts? There was a time when having a person indebted was enough to satisfy him, but now the debts were being called in. Rents were raised even though nobody could afford them. There was no leniency, there was no negotiation. Was the *Padrone* struggling for his own survival, his cruelty an indication of his fragility. Was he as much a fish out of water as the rest of the *paesera*? Dom shook his head. This fish had bite. He was not the same as the starving masses all around, the poor, crying infants, honorable men accepting charity to feed their ailing families. *Il Padrone* had a countryside he could pillage.

"*Signore.*" A quiet voice in the darkness caught Dom's attention. The stars were thick and bright, but the sky was moonless making it difficult to see outside of the fragile yellow aura of the lantern.

But Dom did not have to see. He could feel the breeze brought to him by the singsong voice. He had failed, he had fallen asleep and was dreaming as curs mingled with the mastiffs and frolicked in the trees.

"*Signore.*" The gentle voice once again, only now she stepped into the light. The gold light played like magic along her bronze skin. Her black hair pulled up seemed to capture the gold and shine with its stolen treasure.

"I'm here," Dom said.

"I didn't want to frighten you." Spoke his oread.

Dom shook, his body not cooperating, trembling and rigid. So too did his tongue tremble. Words stuck in his swollen throat. He could not speak. His oread stood before him, looking up at him with gentle, curious, brown eyes. She stretched out her arm and held out a canvas satchel. "I saw your lantern and thought you could use some food."

"Oh...no...I couldn't." Dom cleared his throat. Speaking was a necessity here and he had to get his words to cooperate with his mouth. He coughed. "I could not take your food. I've eaten already." His stomach growled in protest.

She sucked her lips and looked at the ground for a moment. Looking up again she said, "My father said you are not being paid for this job. This is not a handout." She decided not to pursue that argument further, knowing full well that it meant nothing to a man's honor whether he was paid or not.

Her eyebrows arched up on her head and her eyes became sad, but warm, much like Anna's when Dom sent her home. "Please come down and eat. I can't take this food home. If not for you, eat it for me or I'll get into trouble. I'm not supposed to be here."

Dom jumped from the top of the wall landing on agile legs. "If you're not supposed to be here, why are you here?" He asked. He tried to look into her eyes, but his heart would not allow it.

She stuttered, touching her collarbone lightly. "I...well, I just thought you would be hungry. I felt bad for you when Alfredo said you had to stay. *È stupido*. Those mastiffs would chase any cur out of the estate. It doesn't make sense to keep you here." Her face became hot and red. She gazed up at this young man before her and smiled. "I just wanted to bring you some food. Here." She shook the satchel and held it out to him.

Dom took the satchel from her and opened it. It was heavy and full. The first thing that caught Dom's attention was a large, metal container. It was hot to the touch. "What is this?" he asked as he opened the top.

"It's coffee." The woman smiled. "My father uses it when he must work late. It keeps him awake. You must drink it all. He'll positively strangle me if he knew I made a pot for you."

Dom smiled as he smelled the bitter odor of the coffee. He covered it again. "I will, thank you."

"There's some cheese and sausage, too." She pointed. "And bread, freshly baked. Oh, I hope it's enough. You looked like you worked so hard today."

"Yes, *signorina*." Dom nodded, sitting back against the wall, adjusting the lamp.

The young, dark oread stood above him, biting her lower lip. She stared at him not knowing what to say. He did not seem to want to talk to her. He just sat and stared into the bag even though he already had plenty of time to examine the contents.

"Um...I'm Maria.... I mean my name is Maria-Angelina." She spoke quickly.

Her presence struck Dom in unexpected ways. She was no longer a cool breeze to him, but a fever. His body was hot, and his heart was racing. His normally steady hands trembled. He wanted her to go away. He wanted her to stay. He could not understand himself.

"*Mi dispiace*. I'm sorry. I'm very rude...I think. I'm Domico Rossa...I'm a stone carver." His words rushed from his mouth before he could change his mind. Once his sentence was done, however, his throat tightened, and he thought he would stop breathing.

"Well, I'm pleased to meet you Dominico Rossa, the stone carver." She held out her hand. Did a man shake hands with a woman? Dom did not know what to do, he took her hand as if it were a man's hand and shook it, though he was wary of how he squeezed. It seemed so small in his palm, her fingers thin and delicate like a flower.

"Why is a stone carver building a wall?" Maria asked, then covered her mouth. "I'm sorry. Sometimes I'm rude, too. My father says I don't think before I ask questions that are none of my business. Of course, you don't have to answer."

Dom was relieved. 'She's as nervous as I am,' he realized. It calmed him.

"It's no secret," he swallowed. "There's not much call for carvers in these parts anymore. My grandmother, may she rest in peace, well, her family were stone workers and brick layers, so we learned how to lay brick and stone. That's what we do mostly. But I'm a carver. Sometimes we still get work carving. We're working on angels and capitals for a library in Naples right now. Capitals are the decorative parts that go on the tops of columns. Maybe I'll even go north when the time comes. There's carving to be done up north near the marble mines. I just don't want to leave the family." Dom stopped as he realized he was rambling.

"You do good work." She caressed her lower lip, a nervous habit. Dom felt desire he'd never known.

"Uh...um...Thank you for the food. It has been so long since I've had sausage. We had cheese last night, but sausage. I've not had sausage in a long time...and I've never had coffee. I don't even think I remember what sausage tastes like." He stared into the satchel to calm himself.

She smiled. This man liked her. It made him foolish and silly, and she enjoyed his discomfort. Her heart slowed once she realized that he was so unsure. "Then taste it." She said as she laughed jovially.

He looked up sharply from the bag, looking into her eyes indignantly that she would be laughing at his lack of social graces, his ignorance. But when he saw the refreshing, white smile, her laughing eyes, he could not help but laugh with her.

"Go ahead. I brought it to be eaten." she urged, motioning to the bag.

"Please, sit." He responded, then stopped. "No...don't sit...I mean, you'll soil your dress."

She continued to laugh but sat beside him without concern for her dress. He removed the sausage from the bag and cut a piece of it placing it on his tongue. It was cold and spicy. His mouth became wet and hungry for the salt. He was not embarrassed to cut another slice immediately after swallowing.

"So, I guess you **were** hungry, *Signore* Rossa."

"Dom." He pushed out of his full mouth.

"Pardon?"

He swallowed and began to speak but had to stop. He'd swallowed too much and had to wait for the painful ball to creep down his throat and into his stomach. He sipped the coffee to expedite the process and winced at the bitter taste.

"Most people call me Dom." He said. He felt uncomfortable, awkward. He tried to remember to be like stone, but such an axiom was ill suited for this instance.

"Dom." She repeated to herself. "Everyone calls me Maria-Angelina. It's terribly long, don't you think? It's so terribly long. I really don't like it at all."

"It's a pr..." Dom stopped himself. He could not say her name was pretty; that could not be proper. "It's a...nice name. It's a very nice name." He reinforced with more confidence.

"You're sweet, but why don't you just call me Maria..."

"Pratolina..." The word flew from his mouth. He did not remember thinking about it. He certainly did not remember choosing to say it. The word just flew from his mouth beyond his intent. He sat frozen, awaiting disaster.

"What did you say?" She looked at him quizzically.

"Nothing."

"No, you don't." she giggled. "You said something, now out with it or I take the sausage back." She poked him in the rib with her little finger causing him to jump and laugh.

"Pratolina...I said Pratolina. I don't know why. I...I saw you this afternoon. You were picking flowers over by that stand of trees and...and putting them in your hair." He blushed.

Again, she laughed, almost screeched with joy. Her laughter brought the cool, comforting breeze back into Dom's life. He liked her laughter. No, he liked prickly pears; he liked this sausage. He loved her laughter. He wanted to hear it again and again.

"Pratolina. Pratolina." She repeated. "I don't think they were daisies. I think they were mostly weeds."

"I thought they were *prataline,*" he said in soft voice.

"Oh, I love it. Call me Pratolina." She offered a playful bounce and took his hands into her own. His hands were big and thick, strong. They were also gentle and kind despite the heavy calluses. "Please, I love it. It will be our little name. No one else will know."

Dom felt ethereal threads insinuate and tighten between them. He remembered thinking that she could read him when they had their encounter with Little Alfredo. Somehow, she could understand his soul, even from a distance. Something was happening that he could not understand. She was so… beautiful in the truest sense of the word. She was full of beauty, this oread with the long, dark hair and lithesome neck. Beautiful and breezy and…something else. Beautiful, breezy and… …free.

She was free. This made Dom uncomfortable as he understood the limits of his own freedom as a man. Now here was this woman sitting with him in the middle of the night talking about "our little name," and poking him in the ribs, feeding him stolen food and laughing as if nothing in the world mattered. The son of *il Padrone* was courting her, yet she sat with him in the sand, next to a dirty, sweaty young man who had even forgotten to put on the fresh shirt.

And now he could not think of a life beyond the lantern light, beyond her presence. In such a short time, minutes, maybe even seconds, this woman etched herself into his soul. Now there was nothing else, no wall, no *padrone*, no bitterness to the coffee. The world was contained in the gentle, golden lantern light, energized by her girlish laughter, her big, brown eyes. These treasures in the golden light became everything he wanted in his life. It was contentment and it was...wrong.

It could not be right. It just could not be, despite how it felt, how real, how necessary. It just could not be right. She would marry Little Alfredo and soon she would be *la Donna.* He would marry Clara Patrillo and be called *Mastro* Rossa just like his father. She would never have to worry about being brought low, but he would. He would always have to worry about being brought low—about being like stone.

"Why are you here?" He asked. Dejection tinged his voice. He wanted this to be real, but he knew that it could not be.

Pratolina was about to give him the rote answer, 'I thought you would be hungry,' but she looked into his eyes and knew this young man would know that that was not the reason. But she could not answer. She was not free, not nearly as free as Dom thought she was. Pratolina was just another frightened little girl in a tiny glass box yearning to breathe real air, her own air. She was suffocating in the miasma of the archaic gentry.

"Did you see that old peasant today?" She sighed.

Dom nodded and bit a piece of crusty bread.

"He was so sad. I pity him."

"He doesn't need pity. He needs food." Dom responded without thinking. "He needs this." Dom pointed to the satchel.

"I've never seen the peasants before." She did not seem to be listening to him. "I mean not up close. Not like him. I see *gli giornalieri*, but they're not like him. He was so dirty and broken. I've only read about people who were broken, but I've never seen one."

'*Gli contadini* are just over the next hill,' Dom thought.

"*Gli giornalieri* that you see will eat tonight. That old *contadino* will not." He could feel anger rising in his throat. "He may never eat again. That old broken donkey was all that he had. That old donkey is what he used to plow his assigned plot of land. That old donkey was his way of getting around. He probably lives in a dirt hovel on the other side of the hill. Now he has no donkey. There's nothing left. Even the crops have been bad for the last few years. What nature did not take, Alfredo did. Alfredo took it all."

Dom spit the name 'Alfredo' from his lips like bad taste. Then he realized to whom he was speaking. She would be Alfredo's wife. He must watch what he said and how he spoke of the *galantuomini* if he was to talk with her.

"It is so very sad that one should live like that. It doesn't seem fair, does it?"

"No."

"And Alfredo mocking him so. I wonder if Alfredo could live in a dirt hovel and plow fields."

Dom did not dare respond. He shrugged. Pratolina stared at him, stared at him for two long minutes. He refused to make eye contact with her. Her gaze was too strong, too probing. Dom knew that to look into her eyes at that moment would mean surrendering much of his soul. Surrender. Every corner of his heart wanted to surrender, just give himself to her, but he could not.

"My father works for *il Padrone*. He keeps his books for him. I've not spent much time outside of these walls I'm afraid. I've been so terribly bored."

Dom nodded and his chest tightened even as his heart pounded under his ribs.

She stared at him, trying to discern his thoughts, his feelings. He had become silent. 'What is he thinking? Does he think I'm one of them? Please tell me what you're thinking, Dom.' But waiting for a reply was fruitless.

"I think Alfredo is a beast!" she said, folding her arms across her chest and tucking her chin. She peered into the darkness as if facing some unseen enemy. Her eyes were on fire.

Dom jolted and turned his head. He could not believe what she just said. All who knew Alfredo and his father knew what animals they were, but to say it aloud. To say it aloud…

"You mustn't talk like that. He will be *Padrone* someday."

A sly smile crossed her face as she placed her hand on his, reveling in the feel of him. "But he's not here. You asked me why I'm here. I'm here so I can say what I want."

"It's not good to talk like that about the *Padrone*."

CHAPTER 6

"She told me that that was her happiest day. That day she got to know him. She said it was like exploring, like wandering into lands unknown." The woman said, staring into the distant sky, a thin, vicarious smile on her face.

Dom remembered. He did not want to remember. He did not want to think about it. He did not want to go back into a happy past when today his heart was drowning in despair. Memories of past happiness should not be polluted with the sorrows of today.

That moment, that evening of a million stars. The brightest star sat beside him, smiling and sighing and leaning her body close to him. He could see her smile in his mind's eye as if she were sitting beside the gravestone in her grass-stained dress. The feeling of her young eyes dancing along his dirty, ruddy face made his skin warm. She wanted him to touch her. He could feel how much she wanted him to touch her...such simple desire for a touch, a caress on the back of her hand.

He wanted to touch her. His skin ached for the gentleness of her touch. Though they could not touch, their souls reciprocated their desires. That was a moment of no worries, no expectations, no thought for the future. It was a perfect now. Despite the barriers between them, their souls entwined, an angel-making perfection that tangled them both and would not let go—ever. The world of sweat and hammers shimmered into the distance, never gone, but no longer real.

It was a lasting moment, every sensation a part of him. Dom could still taste the sausage cold on his tongue. He could feel the crust of bread crack and flake beneath his teeth. Her white teeth glistened in a perfect smile as he filled his mouth with bitter coffee and winced. She laughed at his folly, his silliness. That tiny microcosm was vivid. The rest of the world did not matter. The *padrone* did not matter. Only she mattered, his *Pratolina.*

A person may have one day, one hour, or one star lit evening that can be described as perfect. For Dom, sitting in the hole of a dismantled wall with this woman whom he did not really know, yet knew completely, was his one and only perfect now. There would be no other. Oh, there would be happiness. There would be moments in his life that he could call good, but never perfect, never flawless, never without something else weighing him down. If Dom could have spent eternity in the air of one evening, it would have been that evening, tired, hungry, sore—and totally fulfilled.

He lifted his large, injured hand, still bandaged and burning, and covered his red, watering eyes. 'Be like stone.' But there was no more granite left in him. He could not cry in front of this woman. He could not contain his tears. To hear her speak of his "perfect now" made it real once again. Over the years this moment receded like a vivid dream, a powerful memory of something that surely could never have happened. He Pulled a lungful of air, his shoulders trembled, yet no sound passed from his tight throat.

"My name is Cecilia." The woman said after a pause in the story. As a girl she learned that men do not cry. As a woman, she had witnessed that this was not true. Men's tears had run over her hands, her face, soaked into her dress. It always took her by surprise. 'They must cry. No human can live under all this sorrow and not cry.' Yet she was always motivated by deep empathy upon seeing a man's tears, knowing as she did the deep shame behind them. The face of the tombstone became damp with this man's tears. Now, as always, she was at a loss as to what to do. Should she continue? Should she leave him alone with his tears and his sorrows?

The man before her, seeking shelter in his drab green uniform stopped breathing. His body became rigid like the stone upon which he leaned his sweating brow. After a long silence he whispered, "Please, Cecilia, please tell me more."

Tears welled in her own eyes, but she felt she could not cry. She could not add to the sorrow before the grave of her friend. She forced a smile. "Pratolina said she was so bold in her youth. She was desperate to see this young man again..."

They never saw the sun rise, as they were on the west end of the *latifundo*. The sky turned a deep blue before the sun showed itself over the parapets of the *palazzo*. As the stars faded, Pratolina knew that she had to leave. Her father would be up soon, if not already awake and there would certainly be questions. Yet returning home meant leaving this young man to whom she was now irremediably connected. She had to look away to say good-bye. Even then, leaving was a physically demanding process of emotional extraction.

As she walked slowly into the *latifundo* fear welled up from inside of her. She may never be able to see him again. There were rules, cold conventions that had to be followed. This was especially true for women—for young, nubile women prospectively betrothed to a wealthy and powerful man. She certainly could not approach him—not in the light of day. What rationale could she offer to justify such a bold action? Yet evening rendezvous were out of the question.

This fear gripped her. Morality contorted against the power of destiny. A connection of the heart that cannot be severed. It must be satisfied. She knew the consequences of following her heart, the fate of disreputable women under the unforgiving eyes of their dishonored fathers. The moral, honorable prerogative must be adhered to despite yearnings of the heart. These bonds had to be severed. These bonds were inseverable. The heart was a formidable adversary, especially when allied with the soul.

As they said goodbye and she turned to walk away the ropes of fate twist around her heart, coiled about her thighs. She was immobile for the briefest second. In this second, her heart usurped the reign of reason. She turned and faced him, the words flowing from her mouth were foreign to her, as if she were listening to her true self for the first time and did not know what to make of her.

"I really like you, Dom." She whispered. Her tired eyes were wide and intense, staring into his, searching for a sign that her words were not Fool's Folly.

She was rewarded. Dom could not speak. That he should hear such words from a woman...he never thought possible. Yet his eyes, black and shining, thick from sleeplessness, betrayed the elation of his heart—a confused ecstasy.

"I don't want to go, but I must." She turned again to the estate grounds. "How will I get to talk to you again?"

Dom was dumbfounded. The thought of her leaving his life...well there was no greater depth of sorrow. The idea of never seeing her again emptied his soul of vitality. However, like most Campanians, even at his youthful age, he learned to deal with sorrow, with a hungry body and a starving soul. Early in the evening, when the first shimmer of desire rose from his heart, he knew that he would never get to enjoy this woman's company again. He learned to accept the gifts of the present as such.

Now, as improbable as it was for a woman of her class and station to bring him sausage and coffee in the middle of the night, this oread was yet again upturning his understanding of what was possible in the world. Now she offered an opportunity for a future. He was just unsure how to grasp it.

"I...I don't know...*Signore* Belan...your father...I don't know." Dom raised his hands. He could not be thinking what he was thinking. He could not think to entertain the defiance that was growing inside of him for the sake of this woman. Yet he knew he would defy. He would defy the constraints of Campanian righteousness. He would defy the church. He would defy the will of God Almighty. For her, he would defy.

She jumped close to him and stroked his dirty face, her hands coming to rest upon his solid chest. His heart pounded defiance under her palm. Her curving mouth pouted, eyes pleading. "Do you want to see me again, Dom? Please say you do."

If he were capable of speaking at that moment, he would have said exactly that, and more. If he could have pushed the words past the lump that grew in his throat. All he could do was nod.

"Dominico, you will need your sleep tonight, but tomorrow night will you meet me? Please say you will." In her desperation the words fell from her mouth in rapid succession. She was almost unaware of what she was saying. Blue spread across the eastern sky, mocking her. Her stomach curled into a knot from the chance that she was taking. The risk to her honor and her dignity was terrible, but there was nothing else to do. There was no dignity, no honor outside of this black-eyed man who had captured her.

"I will." Dom nodded. The words felt like pebbles passing his throat.

"There's a hill to the east of here. It overlooks the town. Do you know it."

Dom nodded.

"Tomorrow night. Can you meet me there tomorrow night?"

Once again, Dom nodded. A wide, white smile lit up her face as she squealed with joy and hugged him. She wrapped her arms around his broad chest. It expanded and contracted with deep, nervous breathing. She pressed her face into his chest, his heart pounded with violence under here ear.

Dom stood there, not knowing what to do. This was not supposed to happen. This was not how women interacted with men. This was wrong. He knew it to be wrong. But...it was not. There was nothing more right than to be touched by this oread with her long, dark hair. Yet he did not return the embrace. By the time he realized that that was what he wanted to do, she pealed herself from him and ran back to the estate, disappearing behind the wall.

His immediate instinct was to chase her, to catch one more glimpse of her. He even took a step in that direction, but then heard a faint bell in the distance. It was Bruzzo's bell, and this perfect moment in his life was over.

"Dominico!" Paolo's voice was the first he heard as his little brother waved to him. His father was walking next to Signore Patrillo who was followed by two of his sons and Georgio.

Dom walked over to them, his pace a little slower than normal.

"Dominico. Papa let me lead Bruzzo." Paolo almost shouted with joy. "He said I did a good job yesterday and I could lead him again today."

"That's good, Paolo. You did do well yesterday." Dom said, forcing a smile, though he found that his mind and his heart were no longer under his control.

"Are you all right, *Figlio*?"

"Yes, Papa."

Enrico looked into his son's eyes. They were heavy, but there was something else. Enrico attributed it to fatigue. "Are you ready to work?"

"Yes, Papa."

Enrico grasped Dom's face, looking up into his eyes. "Are you sure you're alright?" His son's eyes, usually intense, were now distant and unfocussed.

Dom smiled and nodded, "Yes, Papa, *sto bene*."

Enrico laughed as he spoke, "You look delirious!" He whacked Dom on the shoulder sharing the laugh with *Signore* Patrillo. "It's going to be a long day for you *mio figlio*.

It was going to be a long two days. A seeming eternity would pass before Dom could be reunited with his own heart.

It was decided that the Patrillos would build a fence with some old timbers from their woodyard. That would keep the curs out until the wall was rebuilt. Georgio would stay and start digging the drain. Enrico, Dom, and Paolo would walk back to town with Bruzzo and pick up supplies and brick to replace those that broke when disassembling the corner. The Rossa men left the Patrillos to their task after unloading the timbers then started for town. Dom led Bruzzo who seemed to require more finessing than Paolo could give as the animal was reluctant to retrace his footsteps so early in the morning.

On their way along the road Enrico sent Paolo ahead to 'scout the way.'   Once the boy was out of hearing range the father began talking about Clara Patrillo. Dom pretended to be interested in what his father had to say. His mind, now so fragile yet so focused, was content to do nothing more than dwell on the dark-eyed oread with whom he passed the night.

"Now we're not talking about right away, you understand." Enrico said emphatically, waving his hands in small circles. "Mama and I still think you are too young to marry. We think you should wait a couple of years. And Clara will be ready too. It's not good for a woman to have children so young. But Mama and I feel she'll make a good wife for you and a good addition to the family. Don't you agree, Dominico?"

Dom did not know how to answer. This conversation was just another on the list of unexpected events. "I guess so, Papa."

Enrico noticed Dom's hesitation. He nodded and patted his son on the back. "I know, I know. It's a lot right now. You don't have to worry about it for a couple of years, but now your sister, Hortensia. We really don't have much time with her. We want to make an arrangement with *Signore* Patrillo so we can set a dowry aside for her. You don't want her to be *una zitella*, do you?"

"No, Papa." Dom replied from far away.

"Paolo, go see if there are any travelers around the corner." Enrico waved to the boy as he was approaching.

"In a couple of years, you'll be able to run the shop yourself. You'll know the ins and outs as well as I do. I'll introduce you, formally, to all my connections. Then, in your twentieth year we'll announce your betrothal to Clara in front of the church. By that time Clara will be going on eighteen years old. Your Aunt Maria Sossa tells me that Clara will have good hips for childbearing. That's a good thing. If a woman's hips are too small, childbirth can be very hard. But Clara will have good hips. Maria Sossa knows about these things. She's a midwife."

The last thing Dom wanted to talk about was Clara Patrillo's birthing hips. He really did not want to be talking at all. He just wanted to sleep until the following night when he could see Pratolina again. He contemplated how he would get out of the house. He could tell his father he needed to walk before going to bed...

"Now I know that you will be tired, *Figlio*, but your mother has arranged for the Patrillos to have dinner with us again tonight. We want you to spend time with Clara. Start getting to know her. Do you think you will be up to it?"

Indeed, Dominico knew that he would not be 'up to it,' but what was he supposed to say? His parents were arranging his marriage, just as it should be, just as he always knew it would be. This was not an infringement upon him, but the way things were done. Yet there was another element that Dom did not count on when he imagined meeting his future wife. There was this variable in his heart that pulled at him, that screamed at him not to cooperate. Then there was Hortensia and her impending spinsterhood, *una zitella*, that was dependent upon the success of this courtship.

Enrico could sense his son's hesitation. "And she's not bad to look at, either." He smiled.

"I'll be OK, Papa. I just need to keep moving." Dom responded after a long silence lost in thought.

Enrico laughed and struck him on the back, giving Bruzzo a start. "That's my boy. You'll see, it will all work out in the end. You just do as your parents tell you and it will all work out fine. Don't you worry. We'll lead you through it just as we were led through it when I was your age. Of course, by the time I was eighteen I was already married to your mother..."

Dominic lost his father's soliloquy somewhere in the cavernous distances of his mind.

When they reached Dellamontagna's storefront Enrico froze, and Dom's attention was pulled back to earth. The storefront, usually stocked with what goods and produce *Signore* Dellamontagna could display, was conspicuously barren. The door, usually open and welcoming, was closed. Enrico walked over to the door and looked inside then backed away quizzically.

He looked at Dom and Paolo. "They're inside." He said, then stood there a moment. "Paolo, go rest in the *piazza* by the fountain. You need your rest. We have a lot of work to do."

Paolo started to object but knew that when his father sent him away it was adult business. There was a time when Dom was sent with Paolo, but his older brother was a man now and was allowed in the world of men. The mysterious world of men was alien to a nine-year-old boy. He wanted to pout, to show his disapproval of such unfair treatment, but he did not dare. 'Men don't pout.' He said, "yes, Papa," and walked away to the village square.

When Paolo left, Enrico opened the creaking door. Dom was surprised to hear women crying and family members hugging each other in the middle of the store. 'Someone died,' Dom thought, running a quick inventory of who in the Dellamontagna family was old, sick, or pregnant.

"*Mastro* Rossa," *Signore* Dellamontagna called out as Enrico and Dom stepped into the store. "I'm so glad to see you." He hugged Enrico, kissing him on both cheeks, repeating the welcome with Dom.

"What's going on?" Enrico asked the storekeeper. He was a tall, wiry man with sparse, white hair in a patchwork on his head. *Signore* Dellamontagna was not wearing his usual green apron. He looked dressed for travelling. The oldest boy stood by his father and wore similar clothes. *Nonno* Dellamontagna, the eldest of the family, stood by the wood stove, his old back as stiff as the black, metal fluke by which he stood. The old man was restraining tears, his lids trembling yet effectively controlling the expression of deep sadness. *Signora* Dellamontagna and her two daughters cried unabashedly, clenched in a three-way hug. The youngest son clutched his mother's leg yet emulated his pseudo-stoic grandfather.

"I met a man in Salerno, Enrico. This man told me about *Lamerica*. I was there to pick up my stock and he saw that I really could not afford very much. He told me that in *Lamerica* the stores are filled all the way to the ceiling with goods. He told me that he could get me a store, that there was a store waiting for me to get there stocked to the ceiling. He told me this store was right in the middle of New York City where the Astors buy their fruit. He said all I had to do was get on the next ship leaving Napoli, find a friend of his when I get to New York, and they would set me up in the store. I'll work for a little while, save up my money, then the store would be mine."

"You're leaving?" Enrico could not imagine this. He'd heard about people leaving their homes and families for *Lamerica*. He had heard about whole towns depopulated by this exodus, but he could not comprehend it. He never thought it would reach his own *paesera*, the people he had known his whole life, the families that had interacted with for generations. His father bought goods from the elder Dellamontagna. His mother's father built the hearth in *la casa Dellamontagna.* This was the way it was and the way that it always would be. Enrico could not imagine anything different.

"Yes, my friend." The storekeeper said with a combination of joy and sadness. "My oldest son and I are going to *Lamerica*. When we get enough money set aside, we will send for the rest of my family."

Enrico shook his head. A piece of his world was missing, distorting the rest.

"*Mastro* Rossa, *amico mio*. You I will miss. But there is nothing left here. If you were smart you would go as well. Go and take your family away from this, *la miseria. La miseria* does not go all the way to *Lamerica*."

Enrico, with a sad smile, embraced Signore Dellamontagna and kissed him, "*Buona fortuna, commare.*"

"Good luck to you," the storekeeper offered a broad, toothy smile. "You will need luck. I'm going to *Lamerica*!" He laughed and hugged Enrico again.

Before leaving Enrico was able to secure mortar and cement from the Dellamontagna's. He was shocked to learn that *Signora* Dellamontagna would keep the store until they were sent for to rejoin their family in the United States. Enrico was not in the habit of doing business with women and did not approve of the changes thrust upon him. *Signore*

Dellamontagna was not simply leaving his family behind, which to Enrico was unthinkable in and of itself, but he was pulling an important strand from the fabric of the *paesera, Villa de San Giuseppe*. A man was not an individual. He was part of a family, part of a village, part of his country, a Campanian.

Should the *contadine* leave so little would be the loss. But the peasants did not leave. They held on. A storekeeper, however, was counted on to supply your family with what they needed. This was another matter entirely. Enrico could see the ramifications of this. He would have to get his supplies from Salerno himself, as would the rest of the businessmen in the village. It would not be long before more families packed their bags and left for *Lamerica*.

Enrico shook his head and convinced himself that this was an isolated incident. Someone else would move in and open a store in the vacancy left by the Dellamontagna's. 'Yes,' Enrico insisted to himself. 'That is how it would happen. Everything would be all right. My world won't crumble like this.' But deep inside he knew that there was no one to take Dellamontagna's place in the store. He thought about the empty villages.

Dom was equally confused. He'd dealt with death, but never change. The concept of someone leaving was one that never occurred to him. What was happening?

The Rossa's walked out of town with their mule and wagon and crossed a field that, in the spring, was green and thick with soft grass. In the heat of the summer, however, it was yellow brown. What grass there was crumbled under their feet as they traipsed across. Within a few minutes they approached ruins sitting like an omen on the shore of a muddy, yellow river.

Dom and his father picked up their hammers and began dismantling one of the crumbling walls of the ruins. Paolo picked up the unbroken bricks and piled them into the cart. As Dom's hammer plowed easily through the brittle mortar of ancient walls, he could not help but ponder the people who had lived in this place so many generations ago. His grandfather had many stories about the days when Campania was part of a mighty empire that encompassed the entire world. Was this one of the imperial cities with the gilded roofs and marble wonders described by his grandfather? Dom decided that it was not such a grand city. The buildings weren't much different from his own home, or the low dwellings of the *paesera*. This was just another village where people lived and prospered for many generations only to suffer and decay in the passage of time. He looked toward his own village and thought, '*la miseria*'—be like stone.

CHAPTER 7

The setting of the sun did nothing to cool the air that night as the Rossa and Patrillo families supped together. Dominico Rossa felt the weight of relentless expectation settle upon him, pressing upon him as the fatigue of his sleepless night drained the vitality from his limbs and back. His eyes were tired and heavy, but anxiety kept them wide and glassy. He put in a full day's work and though his sinews were young, strong, and resilient this evening they were stiff, aching with exhaustion. His neck and back were unusually tight, pinching and pulling on his spine, causing him to sit erect and uncomfortable. Meanwhile, family and friends sat around him, laughing and telling stories and enjoying the meal.

Nonno, presiding over the meal as usual, performed his normal ritual under the gaze vouchsafed from the icon of Saint Joseph. He then spread his arms his smile broadened, giving special blessing to his grandson, Dominico, and "the beautiful Clara Eta Patrillo." With that, the family raised their glasses of wine, pale pink from being watered down, and saluted the guests of honor. Dominico could not help but feel strange about this attention. He sat at this table for every meal of his life. Clara joined the Rossa table at least twice a week. Attention, let alone special attention was a rarity, but now they were the focus of both families. They were the topic of conversation, *Nonno* smiling and laughing the whole time, adding his anecdotes about how he was introduced to his first wife, how his father arranged the meeting one week before the actual wedding. He was betrothed to her since he was six years old, but never met his future bride as she lived in another village. He mentioned nothing about Dominico's grandmother, the elder Enrico's second wife. She was courted properly, as Enrico was no longer in the care of his parents but was at that point the primary worker. *Nonna* absence in any of his grandfather's stories seemed conspicuous to Dominico.

Signora Patrillo had made some pasta, as *Signora* Rossa was able to secure some olive oil and spices from the Dellamontagna's in exchange for washing and patching some of their clothes with scrap cloth taken from those that Paolo had long outgrown. This allowed the Dellamontagna women to walk with their men and say good-bye to them on their way to Salerno.

It was a sad day, overall. The emigration of a pivotal member of the village hit everyone hard, but the Dellamontagna women would bear the brunt of hardship as they would have to manage the family affairs and the remains of the family business. Such was typically men's work, and the Dellamontagna women felt ill prepared for such burden. But they knew that it was only temporary. Soon, money would start coming in and they would live well. Before they knew it, their men would return, and they would be living almost like the *padrone*. Or they would join their men in *Lamerica* and reap the bounties of the New World. For the first time in the history of this *paesera* hopes and dreams were based on a land far away.

Yet the lives of the villagers were entwined in a complicated web of mutual need. As Sara Rossa ladled spiced olio onto the steaming pasta on her eldest son's plate, Dominico never considered the chain of events that put such relative bounty on his table. He merely wondered at the attention that was being shown. It was unusual for his mother to cater to him. Sara only ever served Enrico and perhaps *Signore* Ugo Patrillo as a guest. Now Dominico was being treated as if he were the Prodigal Son. He was the topic of conversation. Enrico began the conversation by bragging about his son' s skills as stone carver, and how evenly he lays brick and how strong was his back.

Ugo responded by boasting of his daughter, Clara's, cooking and how he was awed by her ability to clean his shirts perfectly white regardless of the stains. The two heads of the family went back and forth, advertising their children's virtues, sound, sturdy Rossa and Patrillo stock. He felt like a farm animal being sold in the market.

His mother pointed out that, "Dominico stayed up all night last night and still put in a full day's work." But her voice was far away to the young man. All their voices were as if they were mere echoes in a canyon far away.

He just could not bring his attention to the here and now. His mind would not connect to that which was happening around him. His attention, his mind, was with his heart alternating between sweet memories under a broken wall, and even sweeter dreams on a future hill with a dark eyed oread—his Pratolina. And these dreams and memories were more tangible than the cant that was travelling about his ears.

Paolo and Anna sat on either side of him. This was an indicator that he was good with children and would not be a burden to a wife's duties of raising them. Paolo sat and laughed with his grandfather in what seemed an uncharacteristic secondary conversation.

Anna, on the other hand, was quiet and pensive. Her eyes travelled slow and alert between her big brother and Clara. She was probing, reading them. Dom felt as if she were reading his mind and feared what she was seeing. Hortensia, her normally long, sienna colored hair tied neatly and conservatively in a ball behind her head, sat beside Clara, separating her from the rambunctious Patrillo brothers. She would prod and encourage Clara.

Clara sat directly across from Dominico. She toyed with the long spaghetti in her plate debating how to eat the oily noodles and still look appealing to the man who would be her husband. Most importantly, she did not want to make any mistakes under the eyes of *Mastro* Rossa. The ultimate decision would be his as to whether she would be Dominico's bride.

The fact was that she liked Dominico. She liked his quiet ways, his solid gracefulness. She liked to look out the window of her home, across the dusty road and into the Rossa work yard, watching her future husband work, stripped to his waste, his back and chest glistening copper under the sun. She liked his smile and the clear and honest look in his gentle eyes. Dominico Rossa was a gentle man, a kind man who would treat his wife with kindness as *Mastro* Rossa tended to his own wife.

In Campania there was always a distance between husband and wife. There was always a certain formality between them. Clara had witnessed the cruelty of many husbands toward their wives. She saw women trying to cover bruises in vain while withholding their tears. It seemed to Clara that this cruelty was increasing in this time of need and poverty, as if being a man were so difficult that they could only pen up their rage until they came home. Then it all came out. The cruelty that men faced every day in the market, in the fields, or at the hands of the *Padrone* was translated into rage toward the only available target, their wives. Even Clara's own father was prone to such disease of the heart. He was much less patient with Mama, Clara thought. Though he never laid an angry hand on Clara's mother, his angry words struck her, hit her physically. When things were going well, however, when father had work or after *una festa* he loved his wife and *la casa Patrillo* was a cheerful home. Clara often wondered about this link between the prosperity of the *paesera* and the attitude of the men toward their families.

She wanted her home to be happy all the time. The Rossa's did not appear to bend so drastically under the pressures of life in Campania. They pressed along and maintained happiness in their families despite their sorrows. Or maybe they didn't. It was impossible to know what happened in the solitude of one's home.

Somehow, Clara knew that Dominico would be kind to her. She even hoped that one day he might even love her. Her mother told her that that was the way it worked. If she worked hard and took care of her husband, accepted his flaws without pointing them out, he would eventually love her. Clara considered her mother's words, then pondered her example as a wife and found Mama lacking, as *Signora* Patrillo's temper was well known. Her mother did not hesitate to point out her father's flaws.

Clara kept her napkin close as she placed the coiled pasta in her mouth. She was careful to take small bites and avoid touching her lips to the oily coils. Oily lips were not appealing. Taking big, gulping bites was not ladylike. She had to be an appealing lady tonight. Both of her parents emphasized the importance of how appealing and ladylike she needed to be.

She also had to see Dominico's eyes. There was something different about him that night. He was rigid and uncomfortable, not graceful, and easy as was his usual manner. Though always quiet he was now silent, a vacuous silence, a shroud that she could not peer under. He looked at her from time to time but would not allow his eyes to rest upon her.

She caught him glancing up at her a few times but shifted his gaze to his plate whenever they made eye contact. His eyes were so important to her as they were the only means of seeing—him. It was the only way to glimpse what was going on in his gentle, yet complicated heart. Clara had the insight that his heart was now more complicated than ever. He had a secret, and he could not show her his eyes, but she could not discern the nature of that secret.

To Dominico the meal ended quicker than normal. Everything was different. Clara stood to help the women clear the table and clean up from the meal, but her mother sat her down with a gentle hand on her shoulder. "We can take care of this. Sit."

Enrico coughed. "Dominico, why don't you take Clara over to the bench and keep her company there while the women clean up?"

This was the first time that Dom looked directly and intentionally into Clara's eyes and held her gaze. They were both terrified. They could see only unease and uncertainty in the other. 'Is this how it is supposed to be?' Clara thought. 'What is he seeing in **my** eyes?'

"Yes, Papa." Dom stood and motioned Clara to follow.

The bench was twenty feet from the table and faced the barley fields behind the village. If the sun were up, they would be able to see the golden fields like a carpet rolling gently downhill, then up along an Apennine slope. This evening, however, the only light was that of the lanterns in the *casa* and the dim sliver of silver from the waxing moon.

Dom looked behind him as they sat on the bench. At the table sat the elder and junior Enricos and Ugo Patrillo. Their eyes were locked on the young couple sitting on the bench. The elders smiled and nodded to Dom, his father waving his hand and pointing at Clara.

Dom looked at Clara and offered a meek smile. She knew that he did not want to be there. In her heart she knew that he would never love her, and her heart folded over her dreams.

Dom's body was waging a strange kind of war with itself that night. His eyes and his body wanted sleep, needed sleep, needed escape from the conscious world. His mind, however, would not cooperate. His mind needed to run through open fields of thought and wonder. His heart, allied to his mind, conspiring against his body as it pounded within his breast. Blood pushed through his body becoming hot, his skin flushed, his muscles weak.

He lay next to Paolo and tried to sleep. He closed his eyes. He tried to clear his mind. He tried counting sheep. He tried to think of a clear lake. He heard of so many tricks for sleepless nights and tried them all, but to no avail. There would be no sleep that night. Instead, he spent that time thinking about his future. On top of all his thoughts was Pratolina's face, her body, her long neck, and wide smile. At one point he tried to think about Clara in the same way, but her image would only fade and transform into Pratolina. His oread stuck in his mind and clung to every thought.

There was nothing wrong with Clara. Indeed, Dom liked Clara. He'd known her his entire life and was not surprised to find that he was to marry her. Nor could he find much to object to in such an arrangement. She was a quiet girl, but quick to smile, of a pleasant disposition. To his knowledge she had not inherited her mother's storied temper. Dom remembered hearing some of the Patrillo arguments from across the street and two work yards. It was mostly *Signora* Patrillo's side of the argument. Clara was a wonderful cook. She seemed talented at making even the scantiest meal tasty.

That and Enrico was correct, she was pleasant to look at. In fact, she was quite pretty. Her skin was dark and even of color, her eyes a light brown and clear. Her teeth were white and straight behind full, red lips. Though she was short, she was solid, lean and healthy, with square shoulders and an elegant curve. Most importantly, she was kind. Dom could see himself married to her. He could see her as his wife. This was not an unpleasant image.

Only…he could not see himself as her husband. Somehow, he did not fit into the picture with her.

The time they spent on the bench was awkward and silent. He had little to say. What could be said? They tried some banal conversation about the weather or how the fields looked. An actual conversation almost started concerning the Wheat Harvest Festival coming next month, but it faded into the night. That time on the bench was interminable, as interminable as the sleepless night. 'Yes, she will make a good wife.' Dom thought as he turned over, closed his eyes and thought about Pratolina.

CHAPTER 8

"Where are you going, Dominico?"

Dom's muscles froze. His mind froze in similar fashion as the unexpected voice jolted it from its clarity of purpose. To hear a voice in the concealing dark, to be struck by the solidity of it, the impassible nature of it, Dom was immobile.

His mind raced to recognize the author of such sound, the specter that held him so. The air caged within his chest eased from his mouth and the rigid muscles of his brow relaxed. "I'm just going for a walk, Anna. Go back to bed, you'll wake up the whole house."

"Can I go with you?"

"No." Dom stepped quietly over to her if only to allow her the luxury of keeping her voice down.

"Why not?"

"You just can't, *Piccola*. I want to be alone. I'll be back and you will see me in the morning."

At that the little girl was satisfied. Her big brother was going for a walk, and he would be back. She could feel his need to leave. It scared her. She did not want him to go. Her big brother always needed to be with her. *Fratello maggiore.* But he said he would be back. He was only going for a short walk. She would see him in the morning. In the morning, everything would be all right.

Anna ducked herself behind the curtain. Dom heard her crawl into bed. He waited a moment, knowing his little sister all too well. He allowed her the opportunity to ask one more question, but she did not. With a fatigued smile he stood up and walked to the door.

"Dominico?"

Dom stopped short, catching his breath just as he was exhaling. His sister's voice resonated through the little *casa*. He knew that everyone was now awake, but he whispered, "Yes."

"Do you like Clara Patrillo?"

Dom winced and shook his head. The last name he needed to hear that night was the name 'Clara Patrillo.' He cursed Anna's penchant for asking him the one question that he least wanted to answer. How could he explain this? He did not understand it himself.

"Yes, Anna. I like Clara Patrillo." His ears tightened on the side of his head. He detected no other movement.

"Are you going to marry her, Dominico?"

He had to get her to stop talking. Paolo, usually still in sleep, began to shuffle. It would be only moments before he woke up, then there might as well be a general announcement on the steps of the church that Dominico Rossa, the son of Enrico Rossa, was going for a walk.

"We'll talk about this tomorrow, OK. Now be quiet or you'll wake Papa."

"*Va bene.*" Her voice was a thick whisper. She was not going to be awake for long, Dom thought.

Once again, he waited, but there was no sound from behind the curtain.

The night was still and clear. A gentle breeze whispered down from the mountains and tickled the scant leaves of the trees. Dom could hear the wheat sway a hypnotic dance, shushing into the night. It was as if the world were telling secrets. Perhaps they were Dom's secrets revealed to the Heavens, to God who was even now watching him, even now passing judgment on his actions. The wheat whispered in the ear of Saint Joseph whom Dom half expected to appear before him and tell him to turn around. 'Go back home, Dominico. This is not for you. You can't have what you want.'

'What I want.' Dom continued this inner dialogue with the village patron. 'I don't even know what I want. All I know is that I want to go to that hill. I want to see her. I want to look into those soft brown eyes. I want to watch her neck curl and her teeth glisten in the moonlight as she smiles. I want to touch her long, black hair.'

The locusts shrieked in the background, a pressure to his ears almost fatiguing. 'No, Dominico, you want more. You want so much more. Go home and forget this for you cannot have what you want.'

'What do I want and why can't I have it?'

'You already know the answers to those questions.' *San Guiseppe* faded into the background, faded into the wheat whispering in the wind.

The answer to the first question was in his heart. 'I want to marry her.' The answer to the second was in his blood. 'I can't, because she is the woman whom I truly love.'

Saint Joseph was sad but vouchsafed an understanding smile as he drifted into the dark wheat. 'No man marries the woman he truly loves.' His mouth did not move and Dominico did not know if the last statement came from Saint Joseph or from somewhere within himself, the wisdom of twenty generations of Campanians that flowed with his blood. He watched the village patron drift into the wheat, standing motionless like his *Nonno*'s icon, but drifting into the wheat as if carried by the gentle breeze.

Yet there was determination in his stride as he walked across the field. 'It has been a long day.' He shook his head realizing that his imagination had taken hold of him again. This was not unusual. Many times, especially while laying brick, a task as simple and repetitive as breathing, he would get so lost in his own mind that he was unaware of what the wall looked like until he ran out of mortar. He had built walls, level and sound, and remembered nothing of their construction.

'No,' he thought. 'Despite *Nonno 's* stories, the saints do not talk to the living anymore.' Dom knew that they stayed in Heaven and watched *la miseria* from their lofty perches. Why would they come down to his dusty world only to be ignored? Why would they come down when they'd already been here, been martyred and ridiculed and persecuted for the miracles they performed? Why would they come down and try in vain to deter him from going to the hill and seeing a beautiful woman? Why indeed?

There, at the top of the hill, Dom noticed a glowing lantern. He had not thought to bring a lantern with him. The lacy light of the thin moon was sufficient for him, as he knew his way among the fields after a lifetime of walking them. The hill was tall and relatively steep, but Dom's young, strong legs kept a steady rhythm. It was not long before he was near the top approaching the golden glow of the lantern. He could not yet see the object of his journey, the dark-haired oread, his Pratolina.

"Dominico." Her voice was soft and sweet. He could almost taste her voice in the air. His heart jumped. It did not dare beat previously lest she was not there, and he would have to face disappointment. "Is that you, Dominico?"

"Yes, I'm here."

As he approached the top of the hill he could see her silhouette in the glow of the lantern, the light holding her, embracing her hips round and graceful, her shoulders covered in loose rills of flowing, black hair. She put out her hand to stabilize his climb, but Dom did not take it. He needed no help the rest of the way.

The hand was still there once he gained level footing, however. At that point he took it, soft and warm, small perfection between his fingers. Without thinking he raised her silky hand to his lips and kissed it gently between the forefinger and middle. This was an act of the soul, not the mind. The mind's joy is in opening its eyes well after the fact, opening its eyes in time to see the humiliation. Dom looked up at her, hand still to his lips, expecting to be skewered with ridicule. She only smiled and thanked him graciously.

The kiss of the hand. Pratolina knew well what this meant in the heart of a Campanian man. Kissing the hand was, in many ways, even more intimate than kissing the mouth. It was certainly more symbolic, and symbolism was reality for the people of the sunny, richly Roman Catholic *Mezzogiorno*. It was a supplication, a statement saying, 'I'm yours.' Kissing the hand was bastardized by men like *Il Padrone* who used it as a tool of dominance. Yet, when performed willingly, without coercion, it was the most tender act. Dom kissed her hand, and its symbolism was made legitimate in her eyes with his sincerity, his purity. The supplication of his soul to hers was proven in the act of kissing her hand. She never thought that her hand would ever be kissed. At least, it would never be kissed with this level of passion and sincerity. With his gentle supplication he had conquered her soul. Her heart skipped and an incessant heat spread from between her thighs to her blushing neck.

His lips found her hand and he knew that he could defy fate, that he could defy *San Giuseppe*. She would be his. He could have what he wanted. He could make her his wife. There would be an oasis of happiness for Dominico Rossa even in the desert of *la miseria*. If he could kiss the hand of an angel, what matter of the heart could he not achieve?

She squeezed his thick, rough hand. Her thin fingers were so insignificant in his. They were powerful fingers, brute strength veiled and tempered with the tenderness of his heart. She knew he would never hurt her. She was safe.

"Come," she held his hand tightly and skipped like a child toward the lantern. Dom was slow and awkward. His body hesitated and this threw off her innate grace as she pulled against him. She led him to a blanket that was stretched under a wide branching tree. A tuft of thin grass grew at the foot of the tree and on the grass was a wicker basket, the contents covered with cloth.

"I brought you some bread. And I have real honey that my father just brought in from Tuscany." She was excited and smiling, and Dom could not help but smile with her.

She dropped onto the blanket and pulled on his solid arm. "Come and sit down. Sit with me."

Her long, dark arm stretched across him as he sat on the blanket. He felt big and cumbersome and knew that he would rip the soft, wool blanket, and all would be lost. She reached into the basket and pulled a loaf of bread from under the cover and placed it in front of him. "Please get the honey. It's in that jar." She aimed a delicate golden finger.

She sat with her legs coiled to her left. She ignored her dress as she sat and a smooth, lean calf protruded from the hem and curved back to her hip ending in a long, white, beautiful foot. There was a freedom to her, her hair down, a carelessness she would allow her dress to rise almost to her knee without a glimmer of attention. Her bare shoulder brushed his arm as she leaned forward to fix the bread, such careless contact, such freedom, such disconcerting freedom.

Pratolina laughed and looked into his eyes. "Dominico, the honey." Again, she pointed, laughing, her eyes full of glee.

He was clumsy and shaking as he reached for the honey. By the time his fingers coiled around the jar they steadied. The spinning of his mind slowed as he regained focus on his world. She was so beautiful. He wanted to just drift into her and somehow, deep in his soul, he knew that he could. The jar was in his hand, half filled with honey, gold and thick. He looked at it, then at his oread.

"You've never had honey?" She queried.

He only looked at her and shook his head.

"It's sweet. It tastes like sugar, but...richer, I guess." She broke the seal of the jar and placed her finger into the gold, translucent cream. It clung to her yet stretched as she raised her finger from the jar, a golden string like hot glass, hung from her fingertip. Dom watched the nectar capture the lantern light. He watched it drift and drip to her full lips, pink tongue glistening and wet receiving the amber gift. Her lips curved and sealed around her finger as she pulled it, glistening, from her mouth, eyelids closed as she reveled in the taste. Then she looked into his eyes. He would always associate her mouth with honey.

"Go ahead," she whispered, licking the last of the honey from her finger. "Try some with your bread."

He poured some honey on his bread and ate. She was right, it was sweet and rich. He could taste her laughter.

Dom did not know what kind of bird it was that woke him, but it was a bird that sang ere the rising of the sun. It was a sweet song, a honey song and Dom woke easily, without concern. His body was renewed, his mind rested, his soul quiet and sated. All felt right as he exited his dream and woke to Pratolina's dark and shining hair fanned across his white shirt. She breathed so deeply, so easily; she was soft and light in his arms as if she had always been there. Dom closed his eyes again and allowed himself to drift into a twilight.

Then the birdsong came and with it sudden, sharp realization. Dom's eyes became wide, and he twisted his neck to look to the east. The sky was a dark blue on the horizon.

"*Madonna mia!*" He exclaimed as he bolted upright, panicked.

Pratolina woke with a start and rolled onto his lap. "What is it?"

"We have to go!" He said desperately as he threw the empty honey jar into the basket. "The sun is coming up. We must go."

She looked concerned, searching for the east until her eyes rested on the opening sky. "We fell asleep?" She had not yet gained reality.

"Yes. Quick. Step off the blanket. I will fold it." Dom held the corner of the soft, wool blanket. "We were talking, and we fell asleep."

Pratolina stepped from the blanket and searched for the lantern. Her father would be awake soon and would not approve of her absence. She had gotten away with it the last time by telling him she merely went for a walk around the grounds, but he scolded her soundly and tugged on her hair.

Dom did not quite fold the blanket. He rolled it and threw it into the basket. "We must hurry."

"Dominico, will I see you again?"

"Yes." He responded without thinking.

"When?"

He stopped. She stood there. There was no haste to her. She stood, gazing at him, her weight on her left hip, her fingers in her hair. Her tired eyes pleading.

"I...I don't know." He said.

"You want to see me again, don't you?" Her eyes continued to plead.

He picked up the basket and held it up for her. "Give me three days. I'll need three days. We'll meet here again in three days." He said, but he was too nervous. His eyes did not reassure her.

"You will see me, won't you?" She stepped toward him and placed a hand on his chest as one hand took the basket. "Please say you will."

He did not have time. Dom knew his father would be awake soon if he was not awake already. He did not know what the consequences were for his being out all night, but he knew that he would not like them. But there she was, those sweet, honey eyes sad and confused, the ripe mouth curved into a subtle pout.

Dom reached down and kissed her quickly on the upper lip, just a touch, a momentary contact. "I will be here." He said as he started to run downhill. "I will be here!"

He ran, his legs sure and quick, down the hill. At the foot of the hill he turned, running backwards and pulling an arm into the sleeve of his jacket. Pratolina was still there, staring at him as he shouted once again, "I'll be here."

She gasped and pointed. Dom was looking at the sky, then the ground as he landed on his shoulders and rolled backwards onto his stomach. In front of him was a rotted stump from a rotted tree long since felled, perhaps a thousand years ago. Felled just to end up under his backward running heels, toppling him in front of the most important person in his life. He looked up meekly and she held her hand up to her mouth, eyes wide and concerned.

Dom sprang to his feet and smiled. He continued to run backwards as he brushed himself off and picked up his jacket which had fallen from his one arm. "I'll be here," he called up to her and watched her laugh before turning around and running forward, stumbling only briefly.

He ran, hoping to be home before his father would wake, but he realized that it was too late for that. The stars were gone, and the dark blue had turned into a deep azure band taking up half of the sky. His father would be awake by now. Yet the thoughts of impending peril were fading from his mind as he recalled that evening. His body would let him do no less than run. If he had wings, he would fly.

The feel of the ground disappeared from under him, and the village before him faded into a mist. They talked in the night. Truly talked. He did not just speak to her like he did everyone else. He talked to her, and she talked to him, laughing with him, feeling his feelings. And he talked and nothing felt more natural than to bare his soul, for she already knew his soul, she already held it in the palm of her hand and tasted it like the honey on her finger.

But that was of no import to Dom at that moment. His daydreams, *sogni*, danced around her dreams as she so eloquently shared them with him. She told him that she read books. Her days were spent either in the garden or reading books. Such was the life of the daughter of a wealthy man in *il latifundo*.

"I'm going to visit Paris." She said as she stretched her arms to the sky, her head back. "I'm going to visit Paris and walk along the French streets, drink French wine, and wear French clothes. I've read all about Paris, you know. Have you..."

He remembered how she stopped, her eyes terrified as she cut off her words. Dom only stared at her and smiled. "What?"

"I'm sorry," she said. "I...do you...I mean..."

Dom frowned, but only for a moment. "Yes," he said. "I know how to read." She let out her uneasy breath. Dom did not want to tell her just how little he read, but he did, anyway. He explained how he did not have much time to read, but he learned enough to ply his trade.

And she did not care. Pratolina just wanted to share her dreams with him. In truth it did not matter to her if he knew how to read. It was more important that she did not offend him. She certainly did not want to alienate him being well aware how men thought of women possessed of a superior skill.

Dom was not offended. Quite the opposite. He was enthralled. He had never heard such talk, never been exposed to such dreams. The denizens of *il Mezzogiorno* were a sedentary people, quite content with staying home and dreaming dreams of home. In fact, Campanians allowed themselves few dreams. Striving for the unattainable was, to a Campanian, a waste of effort. Dreaming was a pleasant distraction, nothing more. To actually reach for one's dreams.

Well, that was folly, and *il Mezzogiorno* had no sympathy for folly. But a rich girl? She could dream. For the rich, dreaming was portend, not diversion.

Indeed, there was a point at which she asked about his dreams. He stumbled and slurred and closed his eyes for a moment.

"Come on, tell me." She said as she poked him gently in the ribs. "I've told you about Paris."

"One minute. Give me a minute."

"How long does it take to think about your dreams?" she asked with laughter in her voice.

Then he opened his eyes and looked at her, shrugging.

"You must have dreams."

Dom shook his head and shrugged again. Pratolina did not know how to react. Dreams were so much a part of her life. In fact, they were the only part of her life that were worth anything. Dreams were the only liberating part of her life, the only part possessed of richness. Dreams were like honey. Everything else in this dry world was shallow and sequestered. That Dom did not have any dreams of his own was, to her, inconceivable.

He explained to her how his life would work. Soon he would master all aspects of his family trade, and he would work with his father doing stonework all around the countryside. He would marry Clara Patrillo. He would have children. He would take over from his father once Enrico was too old to work. He would teach his own sons the trade. In turn, they would do the same as would their children, as did Enrico, as did *Nonno* as did his father and his father's father before him. There was not room for dreaming. There was a plan as old as the Caesars. There was no deviating from the plan.

Dom wondered what these differences meant for them, for their future. If he married her, would she have to let go of her dreams? That was certain. She would lose a part of her soul. It was times like this when Dom realized he should say goodbye. He should give her her dreams and succumb to his own reality.

To her, not having dreams was the saddest thing she had ever heard, but she kept this to herself. It was no use, however. Dom felt her sadness and her sadness was intolerable to him.

"But I do want to know more about Paris." He said with a smile and patted her hand gently with his firm index finger. He may have to say goodbye, but not yet. This world, with her, was so sweet he had to hold on as long as he could.

It was not long before they had curled into each other's arms and the talking was done. The talking was done yet they were communicating so openly with each other. She laid her head on his chest and listened to his heartbeat. He listened to her breathing become deeper until he knew she was asleep. That she fell asleep in his arms brought him unspeakable satisfaction. That was his mission. That was his purpose. His purpose at that time, under that tree, under that sky, the taste of honey still on his lips, was to let her fall asleep in his arms, safe from the real world. It was then that he realized he did have a dream. She was his dream. She was his Paris, where he wanted to be.

And...

...Dom stopped suddenly in his tracks, his home just ahead. He had kissed her. He had kissed her! He could feel the satiny texture of her pouting upper lip against his. He had kissed her...

As he ran through the back door and heard the confusion of his family, reality settled into his mind. Dom had to put his dreams on hold for the moment and face his parents' stern rebuke.

Enrico was the first to see him and he grabbed him by the collar, staring up into his son's eyes. "Where were you? What is going on?" Dom could not make eye contact. He looked away. Anna stood by the stove and stared at him. Her eyes were hurt, and this pierced him deeper than could any punishment that his father might dole out. Enrico shook him, "You will answer me."

"*Scusi, Papa, Mama.* I'm sorry. I'm sorry." Dom held his hands up. His father's eyes were pale brown and locked into his son's. Dom could no longer look away. "I could not sleep. I went for a walk and fell asleep under a tree."

"What tree?" Enrico shook him again.

"Papa." Sara's voice interrupted. When Enrico turned his head to look at her, still grasping Enrico's lapels, she shook her head an almost imperceptible amount. Enrico let go of his son's jacket.

"Since when have you been taking walks in the middle of the night?"

"Every once in a while. Sometimes I can't sleep so I take a walk. I guess I was still real tired from the night before, Papa.

"It's true, Papa." Anna said, her voice fast and frenzied. It was unusual for any of the children to interrupt their Papa when scolding a sibling. But this was a special case to Anna. This was her *fratello maggiore.* "I saw him before he left. He said he was going for a walk and would be back."

"That's enough Anna," Sara said, "Go help Hortensia. Don't get in the middle. Go." Anna left the room.

"I'm sorry Papa. It won't happen again."

"You're right it won't happen again..." Enrico said, his tone still raised, his finger waving. But he stopped and looked at his boy, his oldest son. "Ahhh." He looked at the floor. "I guess if you can't take care of yourself by now then that's my fault. Get some bread and get washed up, we have a long day ahead."

"Thank you, Papa." Dom said, smiling, "Thank you, and it won't happen again."

Enrico nodded and grunted, waving the back of his hand toward the bread and olio.

As his son walked out of the room Enrico walked over to his wife. Her eyebrows were raised, eyes wide. She nodded with understanding, a half-smile dimpled her left cheek. Enrico nodded and smiled as well, patting her round hip before he followed Dom out.

CHAPTER 9

There was something about this morning, this Saturday morning, which brought a strange sensation to Dom's bones, a quaking uncertainty about the future that he had never experienced. Perhaps it was the sleepless nights. Since his meeting with Pratolina three days before Dom found it harder and harder to sleep. His nerves would vibrate, his mind race with sweet thoughts of her honey brown eyes, long dark hair, lithesome neck until fatigue won the war of attrition between his body and mind. Last night was the most difficult. The expectation of tonight's meeting charged him, invigorated him. Fatigue could not get hold of his energized body. This must take a toll on one's wellbeing.

Dom turned the mixer, the crank old and dry tried his arms, but Dom, his body strong and sure despite the fragility of his state of mind, persevered and mixed the mortar. He just could not shake this feeling. Something was wrong.

Enrico set the last brick in place before running out of mortar. He scraped the sides clean, wiped the trowel with an old rag and approached his son to judge his progress.

"How is it coming, *Figlio*?"

Dom shook his head. "Slow. We need to oil this crank." His voice strained as he forced through the driest part."

"Sorry. We are out of oil except the olive oil your mother cooks with."

Dom did not need an explanation. He was not complaining. He never complained. What was, was, and there was no changing it. 'Men don't pout.' 'Be like stone.'

Enrico wiped his hands. "I spoke to *Signore* DeVallo yesterday. He told me of Vitorio, our new king. He said that the library will still be built. It might not be a library, but it is already up, and they want to finish it. They already have workers taking care of the façade, but they are still going to need those capitals. I'm going to try to get some of the facing work, so we might be making a trip to *Napoli*. With a little luck we can get paid and get some oil and some new tools. It will be good if we could get some meat in our stomachs, too, huh."

Enrico smiled and looked at his son whose eyes were far away.

He sighed. "You know, *Figlio*, Clara is a good girl. She will make a good wife, don't you think?"

Dom was tired of hearing about Clara Patrillo's good qualities. "Yes, Papa."

"But you know, a man is inclined to...well, follow his inclinations. I guess we all do that, God help us." Enrico made the sign of the cross and looked to the sky.

Dom continued to turn the crank but stared at his father.

"You understand, don't you. I guess it is understandable to follow your...inclinations, so long as you remember your obligations. You have obligations to your family. You are born with them. When you become a man, you follow through with them. You are a man now, you must learn to follow through with your obligations."

"I know, Papa. I follow through with my obligations."

Enrico nodded. "That you do. You are a man of virtue. But it is easy to get caught up in other things. Things in here." Enrico pushed his thumb into his chest, making a dull thumping sound. "You can't let that get in the way of *familia*."

"I know, Papa." Dominico did not want this discussion. He knew that his father was talking about Pratolina. He wondered how much his father knew, and how he knew what he did. It did not matter. His father did not understand. Pratolina was not one of **those** women, the women whom the men would smile to in the market when they thought no one was looking— the women men talked about when they were alone, out of earshot of their wives. Dominico was just now privy to those private conversations, though he had nothing to add. And he never would because Pratolina was not one of **those** women.

No, his feelings were different, more pure, more real. At least that's what he thought. Was this how it began? A man falls in love with a woman but marries the one who is right for his family. He then spends his life stealing moments with the one he genuinely wanted to marry. Eventually it becomes a crude story with which one entertains his companions. It becomes vulgar, unclean, a lie perpetuated over the course of years—years. His father's friends kept the same mistresses for most of their married lives. Were they the women whom his friends really loved?

Dom even wondered about his own father, but such thoughts did not stay for long. His father never spoke of other women. He never smiled at other women—not in that way. Enrico never took part in the same prurient behaviors as many of his friends. Dom realized his father even responded to his mother differently. There was that distance, but there was also a tenderness that the other men lacked toward their wives—a love.

But that was his father. Enrico did not make any wrong turns. He did not do anything that would jeopardize his respectability in the village. He was the one people turned to when they needed a pillar to lean against. Dom's father was what might be called the spiritual *Padrone* of the village. Even Father Antonio, the embodiment of the spirit in *Villa de San Giuseppe* seemed more distant from the hearts of the villagers than Dom's father. Indeed, one would be hard pressed to find anything about Enrico Rossa that would capture the critical eye.

Was that all there was? Dom wondered. Did Enrico have his own Pratolina once, one day long ago? Did he have his own secret hill?

From here it was not far for his mind to wander on Pratolina again. She crept so easily into his brain and, once there, wouldn't leave.

He felt a tapping on the shoulder, his father's rough fingers. When Dom turned Enrico pointed toward the gate. A mounted man holding a shot gun galloped toward the gate and called to the guards. He was *Il Gabelloto*, the overseer. No one knew his name, for he was always *Il Gabelloto.* His appearances were rare in the village at this time of day, the sun still low in the eastern sky. His place was usually among the orchards of the *latifundo* ensuring that the *Padrone* was getting more than his money's worth from the ill paid laborers. His appearance certainly did not bode well, and Dom could feel that shaky heaviness in his bones again. It was enough of an omen that Enrico stopped Dominic from his work to watch what was happening. Otherwise, Enrico and Dom would have continued working and ignored those things that were not their business.

Il Gabelloto always worked at this time of the day, therefore his presence outside of the walls of the estate was related to his job. This job often included visiting villagers of outstanding dept to the *Padrone* and collecting his fees one way or another. The shotgun was an ever-present symbol of his power, but was usually strapped to the horse's side, or on *Il Gabelloto's broad* back. This morning it rested in the crook of his arm, the twin barrels protruding like cannons from his side. One of the gatekeepers rushed to the side of the foaming steed and nodded quickly and jerkily as the big, mounted man pointed toward the *palazzo*. The gatekeeper then ran and called for others as the overseer rode toward town.

"We'll hear the church bells next." Enrico whispered somberly.

It was not long before the gate opened, and half a dozen mounted men emerged from the estate. Between them was a carriage, pulled by two tall, brown horses. Dominico's arms became weak as he stood and held a brick and trowel at his sides. In the wagon were Pratolina and her father. She looked over at him, a frown on her face and sadness in her eyes. Her father sat erect and possessed of a stern and motionless gaze. Behind them were the women, children and tattered *giornalieri* along with the better-dressed house servants. It seemed the entire *latifundo* was emptied of people.

That's when the bells tolled, the church bells pealing a dolorous rhythm from the belfry of the old, dusty church. Their slow, mournful rhythm could be interpreted as another bad omen, as the ringing that announced the beginning of Sunday mass was of a more joyful tempo. But the message was clear. Everyone was to meet in the town square, *il piazza*. Enrico and Dom placed their last bricks, cleaned the edges, then set their trowels on the unfinished wall before beginning the long walk to town.

By the time the Rossas entered the square the rest of the villagers, townspeople as well as *contadini* were standing in a great half circle facing the front of the church. Don Alfredo and his son stood on the church steps. *Il Gabelloto* paced in front of them, a scowl on his thick jowly face, the shotgun nestled solidly in his great, bulky arms. At the door of the church Father Antonio stood, his hands folded in front of his mouth, his eyes closed in frantic prayer.

Enrico and Dom arrived at the same time as the rest of the Rossa family. The patriarch motioned them to stay in the back of the crowd. He then nodded at Dom who followed him and his grandfather to the front of the assemblage. People let the Rossa men through without question, as Enrico was *Mastro Rossa*, a man of respect in the village.

When Dom reached the front of the crowd his first thought was to scan for Pratolina. He found her and discovered that she had already spotted him. Dom looked at her with the question in his eyes. She merely shrugged and shook her head before turning her attention to Don Alfredo.

Don Alfredo climbed two more steps of the church and raised his hands clothed in gray, felt gloves. The din of the crowd ended, and the world was silent.

"It pleases *Le Padrone* that you could all come with such short notice, "He started. "I did not want to pull you from your labors, however, there is a serious matter to attend to this morning. I hope it will be brief."

Dom stared at the man on the church steps. Something was out of place. He stared at Don Alfredo until he could discern the problem. Don Alfredo was dirty. He was normally so repulsively clean, like a salamander, but this morning he was marred with dust, his face showing traces of sprouting hair.

"Yesterday, one of my people was accosted on his way back from Salerno. This *Brigante* unhorsed my man, hit him with a stick and stole his money, his jewelry, even his wedding band. He then ran off on one of my own horses." Don Alfredo shook with anger.

"I will not allow *brigandaggio* into **my** land." He pounded his chest. "We will not allow this country to become a haven for bandits, thieves, and cutthroats. Pretty soon such outlaws will prey on you as well." His felt covered finger waved at the crowd.

Dom shook his head when he realized that people who had nothing had little to fear from thieves. But they were afraid. He looked around at the crowd and they nodded as if in a trance at Don Alfredo's words.

"That is why," Don Alfredo continued, "I took it upon myself to spend the night scouring the countryside in pursuit of this menace. I decided that my men and I would not rest until this fiend stood before us." Alfredo snapped his fingers and there was movement behind Pratolina's carriage.

A mounted man with a long beard walked his horse at the edge of the crowd. Those who could see gasped as he rode through. Dom noticed the men in the corner looking at each other, shaking their heads and pointing. As the horse jerked into the clearing Dom saw a rope tied to the saddle at the rider's side. The rope was taut and disappeared into the murmuring crowd. On the other end the rope wrapped around two gnarled and calloused hands, gray with the dirt of the fields, but also sickly blue from lack of circulation. The owner of those sorry limbs was pulled, crying from the crowd and Dom's heart sank. He looked at his father whose face betrayed no emotion. 'Be like stone.'

The dangerous, fiendish *brigante* of Don Alfredo's story was no more than the old and wretched *contadino* whom Dom had seen days before surrendering his donkey to *Signore* Belan. The skin was loose on his dirty, leathery face, shallow and pale. As he cried brown streaks coursed through the grooves of his sunken cheeks, tracking dirt from his thin, haggard eyes. The old man's toothless mouth was contorted with fear and white foam gathered in the corners of his cracked lips as he struggled against the rope.

Alas, he knew that there was no hope. There was no escape and when he sank to his knees before Don Alfredo a part of Dom sank with him. The crowd was as quiet as a giant tomb as the people stared at the prostrate man before them. The bones of his shoulders protruded from the canvas that constituted his shirt. His back was permanently rounded at the neck, and this was further exaggerated by the sloping defeat of the man as he knelt and cried before the *Padrone*.

"Behold a thief, a brigand and an outlaw." Don Alfredo jumped from the stairs. His eyes were narrowed and hot, his effeminate jaw quivered. "Make him look at me."

Two burly men followed their patron's directions and grabbed the old man by the thin gray hair, pulling his head up. One of the men grabbed his chin and jerked his dirty face to the *Padrone*. Dom could hear the crackling of the old man's bones in response to this abuse. The rough men would surely break such brittle bones.

Alfredo looked the old peasant in the eye, his own eyes cold and without mercy--*maloccio*. "Do you think you can steal from me and get away with it? DO YOU THINK YOU CAN STEAL FROM **ME**, DON ALFREDO BELAN!"

The old man struggled to speak, his mouth, thick and dry trembled in the burly man's hands. "N...n...no. *per favore* Don Alfredo. I beg you, *per favore*! Have mercy...have mercy on me...please. I have nothing...my children starve."

"Silence him." Alfredo's cold voice directed, and his henchman slammed the old man's mouth shut between stout hands.

Alfredo removed the gray, felt glove, finger by finger, from his right hand and replaced it with a black leather glove. "I would like to, old man. I am a man of mercy." He nodded toward what was left of the old man before him, pursing his lips as if pained by the decision that he had to make. "Don Alfredo doesn't like to discipline his own people, the people with whom he grew up."

'Who did he grow up with?' Dom thought, but his expression was like stone.

"But I'm afraid I cannot allow you to steal." With a nod he directed his men, but Dom did not know what was to happen. The burly men lifted the skeleton of a man, his joints loose and swollen. The old *contadino* screamed upon liberation of his jaw.

"Don Alfredo! *Per favore! Per favore!* My family will starve without me! Please, Don Alfredo! Be lenient."

"Unfortunately, my friend," Don Alfredo frowned, his eyes closed in mock repentance for what he was about to do. "My family will starve if I let everyone in Campania steal from me."

Alfredo turned to the crowd as the old man was bound face first to the wheel of Pratolina's carriage. Pratolina looked at Dom, her eyes wide with fear. Dom screamed at her in his mind, 'get out of the carriage!' Amazingly, she seemed to hear his desperate thoughts. She jumped out, pulling her father with her.

"I am well within my rights under the law of this country to hang this man for his crime." Alfred walked around the edge of the crowd. "But I will be lenient." He followed the arc of the crowd to the end where was placed a square, black box. He opened the box, reached in and Dom could not breathe as he saw the long, leather whip, like a black snake, in the hands of the *Padrone.* "I will give the old peasant a chance. As is my right under the laws of this land, and in the name of his majesty, the ultimate law of a united Italy *Vittorio Emmanuelo Re D'Italia*, I hereby sentence you to thirty lashes to be delivered at two-second intervals for the next minute. After which your debt to this village will be paid and you may go on your way with no further penalty."

"Oh no...Oh no." Dom did not realize that he was speaking aloud until Enrico nudged his arm. But Dom was no longer like stone. His jaw became weak, and his mouth hung agape like an idiot.

The canvas was cut from the *contadino*'s back revealing white, almost translucent, skin. He still spoke, but his words were incoherent from his slathering mouth. Tears flowed, clenched closed eyes and he shook his head pitifully. Occasionally Dom could hear him say 'No,' '*per favore*,' but his pleading became an unintelligible whimper.

Don Alfredo, with deliberation, walked within striking distance of the pathetic old man tied helplessly to the wheel. It was a silent eternity which Don Alfredo used like a brilliant actor sculpting time to emphasize the drama of the moment. The crowd was hushed but for the crying of the *contadino*'s desperate, pleading wife. Another burly man held her. Children, likely the peasant's grandchildren waled and reached for the doomed old man tied to the wheel. The silence of the gathering muffled the sound of their crying. Or perhaps it was the throbbing of Dominico's heart against the wall of his chest as Don Alfredo stepped within distance of the old peasant and drew back his arm, the whip whirling in the air—Satan's tail thrashing about to its owner's cold laughter. Father Antonio waved the sign of the cross in the air then closed his eyes.

The whip floated in the air as time slowed, uncoiling with an oily grace toward the ashen skin of the peasant's naked back. Then there was the crack like the strike of a tiny lightning bolt echoing against the face of the church, echoing among the silent, statuesque crowd. Dom winced to the sound of it.

There was also another sound, an alien, sickening sound that Dom could not decipher. He could not decipher it until the next strike, the next crack that also seemed to take forever. Once he realized what it was, he became sick to his stomach and tried to ignore it, but it repeated itself with every crack of the whip. It was the sound of the old man's skin ripping and splitting as the whip pulled it from his bones and sinew.

It was that sound that Dom could hear, he could almost feel the narrow end of the whip pulling the skin from his own back with every lash delivered by the "merciful" Don. It was this sickening sound that he could hear above the screaming of the old peasant—the banshee like screaming. Screaming so deep that it echoed from the lungs of the very earth on which he stood. Screaming so violent that blood sprayed from the old man's dry throat. It sprayed at first in a fine, brown mist, then in sickening clods of brown into the carriage.

The screaming was the first sound to stop. The peasant's bony frame sagged, a lifeless bag of flesh against the wheel. His arms were stretched, thin, white and bloody. Yet the whipping continued, striking, and snapping, again and again, eleven...twelve...thirteen. Each strike ripped another wide, red swath across the poor *contadino*'s back. Each strike burned into Dom's soul, a scream from inside. Fifteen...sixteen...seventeen...and Dom watched every strike. He watched the thin, translucent skin torn from the old man's back. He watched as the flesh was brutally exposed, torn and hanging, to the hot, Campanian sun. blood flowed in wide streams from the slices in his back, across his bare legs, pooling briefly on the parched ground before being sucked into the thirsty earth.

Nineteen...twenty...twenty-one. Dom found strength in hatred for the *Padrone*. His jaw set and his eyes narrowed, no longer flinching at the grotesque he was witnessing. He was like stone. He was like stone on the outside. Within, however, he burned, he seethed with anger, a volcano, pressure boiling, waiting for release making his muscles tight and still. 'This was no *Brigante*. This was just a man who was trying to feed his family. He was a man at the end of his rope, hopeless and without any recourse.' Twenty-five...twenty-six...twenty-seven. 'How can this happen? Why do we let this happen?' But Dom already knew the answer. This was the way it was. *Il Padrone* was the law. This was how Campania worked. It was how Campania worked in the days of the Samnites, the Roman, the Normans. This was the way it would always be.

'How far will I have to fall before I become that desperate' he thought. Twenty-eight. 'Will that be me one day, tied to a wheel and whipped to death for trying to feed my own children?' Twenty-nine. 'What will become of his family?' Thirty.

Don Alfredo stopped. The whip, once so alive, lay coiled, impotent about his feet. The Don inhaled, his diminutive chest expanding with pride, and stared at the destroyed old man as the cobbles under the wheel soaked red and brown. Within a few seconds Don Alfredo nodded to the man holding the peasant's wife, her tears dried, breathing dulled, face pallid and lifeless. She fell to the earth, her legs too weak to support her, but she crawled to her bleeding husband, wrapped her arms around his bloody leg and held him. A young man, perhaps one of their sons, approached and cut the bonds that held his father, took him gingerly into his arms and lowered him to the blood-muddied ground. Dom noticed the old *Contadino* draw a shallow breath. 'My God. He's still alive.'

"So," Don Alfredo addressed the crowd. "Is there anyone else who would like to steal from me? Is there anyone else who thinks he can take what is mine."

The crowd murmured, but no one stood out to speak. 'Someone should say something.' Dom thought. He looked at his father and his grandfather. 'Someone should point out that it's not right for one man to have all of the wealth when the rest of the population starves or barely gets by.' His elders did not move. They stood and said nothing, did nothing, just stared blankly like stone at *Il Padrone*. 'It's not right for those who work to live like this.' Dom thought, but alas, he too said nothing. 'Is this how it will always be?' He knew that the answer was yes.

Il Gabelloto dragged the peasant, his wife grasped his listless body, refusing to let go. He dragged them unceremoniously from the carriage, brushing the young man aside like a cur. He then motioned *Signore* Mastradelfiori and his daughter to return to the carriage. Pratolina and her father obeyed the unspoken order. Don Alfredo mounted his horse and, with his contingency behind him, trotted through the mass of people.

"*La Miseria*!" Someone shouted. Soon the masses repeated the statement, "*La Miseria*." "*La miseria*!" As Don Alfredo rode through them—untouched. "*La Miseria!*"

They said it not in unison, but as a patchwork of dissention. They spoke as a hundred individuals, not as one unified voice. Thus, they were defeated.

Dom waited for Pratolina at the top of the hill for what seemed like forever. He could not wait for his family to bed down. Instead, he asked his father and mother if he could be excused after the meal, then walked into the dark fields. Enrico understood what his son was going through. He knew that his boy, so new as a man, needed time and space to make sense of what had seen that day. To see a man whipped and destroyed, then to walk away and lay brick as if it were any other day. This was hard on a young man. Enrico had not forgotten what seeing such injustice, such horror, for the first time was like. But he'd also learned that all one could do was walk away from it and concentrate on living, concentrate on working, and accept that the world is not a just place.

His son would have to learn that as well, but that would take time and patience. This was the hardest lesson of all. 'Be like stone.' And that night the family was like stone.

There was no heartfelt intimacy, no jovial story telling in the Rossa household, nor in any other. There was only silence and solemnity except for Paolo who saw nothing of what had happened as he was in the back of the crowd and not tall enough to be a witness to the travesty. He must have heard the screams, but he did not connect with the horror. Paolo tried to be endearing but managed to merit only a sympathetic smile from *Nonno*. Anna hadn't seen the whipping either, but she fed off the emotions of others and was equally solemn that night.

It was a relief for Dom to get away, to walk to that hill knowing that he would see Pratolina. He discovered that when his heart was heavy, he wanted to be with her. He wanted to find comfort in her.

He was sitting with his thighs pulled to his chest, his chin resting on his knees, his eyes staring at the quarter moon. He heard gentle footsteps in the dry grass and soon Pratolina sat beside him. She held the same blanket she had three days ago, but simply placed it on the ground beside her. She too pulled her thighs up to her chest, careful to straighten her dress and cover her legs this time. There they sat, quiet and still, staring at the moon.

"He died." Dom said. His voice was dry and uneven.

"What?"

"*Il contadino*. He died just before sundown. He lost too much blood, I don't know. But he died."

Pratolina swallowed hard and stared at Dom who continued to look at the moon. "I...I..."

Her voice broke. She could not form the words that could come close to expressing her feelings. Dom turned to her, her brown eyes sad and wet and...scared.

"I got...I got his blood...on me." She quivered before her tears took control, shoulders shuddering, chest heaving. "I got his blood on me! I...got..."

Dom reached his arm around her and pulled her close. She wept uncontrollably into his chest as he ran his fingers through her hair and rocked her, doing his best to make the memories of the morning go away. She merely muttered between her sobbing, "I got his...blood...on me..."

'I did too.' Dom thought as he stared into the face of the moon. 'We all did.'

CHAPTER 10

The silence of the little, sunbaked town was aroused by the gentle din of the pipe organ emanating from the church. This was Sunday's final procession of Father Antonio, the pastor and, in fact, the only representative of God in this *paesera*. Father Antonio was a short man, robust of frame and ruddy of complexion. Despite the often-solemn nature of his work he kept a jovial smile upon his fleshy face. During this mass, however, his face was sober and unnaturally pale as if he were ill, as if he'd contracted the crippling, painful disease of the village, the angst of the punished and brutalized. The weight of the *paesera*, a few hundred heavy souls, pressed upon his brow and made his temples ache.

With a slow, deliberate pace, he walked to the back of the church, gently swinging a tarnished, brass incense burner. He just could not get the relic to hold a shine anymore. He polished it often, but the long, brass burner would no longer shine. With slow steps he walked, his back arched from the fatigue of supporting the souls of his parish for the better part of the day, his corpulent body swaying back and forth with every step.

This was a difficult mass, he thought. His parishioners were desperate, angry. He could almost hear the silent questions of the congregation, the critical musing of a people abandoned by their patriarch, their God, their saints. There was nothing left. There was no one to pray to. There was only *Il Padrone* and his long, satanic whip. This pasty-faced demon to whom God vouched free reign over the miserable inhabitants of *Villa de San Giuseppe*. Father Antonio found himself unable to carry the weight of the onerous suspicion of God's motives projected onto the village Priest. 'They're questioning **my** motives.' He thought. 'They saw me on the steps behind *Il Padrone*. They did not see me crying?'

As Father Antonio pressed the great, mahogany door open, pressing it hard as it had warped sometime in the last three hundred years and required effort to move, he heard the congregation stir and follow him out of the church. They let out their breath collectively once the door was open. The old church itself seemed to sigh. With all eyes on the floor, they walked behind their Priest. The silent reverence that they displayed in the house of God was not unusual, but on that day, it felt cumbrous and unnatural. Standing beside the great door, bidding farewell to the congregation as they passed him, the silence was all encompassing.

When mass ended on a typical Sunday afternoon the congregation left the church, and the silence was over.

Laughter began, men found their groups and told stories, children jumped from the church steps and began their ribald play before their feet hit the ground. On that day, however, the stygian silence followed the *abitante* from the hallowed house of God onto the less than hallowed *piazza*. The cobbles where the old *contadino* was whipped were still brown and tainted with blood despite the Rossa men's attempt to clean them. They were a reminder of the previous day's event and were of more symbolic value at that point than the tired, old church.

Yet life continued in town that day. It continued as it always had since the church was built so many countless centuries ago. The people of the countryside gathered in the *piazza* and relaxed after the long day of Catholic ritual and cleansing in the eyes of God. They formed numerous smaller congregations. The men, clad in their best suits of black and gray, gathered into their own groups, talking business or trading salacious stories in marked contrast to their stoicism within the walls of the church. Father Antonio was always amused by the conspicuous silence of these groups of men as he walked among them or even joined them for a moment. The men would smile and exchange pleasantries with the priest, but Father Antonio knew they could not wait for him to leave. And perhaps it was a mortal sin, but Father Antonio enjoyed their discomfort.

The women coalesced into a larger congregation. They usually moved as one body in laying out food and wine around the dry fountain. Between these groups, children played and ran, girls giggling with joy, boys laughing, being chastised by their mothers for soiling their Sunday clothes, some being pulled by the ear while mother whacked their stooped bottoms.

Sometimes there were groups in which the sexes were mixed. They were the young men and women for whom courtships were managed and marriages arranged. Such gatherings were scrutinized by the elder women and chaperoned by the families' older brothers or uncles or cousins—rarely ever fathers. Fathers delegated the defense of their daughters' honor to the eldest sons as they themselves sought their own, small cadres and tended their duties and obligations. The wives oversaw family matters and all responsibility in such matters was deferred to them. Fathers took care of business, work, and the social education of their sons.

Hortensia Rossa found herself waiting by the church steps as directed by her mother. She fidgeted with her hair, hoping that it was tied securely in place and would not come undone. She straightened her dress, mindful of the repairs made to it over the years. The patches and seams were well hidden. In fact, hers was a relatively new and well-kept dress compared to many of the women in this country. Hortensia stood awkwardly by the stairs, not daring to rest her weight on one leg lest she make her hips look too big, or her back look crooked. Her lips, usually full and red, were forced tightly together, and her brow, normally a smooth copper, was wrinkled with apprehension.

"Dominico." Enrico called quietly to his son.

"Yes, Papa."

"I want you to stay close to your sister. You watch out for her today. Mama is going to introduce her to Rafael in a few minutes and you are going to make sure she's okay. This is important work now, Dominico."

"I know, Papa."

"Your Aunts Angelona and Vedora will be nearby watching out as well, but there should certainly be a man's presence there. Remember, this is the first time they've met, so there will be no touching. If this works out, he may touch her hand on the next visit, but no touching today. Do you understand?"

"No touching. Yes, Papa."

"Good." Enrico nodded and patted his son's cheek. "I'll be with Ugo and *Nonno* and Father Antonio. We're going to replace those cobbles tomorrow before we go over to the wall." Enrico waved his hand in the direction of the bloody cobbles visible as none of the villagers would go near the area.

"Yes, good, Papa. That's not good to have around." But Dominico had this queasiness in his stomach as he considered touching the bloody cobbles.

Enrico walked away and Dominico approached his sister. He smiled at her, but she could not smile back. She was shaking, her muscles were stiff. Dom kissed her gently on the cheek and that brought a brief smile and a *grazie*. He then stepped behind her and braced a severe look upon his face.

Shortly thereafter Sara and her older, sterner sisters approached. Behind them was a tall, thin man with thin black hair and a bony, but innocuous, face escorted by an older man and woman. He was Rafaelo Montandenestra. His father, Geraldo, made a good living transporting goods from Salerno, Napoli, and Caserta into this little town. All who lived in this country had to do business with him except *Il Padrone*, who utilized his services in exchange for the privilege of living on Belan land and travelling rough and inadequate Belan roads. *Signore* Montandenestra even had to pay a levy to Don Alfredo for importing goods into the *Paesera,* the cost of which was, of course, passed on to the villagers, making them that much poorer.

Despite this, Geraldo was able to prosper for the most part. He was a well-liked and respected man in *Villa de San Giuseppe*. He was known for his ability to get the best price on goods and pass them on to the struggling businessmen. Lately, however, Geraldo was struggling. Businesses and farms in the area were depressed. There was less demand for supplies from *la citta*. His trips were fewer and further between and what once required numerous asses pulling as many wagons currently required only one.

Still, the Montandenestra family would make a good adjunct to the Rossas, or any such family in *la paesera*. Three of his sons were of age. The two eldest, in their mid-twenties, were already married and had started their families. The third son, Rafael, was highly sought after by the families of the town. But *Signore* Montandenestra was most excited about Hortensia Rossa. The Rossa dowry, as agreed upon earlier in the week, was not the largest offered in exchange for a marriage with Rafael, but the Rossa name was one of respect in this country. The elder *Mastro* Rossa was well known throughout Campania for his skill and craftsmanship. His son, Enrico was also respected as an honest businessman as well as a man of charity and good faith. An alliance with the Rossa family, Geraldo decided, would be in the best interest of his faltering business.

And Sara, Enrico Rossa's wife, was of the Bagliacci family. The women of this family were well known for their fecundity. Their children tended to survive that tenuous five years of life that was so harsh a gauntlet to young Campanians. Sara had only lost one child, a boy born nineteen years earlier, her next child after Hortensia. He was born sickly and died within six months. Her next three children, however, survived with little difficulty. Dominico suffered one fever in youth. Paolo was six before his first major illness. Anna was rarely ill and, when sick, was quick to convalesce. The women of the Montandenestra household noticed that Hortensia had inherited Sara's bodily structure, including her all-important hips. Her back and shoulders and ample bosom were those of her mother's, yet that deep and relentless look in her eyes was Rossa blood indeed. All these facts were contained in the unwritten register of village families, known to all.

"Hortensia, come here." Sara Rossa sang to her daughter. A broad grin spread across her face. The wrinkles beside her eyes and along her cheek only amplified the beauty of her smile.

Hortensia turned briefly toward her brother. She realized how rare it was that she said anything nice to him. She always nagged at him and bit at him with her words. It did not matter how hard he worked—and he did work hard—she would attack him for not working hard enough. It did not matter how he dressed, she would accuse him of slovenliness. But she loved him, and he knew it. He always just blew off her inane and false comments without retort because he knew that she loved him, and he had learned Papa's penchant for not pointing out the obvious and for brushing off the meaningless. He could tell by her smile and by the warmth in her eyes that her words were meaningless and that her love was obvious. Now here he was, tall and stern, to protect her honor. She loved him so much.

"*Signore* Rafael Montandenestra," Sara said as her daughter approached. She bowed and smiled to the young man. "I would very much like you to meet my daughter, Hortensia Saralina Rossa."

Rafael was the least outgoing of the gregarious Montandenestra's and he seemed to fumble with himself about his next step. Geraldo poked him in the ribs with his nubby fingers and with a sunny smile motioned his son to approach Hortensia.

The confused young man bowed slightly and moved to take Hortensia's hand but looked up at Dominico first. Dom shook his head ever so slightly and stared into Rafael's eyes. He'd never stared into anyone's eyes in such a way, as if fire could be thrown from his dark irises. Rafael flinched back slightly then stared back at Hortensia. He produced a bundle of flowers from behind his back—*Pratoline*—and held them out to the Rossa girl. "It is good to meet you."

Hortensia reached for the flowers with both hands, meticulously scrubbed clean. "*Grazie mille*." She smiled and curtsied subtly as she held the flowers to her breast.

Dominico simply stared at the flowers in his sister's hands—*prataline*. His mind, always occupied with the image of his beautiful oread was now bombarded with memories and feelings. His heart raced as he remembered looking for her in church, straining his eyes to look around the congregation without turning his neck. But she was on the balcony with her father and his employer. Dom did not dare turn all the way around to see her, yet he felt that he could feel her gaze upon him. The Rossas sat in the front of the church and were easily visible to all.

Now his attention was riveted on the important duty of overseeing his sister. He could not afford to be distracted from this effort. He was doing well in focusing on his responsibility. He was doing so very well until Rafael brought the dry, pastel bundle of *prataline* into Dom's consciousness. It was all that Dom could do to keep his attention on his older sister and her suitor as they walked around the *piazza*.

Without thinking Dom scanned the crowd looking for Pratolina. He looked toward Don Alfredo who sat in front of one of the shops. Every Sunday he chose a storefront and would sit in front of it in a large leather chair. Townsmen would walk up to him and pay him respect by kissing his hand. They would then ask him permission for something or look to him for a favor or dispensation. Women would bring their babies to meet him or ask for his blessing for their children who were to be married. This Sunday, however, few people visited him. Those who visited did so out of dire necessity.

Dom saw Pratolina's father standing beside Don Alfredo. At times, the patriarch would turn to him with something to say, and *Signore* Mastradelfiori would respond in a stiff and professional manner. But Pratolina was nowhere to be seen.

Hortensia and Rafael seemed to be getting along well. The redness in the young man's face was fading as he talked with Dom's sister. She in turn smiled and listened to what he had to say, rarely interjecting. Rafael spoke of his travels. Compared to those who lived in this country, Rafael was cosmopolitan. The villagers in this country never saw anything outside of their own hometowns and villages. He told her stories about the cities, especially the ports of Napoli. He told her about the ocean that she had never seen. She was fascinated by his description of Mount Vesuvius, the great volcano that overlooks the ancient city. Hortensia nodded, smiled, and was genuinely interested in what he was saying.

Dom was more interested in the discourse between his mother and Georgianna Montandenestra, Rafael's mother. This was the mechanics of marriage and was of much greater substance than anything that Rafael had to say. At this point Sara and Georgianna had the final say in whether there would be a marriage and when that marriage would take place. Rafael and Hortensia had little say in the matter. Dom considered this truth with a new and critical perspective. He was stricken by the dry reality of what was going on behind the sweet façade of a man and a woman walking together. He noticed the listlessness of this transaction in contrast to the ethereal and sensational reality that he experienced with Pratolina on that hill.

And as he thought about his oread on that hill, under the moonlight, there she was—his Pratolina. Rafael and Hortensia brushed passed her under a crowded nun's walk on the rim of the *piazza*. She stood with some women who were watching their children run and play. Pratolina took boundless joy in watching the children and laughing at their foibles. The children were the first to heal from the events of the day before as they were protected from the sight of cruelty. Once free of adult languidness they burst forth in their typical, childish play.

Pratolina was laughing and pointing to one of the little boys as the Rossa party walked by. She stopped talking mid-sentence when she noticed Dom approaching her. At first, she seemed…frightened. Dom sensed that she was frightened, but he knew not why. Then as he drew closer her emotions turned to those of confusion and awkwardness and this Dom understood. He wanted so much to see her, to catch a glimpse of her. Now he was about to bump into her, he did not know what he was supposed to do. He did not know of any rules or customs for defining and regulating this interaction. There were such rules for everything, but how does one learn the proper rituals for this interaction? It was not like he could ask the priest.

He thought about the men who would smile slyly at their mistresses, and he knew that he could not smile at Pratolina. She was not his mistress, but if he were to smile everyone would think that she was. He thought that he should take his eyes off her and brush by as if he did not know her, but that would hurt. It would hurt him not to at least acknowledge her. Approaching her seemed to take forever, yet it was not enough time for him to decide what to do.

As he approached, he gazed into her eyes. He could not take his eyes off her. She was of the same mind. Pratolina looked into his eyes asking him what she should do, but he could not answer. He could only walk by her, looking into her eyes, hoping that no one else would see the questions that peeked from behind them. So, they passed, looking into each other's eyes, wishing that they were on that hill, wishing that they were somewhere away from all these prying eyes. Dom felt that everyone could see the feelings between him and the beautiful oread. He longed for the solitude of the hilltop, for a world in which only she existed. Then he would know what to do. In the absence of the bonds that are other people he would be free and would know what to do.

Instead, he had to live through the awkwardness of it. He would not see her for another two days. For over forty-eight hours he would dwell on this five-second interval. He would replay it over and over...

CHAPTER 11

"Come with us, *Figlio.*" Enrico said as he stood up, slapping the top of the table with his thick palm.

Enrico had been staring at Dominico throughout the entire meal. There was an unspoken question between father and son. Enrico did not know the nature of the question, but as the head of the family he had to answer it and be satisfied with what he decided. Dom realized that whatever his father was thinking, it was a matter of tremendous import. The intense scrutiny, however, was making him uncomfortable. In the last few days Dom was feeling uncomfortable in his own home, like wearing clothes that were too tight.

Primarily, he was uncomfortable because, for the first time in his life, he was keeping a secret from his family. This was gnawing at him from the inside, but he dared not speak of his adventures on the hill. As open minded as his family was, they remained steeped in the traditions and mores of a culture hundreds of years old—older than the stone ruins around laying like old bones around the countryside. He would hold on to his secret and keep Pratolina in that special, hidden place in his heart.

At the same time, his family knew him well. Every day Dom wondered just how much they knew, how many of the details they were gathering from his far away stares and evasive answers to simple questions. He wondered just how much they knew about his long walks every third night. Had they followed him on Saturday? Did they know about Pratolina? He did not think they knew about her, but they knew something.

To which Dom could only wonder, 'why don't they say something? Why don't they ask?' Dom was trapped. He did not want his family to ask about his nocturnal strolls, for he would not lie to them. On the other hand, the thought that they knew that something was amiss and yet held their questions was uncharacteristic. This was the most ominous phenomenon resulting from this experience. Sometimes Dom wished they would ask just so he could shed himself the burden of his secret. He had not realized that a hidden life was so heavy. Every day he debated telling his father the truth about his even walks. His father would understand. He was a man. He had been young before. Yet Dominico could not embrace the fact that his father had once been a young man. He could not imagine the many loves his father may have had or the secret strolls that may continue to live in his heart. This was his father.

Now, with Enrico asking Dom to join *Nonno* and him, Dom felt a stone lodge in one of the vessels of his heart.

'They know,' he thought. 'They're going to confront me on it. They're going to tell me that I can't see her anymore—that I'm bringing shame to the family name.' In his mind, he rehearsed how he would respond. He considered bursting with anger and resentment, even violence against anyone who would keep him away from his oread. This tactic fell from his mind as soon as it bloomed. The reality was that he held his father and his grandfather in too high esteem to act in such a disrespectful manner. The best he could do was acknowledge that he'd done something terribly wrong, agree to never see her again, then make tracks to the hill to tell Pratolina that they had to find another meeting place. This, too, was disrespectful. Something would have to break.

He was to meet her tonight and this break from the routine with his father and grandfather had Dominico nervous. He hoped that he would be able to break away. Dom prayed that he would not be late meeting her and if he were, he prayed with equal fervor that she would wait for him. The boy becoming a man hoped that she would not be angry with him, that she would want to continue meeting him.

"Where are we going, Papa?" Dom asked, following the two men into the shop and out to the work yard. They passed by the angel that sat where they had left it over two weeks ago. It seemed such a long time to Dom. Somewhere, somehow, in that span of time, the entire landscape of his life had changed.

"We're going to *Signore* Montandenestra's warehouse. We'll be meeting the other men of the village there." *Nonno* responded. He had an unusually grim look on his face. His eyes were clearer and stronger than Dom had ever seen, but they lacked the cheer that was intrinsic of his grandfather.

Dom wanted to ask why. He wanted to know what was going on. Most of all, Dom was concerned with how long this gathering was going to take. He had other places to be. Better places than a musty warehouse full of men. But at least he knew that he would not be confronted about Pratolina. He was spared this trial for at least another day.

"Sometimes the men of the *paesera* get together, Dominico. When we have important things to discuss we get together at night and talk." Enrico explained as they reached the main road and started for town.

Dom saw a light to the left of the *piazza*. The moon was waxing a quarter full and provided enough light for the Rossas to walk the craggy road without carrying lanterns.

"Will Don Alfredo be there?" Dom asked.

Enrico looked straight ahead, his eyes narrowing to angry slits. "No," he said calmly, but the coldness in his voice matched that of *Nonno's* eyes. Dom realized he was about to participate in something important. Yet, though his eyes were focused on the warehouse, his heart was reaching to the distant hill with the sprawling tree. "Only the men of the village will be there." *Nonno* said, emphasizing 'men.' Out of instinct, Dom looked around to make sure no one heard such a disparaging remark.

When the Rossas reached the warehouse door Enrico knocked a rhythmic pattern on the door. The old, gray door eased open on creaking hinges. The three men outside scanned the surrounding area to make sure no one was around to hear the squawking hinges. Dom did not really know what he was looking for but knew that he should be looking. When they stepped into the warehouse Dom noticed that there were two flat carts outside. A few more carts were disassembled and stacked in a corner, for they had not been used in many years and there was no prospect of them being used in the future. The warehouse contained very few items yet many, many empty shelves, and pallets where erstwhile goods were stored when times were good.

About two dozen men gathered in the center, some sitting on chairs and boxes and barrels, others standing or leaning against beams or large crates. Dom knew all the men, some better than others. They were all townsmen, craftsmen, tradesmen, and business owners. There were no farm overseers. In fact, nobody in the employ of *Il Padrone* was present in that building.

The omission of *Il Padrone's* representatives may have surprised Dominico, but the absence of *contadini* went unnoticed. The townspeople and skilled farmers never associated with the peasants who were considered unskilled and thus inferior people.

"*Mastro* Rossa," *Signore* Montandenestra approached and kissed *Nonno* and Enrico on both cheeks. "Thank you for being here. *Grazie*! *E tu*, Dominico. Welcome. Welcome." Geraldo held his arms out with warm welcome before hugging Dominico and kissing him on the cheek.

"This will be your first meeting, Dominico," remarked *Signore* Nuovo, the cooper. "You know that you are to discuss nothing you hear tonight, don't you."

Enrico coughed, "My son will keep this to himself. He should be here. This affects him as a man."

Signore Nuovo nodded along with the rest of the men.

"Are we all here?" *Nonno* asked as he scanned the room. "It looks like it. You know why we are here, don't you?"

Donatello Zuollo spoke first. His bellicose voice banged against the walls like a hammer. "We are here because we have seen the last atrocity from the pig on the hill."

Dom winced as he realized *Signore* Zuollo was talking about Don Alfredo. *Signore* Zuollo stood in the center of the group and waved his thick, round, ironsmith arms. "The way he killed that poor *contadino* on Saturday...and right in front of the church..."

"It was just a peasant, and a thief at that." One of the men in the back broke in weakly.

"It wasn't just a *contadino*, Bepe!" *Signore* De Toscanii added. "It's been all of us. I know he has been requesting extra levies from my family."

"Ours, too...He never gets enough...he takes it all when he can..." The men spoke out *en masse*, arms waving and heads nodding assent. "How much can a *contadino* steal compared to *Il Padrone*?"

The voices melded together. Enrico held out his hands and waved, "No...no...we can't continue like this. Let each other talk or else we'll get nowhere."

De Toscanii continued. "*Il Padrone* is taking more from us and tightening down on our actions more and more. How many of you are doing work for Don Alfredo without compensation?"

The men grumbled, but no one spoke.

"You must understand," *Nonno* added. "These are the actions of a desperate man. When a *padrone* becomes desperate times are bad and much blood is spilled. I've seen this before. Enough to know." His thin, white finger waved in the air. The older men with the same memories agreed.

"It won't be long," One of the old men started, "before we start seeing his men come into our houses searching for money or seed or any valuables that they can steal. *Il contadino* was only doing what Dons have been doing for centuries."

"And don't think *Il Padrone* will stop at whipping *contadini*." Enrico said. "He will whip every man, woman and child in this country if it serves his interests. I, for one, am getting tired of submitting to his requests. I'm getting tired of him taking food out of the mouths of my family."

"We have a new king now, Vitorio Emanuello..."

The men hissed at the barer of that news. Enrico shook his head, "it doesn't matter. Forty years ago, we were told that we would be part of a great republic. You were there, Papa," Enrico turned to his father. "I was too young, but I remember...I remember Garibaldi's Redshirts watering their horses in the village."

Nonno nodded, as did the older men. "That was after the union. You were still in the womb when some of us fought with Garibaldi in *Napoli*." Dom noticed two other older men nodding and looking at the floor, their old, leathery arms folded across their chests. "We were told that we would be part of a great republic, that a united *Italia* would regain the old glories—*La gloria da Roma*. One year later we are a kingdom under the first Vitorio Emanuello."

"And has anything changed?" Enrico asked his father.

Nonno simply shook his head and pursed his lips to control a deep frown. Dom stared at his grandfather. 'Nonno fought with Garibaldi?' The landscape changed even more. How much more did he not know?

"And it's not going to change. Do we think we can get any help from *Napoli? Napoli* is just as corrupt and dirty as our town. Vitorio Emanuello is no better than *Il Padrone*. Nothing will change unless we make it change." Enrico's hands clasped into great fists, his knuckles white and hard.

"So, what do we do, *Mastro* Rossa? Are you suggesting that we fight *Il Padrone*? What guns we have are old and misfire more often than not. *Il Padrone* has guns from Germany and America. He has horses when all we have are half-ruined asses. What do you suggest we do?"

"I'm suggesting that if we stick together *Il Padrone* will have to treat us with respect." Enrico said.

The men in the warehouse grumbled some more.

"Let the man talk," *Signore* Nuovo called out and silenced the room.

Enrico continued. "He can't come down and wipe us out. He relies on us. He depends on the work we do. This is making him desperate. Between the droughts and the pestilence and parasites he's been hit hard. And because of this he is even more dependent upon us. That's why he raises our levies and our rent. That's why he feels he must whip us to make us behave. He's afraid. He knows that we don't need him, but he needs us. He doesn't want us to know that. He's afraid of us. He's afraid of what will happen if we stand together. Without us, he's finished."

"He'll fight, Enrico. He'll hang the first one of us who speaks like this."

"Then we all have to speak at the same time." Enrico slapped the man on the shoulder. "He can't hang us all. Aren't we tired of being treated like animals? I am. What will my son go through? He'll be starting a family in a couple of years and what will he have? Nothing. What about your sons? What will they have? Nothing. *Il Padrone* will take it all. And what's worse, he'll take our pride with it. I read a great man long ago who said he would rather die like a man than live like a dog. We are living like dogs right now. My littlest girl must go out in the hills and pick wild plants and prickly pears just so we can have enough to fill our bellies. What kind of life is this?

"And my son and I have been to *Il Latifundo*. It doesn't look like it used to when I was a boy, but there is still wealth there. Much wealth. There's a fountain there pouring clear water from a statue being used for nothing more than decoration. There are fruit bearing trees, and the fruit will be loaded onto ships and sent to other lands while we starve. And then Don Alfredo will come down and take what money we have, what valuables we have and beat us if we resist, kill us if we dare to do the same to him. Is that not being treated as dogs? Is there a man in this room who doesn't feel his heart becoming heavy and his liver getting soft as he stands around and lets this happen?" Enrico's eyes blazed as he looked around the warehouse. Only half of the men would meet his gaze, the rest stared at the floor.

"I talk to *Signore* DeVallo. He brings me news from other cities, other *paesere*. He tells me of villages in *Sicilia* where the people are uniting and driving their *padrone* from the countryside. They are freeing themselves by sticking together. No...this is no longer about a ragged *contadino* being whipped and beaten at the steps of our church. This is about a people who sit back and allow themselves to be destroyed by one man. This is about the backbone of the country, those who work and sweat and bleed and destroy their bodies for nothing. We work for the sake of stuffing the pockets of a man who is already wealthy. I don't mind breaking my back to put food on my table. I wouldn't mind breaking my back to put food on the table of any man in this room. I won't break my back for *Il Padrone*. We should be able to cover our own tables, feed our own children, clothe our own wives."

As Enrico spoke Dom noticed more heads rising, wide eyes met his father's gaze. People breathed deeper, and their hearts pounded harder and steadier, stronger. There was a soul in that room, a unity that was not there when they walked in. Dom realized that this unity was born of his father's words. He'd never heard anyone speak like this and never imagined that his father could be so stirring. He never realized how the simple act of talk could raise spirits and bring strength to the soul.

"We are with you, *Mastro* Rossa." *Signore* Nuovo said, turning to the crowd of men and swirling his arms like two great fans. "Are we with him? Are we united?"

"*Si*!" They cried in one great voice like a song. "We are with you *Mastro* Rossa!"

Enrico shook his head angrily. "Never again!"

"Never again!" They repeated.

"Never again will we allow our own to be beaten."

"Never!"

"Never again will we allow anyone to steal from our families."

"No...Never again!"

"Are we going to stand together?"

"Yes!"

"Are we going to fight together?"

"Yes."

Signore Montandenestra approached. "*Grazie. Grazie. Mastro* Rossa. Thank you. We will be there when *Il Padrone* serves any of us another injustice. We will be there. His actions will not go without resistance."

"There's no other way." Enrico nodded.

It was late by the time the men dispersed to their homes. Enrico's reputation within the village was raised to the next level. One might say that Enrico Rossa was placed in some archetypal arena in opposition to *Il Padrone*. He was the heroic image, a living icon. Dom felt a passion flow in him, as if his soul was set on fire and every breath was a conquest. He was proud. He was proud to be his father's son. Proud for the first time in over two weeks when he watched his father supplicate himself at the hands of the *padrone*.

Enrico could feel the fire burn within him as well. He knew what the meeting was to be about and had opted early to say nothing. He'd grown too cynical over the years. His own political philosophy was one of futility, not unity. He was not a revolutionary, not a leader of men. But as he stood in that warehouse, awash in defeat and a self-loathing that sat and stagnated, a black bile stirred and frothed until it exploded from his mouth in anger. As he spoke, he became lighter in body and stronger in spirit. As he spoke his soul connected to those in the room. One by one their souls mingled with his, becoming stronger. Souls united, strengthening until all were as one and his voice was the all-encompassing reality. For the first time in his life, he felt that things really could change.

Nonno was...tired. He too had been caught up in the energy that pervaded the warehouse. Once they stepped out of the old, gray building, however, he became tired. The energy drained from him. His own cynicism was more ingrained from many years on Campanian soil. Now he was tired, his back bowed at the shoulders from his own weight.

"*Nonno*." Dominico took his arm and walked with him. "I never knew you fought with Garibaldi."

His grandfather looked at him, his eyes betraying the fatigue of his spine. The old, crooked man shook his head slightly. "In the end, it was nothing to speak of."

Dominico ran across the fields toward the hill. He was breathing heavily. His heart pounding in his chest raised a convincing argument for him to slow down, but there would be no slowing until he reached the hill. He had to get there as soon as he could. He had to get there before his oread went home angry and dissatisfied. He had to beg her forgiveness for being late and explain that he could not get away. He had to get there before she left, for he felt that if he missed her, he would never see her again.

His father was too aroused to go to bed and Dominico lay in his pallet waiting helplessly as his father stood up and stared out into the fields. Finally, Dom could wait no longer. He was a man, after all. He was not sure if it was with courage or with desperation that he rose from the pallet and approached his father. "Papa, I can't sleep. I need to go for a walk."

Enrico said nothing but looked into his eyes. Dom knew that his father was trying to read his secret. Perhaps he already knew. Finally, Enrico nodded and waved the back of his hand toward the hills. "Don't go too far and don't make your mother worry tomorrow morning."

Dom bounced. "I won't, Papa. I won't." At that he ran into the dark.

Enrico watched, knowing that his son was running to the arms of a woman. There could be no other explanation.

When Dom reached the hill, his heart sank as he did not see the lantern light that always welcomed him. He scrambled up the hill realizing the futility of it. She would not be there, but still he had to climb the hill and at least breathe the air that held her aura.

Upon reaching the top of the hill, however, he noticed the lantern. It lay on its side, unlit. Just beyond the lantern was the gray and brown wool blanket wrapped around Pratolina like a flower protecting its tender bud. She lay in the fetal position, her knees tucked to her chest for warmth. Her little hands provided the pillow for her soft, crimson cheek. Dom stood there taking the opportunity to soak in her beauty, her peace. His heart raced. He breathed in deep, inhaling her very presence.

With stealth, he walked over to her and lay beside her. He positioned himself that he might look at her beautiful, pacific face, her pink lids draped lace over her eyes, scarlet lips parted slightly. She was barefoot and her graceful, white ankles glistened in the moonlight. He watched her sleep, fascinated, enthralled. He thought he had never seen anything so beautiful in all his life. He watched her sleep, content, wanting nothing more in the world but to be a part of her dreams.

Dom did not know how long he was there, enjoying her beauty, careful not to move too fast or breathe to hard lest he wake her. The moon that had lit his way was almost gone over the horizon, however, when she stirred and her lacy lids opened to reveal the beautiful, honey brown eyes that were the core of Dom's thoughts. When she realized that there was someone else there, she was startled but eased in an instant by Dom's gentle hand.

"I knew you'd come," she said as he wrapped his left arm around her shoulders and pulled her to him. Pratolina rested her head on his broad chest and sighed, her voice a sleepy whisper. "How long have you been here."

"I didn't want to wake you." He replied. "I just let you sleep."

"What kept you?" she asked, rubbing her left temple into his chest and yawning. She was comfortable, content.

"It doesn't matter, I'm here now."

Pratolina was satisfied with this answer. She had a naturally probing mind but chose to accept the moment for what it was.

With that answer Dom told her that he was involved with men's business. On this domain women were not allowed. But he told her in a nice way, much nicer than she had heard the men of the *latifundo* tell their wives to mind their own business and stay out of men's affairs. Dom was a gentle soul. She would not fault him for the vanity of his gender.

Besides, she could feel his fingers gently rolling through her hair. It was not long before she was lost in his gentle touch. This was her world, those hot fingers, strong yet tender, carefully stroking her long, thick hair. He was caring and kind as he caressed her hair, careful not to pull where it was knotted in her sleep.

A strong, relentless heart drummed under her ear, calling to her. She knew it belonged to her, beat for her, yearned for her. Her own heart beat the same rhythm. The fingers rolling through her hair...a sigh...a hand on her cheek. Such a gentle-hearted boy, yet strong in spirit. His quiet demeanor contrasted against a loud pounding heart and deep, full breathing. Her long, dark hair curled and coiled around his fingers...fingers caressing the curve of her neck. His was an old soul in such a young, strong body...gentleness. A finger, strong and gentle under her chin, raising her sleepy face. His fingers coiled in the locks of her hair...his breath deep caressing her face, heart pounding fast. His lips were close. She could feel them touch her cheek. Her eyes were closed...his breath on her face... lips on her cheek. 'Closer,' she thought, 'pull me closer.' Arms tightening about her...gentle...his lips against hers—sweet.

CHAPTER 12

"She told me how good everything felt." Cecilia said, a melancholy smile struggled to relieve the heaviness of the situation. The man before her, his head against the stone was motionless as she spoke. How much did he hear? He seemed wrapped in his own thoughts, in his own memories. She might as well have been talking to the stone itself, cold and gray like the man before her. His tears stopped, but not the sadness, the indescribable woe that was so much a part of him. There were no more tears. He was dry, barren in the truest sense of the word. His soul parched, wanting for life, wanting to be slaked with some substance that would return to him at least a fragment of his spirit.

Reliving her own ethereal memories, she gazed with compassion on the man caressing the stone. "It lasted only a month, she said. It lasted only a month, but she told me that in that month she lived her entire life. She was in love with him, and she would do anything for him. She would have died for him."

'A month,' Dom thought, wishing that he could cry some more. Though he hated the tears they did seem to cleanse him. His tears were his penance. In their absence, in his own spiritual dryness, he knew that there would be no repentance. 'It seemed so much longer than a month. The wall, the rendezvous on the hill.'

"They'd started out meeting every three days, but she said they eventually met every night. They were the sweetest stories you ever heard. She insisted that he needed his sleep, that they should only meet every third day, every other day at the most. He told her that he was unable to sleep. His thoughts of her kept him awake throughout the night. He figured if he was going to lose sleep over her, he should at least be with her. That made her happy, and made her love him even more..."

"Easy, Dominico," Enrico called over to his son. They were finishing the façade, blending the new finish to the sun-bleached surface as best they could. The sun was descending quickly, but the Rossas had so little left to do that they decided to work a little later, work by lantern light if necessary to ensure that they would not have to return in the morning.

Enrico smiled as his son swiped deftly the finishing strokes of the façade. This job had been his cross for almost a month, but it would be done soon, and he could go back to working for his family and putting food on the table. He had two jobs lined up already. No more would he be forced to accept charity from others. No more would he be forced to endure the humiliation of dependence. In fact, what he saw as charity was his own generosity for others was being returned. Still, he felt what was given to his family amounted to charity and every mouthful of charity seemed a swallow of slow, bitter poison. Now that this cursed wall was finished, he could rebuild his life and piece together what was left of his manhood.

He stood back and looked at their handiwork. He'd never seen his son work so hard. Dominico was committed to this wall. Enrico figured that his son was infatuated with the *latifundo*, with the regency that was opened to him, but then he realized that there was something more. He'd noticed the girl, the woman who was walking with the young Alfredo that day a month ago. She always managed to make an appearance in the trees while they were working. Indeed, she was a delight to the eye and certainly Dominico had noticed her, but would he have allowed himself to get involved with her? Enrico put the thought out of his mind and stared at the wall.

It was a piece of perfection, the wall. A slight hump marked where the old wall ended and the new addition began, but Enrico knew that the ground would settle and within a week there would be no difference at all. It would be a flat and continuous piece. The only difference that a returning visitor would notice was the drain. When the rains came the water would rush through the drain, be displaced with gravel, and harmlessly seep down the side of the hill. That wall would last longer than the ruins outside of town ever did. Yes, though it was tantamount to slavery, Enrico was proud of his work.

"Look at what we've done, *Figlio*. This may have been a punishment, but we did a fine job. There's nothing like looking over the result of hard work. It looks good, Dominico. It really looks good."

Dom smiled as his father's arm rested across his shoulder. "We did it, Papa. We're done. Now we can finish those angels."

"And a hearth we'll build for Capoletto." Enrico nodded.

"*Mastro* Rossa!" A shrill voice called from the gate. "*Mastro* Rossa come here."

Enrico motioned his son to follow. Paolo was loading the tools onto Bruzzo. "Paolo, you pick up here. We'll go home soon."

"Yes, Papa."

"It's young Alfredo. His father must have put him in charge of overseeing us. We'll settle things with him and then we are done." Enrico whispered to his oldest son, whom he had just noticed was now taller than him.

Dom nodded.

As they approached the gate Enrico's stride was light. The burden of the wall, now lifted, made his body lighter, his spirit freer. Upon reaching the gate Dom's own soul jumped as he noticed Pratolina standing behind young Alfredo. She was listless until she noticed Dominico standing next to his father. She stared at him and, through the ether, shared their memories of the blissful night before.

The younger Alfredo leaned against a wrought iron slat of the great, black gate that separated him, sheltered him from

La Miseria. In many ways it was this gate that gave him his power, his status. *Alfredo Piccolo* was as sober as a statue, his eyes unfocussed, peering down the length of the wall to the corner that the Rossas had just replaced. His lips were pale and pressed together tightly. The future *Padrone* never even vouched Enrico a glance. Perhaps he knew better than to look a real man in the eye. Perhaps he knew he would see his reflection in those eyes and find himself lacking.

"Yes *Signore* Belan." Enrico smiled with false courtesy. "There is something more that we can do for you?"

"I see you built a drain." The young man's eyes, though unfocussed, were sharp and full of...full of something that Dom did not understand, but it reminded him of a freshly cleaned blade.

"*Sì*. You will have no more erosion there, *Signore* Belan."

"My father told you years ago that he did not want a drain. Redo it." The serpentine youth turned his pale neck. Now, only now that the hierarchy was established and assured could he look into Enrico's eyes. "Redo it." He then turned and walked away, grabbing Pratolina by the arm and pulling her with him. He could only look into a man's eyes for so long.

She tried to look back, to see into Dom's soul, to understand what was going on inside of him, to try to relieve the anguish that she could feel in her own soul. She tried to catch a glimpse of her lover's eyes, but when she turned, they were already gone. Her stomach knotted and her mind screamed an omen of danger. The world was about to change.

When Enrico heard the young snake say, "Redo it," something inside of him...let go. Let go. Yes. This was the correct term. For almost forty years there existed something inside Enrico that held his anger in check, held him in place—his place. Throughout the indignity of rebuilding the wall without compensation, accepting the charity of those toward whom he had once taken pride in being charitable, this thing inside held him. It held back his anger, his humiliation. It held in his pride for the sake of his family, Dominico, Paolo, Anna, Hortensia, Sara, and his father. Bent and twisted were the fingers of this hand, the links of this chain that held his soul in place. They were gone, crumbling like dust in his bowels.

"Papa." Dominico trailed after him. "Papa, it's OK. We'll redo it. It'll be OK. If they don't want the drain, we'll do something else. Papa..."

There was no response. His father was not hearing him. His eyes became as cold as those of *Signore* Belan—a viper's eyes. No, they became sharp, stiletto sharp, but not cold. There was fire in those eyes, fire behind the singular focus. The focus that the young Alfredo lacked was epitomized in Enrico Rossa's eyes. The elder Rossa walked erect and rigid toward Paolo and Bruzzo. Even his limp was gone.; Dom noticed his father's hands clenched in hard, red fists, his arms swinging like steel pendulums from the shoulders.

"Papa, what are you going to do? Papa..." Dominico was afraid, a useless, bodiless fear. "Papa, we'll take care of it. It will be all right! Papa..."

Enrico approached the ass. Bruzzo bucked his disapproval and tried to step away from the fury that was approaching, the ancient survival instincts of his once wild ancestors stirred in his equine heart. Paolo held the reigns, staring wide-eyed at his father. His father was, at the moment, a stranger to him, an angry and brutal stranger.

"Papa let's go home..." Dominico rushed to his father's side.

"Dominico," Paolo shouted, "What's happening?"

Enrico reached for a sledgehammer that hung at Bruzzo's flank, pulled it from its tether and turned a stiff one hundred and eighty degrees.

"No Papa...Don't." Dominico yelled and tried to grab his father's arm.

"Dominico...!" Paolo's voice was that of a boy half his age.

Dom turned, his face red, eyes wide. He waved his hands at his little brother. "Paolo! Go home! Go home now!" He then ran clumsily toward his father, stumbling, his legs uncertain. How does a son restrain his own father? It is not done.

"Dominico...!"

"PAOLO, GO HOME!!" Dom yelled over his shoulder but did not check to see if his instructions were followed.

"Papa don't do this. We'll redo it!"

Still there was no response from his father. Dom had to run to keep up with his gate. He tried to grab his arm but was shrugged off as if he were Paolo's age. Dom, however, continued to beg his father to turn around, to go home, to stop what he was about to do. In what seemed like no time at all, however, they were facing the gate. Alfredo was standing behind the bars holding Pratolina by the arm, his grip tight. She tried to pull away. Alfredo stared with haughty lips pursed watching what was about to happen. Three men with rifles resting in the crooks of their arms stood at Alfredo's left. They aimed at Enrico, but Alfredo held his hand out keeping them from pulling their triggers.

Dom knew that at any minute that hand could come down and he would witness his own father's death. He became frantic, grabbing his father's shoulders, trying to look into his eyes. But Dominico was no longer a part of Enrico's reality. His eyes on fire peered through his son and focused on the great black hinges that held the gate to the wall. Enrico grabbed the handle of the hammer with both hands and reached back. Instantly Dom jumped from in front of his father to avoid the mighty swing. There was an angry clang of steel and spray of mortar and sparks as the hammer struck where the hinge met the wall.

"Papa, Stop! Don't do this...They'll kill you, Papa! Please stop!"

The hammerhead continued to crash against the hinge, crushing the concrete. Enrico held a firm and rapid rhythm as he struck the hinge, his shoulders and arms became part of the great arc that carried the hammer. Dom could not approach his father lest he get caught in the path of the arcing steel head. All he could do was plead and beg his father to stop.

Beg and plead to no avail as the hammer struck the hinge again and again. Mortar sprayed and concrete separated. Again...again...again...the great, black hinge moved. It moved ever so slightly, but it moved. Alfredo's hand was still up, the rifles leveled, unwavering, at Enrico's chest. Again...again...one of the mighty bolts that held the hinge in place was exposed. Enrico started to growl like an animal with every swing face contorted by a vicious sneer. The hammer fell faster and faster keeping time with his mounting fury. His feet came off the ground as he threw all his strength and body weight into the swing...again...again...again...another bolt exposed. The hinge was loose and moving noticeably with every strike.

"PAPA! YOU CAN'T DO THIS...!" Dom yelled as he noticed that the hinge was no longer holding. The gate began to lean and now Enrico was striking the hinge itself, disconnected from the wall.

The bottom hinge creaked as it strained to hold the weight of the great gate. With Enrico pounding on the iron, however, the old hinge simply could not support the weight, and Dom noticed the bolts being pulled from the wall. It swayed slowly, a blade of grass in the wind, but the gate eventually collapsed under its own weight, crashing, and shrieking as it fell to the cobbled ground.

"NO, PAPA, DON'T!" Dom shouted as he pursued his father who stepped across the fallen gate toward the young Alfredo.

Dom heard Pratolina scream, but he could not look at her. All he could think of doing was jump between his father and the rifleman, hold him in a bear hug and physically keep him from moving.

He heard Alfredo yell, "Hold your fire! In the name of God, hold your fire!" as he grabbed his father in that great and desperate hug. His father's hot, angry arms were pinned to his body as Dom locked his hands together behind his father's heaving back. It was then that Dom felt arms around him—gentle but desperate arms.

"*Mastro* Rossa, don't! They'll kill you! They really will!" It was Pratolina, her voice in Dom's ear. "Think about your family!"

Enrico's legs, the legs that dragged Dom at least a quarter of the distance from the gate to where Alfredo was standing, stopped struggling. His body was still rigid, his eyes still burning. But he stopped walking. Dom's arms held his fathers in place at his side. This girl, though her arms were ineffectual, her presence was the reason Alfredo ordered his men to hold their fire. She was in the way! This fact allowed Enrico one split second of reason, one split second to look at his son, to think about Sara and his children. 'Think about your family!'

The stone worker glared at the young snake and his riflemen. "WHAT DO YOU WANT FROM ME?" He screamed, his voice harsh, foam spraying from his mouth with every word. "WHAT MORE DO YOU WANT FROM ME? I'VE GIVEN YOU EVERYTHING YOU PIG BASTARD! THERE'S NO MORE!"

His body lost some of its rigidity and Dom felt that he could loosen his grip, but he still held his father's shoulders. When he loosened his grip, however, Enrico waved the hammer over his head.

"THERE'S NOTHING MORE LEFT BUT MY BLOOD! IS THAT WHAT YOU WANT? IS IT? DO YOU WANT ONLY A CUPFULL OR DO YOU WANT IT ALL YOU...YOU..." With a great yell Enrico curled his body, spun, and threw the hammer at the young Alfredo.

Alfredo never moved as the hammer, spinning gracefully through the air, fell short of him. He simply stood there with his hand out indicating to the riflemen that they were not to shoot. They were not to take a chance of killing his fiancée.

Enrico stood in front of his son, staring at the young snake, breathing deeply and heavily like a lion after pursuing its prey, hands opening and closing with each breath. His eyes descended upon Pratolina, then to his son, then back at the girl. There was concern in her eyes, genuine concern. One of her hands rested on Dominico's arm, an action without thought. It was the kind of thing lovers did unconsciously to tell the world 'This person is mine.' The fire in Enrico's eyes turned to his son, and Dom let go of his shoulders.

"You will marry Clara Patrillo!" His father said before turning briskly and walking toward the felled gate.

CHAPTER 13

Everything was quiet on the hill that night as Dominico laid his head in Pratolina's lap. He was not sure of this position. He had never seen his father lay his head in his mother's lap and was not sure if it was proper. But it was good. It was comfortable, and it was a natural reaction upon seeing this beautiful woman on this still and quiet night. Not a word was spoken. He simply sat beside her and looked at her. She reached her hand around the nape of his neck and gently lowered him to her soft, warm lap. He allowed this without resistance, without hesitation. It was what he wanted—a long needed surcease.

Most of the night was spent in that way, his head in her lap, his eyes closed. Her fingers glided through his thick black tresses. Her other hand rested upon his chest feeling his pounding heart. Silence was the rule for so long. The moment was all that they had—all that they wanted. Pratolina, however, had something on her mind. Something was burning inside of her, but she did not know what it was. She searched inside her heart. For so long the two of them were able to forget the realities of their lives and enjoy each other's company and love. After that day, however, reality revealed itself. The reality of *il* Mezzogiorno and the injustice of the social order blended with the living fantasy of unfettered love. Confusion resulted.

"Dominico, are you awake?"

"Yes." He said softly, his voice a gentle breeze.

"I...I feel like I have to apologize to you."

"Why?" Dom opened his eyes.

"I don't know. I...I always lived a kind of life that never brought me any satisfaction. It did not feel like it was my life at all. It was someone else's life, someone else's rules and all I could do was go along with it. I felt so empty, but I...I never...I was never..."

Dom smiled and brushed her cheek with his rough gentle fingers. "Poor."

Pratolina sighed. "There are many ways to be poor, Dominico. In many ways I thought I was the poorest person in the world. And how selfish I seem. I see what you and your family go through. I see how the people whom I've always known treat the people whom you've always known. We are from such different worlds, with such different emptiness. Yet now we find ourselves together and everything is so wonderful for us on this hill, but..."

"But...?"

"We can't stay on this hill forever, Dominico. When you marry...what was her name...Clara? You won't be meeting me on this hill anymore."

"Or when you marry Alfredo Belan."

A tear fell from Pratolina's eye, and her body shook. "I won't marry Alfredo. He is a viper. He is an evil man. I never really liked him, but after watching him...I despise him, and he will never have me."

Dominico said nothing. Such words were like nothing he'd ever heard. Her marriage was already decided and how she felt for Alfredo Belan was irrelevant to the matter. She would marry him, and he would marry Clara. There was nothing to decide.

"Dominico, I swear to you, I will never be Alfredo's wife. But..." she cradled Dom's head and looked into his eyes. Her lips quivered, "Neither will I be your mistress."

"I would not ask that of you." Dom assured her. In the last month he had been nothing but respectful to her honor, her chastity. Though they knew well the feel of each other's mouths, and the contours of each other's arms, in every other respect Dominico was the perfect gentleman. Pratolina's honor was intact and, as far as Dom was concerned it would remain so.

Pratolina was silent, staring at the stars. "Do you want to marry Clara Patrillo?"

Dom was startled. He had never allowed himself to think about it one way or the other. What he wanted was not important. What was best for the Rossa family was the bottom line and his marriage into the Patrillo family was best. His family obligations would be fulfilled. He wanted to fulfill this responsibility, to take his place as a man in the Rossa family.

"I guess." He said. "It's what I have to do."

Pratolina became frantic. "It's what you **have** to do but is it what you **want**."

"I've never really thought about it."

Pratolina kissed him on the mouth. She was aggressive about it, taking him by surprise. Her lips pressed violently against him, her tongue searching his, her fingers clenched in his hair. She had never so boldly initiated a kiss. Oh, she had initiated kisses from Dominico in the typical subtlety of a coquette, but never in such an overt fashion.

Their mouths parted audibly as she looked into his eyes. "You are the most exasperating man I've ever known. Why can't you answer my question?"

Dom's mind was blank. He was not sure if he remembered the question let alone whether he could answer it.

"Do you want to marry Clara Patrillo? Do you want it here?" She tapped his chest above his heart, pounding rapidly.

"No." he said. 'No,' he repeated to himself as if he'd reached an epiphany. If he was honest with himself, he had to admit that he did not want to marry Clara. He wanted to marry Pratolina. He wanted to walk off that hill with her, walk hand in hand with her into town and announce his intentions at the top of the church stairs.

"Can I make a confession, Dominico?" She asked, staring at the stars.

"Yes."

"I don't want you to marry Clara, either."

Dom was home well before sunrise. He and Pratolina had gotten into the habit of falling asleep in each other's arms and waking just before the birds started singing. Their bodies, when together, were tuned to the rhythms of the Earth and the sky. Everything was in harmony, and they were learning how to read this harmony like a poem. When Enrico stepped into the divided kitchen Dominico looked refreshed and ready for work. Enrico did not smile when he offered his son good morning. He knew that this day would be the end of an era for him and for his family. The seeds were already sown, the script already written. The crop must now grow, regardless of its bitterness. The play must be performed, regardless of how tragic.

"We'll start work on the angels today, Papa." Dominico smiled, trying to stimulate his own father's mood.

"I'll start the second one and you finish the first. By the time you are done you can start the detail work on the second and I'll start the third. We have six to do. We are very behind. We may have to work late and work on Sunday to catch up."

Sara walked into the room and placed the bundled *fascia* into the oven. "You won't have to miss church?" she sounded shocked.

"Yes, we'll have to. We must get those angels done."

"I would think church comes first. God comes first." Sara stared at her husband. For twenty-two years they had always gone to church together, never missing a single week even when Sara gave birth to Paolo late on a Saturday night, she was in church on Sunday morning.

"My family comes first!" Enrico exclaimed. His voice was uncharacteristically loud and course. "*Accidente!* Woman, if this project isn't done on time my reputation is ruined. No reputation, no work—no work, no food. It is really that simple!"

Sara's mouth dropped open, and a great sadness prevailed over her features. Hortensia took Anna and Paolo outside under the premise of collecting kindling.

Enrico struck a wood beam with the side of his fist causing the cottage to shake. "Don't..." he turned to his wife with his finger waving angrily in the air, but once he looked into her sad, wet eyes his words halted with a violent jolt in his throat.

"Papa, let's go to work." Dominico suggested, trying to calm the situation.

Husband and wife stared at each other for a moment, a heavy, emotional moment. Enrico dropped his hand and walked out the door, his head bowed, his gate angry.

Dominico met his mother's eyes, "I love you, Mama," and he turned for the door.

"Dominico!" Sara called her son who stepped back into the room. "Watch out for your father today. Take care of him. He needs you."

Dom nodded, knowing the truth of those words. The enormity of taking care of his father was heavy on his shoulders. This was not the way that it was supposed to be.

The Rossa work-yard rang with hammer's striking chisels, chisels striking stone. The sun was low over the horizon, but the intense workers were already glistening with sweat. White marble stuck to their wet bodies as they worked. Enrico was pale with marble dust as he worked more furiously, striking great shards of stone from the blocks. Expertly he rounded the blocks with deft blows of the hammer and chisel. Once he had the general shape his strikes became less violent, more precise. He would hammer out the general shape of the design. His son would then take over the detail work.

Dominico was less frantic, but just as intense as his work required more precision. His steady hands cut the details of the design alluded to by his father's crude preparation. Thus, they hoped to get the project done within three weeks. They would have been finished if not for the interlude with the wall. The angels would have been done and they would have been the envy of the country. Now speed would have to take the place of precision. The kind of detail that Dominico liked to add to his work would have to be sacrificed.

Father and son worked without rest. So intent were they that they did not notice the riders approaching the work-yard. It was not until Paolo, who was responsible for getting the tools they needed, emerged from the tool shed and spied the approaching visitors.

"Papa, Dominico, look." He pointed down the road.

Dom and Enrico looked in the indicated direction and noticed half a dozen riders approaching. Don Alfredo and his son were at the head of the contingent. The other four men carried rifles. Il Gabelloto took up the rear, his long, heavy shot gun cradled in his arms.

"Paolo, go inside." Enrico said, his voice low and steady.

Paolo did not hesitate. Though his father seemed calm, his voice betrayed an urgency with which Paolo did not want to trifle.

Enrico debated sending Dominico into *la casa* to 'take care of the women,' but he knew that his son had outgrown such station. He'd proven that he could keep a clear head and manage intense situations. 'Hell,' Enrico thought, 'he handles himself better than I do, now.' As much as he wanted to protect his son, this was what manhood was about. Dominico would have to face the cold realities of his gender. He would have to face it now.

"*Mastro* Rossa." Don Alfredo called out as the horse stepped up to the gate of the workshop. In his hand was a large sledgehammer. "It appears you left something at my estate. I've come to return it."

Enrico approached the *Padrone,* his eyes were focused, his features solid. As he neared Don Alfredo, *Il Padrone* held his gloved hand out, palm down, to receive the proper respect from this errant stone worker. Men from the village emerged from their home and workshops and made their way to the scene. They formed a loose crescent around the Rossa work yard. Once Enrico kissed *Il Padrone*'s hand the natural order of things would be restored.

But the natural order was broken. It was broken in the heart of Enrico Rossa and thus the very fabric of the village had changed. Enrico's lips never touched the cloth of the glove as the elder Rossa stood and stared at the man, a foppish salamander astride a noble horse. The men gathered around the scene were silent and staring. None of them had ever seen such a confrontation. They had never even heard of such a situation in the myriad stories and fables.

Don Alfredo was caught off guard. He had never had to respond to true insolence. He responded to petty things he referred to as insolence, but never true defiance. Any resistance to his authority took place behind his back, or in his absence. Such infraction was swiftly dealt with and assured the lower population that *Il Padrone* was all seeing and all-knowing and his retribution was sure. But this! This was insolence direct. It was resistance in his face, under the presence of his wide and all-seeing eyes. There was no pretense of deception, no assumption of invisibility. Enrico Rossa was openly defiant and for this no one was prepared.

Indeed, Enrico himself was not prepared. He was certain of the consequences, however. A part of him screamed for remission, pleaded with his soul to hold in that pride and kiss that damned gloved hand and be done with it. He could hear the pretty girl say, 'think about your family.' But there was nothing more to do. The shackles about his soul were gone and he could not force himself to be supplicant even though he knew it would be for the best. There was just no more supplication to give. One can't coax water from a dry well.

"Well, *Signore* Rossa. You seem to have become bold all of a sudden." Don Alfredo glanced around at the gathering crowd and smiled. Almost every male in town was either standing there or approaching down the road. They were angry and felt the strength of their numbers as they assembled. "To have developed such courage in such a short time. My, my, you must have been kissed by quite the muse, my friend. But be careful. Such hubris has been the downfall of better men than you."

Enrico stared at Don Alfredo. He reached out his calloused hand, covered in marble dust, and said, "I'll take my hammer, thank you."

"Indeed." Don Alfredo held the hammer across his square and bony shoulder. "But there is still this matter of vandalism perpetrated by you on my property. I expect that the gate will be replaced immediately."

Enrico's lids narrowed and his jaw clenched. Dom walked up beside his father but looked at Don Alfredo's contingent with wide, unblinking eyes. They were shifting in their saddles and checking the straps of their rifles. Dom then investigated the gathering crowd. Their eyes were wide but resolute. He could see change coming soon. This would be the end of an era in this village, the beginning of the end for Don Alfredo. Dom's own soul became resolute. The fire of the revolutionary was ignited and burned within his breast, burned throughout his limbs.

"Your gate may be replaced as you see fit, Don Alfredo, but not by Rossa hands." Be like stone.

Il Padrone's face contorted with an almost pained rage. He would no longer tolerate insolence. He spurred his horse and crushed the wooden fence post with a swing of the hammer as the animal burst into the work yard. Dom watched as the hammer arched toward his father, striking a glancing blow across the forehead. He jumped to his father's defense but was knocked to the ground with the butt end of a rifle driven between his shoulder blades. The world spun and the sounds of hooves and distorted rifle shots echoed through his mind.

Dom lay face down on the ground, trying to get his eyes to focus, trying to get the world to stop spinning. He tried to force himself to his feet, but his arms were weak and would not obey his commands. In this swaying world he could see his father trying to move, his back to the well. He was holding his forehead in red, dripping hands. Horses trampled behind him. Gunshots exploded inside the workshop, but also another sharp sound that was so familiar to Dominico reached his ears. It was hammer against stone, hammer against stone.

Somehow, Dom was in a seated position staring into the work yard. In horror he noticed Don Alfredo striking the unfinished marble with the hammer, striking them from the back of his horse. He was awkward and unbalanced, but continued to wield the hammer with is feminine arms. The world was coming into focus as Dom saw Il Gabelloto pull the support beam of the Rossa home with a rope. The dry old beam gave readily to the combined strength of the man and horse and Dominico was paralyzed as the *casa* in which he was born and raised sagged limply into the workshop below.

He was not paralyzed for long, however. Anger welled inside of him and flowed to his fists. As the anger grew, so grew control over his body and his mind. There was a crowd of men there. They would help. They were his father's friends. They swore to fight with Enrico, to stand together against their oppressor. Dom turned expecting to see a seething mass of angry Campanians close upon their shared nemesis.

Instead, he saw them stepping backward from the scene. Many of them were already in Patrillo's work-yard seeking a place to hide. Others stood in the street and watched the pathos. Their only response was the terrified sadness in their eyes. They were otherwise inactive, impotent, a spent fury.

Dom turned to the work yard and ran toward his father, but he was grabbed by the hair by a rider and thrown backwards before he could reach him. One of the overseers stood before him, rifle in hand as Dom jumped to his feet again. He could hear his mother screaming and crying, shouting "No! No! Give it back...give it back!" She pulled on the arm of a big man who held a small cedar chest. It was Clara's dowry, the dowry that was to be used for Hortensia's marriage. The man jerked away from Sara then struck her across the face with the back of his hand. She curled backward and fell in a heap to the ground.

"WHY ARE YOU LETTING THIS HAPPEN!" Dom faced the assembled townsmen. "You can stop this! Stop this!" They only stared at Dominico, shaking their heads. Gone was the collective pride, the honor. There was no more anger in their eyes—only remorse.

"You cowardly sons of bitches!" Dom called to them. He turned his back on his own house and approached the men of the village. "You said we would stand together. You agreed that it was better to die like men than to live like dogs. Now look at you..."

Another shotgun blast, horses whinnying and frantic in the chaos.

"DOGS...USELESS DOGS...ALL OF YOU!"

Then, as suddenly as it began, the assault was over. Dom could hear his mother crying, and the horses being calmed by their riders. The last sound of the confrontation was that of a hammer striking stone. Dom recognized the sickening sound of the stone giving and crumbling, fractured under the hammer. He hung his head, knowing that his family was ruined.

"How could you let this happen?" Dom could no longer face the group of men, but he could address them. "HOW COULD YOU LET THIS HAPPEN!?"

"You really are a young fool." It was Don Alfredo's voice. Dom prepared himself for the sudden shock of pain from a rifle butt, maybe even a bullet.

Dom heard the horse approach from behind. "Did you really believe that there was any fight in these pathetic people? You know nothing. Campanians have been defeated and enslaved for thousands of years. The Samnites, the Latins, the Romans, Vandals, Normans, Bourbons. Whoever came, conquered. Your ancestors were defeated and subjugated throughout history and your descendants will be defeated and subjugated in the future. So don't blame them, *ragazzo*. It's all they know. They don't know how to be anything more than slaves and serfs. Did you really expect anything more from them?"

The young man, without looking at *Il Padrone*, without responding, hung his head and ran to his father who was lying in the sand, a pool of blood spreading beneath his head. Enrico moaned and rolled about, his hands clasped to his face were sticky and dirty with blood, sand and marble powder. "Papa, let me see." He pulled his father's hands away from his face and noticed a swath of skin hanging from the right temple. The hammer grazed him but struck with enough force to peel the skin from his forehead.

Once again, the sound of hoof beats closed upon him and this time he looked up. Don Alfredo was holding the cedar chest under his arm. "I wish to return this." He dropped the hammer to the ground. "If or when your father is coherent let him know that the contents of this box should cover about half of the expenses for repairing the gate. We will be back for the other half at our convenience."

As Don Alfredo's men galloped off Dom ran to his mother who was still on the ground. She was crying, her red face distorted with sadness and weeping. "Mama, it's over."

Her hand reached up and pushed her son. "Go...go take care of your father. I want you to take care of your father..."

"Dominico," *Signore* Patrillo said as he approached. "You take care of your papa. I'll take your mama to my place and my wife will clean her up."

Signore Nuovo spoke next, "Dominico, where are your sisters and your brother?"

"I don't know."

"They're over there," *Signore* Montandenestra announced. "They're hiding in the barley field. I see them. I'll get them and take them to your place Ugo."

Signore Patrillo nodded and helped Dom pick up the waling Sara. "Where's my husband?" She said, "Is my husband all right?"

"Damn you! Damn you!" Dom heard his grandfather's shrill voice, full of fury yet...hopeless. He turned in time to see the icon of San Giuseppe raised high in the old man's dry, trembling hands. He held the beloved statue high over his head, his elbows bent, arms trembling, eyes wide and angry. His hands gripped the icon as they would the throat of a hated enemy. Then the old man's arms arced forward, and the icon crashed to the ground. The porcelain shattered and exploded in a crash of shards and dust. The elder Enrico crushed the larger pieces of this erstwhile treasure under his unsure heal before stumbling away.

Signore Patrillo and Dom returned their concentration to Sara, who had not seen the event behind her.

"Shhhh, *Signora* Rossa...Sara...Enrico will be all right."

Dom looked around at the wreckage that was once his home. The north corner of the house sagged eerily into the workshop that once took up the space below. Bruzzo had run off in the excitement. Tools, some bent and twisted, were strewn along the ground. A broken wheelbarrow lay shattered by the well, the mixer riddled with bullet holes. Then, with an almost prescient dismay, Dom looked at the marble from which the angels were emerging. They were all chipped and gashed, but most of the damage could be covered with the right skill. The one that was almost finished and the block that Enrico had started that morning, were, however, effectively shattered. There would be no repairing them.

Dom remembered his father's angry voice that morning, 'if this project isn't done on time my reputation is ruined. No reputation no work—no work, no food. It is really that simple!' The project was over. There was no way to complete it even if they could afford more marble, it would take weeks for a block to be transported from the north. The Rossa family was ruined. It was really that simple.

CHAPTER 14

Silence, defeat, dishonor. These were the black clouds that engulfed Dom's soul as he plodded wearily toward the hill that night. With every step he trudged through his own spiritual, impenetrable quagmire. His heart was heaviest of all upon his mind and upon his normally quick and agile legs. All was gone within him. That vital, dynamic part of him was gone. It was his home. It was his life. It was everything that he had learned and known. The spirit that was cultivated in him, his manhood so new and fragile, his standing in the community, his identity as a Campanian. It was all gone.

Even Pratolina could not make it better. She had made everything better since he met her. This time was different, however. She would not be able to fix this. She would not be able to reach his soul tonight for it was sunk too deeply within, slinking cowardly into some unknown corner of his heart. This was the first night that Dom did not want to go to the hill. He did not want to see her. She was too good, too pure for him. He was soiled, diseased with dishonor and ruin. Blackness might find its way into her lovely heart, bringing her the same ruin that it had brought him. This was his heaviest burden, the possible contagion of a black soul.

Dom knew how connected he and Pratolina were. He knew that the sickness of his soul could only find its way into hers, as they shared one spiritual entity. Dom did not know the language of soulmates, but he could feel the reality of his ethereal self combined with hers, dancing with hers in some spectral cloud that neither of them could see or sense, yet both could feel in the most personal and intimate reaches of their selves.

Wherever this cloud was, this Heaven, Dom felt that it was characterized by light, by whiteness and purity. It was all that was clean and perfect in the universe, shining whiteness, happiness, and honor. It was vestal and true. Blackness and shadow and shame could not exist there. Yet blackness penetrated so deeply into Dom that he could only bring ruin to spectral joy. He felt that should one grain of dirt, one sliver of shadow, find its way into the white perfection of his love for Pratolina that all would be ruined. He could not let that happen. He could not lose this heaven that he carried around inside of him.

He would go to the hill and tell Pratolina that he could not stay, that he was too tired, that he had work to do at home... rebuilding. Rebuilding. How could she ever understand that? She'd never built or rebuilt anything. Then again, neither had she ever destroyed anything. There was so much to his life, so much to his manhood that Pratolina could never understand.

Yet she was the one that he loved. It wasn't because she was perfect for him—she wasn't. It was not because they had so much in common—they didn't. She was just the woman he loved. She was his whiteness, and he could never allow anything to mar that.

When he reached the hill, she was not yet there. This was not something to worry about. They both had other obligations that often held them up from being where they really wanted to be. It was common to have to wait. Dom sat at the bole of the great tree that overlooked the mountains on the horizon. There was an eerie cast in the sky that night, a reflection of Dom's gloom. It was a gray-blue tint that traced the worn and rolling mountaintops against the dark and distant sky. Dark and distant, Dom could relate to the sky.

'Say good-bye to her, Dominico. You can never have her. You can never satisfy her. Look at you, a ruined half-man from a ruined family. Your dishonor will travel with you. It will travel with your children, too, if you are not good enough to dig your way out of it. Say good-bye to her.' Saint Joseph was standing next to Dom with his hand on the young man's tight and aching shoulders. 'You can never have her. You'll wed another. And Pratolina will not be your mistress. For her sake, say good-bye to her.'

Dom pulled his knees to his chest and buried his face in his folded arms. He did not want to cry, but his eyes filled with tears. 'For her sake.'

"Dominico?" Her voice was sweet in his ears.

He was afraid to look up, afraid to let her see the water in his eyes, afraid to reveal the blackness in his soul that his wet eyes would betray.

"Dominico, I'm so sorry. I heard what happened. I didn't know what to do. I wanted to be there, but I dared not..." She sat next to him and rested her head on his broad shoulder, wrapping her arms around him.

She felt the slight tremor in his back as he choked back tears. She knew that he would not allow her to see him cry but this emotion in a man touched her just the same. "It will be all right. You'll..."

"I won't!" He shouted.

Pratolina looked at him, her eyes wide and wondering. She clung to him.

"I won't. There's nothing left to do." Dom raised his head, his eyes swollen and red. He stood and stared at the gray-blue mist on the horizon and shook his head. "There's nothing left to do."

"Oh, Dominico...don't..."

"I must leave here." The words escaped his mind and ran through his lips before he knew what he was saying. It was so simple, such a pure thought. 'Run. Get away from the pain. Get away from the dishonor...*la miseria.* Get out of Campania.' As these careless words escaped his lips, his mind became suddenly awake, swimming with thoughts and dreams. His mind had been dormant since bandaging his father that morning. Now, dreams filled his consciousness. He must leave.

He could leave. Leaving. The thought had never occurred to him, but it was always there inside, sleeping, waiting to wake. Leaving. He wondered how long and with how much energy he held that thought down only to allow it to escape to that hilltop, a desperate statement, a distant hope.

"Where would you go, Dominico?" Pratolina's fingers clutched at his torn shirt, a reflex upon hearing him mention leaving. She buried her head in his chest. He was warm with sadness, but now there was a different heat, a fire that re-ignited in his soul.

"*Lamerica*!" He pronounced and now his eyes were lost beyond the gray-blue mist, beyond the rolling mountains, even beyond the sky. He was looking into his future the genesis of a grin grew across his face.

Her arms tightened around him as if he would disappear to *Lamerica* by sheer force of will. She had to hold him there, she had to hold him to the ground and keep him from being swept away in his dreams, swept away from her.

"No." She did not realize that she had spoken this thought aloud, but the piteous tone in her voice was a nail in Dom's side.

He held her by the arms, staring into her eyes. His soul was alive again, vibrant, and undefeated. Be like stone. He attributed this turn in his soul to her presence. Only her light, her whiteness could have penetrated the gloom in his heart. Only her passion could have reinvigorated his dead mind.

Before she arrived on that hill that night, he was dead inside. Her presence carried the stuff of dreams with her.

Her eyes were brown, wide, and sad. Her red lips curled in a frown that melted his heart. He was so filled with dreams that he wanted to wrap her up in them and run with her through the barley laughing and dancing...

"Marry me!" The words poured fourth without relent. "Marry me, sweet Pratolina and we'll go to *Lamerica* together. There are no rules that will keep us apart in *Lamerica*. We can buy a house and have children, and nobody will be the wiser. They'll just say, 'there goes Signore Dominico Rossa and his beautiful wife, Pratolina.' 'Aren't they a beautiful couple?' 'Don't they have the most beautiful children.' Marry me! We'll have our own land and there won't be any *padrone*. There won't be anything to stop us."

Pratolina laughed, her eyes flashing like honey in the sunlight. "You're crazy..."

"...of course I'm crazy. You have me crazy! If I stay here, I'll have to marry Clara Patrillo. I don't want her. I want you. I'll be forever in debt to *Il Padrone*. And you will be forced to marry Alfredo Belan. You know your father will make you. It would be too great a dishonor to him if you refused. Only in *Lamerica* can we be together. Only in *Lamerica* can we be free."

"You need to sleep," Pratolina giggled. His joy was tickling her. She could get lost in this. She wanted to get lost in this dream. "You're going to regret saying all of this in the morning."

"In the morning, we can be packing our bags and on our way to Salerno." Dom smiled. "Please say you'll marry me. Please marry me, *Pratolina mia*. Marry me." He placed a kiss on her cheek, "marry me," then another, "marry me," then the other cheek...her mouth...her forehead...the curve of her neck... "Marry me...marry me...marry me..."

Pratolina laughed aloud, "All right...all right. I guess it's either marry you or you'll smother me."

And he embraced her, pulling her to him and holding her. He wanted to be a part of her. He wanted oneness with her. Her hands caressed his back, her hair tickling his neck, whiteness, light—happiness.

Time came in the night when the euphoria had run its course, though the happiness remained. The expression of dreams and desires and hope for the future is a compelling narcotic. To make those dreams come true, however, required planning and an accounting of reality.

Pratolina was the first to cross the threshold into reality. "I can't go with you, Dominico."

Dom knew that this would have to be discussed, but he did not like the reality. He wanted to remain in the euphoria a little longer.

"Not at first, my darling. I have no money, and my father will not allow me to go. He'll never give his consent. You won't be able to afford passage for both of us. It will be hard enough for you to get passage for yourself."

Dom was silent. He did not want to hear this right now. But reality was clear and plain once one stopped to look at it with unclouded eyes. "Then I won't go." He exclaimed. He had no desire to be away from Pratolina. All his dreams involved being with her. If she were not with him, then there would be no sense in dreaming, no impetus to make those dreams real.

"No, Dominico. You must go." Pratolina stared into his eyes. "You must go because it is the only chance that we have of being together. If you stay it will be just as you said and both of us will be miserable for the rest of our lives. No, you must go. Go to America and make some money. You can then send me passage to join you as soon as you are on your feet."

"What if you're married to Alfredo by then?"

Pratolina was silent. She knew that the engagement would be formalized next week, and the wedding was planned shortly thereafter. There really was only one way...

"I will not be married to Alfredo or any man. I will marry you after I get to America. I promise you. No man will have me but you."

"It won't be long." Dominico held her tightly. "It won't be long. There will be land and a little white house waiting for you when you arrive."

Pratolina laughed and held him just as tightly. She doubted that there would ever be a little white house, but it did not matter. There would always be Dominico, and Dominico was all that she wanted.

CHAPTER 15

The family looked at him silently. There was nothing that could be said at that point. Sara and Hortensia stood frozen, bowls and cups in their hands as they were in the process of clearing the table. They looked at each other, neither knowing what to do nor what to say. Anna simply closed her eyes. She did not want this world. She did not want the reality of what was said to reach her, for she could not handle it. Even Paolo, usually ebullient, was silent and grave.

None seemed more transfixed by Dom's words than Enrico. He clutched at his empty cup and squeezed until the pottery fractured then shattered into red dust on the table. His entire body shook. Were there any more ways in which a man could be defeated? This thought in the deepest reaches of his mind, where a charitable man keeps his selfishness. A charitable man hears the muffled complaints of his own selfishness but adheres not to its pleas. He was silent, though his soul was screaming. With a confused look he turned to his father. The elder Enrico stared at the table and nodded, as if he'd expected this all along.

Most conspicuously, Dom was silent. He tried to be strong. He tried to be like stone, but once the words escaped his throat there was nothing left with which to hold him together. "I want to go to *Lamerica*." Such a simple phrase, such little words, a wish, a dream spoken, and the family fabric unraveled around him. He put his head in his hands and tried to control his sobs.

"It's all there's left to do, Papa." He croaked from his spasming throat. "There's nothing left for me here. There's really nothing left for any of us."

"Let's not talk about this now, *Figlio*." Enrico forced the words out, but it he had no more wind in him. *Nonno* stilled his nodding. "Sleep on it, my son and think about what you are doing. You're breaking the family apart."

The palm of Dom's hand struck the table, causing the dishes there to jump and rattle. "I've already slept on it!"

Sara tapped Hortensia and directed her to follow into the kitchen. Hortensia touched Anna by the shoulder with the same direction, but the little girl would not respond. At her age she was not interested in a woman's place and thought little about leaving men to their own business. Her big brother was going away, and she was not going to leave that table until he changed his mind.

"I'm sorry, Papa, I didn't mean to shout. This is hard for me, too. But this is a decision that must be made. Look. We're having a hard enough time making ends meet now. Add to that the broken tools and the angels and capitals that we cannot finish and *Il Padrone*. Lord only knows when he will come back and take the rest of what he thinks you owe him."

"We'll get by. We always get by." Enrico was gruff and commanding, but in his voice, there was a trace of an almost pathetic plea. 'Don't do this to me, son. Don't leave me when I need you the most.'

"We'll get by better if I'm not here. If I go to *Lamerica* I'll find work and I can send you money. You can use that money to put food on the table and pay your debts to *Il Padrone*. Then you can fix the house up and get the new tools that you've always wanted. We can start over as a family. I don't have to stay over there forever. I'll come back when we are on our feet again. It's only temporary."

"Only temporary." Enrico whispered.

Anna moaned a low and pitiful sound. Dom put his arm around her, and she lay her head on her brother's chest.

"Things never work out the way they are planned." Enrico admonished. "What we think is going to be temporary is an illusion, like finding the end of the circle. You always think it's around the bend, but once you get there you find only more of the same."

"Papa, I don't want to leave. I don't want to leave my family, but there's nothing left to do. One of us must go and it must be me. You need to stay here and take care of the family while you are still healthy. If we wait a few years, you may not be able to take care of the family. You know how things happen. Then we will really be in trouble."

With shaking, nervous fingers Enrico adjusted the bandages around his head. He did not need to be reminded about his age, about his injuries, about the fragility of life in Campania. He wanted his son. "No," he responded. "There must be another way. We'll find another way."

Nonno silently pushed himself from the table and walked toward his hovel behind the little *casa*. Enrico watched but was unconcerned. His father did not appear to be upset. He seemed more thoughtful than anything. Enrico figured that he needed time to wade through his thoughts.

Anna's shoulders trembled.

"I've thought of everything, Papa. There is no other way. If we continue like this then I'm only going to be one more mouth to feed. We won't have any money coming in. I can't allow that to happen any more than you could if you were in my position." So, this was what it felt like to be a man, Dom thought. 'My sister crying on my lap, my father distraught. God only knows about Mama and Hortensia. Hortensia!

"Papa, how long will it take us to get up another dowry for Hortensia? It will take a long time. How much longer does she have? And we still must pay back *Signore* Patrillo." The last words slipped out and he quickly regretted the response.

Enrico looked up quickly. "Pay back Ugo? Why? Your marriage was agreed to."

Dom did not know what to say. He stuttered for a moment. "Papa," He said, "Clara is a beautiful girl and will make a wonderful wife and mother. She shouldn't have to wait for me.

What if this takes more than two years? What if it takes four or five, which it probably will? She shouldn't have to wait."

Enrico put his hand up to stop his son. He knew Dom did not want to marry her. Perhaps it was too soon for him to make such decisions. He thought about the girl at the *latifundo*. 'Does she have anything to do with this?' But he would not ask his son though the question would burn in him for years to come and burn in many ways. Still, he would never ask his son that question.

Dom understood the intent of the raised hand. "I'm sorry, Papa…"

"No," Enrico interrupted. "We should sleep on this and talk about it in the morning. There's a lot to talk about. Even if I would allow you to go, how would you get there? We have no money. It costs money to take passage on the ships. And where would you stay?"

"The Dellamontagnia's have that man's card. He could find me a place and a job from what I understand. I can have a job waiting for me when I get there."

Anna's sobbing became more incessant, less controlled. She clutched his leg, her little fingers pinching the skin. Hortensia and Sara approached the table and removed the rest of the dishes. Their eyes were red and wet, and they refused to make eye contact with Dom.

"And to get passage I can find a job in Salerno…I don't know… washing dishes or something. I can get the money in the city for passage. It shouldn't take me long."

"You'll do no such thing." *Nonno* approached the table.

Enrico and Dom stared at him. Dom could feel his heart sink as he looked into his grandfather's stern eyes. If *Nonno* decided against him going to America, the discussion was closed, and Dom's plans were nothing more than a pipe dream.

A red cloth lay open like flower in the old man's pale, wrinkled hands. With his shaking arms the elder Enrico placed the red cloth on the table as gently as his palsy allowed and revealed the contents. Dom looked at his grandfather's face and noticed that he was fighting a frown. His old eyes were always wet, but this time they were red and wetter than Dom had ever seen. The last fold of the cloth was lain flat and in the middle of the scarlet silk was a shining gold watch on a violet watch fob trimmed with gold. The gold of the watch captured the scant moonlight and made the world brighter. On the facing of the watch was an intricate design of horses and deer around a beautiful and curving "R." The name ROSSA was inscribed on the back. It may have belonged to *Nonno 's* grandfather.

"This will get you passage."

"*Nonno,* I can't..."

The old man reached for Dominico, his oldest grandson, and clasped him around the nape. He drew closer to the boy, the man, and kissed him on both cheeks, "*Buono viaggio.*" He whispered, his voice strained and crackling, "*Buono viaggio* and a quick return." The old man waved his finger at Dominico.

Then the frown took control of his gentle face. He turned and walked away.

Anna sobbed.

The decision was made. There was nothing left for Enrico to do. He stood on shaking legs and stared at his son. There were words to say. There was something that had to come out, but they just wouldn't. They were selfish words. Perhaps it was a plea, 'please don't go.' But Dominico would never know. His father walked into the house and down into the work yard.

Dom felt alone, the first sense of loneliness that he would feel in his new life, but certainly not the last. It was at this point of loneliness that he realized that he was stroking Anna's little head. He looked down at her just as she raised her head. Her face was red and wet and wrinkled from being pressed, crying into his legs.

"You said you would always be able to play with me." She said, her voice was even and smooth, but sounded weak, helpless, so much like a lost little girl who'd given up on being found but called out anyway.

There was nothing to say. He just held her.

CHAPTER 16

The evenings between them were quiet since Dom decided to go. He and Pratolina no longer had much conversation inside of them. Not that their time together on that grassy hill, under that twisted tree was any less intense than when they would wile away their time in talk. Indeed, the time was even more intense. It had a finality to it, a sudden realization that time was a scarce commodity that was quickly running out between them. To ruin the spiritual emphasis of their evenings with idle prattle seemed a sin. Instead, they lay in each other's arms, holding each other, absorbing the feel of each other, pressing against each other that they may still feel the heat from thousands of miles away.

Dom was glad for the merciful silence and the tender, tactile attention. His words were mingled too closely with his thoughts, and he could not quite figure out what to say or how to say it. Contradictions pervaded his mind like competing phantoms. This sea of dreams that Pratolina had awakened continued to pull at him, turn inside of him and sunder all reason within. He could not talk. He did not know what he was feeling and thus had no means of expressing himself. How could he explain?

How could he tell her that he did not want to leave her, but he wanted to leave? He could not make sense of the pain that he knew he would feel once he was unable to see her every night. Yet he was drawn to this new adventure, the excitement of it, the adrenaline of it. He felt an innate satisfaction knowing that he would be leaving this dusty land and exploring worlds beyond. Then there was the fear of leaving what was known and comfortable, but at the same time he yearned for the chance to have something, to become someone, to fulfill some inner potential that could no longer be satisfied in this small, Campanian village. He yearned for a chance.

Dom peered into her face. Her beautiful, golden-brown face that was so much more like honey in the moonlight. Her dark eyes were open wide, and her mouth trembling. He noticed a new tremor in her body. Her soft, warm body pressed against his, fit so perfectly in the contours of his own. She was made for him. They were made for each other. They both knew that in their souls. They both knew that if they were to ever be together it meant being apart. Suffering the pains of separation was the sacrifice for a lifetime of happiness in the future. How cruel and unjust the world seemed. In a just world, lovers, true lovers, could love. Nothing should stand in the way when soulmates find each other, bind each other in themselves and synthesize that inextricable bond that is the target for the realities of life.

How tightly those strands hold between soulmates. The relentless assault of life's complexities, society's hypocrisies pulls and cuts at the chains that bind such lovers but can never truly cut them. Pain is the consequence. There are so many battles to be fought. Pain, fatigue, fear, the compulsion to satisfy the whims of society, of God, of every other meaningless abstraction that stands between lovers. How many give up? How many are torn asunder by the strain? Yet those bonds are never broken, never cut. Those bonds are only stretched, and tug at lovers for the rest of their lives with dreams of what could have been if they'd only held on a little longer, if they'd only made it past that last obstacle. How cruel and unjust are the lives of lovers, the lives of soulmates.

Pratolina sat up, breaking herself from Dom's embrace, and stared at the mountains silhouetted in the distance. A bittersweet smile crossed her face, highlighting the mischievous look in her eye. There was much going on in that young woman's mind. Yes, so much that Dom would not understand and would not need to know about until the right time.

She, too, relished the silence and peace that was their blanket every night. It was sweet and serene, and she wished it would never end. But everything ends. This, too, will end. These tender rendezvous on the grassy hilltop would end and all that would be left for a long time would be the hope that something else just as good awaited. So, too, the silence must end.

"Do you love me Dominico?" she asked as she pushed away from him. Her voice was that of a schoolteacher toward a stubborn pupil.

"Yes. I love you." Dom replied as he reached for her. He did not want to be apart from her any more than he had to be.

"Tell me again. Please tell me again. I love to hear you tell me."

"I love you. I love you. I'll tell you a thousand times a day if I can."

She smiled and curled her shoulders, rubbing her head into his broad chest.

"I know you love me." She whispered. "You've loved me since the moment you saw me picking flowers, didn't you?"

"Yes." His fingers glided through her hair.

"I love you, too."

"Shhhhh...enjoy the night."

"You know that don't you?" There was now a subtle desperation in her voice. "You really must know. Do you feel it?"

"Yes, I feel it."

"Where do you feel it?"

"I feel it in my stomach and in my throat."

She looked up and peered into his eyes. "You are the silliest man I know. You feel it in your stomach and your throat."

"They get all...I don't know...tight, I guess. When I'm around you or hear your name or think about you I feel it most in my stomach and throat. Oh, and my legs get weak about the thighs sometimes."

She giggled. Pratolina knew what he meant. That he did not attribute this with the heart she attributed to his lack of exposure to poetry. "Me too." She replied. "I love you, Dominico Rossa. I will always love you and I will always be yours."

Dom ran his fingers through her hair some more.

"Don't forget me when you go to America."

"I'll never forget you. You are the reason I'm going."

"It's so easy to forget when you are away. You will be in a new and exciting place, and you'll forget all about Pratolina."

"Now you're being silly."

Pratolina rested her back against his chest and looked up into the sky, but she was looking at nothing. She was looking into her own mind.

"You'll go to America all big and strong and handsome and all of the American girls will fall in love with you."

"Stop. That's ridiculous."

"I can see you there, in America. You're surrounded by all those beautiful American girls with their painted faces, their golden hair and their long, white fingers." She ran her hand along her own fingers. "They'll all want you and you'll be so captured by their beauty that you'll forget all about poor Pratolina."

"I'll never forget. *Lamerica* has nothing or no one more beautiful than you."

"You'll be swept away. Any man would."

"I won't."

"My hair is not gold, and my fingers are not long and white."

"I love your hair, and your fingers are beautiful." He kissed her right hand cupped like a flower in his own.

"When do you leave, again."

"In two weeks. There's a steamer leaving *Napoli*. It stops in London then goes to New York. I told you this already."

She knew about the arrangements. They were already made. He would meet a man in *Salerno* who would give him the tickets for the ship and an address in New York of a man looking for stoneworkers and willing to provide room and board. From there Dom would start his new life. He would start his life without her but for her at the same time. They would be united in their dreams but separated by many thousands of miles. The impossibility was wearing on her.

Dom would be faithful to her. She knew that. She could see it in his eyes that she was the most beautiful woman in the world, at least to the owner of those eyes. No woman could come between them, could sever that bond that tied their souls. She knew this in her heart.

"Dominico?"

Her voice was meek now. Dom was caught off guard by this as her voice always carried with it strength and certainty. Yet now she was uncertain about something. He would set her at ease, whatever it took. For a moment he was afraid, however, that she would ask him not to go. He would stay if that was her wish. But he very much wanted to start this adventure that would make her his own.

"Yes, what is the matter?" He responded.

Her hand caressed his neck, and she looked up into his eyes as she spoke. Her breathing had become deep, and her face flushed. The tremble was worked out of her body, but replaced by another energy that Dom did not understand.

"Dominico."

He could feel her breath sweet on his face. "Yes, *M'amore*."

She whispered in his ear, and he stood up, clenching his hands and shaking his head. "No. No." He cried. "I can't. Not now."

"Please, Dominico. We must."

"No. It's not right! I mean I want to, but...we're not married. You're not *m'amante*. I want you to be my wife. I want to court you properly."

"We can't court properly, *M'amore*. We never will. I will be your wife. I'm yours. I've only ever been yours in my heart. Please, Dominico." Tears welled up in her eyes. One fell across her flushed cheek. "Please do not leave me without knowing your love."

Dom shook. This was preposterous, insane. A woman, a proper woman did not just come out and ask a man...This was beyond anything that Dom was prepared to handle. He knew what he wanted. He wanted her. He desired her in every way that a man could desire a woman. Her body, her soul, her love—he wanted all of it. He wanted to drink it like wine and bathe in it until she was soaked into every part of him. But there was a way that this was done. All he'd ever known was this 'way.' There was no other way—no other proper way.

Yet there she was, curled on the blanket, fighting tears. She wanted him. She offered him the most valued treasure of a woman, a treasure for which he yearned. It would be so long before he could see her again. So long before he would be able to marry her. Those were the cards that life dealt. That is what they would have to do if they were to do it right. How could she, as a proper woman, make such a proposal? Despite the confusion he reached for her. He wanted her to stop crying.

When he touched her, the crying became worse.

"Dominico," she sobbed, "I know you love me. Don't think less of me. Please don't think less of me. I couldn't stand it if you didn't love me."

"I love you. I don't think less of you. I'll always love you. I've just never heard anything like that from…"

"From a woman." She completed his sentence, the crying subsiding. "Women desire too, Dominico. I didn't mean to offend you. I just don't want to be separated without sharing myself with you. We can't do things the way they 'should' be done. If we did that then we would not be together now, would we?"

Dom shook his head. Her body was curled into his again, her breath on his neck. She presented a good argument. Of course, Dom did not require much convincing.

"It's OK. You don't have to talk." She whispered into his ear again, kissed his cheek.

He felt his body shake and react to her. Fire spread from between his legs, through is fingertips. He burned for her, his heart pounding, fire under his skin. Her lips close to his, starry eyes staring into him, pleading him. Pleading him as his hand traveled softly across the small of her back, to the round of her lovely, soft hip. Lips pressed against hers, tongue-searching kisses wet and full. She lay back, pulling him to her. Her hands pulled him, her mouth pulled him, her yearning pulled him. Bodies shaking under exploration, unknown, untried desires moving their hands.

Her skin reminded him of honey. How that dress seemed a blasphemy as it slid from her body, allowing his hands to revel in the satin-like skin underneath. That such skin should be contained in course fabric. Skin so tight and soft, hot to the touch, hands touching, mouth touching. Her body glided under him. She moved with him, moved for him, dainty hands tracing the tight muscles of yearning shoulders, chest broad and strong. Thighs pressed against him. Could anybody see? His mouth found her neck stretched and wanting as his hands caressed her body, her hips, her stomach, her breasts...her breasts round and soft and yielding. The sounds she made as he touched her, the arching of her body for him, yearning, turning her body for him.

"Take me..." whispered in his ear and he was inside of her, one with her. Wet heat pulling him, driving him wanting more and more. He wanted eternity, arms clasped around his shoulders, legs about his hips, inside of her, wanting her, kissing her aching mouth. Moaning, yelling, her breathing deep and desperate, 'am I hurting her?' Pulling on him as he slowed for her, pulling him harder, clutching the flesh of his shoulders, her body throbbing, rocking with his. They would never again be apart.

Part II

La Via Dolorosa

CHAPTER 1

"It was here that they made love." Cecilia said without apology for speaking so boldly. There was no more innocence left in the world, what with the soldiers returning to their homes incomplete in body, mind, and spirit. There were no more apologies to be made in a world that just saw a whole generation ruined by war. No, there was no more innocence—no more innocence except there, in that spot, with this man crying over a tombstone. His was an innocent sorrow. To Cecilia, his innocent pain justified the existence of a scarred and battered world that otherwise called for extinction.

"It was here that they said good-bye." She continued.

The soldier in muted green held the stone, caressing it with his fingers. She noticed a smear of blood on the stone as his compulsive caress was rubbing the bandages from his right hand. Quietly, unobtrusively, she took his hand in hers and gently re-adjusted the bandages, wrapping part of her handkerchief over the frayed gauze. She wanted to ask him what had happened. His hand was raw and blistered. Cecilia had seen enough wounds to know that his hand was burned.

To ask him to elaborate, however, would have been...wrong. It just did not fit the moment.

He did not resist her attention, barely even noticed her nursing as she kept talking. Her voice became a rare beauty in his life, and he did not want her to stop. She continued the story as she wrapped his hand.

"I guess that's why this was always such a special place to her. Anytime she got a chance she would come here and... well, I really don't know. I guess she would think or dream about him, wonder what had become of him..."

"No, don't...not yet." Dom whispered as he lowered her hands away from the buttons of her dress. "*Appena alcuni minuti più...per favore.* Just a few more minutes please. I want to see the moonlight on your skin."

Pratolina lay back on the blanket that served as their proxy for a matrimonial bed for the last ten days--their haven. Her body, exposed to the evening air and to the moonlight, held a honey glow within its softness. She lay, staring at her man, her lover. Her trembling hands caressed her bare stomach as he gazed upon her, his glistening eyes dancing joyously over her beauty. He drank in her goldness, her softness. A playful, childish smile crossed his youthful face. A new treasure he found, an El Dorado or a goddess icon hidden in the dry, Campanian sands. His enchanted gaze was a physical presence. It pressed upon her, warmed her, her breathing becoming forced and deep.

"Don't look at me so." She blushed and turned away from him, covering her breasts with her tiny hands. "You make me nervous."

"You're beautiful." He took her hands in his like fragile flowers and lowered them to her bronze hips as he gently kissed her breasts, pressing them tenderly between his lips before pulling away.

His hand travelled along her soft skin. They were rough hands for his age, rough and strong. Yet there was a softness to them, like rough leather under a silk stocking. His hands explored her stomach, her hips, her thighs, the moonlight shimmering gold between his fingers.

"I love to look at you. I want to soak you all in so I can carry as much of you as I can with me..."

"Please don't mention leaving. Let's pretend you're not leaving. Just touch me and enjoy me and love me."

"I do love you, Pratolina. I love you. *Ti amerò per sempre*. I will always love you." He spoke these words and stared into her dark and lovely eyes. When he was quiet, however, his eyes continued surveying her body. The sweet curve of her chin, the delicate, upturned nose above red, full lips. There was no part of her he did not want to know. That long, beautiful neck that so attracted him tapered to soft, round shoulders that blossomed lower to round and supple breasts just barely the size of his palm. He followed the curve of her waist, searching for the slight, brown mole situated just beside her navel. He touched it and she giggled and pushed his hand away, but he only touched it again.

"I love you..." he said, looking into her eyes once again. She could feel the rough-silk hands between her thighs. She could feel herself yielding to his presence. She had no decision to make. The stars overhead, the gentle breeze, the crystal-clear evening had already conspired. Closing her eyes as he kissed her, she felt the weight of him, then the completeness of him before the world disappeared and there was only oneness.

When she secured her dress this time, he did not interrupt her. Their time together was at an end. They had no way of knowing how final their goodbye would be. As her body was hidden beneath the shroud of her clothing, he noticed her shoulders shaking and her eyes closed. Soon the sobbing began, and tears streamed from her eyes onto the blanket rumpled beneath her.

Pratolina pressed her lids with her fingers and tears soaked into the fibers of the blanket. She wiped her eyes dry with the backs of her hands. Her face flushed and a mighty frown twisted her usual, pristine features. Trying to control the sobbing was most difficult as she pulled air into her lungs in short, quick breaths between tight pressed lips. If she took a deep breath, she would not be able to control herself. She had to stop sobbing. This was ridiculous. She had known this day would come for a week and a half. She knew she had to say good-bye to him. This foreknowledge did nothing to alleviate the current pain. She was to lose a vital part of her, not a limb or an organ, but the very fabric of her soul—the part of her that mattered most. That is what was happening, was not it? She was losing a part of herself.

Dom reached for her. He reached for her, but she pushed him away. There was no sense in letting him comfort her. One way or the other, Pratolina would have to become Maria-Angelina again and carry on. Being held by him would not help, would at best delay the inevitable. There was only one way for him to relieve her pain. Yet even that would only delay the inevitable. If he did not go away there was no chance of their being together, there was no future. She had to look at it that way. Endure the pain for a future happiness.

That was the Campanian spirit, a sacred faith in the hearts of all the people of the *Mezzogiorno*. Get through today's pain for hope of tomorrow's rewards. Sometimes it was a matter of getting through this life's pains for hope of Heaven's rewards. Would there be a heaven for Dom and Pratolina? Something inside of her said...She shook herself. She would not dwell on that. She would not think the unthinkable. Dom would return. Dominico would become wealthy in *Lamerica,* come back in a gilded carriage, carry her to the church and marry her. There was nothing else for her. There was no other hope to be considered but that found with him. No other heaven but the one they had discovered with each other and consummated vigorously over the course of this last ten days together.

Dom's heart fell as she pushed him away the second time. "Pratolina, don't cry. I will be back for you." He could feel the heat inside of him bursting behind his eyes, but he could not cry. Be like stone.

She looked up. "You will be back. Won't you, Dominico?"

"Yes, of course I will."

She clutched at his shirt, the tears welling in her eyes, streaming down her cheeks. "Promise me you'll come back for me. Promise me, Dominico."

"I promise." He said as he kissed her forehead and held her in a gentle embrace. Her body so close to his...so close.

"You won't forget me."

"I'll never forget you. You will always be there, in my heart." Dom stared into her eyes.

Desperate force of will she looked away, pushed him away from her, turned her back to him. When he approached, she held her hands out to keep him away. She shook her head as she placed her belongings in the basket. "Go, Dominico." she said trembling, yet with authority. "Go now while I'm strong." Still, she would not look at him.

In haste, she rolled the blanket in her arms and handed it to him. "Take this. It gets...cold in New Yor..." She jumped into his arms and kissed his cheek. Before Dom knew what was happening, she picked up the basket and ran down the hill. She never looked back.

Be like stone. He could have cried at that moment. He could have wetted that consecrated ground with all the sorrow that was penned up inside. There was nothing more left to him than a dream. A dream of one day holding his Pratolina and their children and never having to spend another day without her. With this dream, the dam of his tears, he turned his back on the night shadows into which she disappeared and made his way home.

Dom sat on the bench behind the ruined *casa* staring toward the hill that could only barely be seen from the village. The tall, twisted tree under which he and Pratolina made love was but a spare and diminutive shrub at this distance. How distance distorts. How would that tree, that hill, those memories look from *Gli Stati Uniti*? Dom did not want his memories, his dreams, that tree, that hill to be distorted or changed in any way, even in his own mind. He tried to brick the memories into his consciousness so that they would remain unchanged, that they would be his secret castle where he could hide and find solace. The tears wanted to come out. They deserved to come out...

"*Figlio,*" Dom heard from behind as he felt his father's heavy hand land gently upon his shoulder. He spoke with forced excitement. "You're up early. You must save your strength. Today you will be the center of attention and tomorrow you have a long walk to Salerno."

"I'll be fine, Papa." Dominico forced a smile and the tears that were welling in the corners of his eyes dried as if on a hot pan.

"I've always had difficulty sleeping as well, Dominico." His father's words became slow, a somber baritone. "I'm afraid it won't get any better. There's a great deal on your mind, and from this point on there always will be. You are a man now. You know that don't you?"

Dom nodded.

"You're making man's decisions. How do they feel?"

Dom could not respond. How did they feel? He was feeling so much that he could not tell which emotions came from where. He just shook his head. Man's decisions, hard decisions. Deciding to leave his family and everything that he knew for a dream. To satisfy this dream he placed the weight of the entire family upon his shoulders. Their very survival would depend upon his success in *Lamerica*. It was all up to him, and he was alone.

"They feel...lonely." He responded.

Enrico laughed and nodded. "That they do. That they do. And they always will. That's the burden.

"*Figlio*, you know I don't want you to go."

"Yes, Papa."

"But you have to make your own mind, and I guess I have to respect it." A frown curled like an arch over Enrico's chin. "Yes, I guess I have to respect it. But never forget, no matter where you go and what you are doing, your home is here."

Dom stared at his father who was desperate to be like stone. He nodded, "Yes, Papa."

Enrico pursed his lips and pretended to wipe sweat from his brow, "and it will always be here for you," he choked through the sentence before standing rigidly and walking back into *la casa*.

The day was filled with revelry as friends and family met in the Rossa work yard to send Dominico on his voyage the right way. A man had to have merriment before taking a journey. Excess sadness was too much baggage to carry. There was laughter and games and people patting Dom on the back, hugging him, kissing him on the cheek. Wishing him *Buono viaggio* and *Buono fortunato*. They all gamboled about the work yard telling stories about little Dominico and how he was such a good boy, always mindful. He was not the boy they thought would travel across the ocean in a quest for riches and glory.

Dom found himself pulled aside by the men who prattled on incessantly about American women as if they had ever known an American woman. "Yes, Dominico, once you establish yourself, they'll be all over you, you know." Dom smiled and nodded without the slightest interest in what they were saying. Or they would pull him to the side and offer him advice about how to survive in America as if they had ever been to America. They were barely surviving in their own homes.

The older women would grab him by the arm and hug him, laughing and crying at the same time. They would kiss him on both cheeks and blubber about how they knew he would grow to achieve great things. The matrons pulled him to the tables and bade him taste the special food they prepared just for him. The younger women, however, were kept at a distance and would only speak to Dom with their fathers or brothers present. It was not good to have a young man associate with a young woman before setting off for a long voyage. Such would be courting impropriety.

Dom found himself caught in a whirlpool of attention, and for this he was grateful as it kept his mind from the trip, from the thought of being away.

Campania was in many ways a Hell, but it was a familiar Hell from which Campanians were loath to leave. If he were to think about leaving, he did not know how he would deal with the fear. He guessed he would have to deal with fear eventually, but as for now he could distract himself with the men playing *Bocce* or throwing horseshoes. Not only was he the focus, but his own attention was demanded in so many different circles.

The one confrontation that Dom was not looking forward to, however, took place in the very beginning when *Signore* Patrillo arrived. Indeed, *Signore* Patrillo had a legitimate grievance with Dom leaving before being wed to his daughter. The dowry was paid and could not be returned. It was becoming difficult to marry one's daughter to a worthwhile groom in the village anymore. The marriage of daughters was of the utmost importance in *Il Mezzogiorno*.

"Dominico!" He called.

Dom stopped and his heart tried to escape from his chest, "*Signore* Patrillo."

The portly man placed his arms around Dominico and spoke to him in a soft voice. "Dominico, when do you think you will be back to marry Clara?"

The words jammed in his throat. Dom hesitated in his response. "I...I...really don't know, *Signore.*"

"I'm sure, being your father's son, that you will live up to your responsibilities."

"Um..."

"*Oro, oro*. Now, now." Ugo patted his shoulders. "I know a man, far away from his home. A young, good-looking man like you. I don't expect you to live like a monk. I'm not naïve." *Signore* Patrillo pursed his lips and nodded, his left hand was held and punctuated his sentences. "And I know that...well... things happen. Unexpected things sometimes. I don't know what the rules are in *Lamerica*, but I know the rules here. The dowry is paid."

"I know *Signore* Patrillo..." Dom did not know how to reassure him, but he was determined to try.

"So, I want you to know that, as it stands, the marriage is as good as done."

"*Signore...*"

"But let me be perfectly clear, if anything happens, anything **unexpected**, I'm expecting you to make retribution in the amount of the dowry."

Dom was stunned. "Uh...um...absolutely, *Signore* Patrillo. I will not forget my responsibilities."

"And one more thing," Ugo continued. "If this takes more than five years I will have to make other arrangements. Clara should not have to wait past twenty years old for a husband, you understand."

"*Naturalmente.*"

"And at the end of five years, if we should find a suitable husband, I'm expecting to be reimbursed the dowry."

"*Si, Signore* Patrillo." Dom smiled. One small weight lifted from his shoulders.

Ugo kissed him on both cheeks then patted his face. "You are a good boy, Dominico. You will be a man like your father."

There was not much interaction with his own family, however, except for *Nonno* who sat in a chair under the shade of the collapsed work shed. Dom tended to the old patriarch and gave him water, wine, and bread to eat. He made sure the old man was comfortable and protected from the heat. Yet not many words were spoken with his grandfather.

"I want to thank you, *Nonno.* Thank you for making this possible."

The old man waived his twisted hand and shrugged it off. "You go and have fun, Dominico. This is your last day as a Campanian."

Dom thought about that phrase which would hang in his mind for the rest of his life. His last day as a Campanian. Just exactly what did that mean. It seemed a formidable transition at such a young age. If Dominico Rossa were not a Campanian, what would he be? Who would he be? The weight that Ugo Patrillo took from him was replaced—replaced ten-fold. His very identity was at stake.

Enrico spoke and laughed with many of the same men from the ill-fated meeting that seemed so long ago. Dom looked at them, watched his father laugh and cajole with them. In his mind they had betrayed his father, betrayed his family. How could his father be so cordial with them? Though he was, by his father's own admission, a man, there were still many things that he did not understand.

Paolo stayed on the *bocce* court and the older men enjoyed showing the young boy the tricks of the game. How to roll the ball so it would only go so far. How to aim and make sure the ball went where it was intended. They shared strategy and tactics, but Paolo had no interest in such abstracts. He clumsily lobbed the ball that went God knew where, and the older men laughed and tousled his hair. But the laughter was almost feverish when the boy, almost certainly by accident, made a good play, careening another player's ball from the *pallino*. He was the center of their attention and had no desire to be anywhere else.

During a moment of quiet Dom looked around for his mother. Sara was busy keeping the *festa* going and managing the food and distribution of what little wine they had. Indeed, she made herself busy to keep her mind from missing her first son. She removed two loaves of bread from the clay oven in the back and Dom was there to help her carry them to the table.

"Mama, you really should rest a while. Enjoy the party."

Sara shook her head and walked to the house for a utensil. "There is too much work to do Dominico. You go and enjoy yourself." She forced a smile and tried to reassure her son.

Dom looked into her eyes, sad eyes that seemed a little more pale than usual. "I'll miss you too, Mama."

She clutched him. The wet trail of tears tickled his neck as he felt his mother take a deep breath. Mothers know. Mothers always know so much more than they let on. And the things that Sara knew she did not want Dom to feel. She knew that he was in love and that he was leaving to be with her. She knew that it would be a long, long time before she ever saw her son again. She knew...she knew even more, but there was nothing more to do. The path was laid and her son had to follow it wherever it led.

Sara tried to talk. She tried to tell her son 'I love you,' but she could not speak. The emotion, so heavy that it held the words in her heart. She could only caress his face, the first roughness of manhood gently scratching her palm, then pointed to the party and nodded, indicating that he should go.

'Where's Anna?' Dom thought as he stepped away from his mother. "Hortensia!"

His sister turned to him.

"Where's Anna?"

"I saw her a moment ago on the other side of the house. She's terribly upset." Hortensia answered.

"I better find her."

Hortensia watched her brother walk away but called him back. "Dominico." Uncertainty in her voice.

He stopped and turned to her as she approached. "I know why you are going." She said. The smile on her face mocked the sadness in her eyes.

"What do you mean? Of course, you know why I'm going."

"No. I mean I know the real reason. I know about the woman you've been meeting." Dom tried to protest but she stopped him. "It's OK. I don't know who she is, but I know you have been meeting a woman. I've not told, nor will I." She added. "I envy you more than anything else. We should all have as much courage and passion and leave this place. But we won't."

"Hortensia," Dom shrugged his shoulders and stared at the ground. "If I didn't think it was best for the family I wouldn't be going."

She nodded. "Yes, I know. You would be a fool, though. Just like the rest of us are fools for not following you. No, Dominico, you go and make a lot of money and come back and sweep that girl off her feet. Then take her back to *Lamerica* and do not look back at this place again. If we are smart, we will follow. I will probably be the first, so you better set an extra pallet aside for me." She smiled and hugged her brother gently. "No," she grabbed his face between her hands. "On second thought you'll be a rich *Americano*. I want my own room."

"You'll have it," Dom replied, a broad smile shining on his face. Be like stone.

Anna was hiding behind a barrel of masonry nails, sitting there with her knobby knees tucked up to her chin, staring off into the barley waving in the distance. She was not sad, but angry. Her eyes were set like stone, dry and unwavering.

"*Mia Sorellina*, what are you doing here? Why aren't you at the party?" Dom sat beside her and stroked her hair. She would not speak.

"Oh, come on." he prodded. "Don't be mad at me on my last day here. I'll miss you and I'll remember how mad you are. I don't want to remember that."

"I don't care."

"Why don't you care?"

"Because I'm mad at you."

"Because I'm leaving."

"You said I could play with you whenever I wanted. You said it. Now you're going away, and I won't be able to play with you." Her eyes flickered. Water built in the corner but did not fall.

"I know I said that. I'm sorry I have to go. But I do have to go, Little One. I'm going to miss you too. If I could stay and have everything turn out okay, I would."

"I don't want you to go. Why do you have to go?"

Dom knew she would not understand. How does one explain something so complicated to someone so young? He could still remember the child mind where everything was black and white, right and wrong. In many ways he still thought that way. Such simplicity, however, was becoming clouded in a complex world. Did he have a right to bring those clouds into a young girl's life?

"I will be back. I won't be gone forever, Anna. I'm just going to make some money and help Papa. That's all. I'll be back and then you'll be able to play with me just like we used to."

"When will you be back?"

"I don't know, Little One. I don't know, but I'll write to you as much as I can, and I'll send you stuff from where I live. Come, don't be mad at me."

Her eyes glistened and her features softened as Dom stroked her silky hair. She lay her little head in her brother's lap and cried.

"Are you still mad at me?"

She nodded but clutched his leg.

After a few minutes, her crying stopped and her grip on his leg loosened. For a moment Dom thought she had fallen asleep. He bent and kissed her tender, young cheek.

"Dominico."

"Yes."

"When you come back are you going to marry Clara Patrillo?"

CHAPTER 2

Distant lights glowed ahead, and Dom knew that they had to be the welcoming signs of an inn. His father told him about the inn, owned by the Gondelli's, that lay alone and secluded along the route to Salerno. Dom was told that the Gondelli's knew of the Rossa reputation and would be happy to put him up for the night. Signora Dellamantagna had given him a sausage to use in trade for a room.

Ahead, the lights called to Dom, energizing his weary pace. He had not realized just how long the road would be. He had been walking all day and his legs were sore and stiff. It was amazing to the young man that his legs would become tired and ache from walking. He was used to walking. He walked everywhere. It was the only mode of transportation in his village. Why was it that he now felt weakness and stiffness? Because he was walking away from his home, the only place he had ever known, and his legs did not know how to do this. Oh, they could walk for miles around the tiny *paesera*, or around the numerous fields. They carried him lightly to the lovely hill overlooking the town where he and Pratolina...

'no, let's not think of that.' Walking so far from the things he knew, however, was not in his body's nature. His legs and feet objected via aching and tightness and a stubbornness that he had to fight to take his every step.

There, ahead, were the friendly, warm lights of the Gondelli Inn and Dom could feel the soft bed beneath him as each step brought him closer. The thought of laying his head from the weary travel encouraged his aching legs to that next step, and the next step after. Each step was just a little closer to *Lamerica*. As he approached, he could see the sign above the entrance but could not read the faded letters.

The old, wooden stairs creaked as he stepped on them. The rotted planks that were the floor groaned from his weight, threatening to betray him, send him sprawling to the ground. So, too, the door ached like his legs as he swung it open. The interior was bathed in soft, yellow light. The old wooden interior was gilded in lantern light. An old man sat in a dusty chair behind a great oak table that must have been owned by a wealthy family many years ago but was now a graying discard sitting with fading majesty in the middle of the room.

"Welcome." The old man said, offering a mostly toothless smile. "You're going to *Lamerica* I see."

Dom stared at him.

"*Non è duro.* It is not hard, *ragazzo*. It's not hard at all to spot a young man on his way to the land of golden roads." The old innkeeper struggled to stand. His back was arched and tended toward his right. As a result, he always seemed to be staring at the floor, or in the process of asking an in-depth question from someone of whom he was suspicious.

"The knapsack." Dom nodded. It had been on his shoulders for so long that he had forgotten that it was there. It was a light bundle, containing only his clothes, some personal belongings, Pratolina's blanket, an old purse, his grandfather's watch, and the sausage. The loaf of bread was long since gone and the jar of olio emptied and discarded.

"Eh!" The old man fluttered his pale left hand, "Knapsack, knapsack. Everyone who comes here carries a knapsack. No, *ragazzo*, it's your eyes. They are so bright, so far focused yet not confident...solemn even. The look of a young man going to *Lamerica*. So many dreams behind those eyes, so little strength in the soul to make them come true. I have seen those eyes many times. Many times, indeed."

He spoke as he reached into a drawer in an old desk. The drawer stuck and would not come undone until the old man kicked it. Dom was amazed that his rickety old leg could reach that high, especially with his back so crooked. "You have many people going to *Lamerica?*"

"You don't have any money, do you?"

Dom felt like he was engaged in another conversation. He had forgotten his desire for a room with his fascination of the curious old man. Dom shook his head. "My father told me that you would remember him. His name is Enrico Rossa. He said he repaired the family vault."

The old man returned a blank stare, scratching between the patches of lacy white hair on his otherwise bald head. "Rossa...Rossa."

"You are Signore Gondelli?"

"So, what do you have? There's no chicken in your hands. That's too bad. I like chicken. Let's see...salami."

"Pork sausage." Dom reached into his knapsack and removed a bundle of oilcloth.

"Give me, *Ragazzo Americano*." Dominico handed him the bundle.

The old man smelled it then lay it on his desk. From his pocket he produced a small knife that he unfolded and cut into the sausage. The oil glistened on the blade as he licked it clean. He cut the sausage into halves and handed one to Dom.

Dom shook his head, holding out his hands. "No, no...that is for you."

The old man nodded. "And is very good, thank you. You take what I offer under my roof if you are to stay. Tomorrow, you see me before you go. I'm an old man and can't afford to give a room for a sausage. You see me tomorrow morning and pay the rest of your keep."

Relieved, Dom smiled and accepted the sausage. "*Grazie*. What would you like me to do."

"Tomorrow. You see me tomorrow. You're going to bed now. You need your sleep. Now go. Your hopeful eyes have become tiring."

The old man, no longer smiling, indicated the direction of the room and Dom thanked him once again. As he turned his back, he heard the old man continuing to talk.

"Yes, I have seen your kind travelling both ways. I've seen bright eyed young men come from the east and I've seen pale eyed old men walk in from the west. I have seen your kind." Speaking in a mumble the old man was barely audible. "Travelers...golden roads...hopeless dreamers..." His words faded into the sound of the creaking floor.

Dom lay in the bed that sat in the middle of a Spartan room. A real bed! He lay flat on his back and stretched his arms wide. Only his parents ever slept in a real bed. He had always slept on shared a pallet on the floor with his brother. Now, he had a whole bed to himself. He stretched his arms and legs. Though the room was relatively barren. There was a bed, a nightstand, a lamp, and a crucifix nailed above the door, nothing more. This bed, however, was an unexpected luxury.

He lay on his back and closed his eyes, pondering the first leg of his long journey. *Lamerica* was so close in his dreams, yet this long walk jolted him back into reality. *Lamerica* was very, very far away. Infinitely far for a man who had never stepped out of his own village. What would it be like? He had heard the stories about streets paved in gold but was skeptical about such wealth. Dom knew too much about people like Don Alfredo Belan who would scrape every ounce of the gold on the streets and keep it for himself before he allowed people to walk on it. No, Dom did not expect golden streets, but he did expect...

What did he expect?

He expected a place of miracles. He expected a place where a broken family name would not stop him from carving out his niche in the world. *Lamerica* had to be a place in which he could, with enough hard work, make his dreams come true. It was a big place. Such a big place had to have plenty of opportunities for a young man. Yes, *Lamerica* had it all, he expected. *Lamerica* held the key.

Lamerica had...nothing...there was nothing there but vast stretches of land and money. But his family would not be there. Pratolina would not be there. Pratolina...Pratolina... without Pratolina it did not matter if the streets were made of gold and the houses made of diamonds, *Lamerica* had nothing.

There was his family, drifting into his mind as they receded into the distance, disappearing around the many bends of the road. His mother cried, hugged him, refused to let him go. She clung to his clothes and sobbed on his shoulder until Papa and Nonno pulled her from him. Nonno held her and comforted her. "He must go now. He must do this. If you try to stop him, he'll resent you for it. He must know..." Dom could not hear the rest of it past his mother's tears.

She was usually so strong. She did not cry unless someone died. In Dom's half dreaming mind he wondered if he had died in the eyes of his mother. A part of him, that dark part of his mind kept that idea circulating even though his heart knew better. Dom, his eyes closed, the worn mattress soft and pleasing under him, drifted off into sleep. He felt the wetness of his mother's tears on his dry shoulder.

Hortensia held Anna and rocked her gently. Anna refused to let Dom see her cry. She wanted to be strong for him. Her big sister held her face and cradled her little body while Dom said good-bye to Paolo. Paolo was the least emotional. He thought Dom was lucky to be going on such an adventure and did not grasp how long his big brother would be gone. Paolo hugged his brother quickly and asked, "Can I walk Bruzzo? I think Bruzzo likes me to walk him now. You won't be able to walk him for a while, so can I do it?"

"You'll have to ask Papa, Paolo. It's up to him."

As soon as Dom let go of him, Paolo turned to his father and said, "Can I walk Bruzzo from now on, Papa?"

Enrico stroked his head and said, "Not now, *ragazzo*. You talk to me later."

Hortensia then stood, handing Anna to her mother. She hugged Dom tightly, the tears wetting her eyes, trickling down her face. Kissing him on both cheeks she whispered in his ear. "You go, and don't worry about us. We should be going with you."

"I'll be back." He said.

Hortensia just shook her head. She started to speak, but the words wouldn't come. Instead, she coughed a little and turned to Anna.

"Anna, are you going to say good-bye to your brother?"

Anna shook her head, refusing to show her face nuzzled into her mother's apron.

"Come now, Anna, you must say good-bye. He's going away. You won't see him for a while."

Anna's little shoulders shook violently, but she refused to move.

Dom looked at Enrico who closed his eyes and nodded. He pointed down the road.

"I'll write to you, *Sorellina*. I'll write you as soon as I can. I wish you would say good-bye."

Still, Anna refused.

"Let's go, *Figlio*." Enrico motioned down the road. "It's time to go. She'll be all right."

Dom and his father began the long walk. Enrico decided to travel with his son for a few miles. Dom felt that there was something that his father wanted to tell him. They walked through the town but before they got to the edge of the village Dom heard something behind them. Before he could turn around, he felt the weight on his left leg, and he almost stumbled backwards. "*Arrivederci, arrivederci Fratello...arrivederci*." Anna cried as she clutched his leg and cried. "I'll miss you...good-bye..." Dom knelt and picked her up, holding her against his chest she covered his face with salty wet kisses.

Dom and Enrico passed from the village. Around the next curve was the south wall of the *latifundo.* Dom stared at the walls. They seemed taller in his mind. They seemed taller and the sky seemed bluer and cooler. He could not feel the heat that plagued him the whole journey. His father walked silently beside him. Dom felt like he should say something. They should talk about something, work, women, something, but it did not seem right...

...And then, there she was. There she was, standing barefoot under the tree that shaded the tuft of grass. In her black hair the wildflowers were like tiny angels floating about her face. She was placing a yellow flower in her hair when she noticed him. Her eyes brown yet...gold and light, her honey mouth a gentle frown, and the wildflowers set in dark tresses.

Dom stared at her but kept walking. His father walked beside him. Neither of them spoke. Dom did not know what his father saw if he saw anything. But his father knew. Dom felt that he knew. As Dom lost sight of Pratolina around the next bend in the road he thought, 'Papa and I should talk.' But what words?

Alas not a word was spoken for another three kilometers. There they reached the crossroads. The sign pointing west said Potenza, the sign pointing east, Salerno. To Dom, however, this crossroads was more significant. Potenza and Salerno meant nothing to him at this point. All he could think was, 'we should say something.' This was the crossroads. This was where Dom's life became something that he could not recognize. He did not know what was waiting around the next turn. He could count on nothing. Nothing at all.

Enrico stood proud before the signs. His father pursed his lips, his eyes dry but squinting. His normally graceful hands fidgeted. He just looked at his son and nodded. He forced his chin out and swallowed hard.

"Papa, I..."

Then he was in his father's embrace. Enrico's mighty arms tightened about his son's shoulders, his big, calloused hands stroking his son's back. Dom returned the embrace, holding his father tightly, not wanting to let go of the last stable footing on his journey. But his father pushed him away, clenched his jaw and said, "Be like stone, *Figlio*...be like stone." Then, with nothing further to say, head held high and proud, he walked back toward town.

CHAPTER 3

"She never heard from him again. Once he left, he was gone from her life forever." Cecilia pouted. Her hands shook and eyes watered as she could feel the immensity of what she had said, and to whom she knew she was saying it. Cecilia regretted that her words could be interpreted as an accusation, but it was too late.

The soldier, his forehead resting against the stone, became suddenly rigid and vital. Anger flooded his eyes, washing the sadness like wildfire through dry leaves. Once tender eyes flashed black and burning in Cecilia's direction.

"She never heard..." He clutched her high on her arms, the bandages of his wounded hand became saturated with blood, smearing the green fabric of Cecilia's dress.

It was night before Dominico reached Napoli. The sea's salty smell wafted to his nose. Gentle Tyrrhenian breezes carried the ancient pungency of the city. The combination of salt and city life became stronger in Dominico's nose. He was getting closer. He was about to knock on the door to another world—a strange world, a new world of promise and profit. Would he be welcome?

He traveled long, feeling the dusty, grainy dirt of the road beneath his feet. The compacted dirt soon gave way to cobbles and Dominico had visions of the piazza before the Church of *San Giuseppe* back home. That was the only cobbled area in the *paesera* outside of the walled *latifundo*. Yet these cobbles had a different feel to them. They were thick and stout, yet uneven, a subtle wave in the road, the result of centuries of carrying the burden of carriages, horses, armies both friend and foe. Proud, gilded war chariots of mighty Rome once shook these stones. Today, these cobbles marked the path for shaky gray wagons of dejected masses in exodus.

Dominico had heard tales of Napoli from his father and his grandfather. They had been to *Napoli* and *Roma.* To Dominico such stories were akin to tales of world travel. *Napoli, Roma, Paesera de San Giuseppe*. These were the boundaries of Dominico's world. He dreamed about his first trip to Napoli someday. Imagined that he would travel with his father, Bruzzo grumpily pulling the wagon and tools along the way. He and his father would build a great wall or face a cathedral or government building. They would leave the Rossa mark in stone that would last forever, as his family had always done.

And *Roma*! Dominico dreamed of the Eternal City with its grandeur and awe-inspiring history. Yet *Roma* seemed impossibly far away, like travelling to the Moon. He marveled at the tales of those who had been there. One old man traveled through the village one day with a message from the Pope. The people gathered around and called out in rage at a government that would virtually imprison their spiritual leader, the representative of God on Earth. They cursed Roma and all her godless denizens. Yet even under the guise of anger Roma inspired passion in all who heard her ancient name. *Roma*! *Roma*! The impossible dream.

Yet here he was, in *Napoli*! In *Napoli*, alone with no intent of leaving the Rossa mark. Indeed, Dominico was only in *Napoli* with the intent of leaving this ancient world behind. It was his doorway to another life and the hope that he could someday marry the woman he loved and bring respect to his frayed family name. His soul was twisted to the point of being rent as he heard his shoes click along the cobblestones. At once his dreams and hopes turned to the wonder of what lay ahead. He would cross an ocean and step into an unknown world. Fear and excitement burned in him, pushed him closer to the ocean, and the pungent sea air. On the other hand, he yearned for what he left behind, and loneliness tainted the exhilaration of travel.

That which he left behind was still just within reach. He could turn back. He could return to the village and sleep in the security of the pallet that he shared with Paolo, the bliss of his mother's cooking and Hortensia's snide comments. He would stretch his limbs, becoming tighter and harder with approaching manhood, and follow his father into the work yard. His muscles would ache from working on stone, his hands tingle from the constant vibration of the chisel and hammer. He could find his way to the hill and the gnarled tree. There he would lay in Pratolina's arms and feel her skin against his, her lips, her long, black hair tickling his bare shoulders. All he had to do was turn back.

'Turn back and then what?' he asked himself as he made his way along the narrow, dimly lit streets. The Rossa work yard was barren but for the broken blocks that were to be angels and capitals. That would not change. There was no longer a reason to stretch his muscles. There was nowhere to follow his father. His palms would not tingle with the feel of stone and steel for the foreseeable future. His mother's cooking would be without spice or salt or luxurious meat.

As for Pratolina...Pratolina...ah, how the mind is haunted and tortured most by the sweetest memories. He tried not to think of her because when he did, he could feel every mile of his travels. Yet he wanted to think of her and nothing else for fear that such memories might fade, and he would have nothing left of her but the blanket which he kept tucked in his rucksack. Oh, to turn back and find solace in her arms just one more time. But to turn back would be folly. Without money, without *Lamerica* he could never have her. He would suffer the pains of marrying another...Clara Patrillo. Worse, he would bear the cross of being witness to her betrothal to another.

He saw her with Signore Belan, the son of *Il Padrone*. Little Alfredo was an insect, his bony fingers touching her where

Dominico had once touched her. No, he could not be witness to such tragedy. *Lamerica* was his only hope, the only chance he had of happiness. There was no turning back. Turning back would only be one more dishonor, one more defeat for his already beaten family.

Dominico made his way along the streets. His eyes were wide, those of a lost and startled animal. He tried to make sense of and memorize every site, look for signs that would show him his way. He could hear families in their apartments overhead, the windows glowing yellow and orange with candlelight. The windows were open to maximize ventilation in the heat of the summer, and the songs of a thousand families danced incoherently in Dominico's ears. To live in such a place, so close together, stacked one on another like caged beasts. An occasional stranger passed him on the street but vouched him only a cursory glance. How different this place was from his cozy little village. How immense and somehow menacing the night became to a young man who had only recently known his first night alone. How strange it was to be alone yet surrounded by voices.

But it was not long before Dominico could feel the weight of his travels pressing on his shoulders, pulling at his eyelids. He needed rest, but he had no money left. Without knowing what to do Dominico followed the salty air, maintained as straight a course as he could until he heard the gentle sound of waves rolling against a stone wall. In the moonless night Dominico knew that he reached the sea only by virtue of the shipboard lanterns glowing yellow in the dark waters of the bay.

He walked along the shore, listening to the waves, entranced by a sound that was alien to him. The song of the sea caressing the land with gentle shush...shush...shush, a gentle, giant mother easing her frightened child to sleep. He thought about his hand filing the details into a stone piece. There was a rhythmic quality to his work when he was lost in it. A true blade along well worked marble made a sound close to that of the sea washing against the shore. This made sense. After all, the ocean worked the stone, slowly carving its vision over millennia.

He made his way to a pier jutting into the bay. The pier was lit with gas lanterns and Dominico noticed a pallet covered in oilcloth. He did not know what was underneath, however he did find that it comfortable to sit on. There was a fair amount of light and a place to rest his head, so Dominico fashioned himself a small place to sleep atop the pallet and propped his feet up, removing the thin-soled shoes and curling the ache from his toes. His feet cooled in the sea air, but his shoulders and back were awkward and ached in protest. It would be some time before Dom would allow these bones to relax. He had one more task to complete.

In his rucksack Dom removed some wrinkled pieces of paper and an old pencil that *Nonno* gave him. On that pallet, under that gaslight, the sound of the sea washing against the shore, the creaking of an old fishing boat as it rocked with the tide he scratched his first words home—to Pratolina.

CHAPTER 4

The sound of the bustling city wharf woke Dominico long before sunrise. The sky glowed over a purple sea washing listlessly against the ancient floodwall. The world came to life as a thin azure strip spread from behind the dark mountains. Vesuvius reached for the first delicate rays of the still unseen sun. Gulls preened themselves as they prepared their daily quest for food around the masted sailing ships. With the gulls the men worked along the wharf preparing their equipment for the long day ahead. They unrolled their nets and unfurled the sails as the gulls pulled and sorted their feathers, making ready their own equipment.

A pale, silver curtain eased across the sky. The morning mist lifted with the first glimmering rays of sun. Chattering and squawking gulls were the first to break the silence, a crescendo played homage to the rising sun. The chatter and laughter of the men, the clink and clatter of their tools provided the beat and rhythm. The sky became brighter, bluer, in response to the romantic music. Planks creaked and bells tolled as the ships lurched toward the blue Tyrrhenian. The gulls lifted into the air and found their places among the forest of masts and billowing sails.

Dominico gathered his few belongings and wrapped them in the soft blanket that still retained Pratolina's scent. His ears were full of the ticklish sound of the sea brushing the gray and green uprights of the pier under which he slept. That night the pier seemed the perfect place to lay his head once the pallet became unbearable. Soft sand and the curious sound of the ocean against the rocky wharf lulled him to sleep. Such a beautiful, caressing sound, like Pratolina's sweet whispering in his ear. In the morning, however, as the heavy-footed seamen prepared for their day this idea proved ill conceived. A dull, rhythmic pounding overhead interrupted the caress of the waves and, with violent hands, pulled Dominico from his sleep.

As he emerged from the confines of the pier, he noticed the silhouette of a man stooping in the distance. Dom stretched as he approached the man, pulling in his first long breath of the day. The air was salty, full of brine and decay, the odor of drying fish wafted through the cool breeze. Dominico thought how he hated the odor of dried fish back in his village. Yet it was somehow clean. There was a flash of light as the stooping man before him lit a match and lowered the globe of a small kerosene lantern. Once his eyes were adjusted to the new, invasive light he noticed that the man had a small wooden cart. The absence of a mule indicated that the man pulled the cart by hand. The cart was filled with baskets.

The man was old and weathered, his face dark with the texture of well-worn leather. His eyes were sunken beneath a bony, brown ridge capped with long, matted, white eyebrows. He really was a skeleton of a man aged beyond his years. He lowered his creaky body upon a small stool, his bony knees jutted up and his black, tattered pants rose high above his ankle revealing stringy brown legs.

Dominico slowed his approach, but the old man looked up at him, his old eyes still sharp and white around the edges. "*Buon giorno*," his raspy voice carried a cheerful toothless smile with its words. "*Buon giorno, buon giorno*. Why, it's a boy, big and strong and full of life. A meaty boy with a healthy chest. Why you'll be a fine fisherman, you will."

The old man lifted a half-finished basket and though his fingers were crooked and spindly, they were deft in weaving the basket in a smooth spiral. "Come, come young fisherman. You'll need a basket before you go. *Per favore, per favore*, take your pick. They are fine baskets, and they'll last you many trips. Yes, many trips. *Per favore, per favore*."

"*Grazie*, but I don't believe I'll need a basket…"

The old man leaned close to Dominico and sniffed. His nostrils inflated dramatically with every pull of air. He nodded, "I don't smell the sea in you boy."

Dominico smiled and shook his head.

"You must be going to *Lamerica*." The old man croaked *Lamerica* and his toothless grin creased his face. The mist was disappearing and the silver-white was giving way to its first traces of blue. There were no longer any gulls on the ground. They were all squawking and flying in gentle circles overhead.

"*Si*!" Dominico smiled.

"*Va bene, va bene*! You go to *Lamerica* on those ships there." Dominico followed the old man's bony finger and noticed that the aesthetic of the ships changed.

Like giant ghosts appearing from the mist the great iron ships appeared before him. They were huge and lumbering, black and gray hulks planted and immobile in the wavy sea. A visceral uncertainty rolled through Dominico as he could not see how such behemoths could float. He knew they did. He had heard about the great ships that crossed the ocean, but never imagined the sheer, overwhelming size of them.

"Yes, impressive they are." The old man smiled. "That's where you'll go if you are going to the land of plenty and golden streets." He laughed and Dominico thought the old man would fall over from the strain.

"I'm looking for a man named *Signore* Petrocchuli. Do you know where I can find him."

The old man shook his head and closed his eyes. His hands, like long, brown spiders, continued to weave the basket. "You go there. You go there and you will find your way."

"*Grazie mille*," Dominico responded and, with his blanket under arm, continued his journey.

It was not long before the cacophony that was *Napoli* pressed in around Dominico, an indescribable weight that pushed from inside and from outside. It started with the almost demonic retort of a steam whistle as a great barge approached the bay. Dominico turned with a start and stared at the slow, lumbering ship crawling like a great snail over the surface of the sea. The sea was turning a deep blue as the sun appeared from the east. To the west Dominico saw the thin line that separated the water from the sky. It was so far away—impossibly far. He lived in a village surrounded by mountains. There was never a time in his life that the horizon seemed impossible to reach. All he would have to do is cross the next hill and he would be there, on the horizon looking down upon the entire world. On the sea, he realized just how far away lay the horizon. His dreams were many hundreds of kilometers beyond that thin line. How would he ever get there? The impossibility of what he was trying only added more weight upon his heart.

He did not have time to deal with this weight, however, as the din of the people reached his ears. People were pushing past him, scurrying about the wharf. Many were shouting and responding to the shouting of others, zephyrs too engulfed in people to be seen. As the sun rose the people became more numerous. Shouting and laughing and throwing their hands in the air. Two fat men in reed hats argued over a piece of sidewalk, each wanting to place his cart of goods in the same spot as the other. Their arms waved in violent circles as they swore at each other. It was not long before one of the men lumbered away with his cart of goods. Women dickered over the price of food and textiles. Brutal and profane foremen directed bulky men struggling under the burden of heavy sacks. One large, bear of a man was being berated by a little, rat faced man with a clipboard pointing and waving his hand at a palette of wheat sacks.

Gulls shrieked overhead and lunged for what edible morsels dropped by unknowing visitors to the marketplace. They flew through the buildings and weaved under ropes lashed across the street for drying laundry. Such marvelous acrobatics.

And such buildings, thin canyons of people. Dominico was amazed that people lived so high up in the air. They were stacked one on top of the other and so close together that it must have been impossible to breathe. He stared at the buildings as he entered the street. His musings did not last long as he was engulfed by the throng of people doing business in the early morning, purchasing goods for their fishing vessels, or food for their families, massing around carriages barely half-full of fruit and bread and dried fish.

An old woman complained about the quality of the fabric from a vendor who was trying to explain that she would not find better quality in all Campania. She cursed him like Dominico had never heard a woman curse, her hand waving in front of her face. She told him that he was probably right as she walked away in disgust. She would be back moments later to buy a few meters of fabric.

Eventually Dominico found his way along the thin winding streets. He felt like he was in a cave. The sun disappeared behind the buildings looming over him, threatening to fall in on him, crush him and the throng of people who plowed past unconcerned of the imminent danger. Babies cried and everywhere people were loud, whether they were steeped in an argument or laughing from the punch line of a lewd joke told only among men. They were so loud as if they had to shout over each other to be heard.

Dominico decided that he was on the right street. He received directions from a tall seaman who read the address on the card and pointed him in the right direction. Yes, this was the street, but what building? Where to go? The buildings were very old, dingy yellow and orange, gray and brown, stained black from centuries of fires and other pollutants--stained by the breath of the people who lived there. The numbers on the crumbling, ashy buildings were hard to read. Finally, Dominico narrowed it down to a handful of buildings then asked directions to each. At long last he found someone who knew *Signore* Petrocchuli. He pointed Dominico to an old, gray building across the crowded street. On the door was a sign that read, "EMIGRAZIONE: SIGNORE PETROCCHULLI."

The office took up the bottom floor of what Dominico thought was probably the oldest building in this ancient city. This was the most crowded of all *Napoli* and Dominico struggled to breathe. The air was thick with the odor of people, breath and bodies packed close together in the summer heat.

Babies cried and the smell of their urine saturated the walls. Grayish blue cigar smoke gathered thick at the ceiling and soon encompassed the faces of all inside. Dominico's eyes burned, and his breathing became labored.

Inside, the noise was surreal as families, carrying all their worldly belongings thronged into the crowded room arguing and caterwauling among each other. They carried with them all their anxieties and fears and hopes and desires. Such emotion crammed into a smoky stench of a room could only result in high drama. Some broke down and cried from disappointment. Others argued about their rights and their health, demanding some kind of satisfaction. Children clung to their parents' legs, fear in their eyes as they looked around the room and knew that they would be lost with the slightest misstep.

Dom was pushed along by the inescapable tide that was the mass of people. Though this seemed a scene of chaos and confusion, there was a definite direction, a destination that Dominico could not see, but to which he was being guided. All who surrounded him seemed just as confused as he was, confused and worried. Scared. What was this journey that they were taking? Why would human beings cram themselves into a room to leave their homes and travel to an unknown land? It was as if all of Campania were trying to fit into this one crumbling, gray office.

"Your first time." A stranger in a new suit and a fine, black suitcase smiled at Dominico.

"Si." Dominico responded, embarrassed. The man was older, possibly in his thirties, though it was difficult to tell in the hazy and dim light of the office. What was obvious was that there was a certain glimmer in his eye, a cocky smile on his face and an air of superiority that Dominico new was more than attitude, but simple fact. He seemed...American.

"Not to worry, young man. You will be fine. Just do everything you are told, and you will be in America before you know it." He patted Dominico on the shoulder and stepped forward.

"You've been there?"

"Of course. I've been there for ten years now. I'm very successful. This is my fourth trip back to the old country. I've come to visit my parents and help build a barn for them."

"Why are you going back? If you are successful, why not come back to stay?"

"Why would I come back here? That makes no sense. There's nothing here for an enterprising man. Besides, my wife and children are in America." He leaned in close to whisper. "She's *Siciliano* and my parents wouldn't understand why I married her." He put his finger to his lips as if his parents were in hearing distance, then offered a cocky wink.

Indeed, Dominico did not understand the marriage either. He'd heard about the vile *Siciliani*. The conversation was cut short, however, as the man stepped up to the desk, unfolded some paperwork from a leather pocketbook and was quickly authorized to leave through a door to the left. "You do as you are told, young man, but be careful. There are as many pitfalls in America as there are opportunities." And the man disappeared through the door into another swaying mass of people.

"You're next..." a gruff voice demanded Dominico's attention. "Do you have your papers?"

Dominico froze. In front of him was a harsh looking man with steel gray eyes and a gray suit. He stared at Dominico who was afraid to admit that he did not know what papers the man was referencing.

"I...I...was told to see *Signore* Petrocchuli."

"A new traveler. You go through that door to the right and wait for your physical. You must have a physical before you go see *Signore* Petrocchuli."

Dominico shook as he stepped through the door on the right. The room was no respite from the smoke or the smell of urine and sweat. The people were divided into two lines, one for men and another for women and children. The lines diverged and were eventually separated by a long curtain that only barely maintained the dignity of both sexes. But the most dramatic aspect of this room was the crying. Intense crying and cursing contrasted with the deathly silence of those who awaited their fortune in silence.

The biggest complaint was about the eyes. There was something wrong with some people's eyes. Dominico did not know what it was, but this illness was sufficient to keep them from pursuing their dream of America. Dominico saw a family split in half as two members out of five were not allowed passage. In the time that Dominico waited in line this family cried, then decided to send the father with the oldest boy to America. The mother, the second oldest son and their older daughter would remain. There were more tears, desperate clutching and hugging as the man and the boy passed through the door on the left. The mother sobbed reaching for her departed husband as the second born son, no more than thirteen, now the man of the family, walked her through the door on the right that led to the street.

"Take off your shirt, *signore*." A man in a white coat instructed Dominico.

"*Scusi*?"

"Your shirt. You must take off your shirt for the physical."

The young man who refused to wear his shirt while he worked in the noon day sun was now embarrassed by his nakedness. He slowly unbuttoned the shirt but was directed to make haste.

"Just undo the top buttons and pull it over your head. There's quite a line today. What is your name?"

"Dominico Rossa." The man approached and looked at his skin, specifically on his arms, shoulders and back. It was smooth and even. He then tapped on Dominico's broad back and chest. The man placed an instrument in his ears the other end of which he held up to Dominico's chest. He instructed Dominico to inhale.

"Have you ever had a cough that took a long time to go away? Have you ever coughed blood?"

"No."

The man ran his fingers through Dominico's hair, inspecting it carefully. "Have you ever had a fever, a very high fever."

Dominico had had fevers, but none that he would consider very high.

The man in the white coat instructed Dominico to open his mouth and stick out his tongue. He stared into Dominico's mouth much the same way he would inspect a horse.

"Have you ever had difficulty seeing?"

"No."

The man's hot hands grabbed Dominico's face and pulled his lower eyelid down, then raised the upper eyelid, staring into his eyes one at a time. He instructed Dominico to look up and down and left and right.

"Are you travelling alone?" The man in the white jacket asked, a stern look in his eye.

"*Si*." Dominico nodded.

"That's good. It's better to be alone."

Dominico stood and worried for a moment as the man in white wrote something onto a sheet of paper. He handed it to Dominico who was holding his breath. The breath came out as the man in white handed him his shirt and directed him through the door on the left. Relief, his journey was not ended before it started.

"*Signore* Rossa." *Signore* Petrocchuli spoke his name with a breathy, ironic voice. "So, you wish to go to America, do you?"

Dominico was tired. Upon leaving the room in which he received his physical he waited in another crowded and pushing line. This man's greasy smile did nothing to relieve the fatigue. Dom nodded.

"Do you read and write?"

"*Si.*"

"That is good. That will make this go a lot faster. Now, for the important part. Is your paperwork done?"

Dominico's eyes widened. The only paper he had was the one given to him by the doctor. He handed that to *Signore* Petrocchuli.

"No, no. This isn't the right paperwork. You must have permission to go to America. If you do not have permission, you do not go."

Dom tried to control his panic. Was his voyage to be ended so soon? He could not hide the fear that traveled across his face.

Signore Petrocchuli noticed the expression and put up his hand with a reassuring gesture. "Don't worry. *Non preoccuparti*. I'll get you what you need." He shuffled through some papers on his desk. He handed a few to Dominico and instructed him to fill them out. He assured Dominico that he would take care of everything.

"Now, *Signore* Rossa. Where are you from?"

"*Villa de San Giuseppe.*"

"That's here in Campania. Now do you have a trade?"

"*Si*. I'm a stone worker."

"Very good. Very good. A trade. That is very good. There's always use for skilled tradesmen in America. There shouldn't be a problem."

Dominico continued to fill out the forms as *Signore* Petrocchuli interviewed other people. Eventually Dominico was able to return to line and once again face *Signore* Petrocchuli. His hands shook as he handed the forms to the greasy man.

Signore Petrocchuli stared at the papers then smiled and sat back in his chair. "Ah, yes. Young *Signore* Rossa. I will take care of this for you. You just pay your fee and come back tomorrow, and everything will be taken care of."

Once again panic struck Dominico. He was not planning on any other fee but his passage. "All I have is this." He removed the watch that his grandfather gave him. "It's real gold." He handed it to *Signore* Petrocchuli who swiped it from the boy's hands, a scowl on his face. He opened the cover and looked at the pearly white face. "It's real mother of pearl face."

"Hrmph!" *Signore* Petrocchuli scowled. "This will cover the fee but will not get you passage."

"But it is real gold!" Dominico panicked. "It must be worth more than some paperwork."

"People are selling their whole lives to get passage. One watch is nothing in this business. You can go and sell it and come back with the money, but I guarantee it will not cover your passage."

"But...but I can't go back. What do I do?"

Signore Petrocchuli shrugged, his eyebrows raised and a frown on his face. He shook his head as he sorted through Dominico's papers. Then he looked up from the desk, a hopeful expression on his face, his greasy smile broad and toothy. "It says here you are a stone worker, yes."

"Yes, yes. I'm a stone carver." Dominico stammered. He was holding back the tears but could feel control over his emotions slipping away.

"I'll tell you, *ragazzo*, I know a man who could use a stone carver. Eh...are you any good?"

"I'm a Rossa." Dominico expressed, not without the right amount of indignation.

"Of course, of course." *Signore* Petrocchuli raised his hands and nodded. "A Rossa. Look. I know a man who really needs a good bricklayer. He's in New York. Now I can talk to his people here and see what I can do for you. I'll tell you what I'll do. This is only because I think you are a good boy, and I like you. You see this man tomorrow morning." He scribbled a name on the back of his own card. "You see this man, *Signore* Falzotte. He'll put you up for the night. Then you come back tomorrow morning, and I'll let you know what to do."

"Tomorrow morning. I'm supposed to be on this ship this afternoon."

"It's not going to happen today." *Signore* Petrocchuli shook his head and pursed his lips. Without thinking he opened a sticky drawer in his desk. The drawer was jammed full of gold watches, twisted necklaces, jewelry, shiny music boxes and various assorted riches jumbled in an ignominious pile. "You come back tomorrow. I think we can arrange something." With ignominy he threw *Nonno's* watch into the pile of shining, twisted metal then slammed the drawer closed.

Still shaking Dominico stepped into the street.

CHAPTER 5

"Just turn back, Dominico. Don't be a fool. This trip, this folly.' Dominico thought. That voice in his head became stronger, more fervent as he lay on the pallet on the floor of an old, decayed building down the street from the emigration office. 'The trip is as much as over anyway. You do not have passage, you do not have a ticket, and you won't get one. You saw the look in that man's eyes. He doesn't care if you come or if you go. Go back home and help your father rebuild. That's what you should do.'

Dominico turned and rolled on the uncomfortable mattress beneath him. He could only imagine how many people had slept on that very board, with these very sheets drawn over them. The thought only worsened his discomfort. He was used to his own pallet that he shared only with his brother. No one else ever slept there, sweated there, cried there--no one but him. He could smell the odor of people all around him, jammed into one room where they shared each other's breath, each other's sweat, the smell of cigars burning above him. Dominico began to hate the ubiquitous smell of cigars.

His body itched from the closeness of all those people, all those lives. A room as full of bodies as it was with dreams and hopes for something better. This old, crusty building not only housed the dirty, bedraggled, desperate people, but their battered souls and the embattled faith that held their spirits together. The insects that scurried along the floor and through the bedding, however, were not moved to mercy by such hopes. Dominico felt guilty for the negative thoughts that pulsed through his mind. So many people pinned all hopes of their future, of their families' futures on the quest for *Lamerica*. Little did he know that his were not the only thoughts of despair and impending disaster.

Few people in the crowded confines of these flaking walls and faded paint slept that night. It was not the babies crying, the incessant coughing, or even the cigar smoke that robbed them of sleep. It was the voices of doubt in their minds that shouted at them, cursed them to make them turn around, return to their villages, submit to the indignities of *la miseria*. This kept them awake, tormented them, oppressed their bodies' necessity for sleep and rest.

Such voices they were. They were the voices of a two-thousand-year-old tradition. They were the voices of generation after generation of Italians who remained in their place. Sedentary urges to remain in the villages and marry and produce sedentary children who would take the place of those who died...died perhaps in the very bed in which they were born without ever straying outside the confines of their *paesere*. And when the invaders came…and they always came…and destroyed the villages, set afire the grass huts of the *contadini*, trampled the crops, stole the livestock, and raped the women before leaving the skeleton of a society behind, it was these voices that said, 'stay, and rebuild.' And they stayed, they rebuilt, they picked up the plow, herded in what strays they could find and pretended that their wives and daughters weren't ruined by the ravishing foreigners. Such was life in the *Mezzogiorno,* and such were the voices that appealed to the souls of this swarthy and hearty people to remain.

In many instances the voices turned the soul once intent on shedding the bonds of *la miseria*. At least half a dozen times during the night Dominico watched as men roused their families, picked up their belongings and passed without speaking down the stairs, onto the street, to return to their villages and make do with the ruins that were their lives and livelihoods. As dark as the room was, he could not see the eyes of those who left. That did not keep him from noticing the dejection. It was as clear as if under the noon sun. The defeat was obvious in the stooped shoulders and shallow footsteps of the men. It was there in the condescension of the women. Even the confusion of the children, who really did not understand what was going on, contributed to the ultimate aura of disappointment, the darkness of the defeated soul.

During such moments, the voices became more arduous, more intolerant of any assertion of will. 'They've left. They've come to their senses. They will return and all will remain as it should. Go back, Dominico. *Lamerica* is not for you.' Dominico pulled on the blanket and reached for his belongings. He would go back. He had to go back. He had to be with his family. They looked so sad when he left—when he turned his back upon them.

'Pratolina.' He thought. "Pratolina," he whispered and prayed that the stale air would catch a miracle breeze and carry this word back to the village into the ears of the one he loved. Pratolina. How could he return and face her knowing that he could never marry her, never make love to her again? How could he walk to the market with Clara Patrillo and see Pratolina on the other side of the square and live with the fact that he failed her? No, there was no turning back. There was no more room for dishonor. If having Pratolina meant descending into hell and carrying the brimstone in his teeth then that is what he would do without hesitation. He would have Pratolina. He would go to *Lamerica* and there was not a force on earth that could stop him.

Signore Petrocchuli smiled when he spotted Dominico in the crowded, heaving mass. He smiled that greasy smile, his tongue slightly pinched between large white teeth. His pale lips creased across his face. He spread his arms and stood from behind his desk. Dominico remembered the cluster of watches and jewelry in the left-hand drawer and imagined his grandfather's watch lying among the twisted gold and silver and copper as if it were nothing special. Dominico hatred *Signore* Petrocchuli. He said nothing as he shook that sweaty cold hand. 'How could skin be so cold when it is so hot outside.' He remembered holding a salamander once, but shook the memory before it could take hold.

"Young *Signore* Rossa! *Buon giorno, buon giorno*! I've been spending an awful lot of time on you, young man. I have some good news for you, some very good news for you. Are you ready to go to America?"

Dominico's eyes lit up and an incredulous smile crossed his face despite the cold feeling that he received from the man before him. "Yes!" He jumped, "Yes I am. It's all I want--a chance. Just give me a chance." How quickly hatred can evaporate.

"Well, sir, you will get your chance. I have made arrangements, and all your paperwork should be in order in two weeks. We have a ship coming to port in two weeks that will take you to America. She's a fine ship, a German ship. She'll get you there in no time flat. And it will only cost you forty lire." *Signore* Petrocchuli raised his clammy hands with all fingers splayed in reptilian fashion.

Dominico frowned and slumped in his chair. Shaking his head he responded, "I don't have forty lire. All I had was the watch that I gave you. I thought that would be enough."

Signore Petrocchuli frowned as well and scratched his chin, but Dominico saw little that he could call empathy in the man. "Ah, I see. That does present a problem. Well…let's see…"

then he sat up with a snap and clapped his hands. "What the hell. *Signore* Rossa...you are a Rossa after all, aren't you?"

Dominico nodded.

"I like you, *Signore* Rossa. Here's what I'll do. Now mind you, I don't do this for everyone, but I see something in you. It's something I don't see in anyone else around here. I am willing to forward you the money on loan. I'll pay for the travel papers and passage. You have two weeks to earn the money to pay me back before you leave. How does that sound?"

"Well...it...I..." Dominico could not speak. This was not how things were supposed to go. He was not supposed to end up in dept. His father always warned about being in dept to another. 'Then the man owns you,' he recalled his father saying. "How can I pay you back?"

Signore Petrocchuli turned and waved to a large man who was standing behind him. "Gordo, Gordo, come, come." The big man approached.

"I believe that *Signore* Falzotte has work for a young man such as yourself. Gordo will go with you to see him and extend my word to him to hire you on for a couple of weeks. When you are done you will be able to pay me, pay him and maybe even have a little left over for the trip."

"*Grazie*," Dominico bowed. 'Two weeks.' He thought. He hoped he would be on his way sooner, but if he had to wait two weeks, he would do it. He knew that this was going to be a long endeavor when he started out--be like stone.

Signore Falzotte pursed his lips and eyed Dominico as Gordo whispered in his ear. He was an old man, balding with a wrinkled and frowning brow. In fact, his whole sagging face supported a perpetual frown. But his eyes were not sad. No, they were not sad. They were angry and cynical. The eyes of a man who had been betrayed many times. Perhaps they were the eyes of a man who had betrayed others and therefore expected the same.

He pushed himself from his chair and approached Dominico maintaining his scrutinizing gaze on the boy. He walked around Dominico, looking him up and down. "So, you wish to go to America, do you?"

"Yes, sir." Dominico tried to keep his voice from shaking.

"You're going to become a rich *Americano*?"

"No, sir. I want to make enough money to come back and...be respected."

Signore Falzotte's frown deepened as he nodded. Standing in front of Dominico he thumped the young man's chest with his fist twice. Dominico did not react with more than a slight flinch. The old man pursed his lips and whispered, "solid." Then he turned to Dominico, "What is the most important thing a man possesses?"

Without hesitation Dom replied, "His word, *Signore*."

The old man nodded, but still scowled. "The boy's been raised with character." He said these things to himself as if thinking aloud. "I think I may have work for you."

CHAPTER 6

After a week and a half Dominico was used to the ride along his route. For Signore Falzotte, Dominico was to pick up merchandise from various merchants around the city and deliver them to a designated ship on the pier. Overall, the work was not difficult. The lifting was easy for a young man used to dealing with rock and concrete. He made his way along the crowded Neapolitan streets, picked up his wares and dropped them off. Despite the apparent simplicity of this job, however, Dominico knew that nothing in *Napoli* was without complexity. Everything in this city was covert.

Signore Falzotte assigned him a route and a carriage drawn by an old, gray mule not unlike Bruzzo. Indeed, *Signore* Falzotte was amazed at how easily Dominico handled the historically recalcitrant animal named simply *Mulo*. He noted how the boy put the animal at ease with a touch under the jaw and a scratch behind the ear. It was the ruination of *Signore* Falzotte's joke to give the new boy the unruliest animal with which to work. *Mulo* was a great asset to *Signore* Falzotte. He forced his workers to work harder but cut down on the amount of compensation that *Signore* Falzotte had to pay at the end of their tenure.

Of course, Dominico was not aware of this behind-the-scenes skullduggery. He was simply given a job, a place to sleep, one meal a day and an opportunity to make the money that he needed to buy his ticket. As yet, however, he'd not seen any money. Signore Falzotte arranged to pay Dominico at the end of two weeks when he was to buy his ticket and leave for *Lamerica*. In the meantime, Signore Falzotte guaranteed that anything that Dominico could get anything he needed from him. All expenses would be deducted from his final pay before Dominico left, his account being squared. This satisfied Dominico's desire to be debt free as his father had instilled in him the importance of being beholden to no man regardless of the necessity.

Now, however, as Dominico circled along the western corner of his route he could not help but fear for his future. While in *Signore* Falzotte's employ, Dominico made the acquaintance of one Roberto Dunna. He was skinny and pale. His hollow eyes betrayed his anger with the world and all that was in it, especially the despicable creatures known as *I Ricci*. He spoke often of the scavengers, the disgusting wealthy who preyed on their own people like eaters of carrion, picking even the whited bones clean.

When thinking about the wealthy Dominico's picture was always that of Don Alfredo and his son. Roberto expanded that vision, however, in his description of *Signore* Falzotte. Dominico never considered the old, frowning man wealthy.

"Oh, he's wealthy all right, the old Buzzard. Filthy rich in the strictest sense of the word." Roberto spit on the ground as he spoke with his new, young friend. Roberto decided to take the boy under his wing and teach him the ways of the world.

"He doesn't look wealthy," Dominico stated. He never remembered seeing the old man shaved or wearing any more than an undershirt over his gray, hairy chest. The hair on his head was wispy, thin, and gray, rarely ever combed. This was a contrast to the almost sickeningly clean Don Alfredo whose very person seemed to repel dirt and whose hair was always perfectly groomed. *Signore* Falzotte lacked all of the refinery characteristic of the landed gentry of the *latifundi*. Dominico could still see the Don's feminine, white hands safe beneath felt gloves. He contrasted them to Signore Falzotte's stubby, hairy fingers, callused and dry with dirt under chipped nails. No, Signore Falzotte did not look the part of a rich man.

"Of course he doesn't look rich." Roberto growled. "Those are the worst kind of wealthy because they make you think that they are one of you. You think you can trust them because they have some dirt on them, or because they wear worker's clothes. But let me assure you, when the wealthiest men in *Napoli* get together, he is among them."

Dominico simply nodded and accepted what Roberto had to say. He was glad for the company. Roberto was an older man. No, not older in the chronological sense. In years, he was not much older than Dominico. He was twenty-one, twenty-two at the most. He was much aged, however. His eyes were old and tired. His skin was thin and lacking in sensitivity. Most significant, however, his mind was older--ancient. His mind was that of a man who had been at war for many years and lost more than he won.

Often his anger repulsed Dominico who would then avoid him. Dominico was too full of dreams to allow cynicism to enter his heart. When he was around Roberto, however, there was nothing more than cynicism in the air as if all hope had been snuffed out by his presence. Cynicism was all around him, in every breath. It was difficult enough for Dominico to remain positive and focused on what he wanted. In his most difficult moments, he rested his head and remembered his hands, his mouth wandering, searching along his sweet Pratolina. He would not allow such wonderful thoughts to be polluted by Roberto's rage.

Thoughts of Pratolina, however, were clouded with responsibility as Dominico made his last stop before carrying his haul to the pier. From a merchant's warehouse Dominico lifted four barrels labeled 'olive oil' onto his shoulder and carried it to the wagon. *Mulo* waited patiently as the heavy barrels jarred the carriage when dropped onto the graying, splintered wood. The merchant counted the barrels as Dominico loaded them, marking each one on the invoice.

"That's good, that's good," he said as he slapped Dominico on the shoulder. "You be careful now you don't drop those barrels or put them down too hard. The olive oil. It will bruise if you put it down too hard."

Dominico found this unlikely, but he was now certain that the merchant had ulterior motives for the care that he requested of his merchandise. Eyeing the barrels suspiciously Dominico climbed onto the creaking seat and flipped the reins.

"You think *Signore* Falzotte makes his money in shipping? You really think that Dominico?" Roberto once exclaimed, his lips red and wet from drinking grappa well into the night.

Dominico shrugging, not knowing what to say, yet not wanting to appear as naïve to the ways of the city as he was. This was of no importance to Roberto who dropped another swallow of the coarse grappa, belched and continued his diatribe.

"You're a fool if you really think that man makes an honest living. You're a fool if you think any man of means in this country actually makes an honest living. You really think all those crates and barrels have in them what's on the label? I'll tell you what. If you're ever stopped and searched by a constable and he decides to open one of those things whatever you do, don't let him search the crates too deeply. They all have false bottoms. You take the olive oil barrels for instance. They're only half full of olive oil, the top half. You put a dipper in there, it'll only go halfway down. Underneath the olive oil is all kinds of stuff that's been stolen or stuff that's illegal in certain countries."

Dominico shrugged once again and turned his pasta and a piece of trash fish on his plate.

"You don't believe me, do you?" Roberto slugged another shot of grappa and winced. "You will. A friend of mine and I, we opened one of those boxes one time. Yeah, we opened one, but we were in a hurry, and we opened the crate upside down. We were going to steal some sardines. That's what we thought was in the box. You know what was in the box? You'll never guess." Roberto started to laugh, his pale cheeks becoming ruddy with alcohol and humor. "*Preservativi*! Safeties!" He struck his knees and tried to draw in a deep breath as his laughter was coming out uncontrollably, his eyes wide in their hollow sockets. "Hundreds of safeties. Imagine what old Leo would say if he saw those. Heh, perhaps they were going to him." Roberto laughed at his latest blasphemy at the expense of Pope Leo XIII.

"Don't talk like that, Roberto!" Dominico put down his fork and exclaimed as he performed the ritual sign of the cross over his heart. "You shouldn't talk like that. His Holiness…you just shouldn't talk like that."

Roberto shook his head and threw back yet another mouthful of grappa. "It's no use, Dominico. I'm damned anyway. It makes no difference what I say. It really is quite liberating to be damned, actually. You'll see. You'll be damned soon enough. Then we'll drink together."

Dominico shook his head. "Never. That'll never happen to me."

"Oh!" Roberto exclaimed, almost falling backwards over his pallet spilling the yellowish-brown whisky onto the tattered sheets. "You think you're better than me, do you! You think you're better than me! Dominico Rossa with your father's honor and good name to carry around with you. You really think you're better than me. You think the stuff that has happened to me can't happen to you? Do you think that Dominico Rossa?"

"I don't want to start an argument, Roberto. I just want to eat my dinner and go to sleep. Let's call it a night."

"No, no! You started this *ragazzo* and now we're going to finish it. Do you think what happened to me can't happen to you?"

Call it hubris, call youth, but Dominico put his fork down, the pasta and fish still speared in the tines. He looked Roberto in his red, whiskey running eyes and said, "No, Roberto. I'm going to *Lamerica*. I will make something of myself. I won't become like you."

"Ahhhh!! Now *il piccoletto con I grossi testicoli parla!*" Roberto laughed and punched Dominico on the shoulder. "It's a good thing for you I don't think I can take you. At least not in the state I'm in now."

Realizing his mistake, Dominico decided to remain quiet and continue eating. He knew that his friend would never remember the conversation in the morning anyway. This was good, as Dominico was embarrassed by his boastful words. Dominico felt no need to continue this conversation further. Roberto knew that his was a wasted life.

"You want to know what happened to me?" Roberto was slowing down and slurring his speech. His red eyes stared at nothing is some distance only he could see. As if according to some inner clock the whiskey was going through its stages. Roberto started out quiet, then moved to angry. Shortly after anger everything became funny. At that point it was not long before everything became somber. The grappa was doing its job. That is, it was anesthetizing Roberto into a sound sleep—one he would not enjoy otherwise.

"You really want to know...what happened to me?"

Dominico tried to finish his meal without saying a word. Too much of a conflict with Roberto and he might just remember the details. That would cost Dominico an acquaintance, the only member of *Signore* Falzotte's workforce who deigned to talk to him.

"I'll tell you what happened. That *stronzo di capra* Falzotte is what happened to me. He and Petrocchuli. They're in it together. They find suckers like me and like you. Young guys with dreams and they rip out your soul with your own dreams. That's what they do. You'll see. You'll be sitting right beside me with the grappa at your lips thinking about that woman back in *Villa de San Giuseppe* and how you'll never..."

"Don't say it, Roberto. Do not say it." Roberto tended to become vulgar when he drank. He became especially vulgar when discussing men's interaction with women. Roberto made a big mistake in using the most vulgar term to describe

Pratolina and found himself lifted from the floor and peering into the angriest black eyes he'd ever seen.

Fortunately, Roberto was not so drunk that he could forget that moment, and those eyes. 'I guess blaspheming God and the Pope is one thing, but not Pratolina. No. One does not blaspheme sweet Pratolina in the presence of this young man.' Despite his naivete, Dominico was strong and solid and quite the force to be reckoned with once riled. Both Roberto and Dominico discovered that. It was more a surprise to Dom than to Roberto. "*Non ti preoccupare*. I won't say it, but you listen. I'll tell you your future.

"You see, Dominico, I was just like you a few years ago. Young, strong. I was going to *Lamerica* just like you. Just like you I needed to get some money together so I could get my ticket. Oh, Signore Petrocchuli was just as pleasant as he could be. Yes, he was. He got my paperwork together and got me a job here with *Signore* Falzotte."

Dominico reached into his pocket and found the paperwork that *Signore* Petrocchuli had given him just the day before. A panic started to overcome Dominico as he thumbed through the papers that rested safely in his pocket. Suddenly he was no longer interested in finishing his dinner. He was no longer interested in going to sleep. Dominico decided that it might just be in his best interest to listen to his friend's story.

"Yeah, I came to work here and everything I needed *Signore* Falzotte would get for me. I needed a little more meat, he got it for me. I needed a shot of grappa, he made sure my throat was never dry. Yes, old rat bastard Falzotte took care of me. He really took care of me!" Roberto threw the grappa bottle across the room where it crashed against a broken pillar and shattered. It was empty, of course.

"What happened?" Dominico encouraged.

"What happened? What? All of a sudden, you're interested in the story?"

"Just tell me what happened. I do want to know."

"Well, I'll tell you what happened." Roberto rocked and Dominico feared that he would lose consciousness before he had a chance to finish the story. Roberto steadied himself, belched a fowl smelling air and continued.

"I go to him for my pay. Met him right outside the emigration office. My ticket was sitting there waiting for me in *Signore* Petrocchuli's sweaty hands. I could see it, but he wouldn't let me touch it. I never even got to touch it. *Signore* Falzotte, he goes through my account. He tells me I earned twelve lire from him. Just enough to pay my passage with a little left over--just enough. Then he started going over my bill. One lira...two...three...Oh, look, another bottle of grappa, four...look, some sausage...five...six. Before he was done, I owed him over twenty lire. Twenty lire! How was I supposed to pay him back?"

Dominico stared at him.

"I'm still here aren't I, Dominico? I'm still here. Still trying to pay that bastard off. And the more I work the further behind

I get. I even tried to starve myself. It didn't work. So, I'm still here.

"Now in ten days you'll be in the same position. He is not going to let you leave. A big, strong boy like you. No. You'll be sitting here with me on day eleven watching your ship sail away, watching your dreams sail away."

Dominico thought about this conversation as he eyed with suspicion the casks of olive oil and proceeded toward the pier.

"Oh, Dominico!" the merchant called out. "Dominico, here, you did a fine job. A fine job." The merchant held out some money for Dominico and pointed to a freshly plastered wall. Dominico had suggested having the plaster redone and offered his services to the merchant for a small fee. After eating dinner, he returned to the warehouse and plastered the wall. It was not long before he had a number of small jobs lined up all around the city along his route. 'I am going to *Lamerica*,' he thought to himself. 'I will not be conned. I will not end up like Roberto.'

"*Grazie*," Dominico tucked the money into his pocket and shook the merchant's hand. In the back of his mind, however, he wondered just what his cargo really was.

> Dearest Pratalina:
>
> This is my last day in Italy. Tomorrow, I get my pay from Signore Falzotte then get my ticket from Signore Petrocchuli. Roberto tells me that they are going to try to keep me here. That they will pull some trick so I cannot get on the ship. I make this promise to you as I live and breathe. I will be on that ship. Tomorrow I will be going to Lamerica and there isn't anything in the world that can stop me. As much as I miss you now, I will miss you that much more when the ship takes me over the water away from you. Then I will truly be separated from you. Then there is no turning back. All I can do is hold you in my heart. That is what I will be doing until I see you again. Do not give up hope. I will be back for you soon.
>
> Love always, Dominico

"Be like stone, Dominico.' He thought as he approached the emigration office. 'This is when the truth will be known. Will my patrons try to take advantage of me or was Roberto only speaking nonsense in a drunken stupor.'

Dominico walked with long strides. His ever-broadening shoulders were pulled back, and his powerful, bronze arms swung at his sides in great arcs. The night before he had not slept. Instead, he spent the night counting the money that he had stashed away. It represented the work of about a dozen odd jobs that he did along his route, patching walls, filling plaster, even sweeping floors, and organizing shelves. Anything he could do to put more money into his pocket he did. Most importantly, he kept his scheme secret. Even from Roberto. Though he liked Roberto he knew he was unstable, especially when he needed another bottle. He could not trust this kind of sensitive secret to such a man as Roberto.

Now, the money rested in his pocket as he wove through the crowd of the emigration office. He walked right up to Signore Petrocchuli's desk and tapped on the greasy man's rounded shoulder. Signore Petrocchuli looked up from his papers and upon noticing Dominico smiled widely. For the first time Dominico noticed some molars missing from Signore Petrocchuli's mouth. The man seemed older now for some reason.

"Ah, yes...Signore Rossa. It is that time at last. Are you ready to go to *Gli Stati Uniti*?"

Dominico smiled and shook the man's clammy hand. "*Si*! I've been ready for a long time. Where is *Signore* Falzotte?"

The greasy man snapped his fingers, and another large man approached. After whispering directions, the man nodded and ran off. "Signore Falzotte will be here momentarily. Here is what I have for you. This is a ticket for the German liner *Halzbad*. She is a fine, fine ship. Of course, you will be travelling steerage, which is lacking in certain...amenities, but that shouldn't bother a strapping young fellow like you. This is a card for a Don Gabriel. He'll have work for you when you disembark. He'll take good care of you."

Dominico nodded, but the smile ran from his face. He was not expecting to hear the title 'Don' used in *Lamerica*. There was no time to ponder this, however, so he placed this curious disappointment in the back of his mind.

Soon the large man returned, whispered in *Signore* Petrocchuli's ear, and jerked his thumb toward the back of the building.

"*Buono...buono*. Signore Rossa, Signore Falzotte is in the back and he's looking forward to settling your account. Let's go."

Dominico's heart jumped into his throat. 'Be like stone. You must be on that ship today.' The young man followed *Signore* Petrocchuli to a lopsided door in the back of the emigration office. Upon walking through the door Dominico found himself in a small square surrounded by ancient brick buildings. The only unbarred door was the one leading back into the emigration office. The rest of the doors were walled in or boarded up. Crates were piled around the small plaza covered in oilcloth tarps. Overhead, sheets and clothes hung from clotheslines. The lack of ventilation, however, lent the plaza a moldy, dead smell. A small square of blue sky overhead provided the only light.

'This is where it is all going to happen. They've brought me here to intimidate me, bring me onto their own ground with only one means of escape.' With that thought Dominico noticed two large men in black shirts, the one man, Gordo who first introduced him to *Signore* Falzotte and the man whom *Signore* Petrocchuli had spoken to most recently. They stood by the door with their great arms folded across their chests. *Signore* Falzotte sat on a crate marked '*Vino*' a plank laid across two crates served as a makeshift table. He was staring at a piece of paper and marking it with a pen.

"Oh, Dominico! You know, Signore Petrocchuli, I'm going to hate losing Dominico. He was my best worker."

"He's going to be an *Americano* now." *Signore* Petrocchuli smirked. "Soon he'll be making more money than either one of us."

Both men laughed, but Dominico noted their mocking tone. He was offended by their good humor. Dominico did not know the source of all this cynicism. Somehow, during the last two weeks with Roberto he inherited a certain amount of street wisdom. Roberto had vouchsafed a great deal of advice on his young friend, what tricks to look for, how to walk, how to talk, how to act. It was Roberto who taught Dominico to first look for a means of escape. Would this imparted knowledge serve him well?

"Now all we have to do is settle up accounts." *Signore* Falzotte looked at the paper and pulled out a roll of battered money. He dipped the pen in a small jar of black ink and scrawled on the paper in front of him. "Let's see, you've worked for fourteen days…"

"Fifteen days." Dominico corrected.

"No…no…" Signore Falzotte responded, "we don't count today. You didn't work today."

"It's fifteen days. August twenty first through September fourth which was yesterday. That's fifteen days."

Signore Falzotte scratched his head. He was not used to dealing with people who could add. Usually, such people were prepared for the trip and had no need to do business with the likes of him. "Indeed. My mistake. I must be getting old. So that's fifteen days, three lire a day is forty-five lire." He scratched out some figures on the paper.

'More than enough for the ticket,' Dominico thought with relief.

"Now I'm looking at your credit account, Dominico." The old man scratched his head even further. "It looks like you were pretty frugal this last couple of weeks."

Frugal indeed, Dominico had gotten by on the barest minimum. That minimum was eating one meal during the day, drinking goat milk rather than wine. Not once did he fall prey to the desire for alcohol, or fine 'American' clothes that were being pushed in front of him. "You don't want to go to *Lamerica* looking like a greenhorn, do you? *Americani* are very particular about their clothes. You must look like *UN Americani*. You must smell like *UN Americani*." But Dominico could not afford to be *UN Americano* at this stage of the game. He simply wanted to go to *Lamerica*, find some honest work, then return. The state of his clothes should not matter.

His only 'extra' expense was for postage. He had sent at least one letter a day to Pratolina. So far, he had sent none to his family. He would send them word once he got to *Lamerica* and had some good news to report. Pratolina, however, he 'needed' to write to Pratolina. If that meant skipping meals, that was fine with him.

"So, when I take away for the credit used that leaves you with thirty-two *lire*."

Dominico let out a sigh of relief. So far all was going well.

"Unfortunately, Dominico, there was some damage to the wagon that you used on your route." Signore Falzotte frowned. "I like you Dominico, but I can't afford to just let a good wagon go without repair. It will cost twenty *lire* to get it fixed."

Dominico's eyes widened. He had been lulled into a false sense of security and now the load was dropped right on his head. "What...what was damaged? There was no damage to the cart when I turned it in yesterday. I've done nothing to damage the cart!" His voice became embarrassingly high pitched. He would have to control his tenor.

"*Mi scuzi*." Signore Falzotte put on the air of sincerity. "The rear left wheel. It's all twisted, and the bearings are crushed. You must have hit something."

Resolve was growing within that young heart. The surprise had worn off. He was over the initial sting. "I hit nothing." His former falsetto deepened into a growling tenor.

Signore Falzotte simply shook his head. The two large men by the door shifted their body weight. Dominico knew that this would be ugly before all was said and done. "So, it looks like I owe you twelve lire."

Signore Petrocchuli sighed with feigned sadness. "I can't sell you a ticket for twelve *lire,* I'm afraid."

Signore Falzotte snapped his fingers and smiled, putting his hairy hand gently upon Dominico's broad shoulder. "I can let you work for a few more days and you can make some more money. Signore Petrocchuli, when does the next ship leave?"

"I can get him on in about ten days." *Signore* Petrocchuli blinked and tilted his head mocking utmost concern for young Dominico's wellbeing. "It's not so bad. Only another ten days."

"No." Dominico said as he reached into his pocket. The two large men in the black shirts unfolded their arms and glared at him, preparing to spring on him like lions. "I can pay."

With his thumb Dominico flicked the money in his pocket. He did not want the men to know just how much money he had so he counted out twenty-eight lire in bills and coins by feel and removed them from his pocket. After making sure he counted correctly he handed them to the sweaty old man in front of him.

"Where did you get that?" *Signore* Falzotte asked.

"Odd jobs. Here and there."

Then Dominico turned to *Signore* Petrocchuli, "So now I can have my ticket."

The greasy man stuttered and stared at the small pieces of paper and coins in his shaking hand.

"Uh...no...wait..." *Signore* Falzotte interrupted. "Wait... wait...wait. You...well you can't just work without a license. There's a tax, I'm afraid. Now we have to add the tax into your account. But don't worry, I'll take care of everything."

Signore Petrocchuli shook his head and slapped his skinny thighs, "The tax. You have to pay the tax."

Dominico stared at *Signore* Petrocchuli. He could hear the large men shuffling behind him, but it was of no significance to him any longer. He would be on that ship today. His hands clenched into fists and his coal black eyes narrowed and pierced into *Signore* Petrocchuli's. The greasy man did his best to look away from Dominico, but he was caught by the young man's eyes as dark as night and absorbing him, drawing the strength out of him.

"I'm going to be on that ship, *Signore* Petrocchuli." Dominico's voice was calm yet frigid. The greasy man's blood stopped. It was many years since this veteran *truffatore,* con man, experienced the sensation of his blood stopping, but here was this boy, so calm, so calm and sure in the face of intimidation. There was something not right about this boy.

"Now let's just calm down," *Signore* Falzotte tried to console Dominico. "We can work something out. You can get the next ship. There's no reason for this to become difficult here."

The large men picked up two axe handles and struck their palms creating a resounding slapping noise that split the heavy, moldy atmosphere. Yet Dominico's eyes remained trained on *Signore* Petrocchuli. They did not deviate. They did not even quiver.

"We're all gentlemen here!" *Signore* Falzotte forced a rasping laugh from his fat, hairy throat. We can settle this like gentlemen."

"You're not going to take food from my family's table, *Signore* Petrocchuli."

Sweat beaded along the greasy man's brow. A twig of oily hair fell out of place along his wet forehead. Signore Petrocchuli shook. He could feel the young man's hands grasping his throat. Oh, his men would do a job on this lone boy. That was a given. But this boy. *Signore* Petrocchuli had a feeling that this boy would not let go of his throat no matter how many times he was hit with an axe handle. He would keep squeezing and squeezing. The harder he was hit the more the boy would squeeze, squeeze until that throat was crushed beneath his thick, brown fingers.

Then Signore Petrocchuli considered the fact, in his mind unquestionable, that this boy would not let go of his throat until one of them was dead. His men would certainly be the deciding factor in that, striking the boy in the back of the skull as a last resort to save their boss, their one source of considerable income. The boy would be dead and there would be inquisitions. His body would have to be disposed. Constables would have to be paid off. This situation could escalate into something far more costly than the fare for passage, for which he was overcharging to begin with.

Signore Petrocchuli smiled his wide, greasy lipped smile and raised his hands. Dominico's eyes remained locked on his. "Dominico...*Signore* Rossa. *Signore* Falzotte and I can settle this. We'll take care of the tax. It's not much of a tax anyway." He offered a nervous laugh as he glanced at Falzotte who shrugged and frowned as if to say, 'it's your call.' "We like you, Dominico. Good luck in *Lamerica*." *Signore* Petrocchuli extended his left hand with the ticket and the card for Don Gabriel.

Dominico hesitated a moment then slowly, warily removed the ticket from Signore Petrocchuli's hand. The ticket and the card were stained from his sweaty hands. He stared at the man for a few more seconds, seconds that seemed interminable to *Signore* Petrocchuli.

For the first time in this situation Dominico was scared. His future was in his palm. He now had something to lose. Only seconds ago, he was without option, without anything but heart. Now there was the ticket, and that small piece of paper could be taken snatched away from him before he had time to revel in it. Dominico knew the odds should *Signore* Petrocchuli suddenly change his mind and snap his fingers. The two large men would descend on him and pummel him beyond resistance. Dominico would then lose everything, the ticket, his money, everything.

Dominico turned and faced the two large men. They were still holding the axe handles. A signal from *Signore* Petrocchuli, however, and they placed the handles against the gray wall and folded their arms again, staring down at Dominico with wry smiles. One of the large men even vouched an admiring half smile. Dominico knew, however, that this admiration would not elicit the slightest hesitation should the order be given to bash his brains in.

With a nod, toward *Signore* Petrocchuli and *Signore* Falzotte Dominico stepped past the large men and disappeared into the crowded emigration office. He had learned much from his time in *Napoli*. He learned about anger. He learned that focused anger was a weapon against treachery. He learned that he possessed anger, that anger resonated in his eyes. He learned that people, treacherous people responded to that anger. Now he would carry this anger to *Lamerica.*

CHAPTER 8

The muscles in his neck cramped as he turned his head to face her. His face was twisted in rage and confusion. Cecilia had seen a great deal of grief in the eyes of many men, but the dire loss and rage in this man burned in his dark, wet, bloodshot eyes. Her first thought was to run, get away from him. It was not uncommon for a soldier to go mad, violently mad, when faced with such sorrow. Violence and sorrow were hopelessly intertwined, the one variable eliciting response from the other. But Cecilia was a courageous woman who had been through a great deal in her own right. Though she jerked with a start and gasped she did not run. She did not lose the composure that had seen her through many hardships.

"What do you mean by that...accusation!" the man yelled, spittle spraying from his mouth, his voice hoarse with grief. Anger, directed by years of experience, exploded from his eyes.

"Dominico..." she said, reaching her gentle hand to his shaking, rigid arm.

The anger abated with her touch. The war required much from his anger, tapped it, focused it, then sapped it of its perspicacity. He lowered his head in hurt and shame, licking the dirt and spit from his lips.

"Yes, Dominico, I know who you are. I knew the moment I saw you here at this grave. That's why I came here."

"I wrote to her. I wrote to her many times." He cried, barely able to speak.

"She never received your letters. Any letters that you wrote would never reach her..." Cecilia stroked his arm. The shaking subsided.

"But why? Why wouldn't she receive my letters?" Dominico looked into her eyes. This was the only connection he had with his beloved, this mysterious, kind-hearted woman who proved capable of soothing his shattered heart.

Cecilia shook her head, her eyes filled with sorrow. From under her apron she produced a small book, leather bound and tattered. The pages were yellowed, dry and uneven. "Perhaps she should answer that herself." She handed him the book. He reached for it with his good hand and caressed the top cover with his great, callused thumb. The book was small, delicate, much too small and delicate to rest in his broad, harsh hand. He thought for a moment that his rough skin might somehow damage the soft leather, scratch it.

Dominico stared at the book for almost a minute before looking up again.

"Hers?" He asked.

"Yes."

The ship loomed large and black above the purple water. The morning mist lifted, wisps of cloud dispersing like silent ghosts over the masts. On the pier, throngs of people flocked and fluttered hither and yon, a confusion of arms and legs and voices shouting and laughing and crying and wailing above the constant din of the gulls overhead. Merchants sold their wares along the pier. Most notably were the salesmen dressed in well-tailored suits and top hats selling *Americani* clothes and shoes and various other disguises that might camouflage the gullible *immigrante* from the ruthless opportunists who awaited them on the opposite shore.

Other merchants were less well dressed, less conspicuous. Their eyes shifted endlessly across the wharf searching out potential problems as well as potential customers. These were the men who sold tickets picked from the pockets of unsuspecting voyagers before they were able to board. Dominico clutched his ticket in hand, mindful of its feel between his fingers. Among other things one could purchase at the wharf were false identity papers, work papers, certificates of inoculation. Dominico rubbed his arm where he remembered the soreness of the needle.

All around was noise and movement, though now Dominico noticed the islands of still people among the sea of those moving along the wharf. These were the families. Those who were preparing to board *en toto* were silent, eerie, fatigued from the journey before it even began. Heartbreaking, however, were the families that were splitting up and saying goodbye. They cried and clutched at each other until the very last moment, loosening their embraces through desperate will, reaching, crying, lamenting for those who were leaving the comfortable folds of the family.

Dominico was not interested in these things. He looked only for one person. Soon he found him right where he was supposed to be. Roberto waited with Dominico's bundle tucked under his arm. He noticed a family with a couple of young girls, and he stood back and admired their thin waists, fragile looking arms, and flowing black hair.

"Roberto!" Dominico shouted.

Roberto reacted as if ready to flee. 'Perhaps shouting was a mistake.' Dominico thought.

Roberto ran to his friend, staring at him with expectant eyes. He shrugged, palms up with one question.

Dominico smiled and laughed. "Yes, *m' amico*. I have my ticket." He held the small, yellow strip up, pinched tightly in his right hand.

Roberto smiled and inhaled deeply as he looked over the ticket. "I never would have believed it. How did you do it? There's no way those two bastards would let you go."

Dominico shrugged, "We just settled accounts. There was a little trouble, but not much."

"Are you alright?" Roberto checked his friend's face, lifted his arms, his legs looked strong. "Was there a fight?"

"No, no. No fighting." Dominico laughed. "I'm all right. I'm going to *Lamerica*."

Roberto laughed and jumped, dropping the bundle to the ground as he raised his arms. "YOU'RE GOING TO *LAMERICA*!" He shouted.

"I'M GOING TO *LAMERICA*!" Dominico shouted in return and hugged Roberto, both men jumping like children at play.

"I don't know how you did it, my friend, but you did it." Roberto's face was that of a victor. A victory, even vicariously, was enough to instill a glow to his sullen, pallid features.

Dominico punched him in the arm. "I did odd jobs, Roberto. Those nights when I was late..."

Roberto nodded and offered a wry smile, "I thought you'd found a little *puttana*. I was mad you were keeping her to yourself."

Dominico blushed and shook his head. "I was working, doing everything I could. Roberto, stay away from the *grappa*...and the *puttane*...and do what I did, and you'll get your ticket."

Roberto shook his head. "No, Dominico, it's a little late for me. I'm too far in the hole. But I'm going to leave here. I'm going to go to *Roma* and see if I can't jump on a train to *Genoa*. I think I can catch a boat from there."

Dominico smiled and then frowned, then forced a smile once again, "I hope to see you again, Roberto. You were right about Petrocchuli and Falzotte. If you hadn't told me about them, I'd have fallen for it." It was not fitting of Roberto's character to be modest, but a sincere thank you was rare in his life. He did not know how to respond. "You come and find me when you get to *Lamerica*," Dom continued, "You come and find me."

Nodding Roberto hugged Dominico one last time. "*Buon viaggio, m' amico. Buona fortuna.*"

Dominico returned the embrace, kissing his friend on the cheek. "I won't need 'luck,' Roberto. I'm going to *Lamerica*."

Roberto's laughter was sad, his eyes focused on the ground at his feet. There was nothing more to say so he pushed Dominico away, "Go...you go now and get on your ship. Make a lot of money and then help a poor friend with a taste for the spirits when you return."

The gangway to the ship was long and bent with the weight of the people who climbed it. It seemed an eternity that Dominico waited on the plank, leaning against the glistening, black hull of the ship. His bundle was tucked tight under his arm. All around him were the haggard and dirty remains of the passengers. The weight of their unspoken fear and wonder held the émigrés in silence. The weight of leaving the only land they had ever known for a promise--just a promise. Such a foolhardy thing to do. Yet it seemed that so many were taking this leap, taking the chance of something better.

To Dominico it looked like the entire country was emptying out, ship by crowded ship. It could not be long before there was not a single person in this new nation called *Italia*. *Italia*--the concept of nationhood had not yet sunk in to the people of their respective regions. Only thirty years old, the fledgling country seemed destined to fall from lack of interest.

'But I'll be back,' Dominico thought. 'I'll be back, and I'll be a man of respect. Maybe even a man of importance in this new *Italia*.' Perhaps there was some hope left. Vittorio Emmanuelo was the new king. Perhaps he could save the tattered remains of what was once a mighty empire and sew them back together. Perhaps there was greatness waiting for *Italia* sometime in the future. It was a shame that Dominico could not wait for that to happen. He had to find his own greatness.

Upon reaching the top of the gangway Dominico was stopped by a well-dressed, well shaven German sailor. He checked Dominico's ticket then muttered some guttural nonsense that Dominico did not understand. However, he was pointing in a direction to the rear of the ship and Dominico understood his intent. There, the third-class passengers gathered and waited until given further directions. More passengers boarded, and the deck became insufferably crowded.

On the decks above, Dominico noticed the well dressed, the clean men and women in suits and white dresses and parasols staring over the rails, waving and smiling at others who waved back at them from the wharf. The men chomped on big, black cigars and stared officiously at the unkempt crowd of the lower deck.

'The next time I'm on one of these ships,' Dominico thought, 'I'm going to be up there.'

Shortly a gallant looking man in a blue uniform stood upon something that elevated him above the crowd, his hands behind his back. Another man, younger, but just as gallant looking and in the same uniform stood next to him. The older man began to speak, but none could understand him. Fortunately, the younger man spoke after him in high Italian. There were some nuances of the colloquial language that the young sailor did not seem to grasp, but the crowd understood well enough.

"Welcome aboard the *Halzbad*. I am Lieutenant Khent. I will oversee third-class steerage passengers. That would be you. In a few minutes, the *Halzbad* will be disembarking for New York City, the United States. When you hear the whistle blow you will be allowed to go to the gunwale and wave to your family. When you hear me ring this bell," The older man in the blue uniform pulled a weighted cord and a bell tolled above their heads, "Then you will make your way to the steerage section located through those two passageways aft starboard and aft port." Both men pointed to the back of the ship, but Dominico could not see the passageways they referred to through the mass of people.

"Anyone remaining on deck by the time the bell is wrung the second time, an interval of fifteen minutes, will be arrested and placed in confinement for the rest of the journey. It is my hope that this unfortunate circumstance will not be necessary." The younger man was a surreal echo of the older.

"You will notice your designated bunk on your ticket indicated at the top of the stub. That is your designated bunk for the rest of the trip. You are expected to keep your area clean.

"You will be served two meals per day. Breakfast will be precisely at seven a.m. Dinner will be at precisely five p.m. At precisely ten a.m. you will hear this bell." Once again, the older man pulled the heavy bell. "When you hear this bell, those of you with green tickets will be allowed on deck. At precisely twelve p.m. you will hear this bell again." The bell tolled yet again. "At this sound, those of you with green tickets are expected to leave the deck. Anyone left on deck when the third bell rings will be arrested and placed in confinement for the rest of the journey. At precisely two p.m. you will hear the bell again." Again, the older man pulled the cord invoking the bell. "Upon hearing this bell those of you with yellow tickets will be allowed on deck. At precisely four p.m. you will hear the final bell." Dominico waited for the peal of the bell yet again and was not disappointed. "Upon hearing this bell those of you with yellow tickets are expected to leave the deck. Anyone left on the deck when the third bell rings will be arrested and placed in confinement for the rest of the journey."

'These people think we're fools.' Dominico thought, 'speaking to us as if we were children.'

"You will find that conditions aboard the *Halzbad* are quite pleasant as compared to other ships. Only aboard the *Halzbad* will you receive two hours of deck time. You will find the cooking exceptional in comparison to other ships of the same line. You will find the mattresses and the sheets are clean, in comparison to other ships. Oh...and beside every bunk there is a bucket. This bucket is for the convenience of those who become...ill...during the trip. Please dispose of any refuse over the side during your deck time.

"Aboard the Halzbad we are concerned with everyone's comfort. However, we must accommodate many passengers. Please cooperate with us to make this voyage as pleasant as it can possibly be. Have a good trip."

As if on cue, the whistle blew with Lieutenant Khent's last words. "You may go to the gunwale." He nodded. The mass of haggard, dirty people, men in moth eaten hats and overcoats, women in stained and threadbare dresses, dirty children with unkempt hair and torn clothes, many shoeless, ran to the sides to say their final goodbyes to those waiting for one last look at their loved ones.

Dominico had no one, so he sat and observed those on the upper decks, the clean people. They waved and laughed and cooed as the ship's engines started to grind and trouble the water. The dainty, gloved hands of the women flapped as if boneless, their mouths open in joy. The men pointed and tipped their hats and smiled beneath their thick mustaches. Those of the lower deck laughed and waved their dirty, dark hands, broken fingernails, and frayed sleeves. Yet their laughter was more bittersweet. Their hearts were heavy with the hope and uncertainty of the future. The upper deck was not burdened by such weight. They were not motivated by hope, but by the pursuit of pleasure.

The harsh, grinding sound at the rear of the ship appealed to Dominico's curiosity. What could make this great ship move? Pushing through the crowd he made his way to the back of the ship and looked down. Some great forces were churning the roiling water as if a great sea monster were rushing, roaring to the surface. But Dominico knew that it was the turning of a great rotor mechanism so powerful that it could move this giant mass of iron across an ocean, to another world, to another dream.

Once again, he stared at the people on the upper deck, then down at the dirty, third-class passengers. The same mechanism moved both parties without prejudice. He admired the well-dressed as he looked at himself. His own clothes were worn and tattered. He recognized every stain, every stitch, every patch a little piece of his life. His hands, though supple with youth, were the hands of a worker, strong and thick with stained nails. Chunks of plaster still clung to his straight, oily hair. The patchy sprouts of a young beard were poking erratically across his face. His shoes were thin in the soles and tight as he had grown since he received them from his father some months ago. Dominico was third class all right.

The great rotor pulled the ship backwards, churning and frothing the green waters. The ship's motion was smooth, barely noticeable at first until Dominico perceived the buildings to be moving toward the front of the ship. Then he became oriented to the motion of the great vessel. The clean people of the upper deck cooed and laughed. The dirty people of the lower deck waved, tears and hope in their eyes. Then there was Dominico...dirty Dominico...third class, steerage.

He would not be third-class for long. Dominico knew nothing of the people on the upper decks, but he knew one thing. The next time he was on a ship like this, he would be with them.

CHAPTER 9

urgatorio. There was no other word for his voyage along *la Via Dolorosa*. Indeed, many of the women spent considerable time deftly working their way through the rosary, their fingers cold and thin. They mumbled their prayers of repentance for the sin of leaving their homes. They mumbled their prayers in hope for deliverance from their punishment, their purgatory. They prayed for the hope of New York, the hope that America would be their heaven. Though these prayers were muttered in low, sad voices, their constancy combined with the hum and pounding of the engines, the scraping sound of the rudder just behind, became a hellish symphony in the stagnant air of steerage.

The constant praying replaced the ubiquitous crying and pathetic urgings to make the men turn the ship around. "I want to go home. I don't want to leave my home…" Weeping from the degrading conditions under which they were forced to live. "Animals, we live like animals," one man cried over and over throughout the second day of the trip. This was no exaggeration, as the emigrants would find that they were of the same status as the livestock with whom they shared the compartment. As time went on things would only get worse.

Over six hundred people, men, women, children were crammed into the impersonal quarters. Each person was assigned a crate on which he could store his belongings and over which he slept. Those who were wise enough to bring mattresses enjoyed one less discomfort. Those without spent the voyage sleeping on the hard wood surface.

Separate sections were not cordoned off for men and women. Facilities offered little privacy. Some families stretched linens across the compartment to afford them some little modesty. Men and women cared for their most personal selves separated by little more than a sheet. Modesty could not be an issue in steerage as men and women became accustomed to the most intimate exposure to each other.

Domestic animals ran amok through the compartment, chickens, ducks, goats, and pigs. They spoiled and scavenged for the packages of meat and dried foods that were brought along by the better prepared. The evenings were often punctuated by a half-dressed man chasing a pig or goat from his pallet, the animal with a sausage or salami in its mouth, the desperate man trying to rest it from him. People rolled from their pallets as the two combatants rushed through the crowded compartment, knocking over belongings, jumping over the confused and rattled families in their makeshift beds. The profanity and shouting overwhelmed the constant pounding and scraping and churning of the ship. Then the crying, then the rosaries came out and the great cacophony clattered and hummed and wailed throughout the tiny chamber.

But it was the odor. The foulness of the odor was the worst part of *Purgatorio*. The air was putrid. A malodorous haze settled with the scent of animal feces and urine. Rats, killed by the pigs decayed under the pallets. People were soon afflicted with dysentery bearing the humiliation of incontinence. The cleaning facilities were such that many went without washing for days. The smell of living animals and dying humans co-mingled to create something indescribably rotten. The smell of vomit clung to the fabric of one's clothing, to one's hair. This was the most intolerable.

The vomiting. Now there was a sensation. Relentless vomiting of those who had never experienced the rise and fall of the sea's swales. At first Dominico thought that he would be all right. His first day at sea was one of relative calm. Though he had heard the strained and desperate sound of retching all around him from the beginning of the voyage he did not think that he would be so afflicted. Come the second day, the sea became more dynamic. The ship, once so huge, was but a thimble in the mighty, swirling sea. The horizon moved! The horizon, the one constant thing on which those born of the land could rely was moving. The horizon was not supposed to change. It not supposed to lift or fall or cock to the side swaying one way then the other, then up, then down always so damned slow and smooth. The movement of the ship was gentle, musical—sickening. That next morning Dominico filled his bucket.

Unfortunately, Dominico did not foresee a use for the bucket, so another had already used it. Dominico gave it to a poor, pale man who had turned green. Dominico feared for him. Could one become green and not die? He would soon find out.

He stumbled, blind in the morning darkness, for there were no windows in the compartment and the gas lamps were not yet lit. In desperation he searched for the bucket, finding it in time to only accommodate half of his illness. The rest spilled to the floor with a sickening splash. All around him he heard the guttural sounds of vomiting and now he was contributing. A more fervent contributor could not be found. It was not long before the bucket was full, but Dominico was not yet emptied and there was nowhere left to regurgitate but the floor.

"My, young man, here," a woman's gracious, matronly voice sang to the sick boy as he began to dry heave. "You must eat this." She handed him a chunk of bread smeared in olive oil.

Just looking at the bread made Dominico's stomach turn. He shook his head and pushed the offering away.

"You will eat, or I'll have my son's hold you and I'll cram it down your throat." she said in a surprisingly pleasant tone. This tone only made her words that much more menacing. She was a slight woman with hair that would have been pearl white if not for the streaks of dirt and soot that settled into it. Her skin was pale and smooth, with the gentle wrinkles of an experienced and difficult life. It was her eyes, however, that revealed the depth of her spirit. Her eyes peered into the hardness of reality, stared it down, but never lost their compassion. Dominico took the bread and chewed it carefully before swallowing.

"There you go. That will make you feel better..."

Dominico vomited on her shoes.

"It's all right dear, breakfast is coming soon," she smiled as Dominico wiped mucous from his mouth and moaned when she mentioned breakfast.

She made him eat. Breakfast was a paste, made from oats, and an aged apple with water. The woman, *Signora* Guglielmo, stood by and ensured that he left not a spot in his bowl. Though Dominico sat, she stood beside him and was no taller than he. Yet, somehow, she seemed taller. It seemed that the compartment could not contain her, that life itself could not contain her. When he finished, she gave him her serving and smiled as he choked it down, forcing the nausea under control with every swallow. Every swallow provoked an opposite reaction that he was determined to beat.

"That's a good boy, Dominico, you hold it down. Here, you drink this." She handed him some water that she had heated over a gas lamp. In the tin cup was a small cheesecloth with brown stuff in it.

"What is it?" Dominico sniffed the cup. The smell was little better than the fetid surroundings.

"You don't worry. It'll make the sickness go away. Drink it down."

Dominico drank and as soon as the hot fluid touched his throat, he knew that there was no salvation on this earth. His throat expanded and his abdomen tightened as if a mule had kicked him. He spewed forth the most voluminous quantity of vomit that any two men could produce on their worst drunken morning. Then he vomited again, and again until what was left of his stomach was nothing more than a great knot and his abdomen was so tight that he could not straighten himself. And all the time *Signora* Guglielmo stroked his heaving back and said, "your mother would be so proud."

"There you go," *Signora* Guglielmo said during a break in the spasms, "Now quick, you eat this." She handed him half a loaf of bread.

"You've got to be crazy, *pazzo*!" He could barely speak, but he was not about to put another thing in his mouth.

"Don't be disrespectful. I may be crazy, but it is rude to point it out. You eat, you'll get better, I promise you'll get better."

"I'm dying," He felt the urge welling up inside again, but restrained it.

"Eat!"

Taking small bites Dominico chewed on the bread. After the first three swallows he noticed that it sat on his stomach without discomfort. The knots and the pain from the trauma of seasickness were still threatening nearby, but the bread stayed on his stomach. He took the next bites with more confidence.

A diminished Dominico climbed the steps onto the deck as suggested by the slight old woman. Three days had passed since his illness and still his stomach felt weak. *Signora* Guglielmo was there every morning and every evening to ensure that he ate everything on his plate. Dominico knew that he was back from the dead because of this woman. He was willing to listen to her in matters of his health. She proved to be wise as well as amusing. Sometimes here lack of restraint embarrassed Dominico. From any other woman this behavior would have been appalling, but from her it did not seem so. Her words were the truth, and they carried with them the air of truth regardless of their propriety.

The two o'clock bell rang, and he took full advantage of the time away from the stinking hole to spend some time under the blue sky. Not that the aft deck was much better than life in steerage. That deck was where the animals were slaughtered for the feasts of the first-class passengers. Dominico often found his shoes slippery with blood by the time the bell rang for him to go below. Nor was his, or any of the emigrant's, presence respected on the deck as crewmen took any opportunity to "accidentally" knock them down, spill offal on them, or otherwise demean them.

Even his quest for fresh air was often frustrated. The deck on which the emigrants were allowed to gather was right in line with the black tails of sooty smoke emitted from the smokestacks. Often, by the time his allotment on deck was over he was unable to breathe, and his eyes burned with every blink. His very tears were black from soot. This day, however, was clear and the smoke was carried southerly by a stiff breeze blowing abeam.

He took this opportunity of clarity to write Pratolina. It was best, he thought, not to trouble her with the details of this hell he was experiencing. This journey was for her he kept reminding himself. There was no hardship that he could face that was not worth her, Pratolina, with the beautiful brown eyes and the honey-colored skin. This pleasant train of thought was interrupted with a shriek and terrible crying.

He turned in time to see a young girl, maybe fifteen, running toward him crying, mouth agape with terror. She clutched the top of her dress, which was torn from the shoulder. Limping, she ran and would have fallen had Dominico not caught her in his arms, lowering her to the deck. Her brown face was streaked with tears and dirt. Her long dark hair knotted and sprawled across her face. From the side of her mouth a trickle of blood fell and stained Dominico's shirt. The girl struggled with him a moment, pounding his chest with her tiny, brown fists.

"Shhhhhh…" Dominico held her close and tried to comfort her. She buried her face in his chest, clutching his shirt in fear and rage, nails scratching into the skin of his shoulder.

Occasionally, she struck him with her hand, but she mostly cried and did not lift her head from his chest.

A crowd gathered around Dominico and the young girl. Dominico, searching for help, looked to the deck above. There was a large man, his close-cropped hair blond, and eyes a pale blue. He had a square chin and arrogant air as his eyes locked with Dominico's. It was his uniform that caught Dominico's attention. The crewmen were very meticulous about their uniforms. This crewman's uniform was disheveled, shirt untucked, pants twisted, belt unfastened. On his shirt a smear of blood made a slight red streak across his chest. Two red scratches glowed on his neck. He gazed down at Dominico and the girl, his great chin thrust out and snorted with contempt at the chattel below before turning his back and walking away.

"What is this! What have you done?" A boy approached and tore the girl from Dominico's grasp, pushing her away. The boy then stepped up to Dominico, his fists clenched. He was a little older than Dominico, but still retained some boyish qualities whereas Dominico was shed of most of the vestiges of boyhood. As such, the boy did not intimidate Dominico. He was, however, confused by the circumstance and unable to respond to the boy's questions.

"What have you done to my sister?" the menacing words struck Dominico's ears.

Then the crowd responded all shouting and pointing fingers their voices a meaningless contortion of speech. The girl cried into her brother's dirt-streaked shirt and clutched at him as she had clutched at Dominico earlier.

Signora Guglielmo then emerged from the crowd and the cacophony faded with her presence. She was not supposed to be on deck, but she had heard that 'her boy' was in trouble and hastened to Dominico's side. As soon as she laid eyes on the young girl, she knew the tragedy. "Oh, poor thing." She said in a soothing voice, stroking the girl's hair, "Come with me, dear. You come with me." She looked at the boy holding his sister. He relinquished her without protest.

"What happened?" He looked at Dominico, now more confused than angry.

"I don't know. She just came running and almost fell. I caught her. She was crying…I don't know." But he thought it best to follow *Signora* Guglielmo into the steerage compartment.

Below decks *Signora* Guglielmo made a small room with linens stretched for privacy. Most of the linens were not her own, but she received no protest from those who owned them. For more than two hours she sat with the young girl while her family and Dominico waited outside. *Signore* Guglielmo paced, waiting for his wife to appear. He was bald, only slightly taller than his wife, but thick of limb and body. He said nothing.

Finally, the curtain was disturbed and the diminutive matron stepped into view, looking at the crowd gathered about her.

"What happened?" asked the girl's father, a *Signore* Sanglicisto. He was an average man with sloped shoulders. His son, Cologerro, was taller, square shouldered. Cologerro's boyish looks were inherited from his father.

"What do you think happened? She's been ravished by a bully sailor." She said in her typical matter-of-fact manner, though the anger in her voice betrayed her sense of compassion and pity for the girl. Not one scrap of pity was reserved for the men. No. Too often the men were pitied for the loss of their daughter's maidenhood as if this purity somehow belonged to them.

The father clutched at his coat, twisting the fabric in his hands. His face contorted with rage he turned to his son, "How could this happen? You were supposed to keep an eye on her."

Cologerro shook his head. He did not know whether to be angry about his sister or afraid of his father's wrath, for the sloop shouldered, boyish looking man was tall and square and masculine.

"We got separated...I...I looked for her and couldn't find her...Papa I tried..."

Signora Guglielmo waved her hand at the father and son dismissively and turned her attention to Dominico. She tried to wipe the dried blood from his shirt. Her husband looked as though he had something to say about this, but in short order he thought the better of it. "You men." She said, "You'll act like wild dogs, but you've a little girl there who needs your help."

Signore Sanglicisto stuttered, "Can she…will she…will I…"

The old woman shook her head. She knew the thought behind his lack of coherence. "She was taken completely. She'll be able to have children. That's all I can tell you." She knew well that the young girl was ruined, that the likelihood of her marriage was now minimal.

"Did she tell you who did this?" He forced the words from his tight throat. His son sat on the nearest pallet and pulled at his hair.

Signora Guglielmo shook her head and continued to wipe at Dominico's, her boy's, shirt. "She said she scratched him on the neck or face."

Dominico hesitated as she looked into his eyes. "I…I know who did it." He stuttered.

Signora Guglielmo looked away, wiped Dominico's shirt the best she could and shook her head.

CHAPTER 10

The gray ocean roiled and rolled with less rhythm as the days passed. Waves grew, misshapen demons rising from an amorphous underworld intent on engulfing and devouring the rocking craft. To the northeast the sky loomed dark. Blue-black clouds billowed, lofty towers on the horizon. Yet overhead the sky was clear for the steerage passengers who spent their sunsets and sunrises in the windowless world below decks. If they had not been so confined they would have noticed how dark the mornings were and how bloody red the Western sky in the evening.

On deck that afternoon Dominico felt a return of the nausea that he thought he had left behind. The pitching of the ship grew merciless, but Dominico knew that he could keep himself and his bowels under control to accomplish his task. In fact, whether he was ready or not, the plan was in motion. There was no going back. Too many people were counting on him to do his part to defend the honor of his people--Italian people. Italian people. Dominico had always considered his neighbors living in *Villa de San Giuseppe* as his people. The broader notion of an Italian people was alien to him. Now, this notion of his people was expanding to include his neighbors in steerage, Calabresi, Abruzzesi, even Siciliani, had claims to being his people.

As he approached his target the muscles around his stomach contracted, accentuating the nauseous rumbling. His fingers, white at the tips, clasped about the handle of the bucket. They shook despite his attempts at bravery. It was not a little disturbing to Dominico that the functions of his hands were at the edge of control and apoplexy. Every footstep was heavy, laden with uncertainty. The swaying vessel only accentuated his sense of insecurity.

Ahead, one deck above, his target was securing equipment from the storm. His broad back was to Dominico and the young man, feeling the weight of his recent childhood, hoped that he never saw more than the giant man's back. Vomit sloshed and splashed in the bucket as he approached the sailor's back. Holding the bucket out to the side, careful not to spill the mess on his leg, he neared the unwary sailor.

A third-class passenger carrying a bucket of vomit to the rail was not an unusual site and provoked no alarm. That Dominico was walking to the upper deck, rather than the closest gunwale did not arouse suspicion. Just another ignorant émigré who did not know which way to go. No one paid attention to Dominico except for the men in the shadows of the steerage bulkhead. These men eyed him closely, eagerly expectant of the boy's mission.

Dominico felt their eyes on him, especially now that he was in reach of his target. There was that moment of hesitation. 'Should I do this?' then the realization, 'It's too late now.' Those eyes on his back pressed as if lifting the bucket with the power of their expectation. Dominico lifted the bucket, gripped its slimy bottom. A sickening, sticky moisture smeared on his fingers.

The sailor became rigid and erect, as if something tapped him on the shoulder, warned him of what was about to happen. He turned to identify the presence he could feel behind him. His square jaw, set like concrete, peered over his shoulder through pale eyes under a broad, rugged brow. He was just in time to see a dark figure propel an unctuous fluid that splattered across his legs and waist, dripping from the cuff of his pants to the deck in sickening plops.

Dom was supposed to run, but, in that split second of stunned stillness he could not get his legs to move. The great sailor stared at him, anger burning behind black and dilating pupils. The sailor was struck equally immobile as it took time for the unbelievable yet undeniable reality to strike his consciousness. Finally, his cliff-like brow furrowed, and his right eyelid twitched as the odor of the vomit wafted from his clothes and penetrated his awareness. That one twitch of the eye was the signal that fired the sailor's nerves. He launched himself over the rail, onto the lower deck, his teeth set squarely in his mighty jaws, his fists clenched as if he already grasped the insolent young émigré's throat between his fingers.

But this émigré was not there. Fleet of foot he was running hell bent for the bulkhead. All around the air was mixed with cries of the angry, tattered masses from steerage. *RAPIST! ANIMALE! UCCIDALO!* KILL HIM! Had the sailor known Italian he would have picked out some of the words and known his fate. Instead, motivated by blind rage he pursued the boy to the bulkhead and down the stairs into steerage.

Dominico was not a fast runner, but he managed to reach the bulkhead before his lion-like pursuer and jump down the steps into the steerage compartment. The aggrieved sailor pursued into the dark hold and sealed his fate.

Upon reaching the floor Dominico turned in time to see the sailor struck in the abdomen by a man wielding a pipe wrench. The blow seemed to split the sailor in half. His angry, blue eyes became wide with shock and horror as he doubled over and fell prostrate to the floor without wind or reason. At that point, the limbs of an enraged mob obscured Dominico's perspective. Dominico remembered seeing curs in his village surrounding a piece of meat and tearing at it in a great mass of teeth and barking. What he saw before him was much the same but the barking, teeth baring mass was human, and this made it that much more horrible.

Men massed around the sailor, balled up on the floor. They kicked him and struck him with sticks and pipes. They swore and spit, dogs rending a piece of meat. That's what the sailor was, a piece of meat to be torn and distributed as a matter of simple justice. The men, blind to rage and deaf to the desperate gasping pleas of the rapist, struck and pounded him, tearing their own clothes. Arms and legs flailed, punctuated by the dull thud of shins along the rib cage, sickening crack of bone. Occasionally a bloodied hand reached from the mass of anger only to be stomped and broken under the heel of a worn and ragged shoe. When the gasping and reaching and struggling stopped, the kicking and striking continued. The giant sailor was no longer large, just a small, inconceivable mass at the foot of men who just moments ago did not reach his broad shoulder in height.

Dominico witnessed the scene with a mixture of horror and excitement. He knew that the sailor deserved what he was receiving, but the sheer ferocity of this attack was unbearable to the heart of a decent man. He knew his part in this attack. He was culpable, perhaps in the eyes of God even guilty, of unpardonable sin. He had never experienced such a mixture of emotion, feelings of righteous retribution, of moral uncertainty, of sin. Oh, he had had violent thoughts. These were the topic of many confessions for which he performed the appointed penance. When Don Belan attacked his home, he feared such thoughts would burn into his soul to the point where atonement was impossible. But thoughts were all he could savor. Always the taste of justice eluded him. Now he tasted justice, violent justice. He felt it warm on his tongue, in his throat, and it tasted like blood.

One thing was certain. Dominico was no longer a Campanian in and of itself. His own identity, the son of *Mastro*

Rossa *Della Villa de San Guiseppe* was no longer enough to describe who he was. He knew himself now to be something broader, more inclusive. He watched the men kicking and pummeling the now swollen, broken body. All the men looked very much the same, dark, sweaty, dirty. Some men were large, bulky, covered in hair. Some of the younger were lean and muscular, not much different from Dominico himself. Most of the men were just men. Average, working men with calluses and scars from their labors. Indeed, their dark eyes were the same, slit thin and angry.

Listening to the men in the violent cluster there were some differences. They were differences in dialect, in tone. The difference was in their profanity, their epithets, and the diverse means of cursing and profaning the hated sailor. Many of the words were spoken in unfamiliar ways. The words and dialects were new to Dominico. Yet their anger was the same—the focus of their rage the same.

Dominico looked around the steerage compartments, the vomit covered floors, the smell of urine ignored in the angered senses of those who witnessed the scene. Dark eyes in white flames were gleaming mirrors of each other. Some blue eyes and fair hair were mixed in with the swarthy crowd. Tuscani, Abruzessi, Latini, eyes all looking in one direction. The young girl who had been savaged was from Caserta. But none of that mattered. Not anymore. Their identities were lost in the deep mist of anger, the desperate quest for justice even at the cost of their own souls. All were united in their search for something better, suffering for the hope that they could find a place where they were valued, they were human, they were respected. All were united in the hope of raising their children, eating decent food, doing meaningful work. Where they were from no longer mattered, only where they were going, only what they were looking for. This was the uniting factor in their lives.

No, Dominico could no longer, in his heart, see himself as a true Campanian. He had been living in the filth of many peoples, shared their dreams, embraced their anger, conspired in their revenge. He was one of them. As the angry mass of men stepped away from the bloody and battered piece of meat on the floor Dominico reached this life-altering conclusion. He was something more, something he never thought possible. He was an Italian. The unity that Garibaldi could not bring about on Italian soil was realized in the steerage hold of this German vessel in the middle of the Atlantic. Dominico Rossa was an Italian. He was not sure if his soul was ready to accept this.

CHAPTER 11

17 Settembre 1900: He's gone. It seems as quickly as he came into my life he has left it. I let him go. The fault is mine. That is what makes the pain of this separation intolerable. I let him go! I love him so and I want him so, but at what cost? Would I not rather be able to see him in the marketplace around la paesera knowing that I could never have him than to lose his presence altogether in the vain hope that one day it might be. It might be. Every day I wake to remind myself that it might be. Yet there's that something inside, that feeling I can't describe and cannot ignore that says that I will never see him again.

It's not that I fear that his love is not true. I know it burns in him as deeply as it does in me. I know that he will return. But will it be too late? Fate has a way of playing with people just as a cat plays with a mouse. Fate dangles what you want in front of you, gives you a moment of freedom to reach for it, then strikes you down with bared claw just before you achieve what you want. I so desperately want him. That's what makes me feel that I will never have him. It's the desperation of my desire that will set the Fates against me. But he will return, and I will wait for him.

But then there's Alfredo. He's such a silly child in the shell of a brutish man. My father despises him as much as he despises Il Padrone. Of course he will never utter such words, not even to me. But I can see it in his eyes.

> *His hatred is there in his eyes even as he speaks to me of the virtues of marrying the pig.*
>
> *Alfredo will never have me. I may lose all I have and all I know, but upon all the love I hold for Dominico I swear that Alfredo will never have me. Indeed, after I tell him, he'll never want me. Nor will anyone else. I'll be alone with the knowledge that Dominico loves me, and he will return to me.*
>
> *--Maria Angelina Mastradelfiori*
> *"Pratolina Rossa"*

Useless...Dominico, laying in his bunk stared at the rotting wood above him. The course, straw mattress caused his sweating back to itch, but Dominico was suffering worse misery at the hand of this roiling, rolling, pitching vessel that at one time was so impossibly huge. Now the waves battered it, juggled it like so many eggs in the hands of a capricious god. Dominico's only hope was to stare hard enough at the bottom of the bunk above him, to stare into the grain of the gray wood, ignoring the moans of the suffering man above. If he could just stare hard enough at the one part of the ship that seemed still, he might get caught in the delusion that all was still. Perhaps then he could trick his body into relieving him of the interminable nausea.

Such a strategy was of no use. As the storm drew nearer the woeful vessel lurched and rolled in such a fashion that even the hardiest travelers found it difficult to keep their paltry meals down. That incessant motion of waves flowed through his bowels, turned them, made them feel as if they were water themselves—as if the waves of the ocean had somehow gotten inside of him and was now turning his guts into bilious fluid. No use, Dominico closed his eyes.

Closing his eyes only heightened the sensation and brought the other horrors of the steerage compartment to life in his senses. There was no escape. Since the storm was upon the vessel the captain ordered that all third-class passengers stay below decks. For a day and a half there was no respite from the hold that was so much like a sewer. There was no chance for even the luxury of the polluted air behind the smokestacks above deck. Instead, one was confined in an area crowded with unkempt, unbathed bodies. The odors that permeated each man, woman and child could only be alluded to, not effectively described, as each passenger's body was caked with its own fetid oils and excrement. The tattered clothes were so covered with vomit and bodily fluids that there was no redemption for them but to be burned in a great pile when they finally reached their destination. Lice ran rampant from head to head and crawled in the beards and mustaches of the men. In such close quarters vermin reigned and could select from a variety of human hosts.

Yet there was no escape from such degradation as the very world that was the source of the misery. The floors were sticky with bile, vomit, urine, and feces. One dared not step barefoot on the floor. Rat feces mingled with that of the humans with whom they competed for food—usually successfully.

Insects crawled and multiplied under the weary passengers' mattresses and baggage. Even the food that they were given, scraps of tuna and scrod that the chefs above would not use for the real passengers, added to the dreadful odor of the compartment. The walls were smeared black with carbon from the gas lamps that provided them light, but also ensured that not one man, woman, nor child would go without a headache.

More consequential were the microscopic creatures that thrived in such filth. Creatures of which the passengers were ignorant preyed upon them. The steerage compartment became one giant incubator for a variety of bacterium and viruses. They pervaded the air and were sucked into the lungs of unsuspecting passengers, making homes in the spongy tissue. They reproduced in the food that was dispersed to all. They piggybacked in the fur of the rats and the spiny legs of the roaches. They populated the cough, the sneeze, the sweat of all with whom one came in contact. They entered the body through the pores, the mouth, the tear ducts. At no time were less than half of the steerage passengers afflicted with illness. By the end of the trip scarcely any passengers would have made the voyage without having experienced some fever.

From this there was to be no relief, as no member of the third class was allowed above decks until after the storm. So, this was to be his punishment, *purgatorio*. Lying trapped within a diseased coffin pitching and rolling and turning his insides into a sloshing mass. Dominico would sleep in his own vomit, vomiting himself to death as had happened to the old

Czech woman. It had only taken a few days for all the water in her system to dry out. Maybe he would die in his own feces as dysentery ran rampant throughout the compartment. Maybe the fever would take him, eating away at his body until there was nothing left but a mass of skin and bone. Regardless, this was to be his trial, the penance for all the sins that he had committed.

Dominico was beginning to feel the full impact of sin. Sin was always an all-pervading force in his life, the life of a rustic Roman Catholic whose only contact with a higher spirituality was the church. At seventeen Dominico understood that sin was ruination. He was born with the taint of sin and all his life was a ceaseless struggle to cleanse himself in preparation for a higher reward. He needed to cleanse himself of all that was impure, all that he did, all that he did not do, all that he said and all that he thought. Many hours Dominico sat before the priest and confessed his sins hoping for absolution that only a man ordained by God could vouch. Dominico was in the habit of reviewing how he lived his life to give a full account of himself to the priest on Sunday.

Yet, Dominico realized that he never fully felt the impact of sin. In the eyes of God, he sinned with Pratolina, the betrothed of another man. Yet when the time came for him to account for his behavior at the foot of the priest, he...he choked. It was not from shame that Dominico could not confess his deeds to Father Antonio, his confessor. No, it was not shame. It was something else, something disconnected from religious piety.

Somewhere in Dominico's heart he could not bring himself to accept that what he did with Pratolina was sin. Their romance was the most beautiful and pure experience. How could such purity be the result of sin? There were times when Dominico tried to confess his love, but his heart would not allow the memory of her, of her body, of her breath on his neck, to be tainted with the label--sin.

Now, in the hold of that tossed ship, there was no escaping from sin. Upon landfall he would have a great deal to confess. To leave one's family must certainly be sinful. Leaving them behind to starve and wait for years under the thumb of a tyrant in the name of achieving fortune? For this there must be a penance. There must be suffering. One doesn't just leave... it just was not done.

Then there was the sin of taking a life. The young man reviewed and rehashed his role in the sailor's death. Was it murder? He ran it through his mind over and over, experiencing each kick, each blow, each spitting epithet. His stomach churned. Guilt? Seasickness? There was no doubt that the beast deserved what came to him. But Dominico could not shake the sense of guilt he felt as he gazed upon the sailor's still and lifeless body. He remembered his own stunned numbness as he turned his head and walked to the furthest corner of the compartment, his head against the blackened wall, his eyes wide, but seeing nothing, feeling nothing. He could not feel. The impact of what he had done had yet to make its way to his soul.

It was Signora Guglielmo who put her arms around him and kissed him on the cheek. "You know, sweet Dominico, there are times when a man must take action, even when that action is brutal and ugly."

Dominico shook his head, refusing to look at her.

"Being a man is a sorrowful thing. You'll learn. You are a good boy. You will be a good man. There will never be a time when you take life for granted. That is the sign of a good man. As a good man, you will feel the weight of all the bad in the world." She laid her gentle hand in the center of his chest. "Come...you must confess and find absolution. Absolution is the only refuge for the good man. No one can bear the weight of what he must do to survive against the desire to preserve his soul without atonement." She led Dominico to an old priest who took it upon himself to voyage with the émigrés to provide comfort and solace in their time of need. His name was Father Rocco Saluzzo from Caserta, and this was his twelfth voyage.

With Dominico he prayed to *Santa* Anna for the boy's absolution and safe journey across the waters. When the praying was done, Dominico made the sign of the cross and Father Saluzzo bade him absolution. This brought some relief to Dominico's soul, but the pitching of the ship and vileness of his quarters made him realize that it took much, much more than the words of an old, frail, very mortal priest to provide absolution. Suffering was the only way to cauterize the wounds inflicted by some sins upon the soul.

'*Per Pratolina*,' Dominico repeated to himself, '*Per Pratolina*.' He refused to think about her directly, for he did not want the dream of her to be tainted or in any way associated with the filth in which he lived. Yet he had to find some strength in his purpose, for it was in the hopes of winning a life with the woman he loved that he began this journey. Her name was his only consolation, his one reminder of what awaited him when he ascended from this hell, stepped foot in *Lamerica* and made his fortune.

Beyond the droning engines and the whining of the ship's own iron against the pressure of the storm, Dominico heard a different cacophony, a tumult of voices and profanity from the other side of the chamber. Soon he heard the telltale signs of a struggle. Wooden cots were disturbed and displaced. Cooking utensils fell to the floor. Chickens and other small livestock rustled and shrieked. Such disturbance was common. Dominico was not aware of experiments in which rats were crowded into cages until their agitation became so great that they tore at each other without provocation, but he knew instinctively that such was true of humanity. Many people, people of numerous cultures, were trapped, crowded in filth and forced to face the painful tribulations of their own choices against their own hopes. These people could find no solace in solitude. They were forced to entertain their own self-doubts, their own fears, while at the same time interacting with a pervasive tide of other people. Often such interaction was that of anger, the combustion of fear.

Dominico felt no need to be around the conflict. He had seen enough already and was too miserable and ill to remove himself from his bunk. But he bolted upright when he heard Giulio Guglielmo shout, "Mama! Don't...Dominico, come quick! Come! Come!"

Ducking to avoid hitting his head on the bunk above, he ran. Twice he fell from a combination of objects and livestock underfoot and the pitching of the ship. He soon regained his footing, ignoring the sticky matter on his hands. When he arrived, he noticed a large man with a piece of wood raised menacingly above his head. The scowl on his face was directed at Giacomo Guglielmo, as was the profanity that was spewing from his mouth. Giacomo was pinned by his father against a bunk while *Signora* Guglielmo pulled the angry attacker's thin hair. Her stout frame compensated for her short stature and lent weight to her tenacity. Desperately the man struggled against her, but between her weight and the rocking vessel he made little progress.

His only hope was to strike his clinging anchor with the wooden pummel in his hand. When he attempted this, a solid, bronze arm stopped the heavy club's descent short of its mark. Dominico pushed the man abruptly, causing him to lose his balance and fall to the viscous floor.

"That *figlio di puttana* stole my salami!" the man shouted in a dialect that Dominico found difficult to understand at first. "He stole my salami. He takes food out of the mouths of my children!" He lay on the floor waving the piece of wood.

Giacomo shook his head. "*Non era me*...I swear it wasn't me."

It was at that point that *Signora* Guglielmo reached under a blanket and with a surprised expression held in her hand a long salami, cut and partially eaten. Her eyes grew wide as she realized what she had in her hand. They narrowed directing anger at her son.

Giacomo hung his head just as his father slapped him across the face. "*Ho generato un ladro!* I've sired a thief!" shouted *Signore* Guglielmo.

"No, Papa...I was...I was just..."

"He was just hungry." Dominico added before the irate father could strike his son again. "We're all hungry, *Signore* Guglielmo..."

"I'm hungry too, and so are my children." The indignant man replied as he picked himself up from the floor, falling once more as the ship lurched in an unexpected direction.

"Here..." *Signora* Guglielmo threw the meat at him, "You have a problem with our children you come to us first. We'll make up for what's been eaten."

The man struggled to his feet and tried desperately to rub the filth from his fingers while at the same time keep the valuable meat from hitting the floor. He ran his fingers across his brow to put his dirty hair back in place. "No...no," he waved his hands as if defeated. "We are all going crazy," he said as he walked away *"Siamo tutti che vanno pazzeshi!"* The slump of his shoulders revealed that he felt less a man for this confrontation.

Dominico turned his attention to *Signora* Guglielmo. "Are you alright?"

"Si." She nodded. But as she spoke, she took a deep breath and wiped the sweat from her forehead. "I'm just a little wore out."

Dominico was just pondering how odd it was to hear such a stout and hearty woman state that she was "a little wore out" when a terrible sound broached his ears. *Signora* Guglielmo, at the end of her breath, coughed. She coughed briefly, just once, but Dominico could hear the fluid rattling in her chest and knew that things were to become much worse.

CHAPTER 12

The sound of that cough haunted Dominico. Such an omen could only portend evil. Its fluid, gravel sound resonated within his mind. It was as if the entire world stopped for just that moment and all his attention was given to that horrendous sound. Many times, during the voyage he had heard that sound in the throats of others. Many times, he had witnessed brutal fevers, the pallid skin, the loss of weight. Too often the stricken would succumb to the illness and give up their ghosts into the hands of the Holy Trinity. He resolved to spend as much time as he could with *Signora* Guglielmo and her family.

He hoped that his presence would be enough. God willing, his love for this matriarch, under whose protective embrace he had only enjoyed for a week and a half, would be enough to keep the Holy Ghost at bay. Surely, God would not take someone who as strong, as sure, as full of fight as was *Signora* Guglielmo. This, of all women, was made to walk the earth for a long time. To Dominico, she was like the mountains, like his own grandfather.

It was true that his presence brought her considerable joy. Dominico never knew just how much this old woman loved him, how he reminded her of a son whom she never knew, a son taken by cholera many years before, just as he was beginning to grow long and lean under a crop of thick, coal-black hair. She reveled in feeding him and imparting to him strength and compassion. Each night she thanked God for giving her the chance...the chance...the chance to know the feel of her first born one last time. Yes, she had other sons. All her children were boys. But the one she lost, her first born, left a void that could never be filled with even twenty sons. This boy, however, Dominico Rossa, son of stoneworker, somehow filled the void. *Signora* Guglielmo could no longer turn him away than she could let go of her first-born's lifeless body so many years ago. In many ways, she was holding that tiny body in her arms still. She felt the baby's phantom weight in her arms until the day Dominico climbed down the stairs into steerage, wide-eyed on uneasy and frightened legs.

As of yet, *Signora* Guglialmo's only symptom of ill omen was an occasional cough. She hoped this symptom could be relieved with some honey and fresh air. This was not to be.

One morning, twelve sailors entered the steerage compartment, followed by the captain and his entourage. Among the officers were the lieutenant and the interpreter whom the émigrés had first encountered upon boarding the ship. This was the first time the steerage passengers had set eyes upon the captain. The man in charge of the vessel that was bringing them to a new life was nothing more than an invisible entity up until now. He was a tall, square shouldered man with a thick, steel gray mustache and a jutting, scarred chin. His deep, gray eyes scanned émigrés as if scything wheat. The émigrés gathered around, staring at each other with dismay. Their eyes carried the weight of their secret, their collective sin.

The captain waited until all the able-bodied passengers were within his field of vision before he began to speak. His voice was as harsh and unforgiving, as accusatory as the very language that bellowed from his thick throat.

"*Ich bin Kapitan Gosse des Halzbad.*" His voice was gravel and tacks.

Instinctively the crowd turned their eyes to the interpreter who stood motionless. The interpreter appeared visibly shaken. "I am Captain Gosse of the Halzbad." The interpreter waited as the captain continued his next sentence.

"*Als Kapitän dieses schiffes ist die gesundheit und sicherheit meiner passagiere und männer von größter bedeutung.*"

"As Captain of this ship the health and safety of my passengers and crew is of utmost concern."

'The health and safety of his passengers?' Dominico questioned this utmost concern as he looked around at the filth, the very foul matter that gathered at the captain's feet. Dominico imagined the captain throwing his soiled shoes overboard while lauding the virtues of maintaining the health and safety of his passengers.

"It is in this interest that I approach you today," the interpreter continued. "A member of my crew is missing. He was last seen in a conflict with a young man among the third-class passengers."

Signora Guglielmo stepped in front of Dominico and pushed him behind her. Her husband did the same, followed by their oldest son and three other passengers whom Dominico did not know. With the slightest, imperceptible shuffle of bodies, Dominico disappeared into the crowd. He was motioned to sit behind a hanging sheet used to provide modesty for a female passenger.

"It was reported to me that my crewman entered steerage and has not been seen since." The captain scythed wheat with his eyes again as the interpreter punctuated his sentence in the same manner as the original speaker, with an emphasis on the word 'since.'

"Of course, you can imagine that there are many questions I have in regard to this matter. Is there anyone here who can shed light on this matter and answer these questions?"

All in the compartment remained silent. Dominico swore that the captain would hear his heart pounding and recognize him as the guilty party.

The captain's shoes stuck momentarily to the floor as he began to walk, but he paced through the crowd as they parted for him, giving him ample room. He scrutinized all who fell under his bladelike eyes. He asked, leaving his interpreter " *Gibt es jemanden, der erklären kann, was passiert ist?"*

The interpreter struggled to keep up with his captain. "Is there anyone who can explain what happened?" Again, the émigrés remained silent.

A large man stepped in front of Dominico as the captain approached his location. A younger woman pushed down on Dominico's head and threw a blanket over him. She sat on his stomach pretending to sew a patch into an old shirt. Dominico watched through the mesh of the tattered blanket as the captain's blue uniform glided toward him, stopped, turned facing the girl. Were his feet sticking out? He wondered. He tried to make himself disappear into what little mattress there was beneath him. He knew the captain could not hear his heart at that point because it had stopped beating. Indeed, if the captain found him hiding it would be certain proof of guilt. He would have been better off had everyone left him alone. Now he had to suffer the uncertainty of hiding.

"Ich versichere Ihnen dab, " Captain Gosse continued, *"die nichteinhaltung in dieser angelegenheit würde am meisten als...respektlos."*

"I assure you," interpreter continued, "noncompliance in this matter would be considered most...disrespectful."

Still not a sound from the bedraggled passengers.

The captain nodded, a sardonic sneer directed at everyone in steerage. He pursed his lips under his thick moustache. *"Das ist, was ich dachte*. That's what I thought." He continued to nod. "Since there is doubt as to the integrity of the third-class passengers all of you are hereby relegated to the steerage compartment until the end of the journey. Upon reaching the United States you will all be detained until this matter is resolved to my satisfaction." The captain shouted, his ruddy face darkening to the complexion of a beat, his eyes turning a cold, pale gray. "Food will be provided at the sustenance level only. No more luxury." The interpreter did not seem as emphatic in this statement as was the captain, but the message got through to the passengers. For many, being trapped in such a septic environment without access to fresh air was a death sentence, yet still not a murmur was heard.

The captain scythed the wheat one last time, waiting for one sign of infirmity, one weak link upon which to pounce and force confession. He found none. He spied only stoic, unwavering faces. Then, with screwed up countenance his spat the only Italian word of this discourse before climbing out of the steerage, "Feccia!"--"Scum!"

CHAPTER 13

Villa De San Giuseppe 19, Settembre 1900

Dominico has been gone for two days. I know that it will be a long time before I see him again. Life has become so complicated. To fall in love with a man whom most would call a mere commoner, but there's really nothing common about him. He's a man of matter and promise. He's a man who can become someone if he's allowed to break the shackles of his status. It's unfortunate that he cannot do that here, where I can hold him and love him with all my heart. Instead, I must wait for his return, when he's achieved the status that is rightfully his and he can, legitimately call me his bride. Though I must admit that a part of me wishes he stayed and called me his lover just so that I would not have to be without him.

I'm glad for him that he is going to America, where he will be able to blossom into the flower that I know he can become. I only hope he hurries back. If not, I wish for him to send for me. I will go to him. I will go to him if I must sell my labors on a steam ship as a maid I will go to him. It would be an escape from this hell.

Alfredo is becoming more persistent in his courtship, and my family is preparing for the eventual marriage. If only Alfredo knew. If he knew…if he knew all of it there would certainly be no marriage. It would also be the end of my life here. I will be cast to the street, which is a place I cannot afford to be. Not as it stands.

I'll wait for word from Dominico and pray his safe passage. I'll pray too that his absence will not be long. Only he can help me now…

Dominico shook. He could hear her voice in the words written on the yellow paper of the diary. Before he could read more, he closed his eyes and whispered a faint apology to his beloved. 'I know I've failed. I didn't become the flower you thought I would. Perhaps you saw something that wasn't really there.'

Mandolins, strummed by deft fingers, filled the stagnant air with an obstinate life. For five days the passengers in third class were without the benefit of sunlight or even the smoke-filled sea air of the aft deck. Their confinement kept them within the bowels of the ship, yet also served to stir the beginnings of solidarity that would be so important in their new homes. The bonds of prison became the bonds of fraternity. None complained, none protested. All endured their punishment, finding comfort in their folk music, songs and countless rounds of *mora*.

The *purgatorio* that was this voyage became *una communità*. The captain's hopes that the peasants would crack under such pressure and hand him the perpetrators of this still mysterious crime was short sighted and ill conceived. Here were a people whom the captain scorned, but for whom he was ill prepared to contend. Their ways were not his ways. Their mettle was not the rigid mettle of his country, but a malleable substance that would twist and bend, but never break. The captain did not understand that the émigrés sense of justice was molded in a land without justice. Those of *Il*

Mezzogiorno knew that they would not receive justice in the hands of anyone representing an authority. Justice was something to be taken, not something to be received by wise and solemn rulers. In their collective consciousness, reporting the misdeeds of a crewmember to the captain would bring nothing but sorrow. That he was a rapist would be of no concern to the captain. He was a part of the machine which the captain relied upon for his profit, just as the *camorra* and *padrone,* who preyed upon the people of Southern Italy, were vital parts of the political complex and thus above the law. It has been thus since time unremembered. So, it would be for the rest of their lives.

No man, woman, or child, born and bred under the sun of Southern Italy, under the fist of the *padrone* or within the blackmail and extortion of *la camorra* would ever consider informing on another's crimes. Neither hope of future comfort nor threat of death could encourage such betrayal. Confession was reserved for the Priest, or the family member who could avenge a wrong, not for the authorities. If a priest or trusted family member could not be found, then the truth was oft lost on the deathbed of a victim whose only comfort was that no authority would cause harm to his family. This was justice in *Il Mezzogiorno*.

The steerage passengers, imbued with this ethic, accepted their hellish lot for the duration of their journey. For a people steeped in the traditions of Roman Catholicism, suffering for their crimes, even their own quest for justice was a cleansing for their souls. It was a sublime contradiction in the lives of the Southern Italian that his only hope for justice lie in actions that were mortally sinful. This harsh Catch-22 was bearable only with the promise of penance and forgiveness of sins. Otherwise, the soul of a Southern Italian who strived for justice was lost.

To be deprived of daylight was, to those who lived under the warmth of the Mediterranean Sun, a suitable punishment for the outrage of murder. The only way the passengers could keep track of time was by counting the delivery of food every day. Whether this happened in the morning or in the evening was unknown. A barrel of trash fish and stale bread was brought down with a cask of vinegary wine and water five times during their interment.

So, the songs of the condemned continued. Some songs were sad. Most were sung badly. Still, they were not without a certain amount of cheer and hope that this punishment would end upon reaching *Lamerica*.

Dominico sat by *Signora* Guglielmo's bedside as she listened to the mandolins and forced a smile on her face. Sometimes she tried to sing the songs that were familiar to her, but her throat was swollen and would not allow for song. Still, she smiled and cheered her children, assuring them that she would be all right. She told them that she was getting better, getting stronger, that she would be on her feet soon. She told them to run along and make the most of their time. Dominico and *Signore* Guglielmo, however, knew the dire signs of her illness and never left her side.

She was not getting better. Indeed, she was rapidly getting worse. By the time the fifth barrel of food was received the once robust woman had lost half her body weight. She was thin and pale, her eyes sunken and dark within bony cheeks. Her fever became a fire under her thinning, parchment-like skin, yet still she shivered. Her body was lost under a pile of blankets donated by half a dozen passengers.

Many of the women in steerage were well versed in the healing arts of their regions. Each offered her services to the woman who was once the matron of all steerage passengers. *Signora* Guglielmo found herself the recipient of poultices and herbs, teas, and tinctures. Olive oil was spread over her body, leaches applied to the poisoned areas around her throat. Reams of garlic abounded about her neck. This great pharmacopoeia failed to relieve a single symptom.

One *maga* suggested that that *Signora* Guglielmo suffered from the effects of *malocchio*, the evil eye. The old, self-proclaimed witch stared at *Signore* Guglielmo with pointed, bony finger and deep blue eyes and crowed that the German captain possessed the dark power and infected her because he knew that she was hiding the boy. Dominico shut his eyes and screamed inward. He knew this woman was most likely insane, but then there was a thousand years of tradition to fear the *mage*, women born after midnight, Christmas morning and possessed of great powers. The old *maga* claimed that she could cure *Signora* Guglielmo if she lay atop her and chanted invocations in a language unknown to any in the hold. When she rose some hours later, she breathed heavily and shook her head. She said that the captain's curse was strong. She would need some of his blood to save the sick woman.

It was not long before women gathered around her and performed their rosaries, laying their hands upon her as they beseeched Saint Anne to see this fine woman to the end of the voyage. It was not long before *Signora* Guglielmo lost her patience with these women. She wanted to be alone with her husband, her sons, and with Dominico. Though weak and sick she was able to assert her will on seven devoted women and made them leave.

All knew that none of the magic applications, no amount of prayer or witchcraft would resolve her illness. She would either get better, or she would die. *Signora* Guglielmo was resolved for either happenstance. Throughout the process she continued to get worse, burning hotter. Her voice became weak before disappearing. Dominico held her hand, slept seated beside her. He did his best to keep a cool, wet rag upon her burning head. Her husband wiped the sweat from her face and arms and cleaned around her when she vomited. Toward the end, she could not vomit as there was nothing inside of her. The very act of keeping her eyes open fatigued her.

On the fifth day her fever was abating. The healers, even the old *maga* considered this a good sign. It was a sign that the evil was being repulsed from her lymph. Dom and *Signore*

Guglielmo, however, felt in their hearts that the lack of fever indicated not a return to health, but instead the fact that there was nothing left to burn. Realizing this her heartbroken husband spoke with Father Capasetta, then broke down and cried. Unable to bring himself to watch the proceedings he walked away as Father Capasetta administered *unction extrema*. Dominico remained at her side.

He listened as she confessed her sins. She did this not by speaking, as her weak lungs could not force words through her swollen throat. Instead, Father Capasetta recited a list of sinful categories and *Signora* Guglielmo nodded when he mentioned one relevant to her. Holding her head, feeling her nod, he could not believe that this was happening, that he was losing one who had touched his life in such a brief time. He felt like he had known this woman for his entire life. She was his self-appointed mother, a matronly love without the influence of which he imagined he could not have completed this hellish trip. He listened to the alien Latin flowing from Father Capasetta's lips. Dominico shut his eyes and tried to instill strength into the hand that felt like so many wilting flower petals in his own. He had to impart this strength so she could survive, so she could conquer this evil within and walk into *Lamerica.* She deserved as much. If he only concentrated enough, he could get her there.

The Priest continued his somber labors. To Dominico he was sealing her fate. He realized that this was not rational. Indeed, if it were in Father Capasetta's capacity to offer her a hundred more years of life he would do so. Father Capasetta loved *Signora* Guglielmo as a sister. His hands shook with the weight of the task that was his misfortune bear. Dominico knew only his own sorrow and realized that Father Capasetta's role would be the last kindness done for her. There was no more. To Dominico that seemed final, seemed like giving up. He found himself hating *Signore* Guglielmo for giving up and for his cowardice in leaving his wife to die in the hands of this Priest. He hated them both. Then guilt pierced him for thinking ill of a holy man and of the husband of a dying woman.

Father Capasetta dipped his thumb in holy oil, placed it on her forehead and made the sign of the cross on the thin skin. He prayed in Latin, the sounds of mandolins played in the background. Then—stillness.

The world that for two weeks was in perpetual motion was still, though the émigrés continued to feel the motion in their uncertain limbs. The steerage passengers heard the great engines whine and groan. The mandolins stopped. Those playing *mora* held their fingers out but stared at each other as the great ship stopped, swayed slightly, then was still.

The hold was silent until two young men shook the confusion from their faces and began to shout, *"Lamerica! LAMERICA!"* Soon all in steerage, almost eight hundred voices, called out in unison, *"LAMERICA!"*

Father Capasetta, after a brief pause continued the rites, but none could hear as his brassy voice was drowned in the joyous cacophony.

Then, to Dominico's surprise, a mass of steerage passengers ran to exit the compartment. Bunks were overturned and animals were scattered in the rush to see this new and wondrous land. The two men assigned to guard the doors realized that they would be overwhelmed by this ecstatic mass and made their retreat. Like the bursting of a dam, the crowd pushed through the door and rushed onto the deck.

Dominico remained with *Signora* Guglielmo, however, as did Father Capasetta. *Signore* Guglielmo emerged from behind a stack of belongings and joined them, his face graven, but dry. It was not long before they were the only people remaining in the compartment.

Signora Guglielmo offered her husband a weak smile, the oil still glistening with the sign of the cross on her forehead. He looked into her eyes, was taken by how they seemed to shine after five days of illness. "*Ti amo*," he said and held his head high so she would not see him defeated. She smiled wider and nodded, returning his love in the only way her emaciated body would allow.

She then turned to Dominico. Her eyes gleamed with joy, a rapture that he could not understand. She struggled to raise her hand toward him, but lost strength before she could touch his tear-streaked face. Dominico looked at her hand then turned back to her eyes. The fire was out. Her eyes were but glass impressions, blank, without life.

La Via Dolorosa was over.

Part III

Lamericano

Sept 1900--Dearest Pratalina:

I'm afraid I've failed you. I don't believe I'll ever set foot in this country. My ship has been sitting in the harbor for three days and there seems to be no hope that we will be allowed to disembark. The authorities are looking for someone among us who has committed a crime. In fact, what was done was not a crime but a retribution. None in third class will speak to the authorities. Three days ago, we were so comforted by the vision of Lady Liberty before us despite the sorrow we felt in our hearts for Signora Guglielmo. But I guess Lady Liberty is not for us. I would give anything to be off this ship. I feel myself becoming weaker, but I will not betray those who've suffered with me. I imagine that I will be home shortly, in failure. Should this letter arrive before that time know that I am deeply sorry for this failure..

I will always love you.

Dominico

"Dominico, Dominico! Wake up! Wake up."

Dominico bolted erect, eyes wide, brow glistening with sweat. His eyes, large as eggs, saw nothing of his fetid surroundings for some seconds. First, he became aware of his

356

trembling body, then he felt the coldness of his skin. His heart, like a hammer made it near impossible to pull in a breath.

"Dominico! You were having a bad dream!"

Reality drifted into focus, a menace from the distance, drawing closer. His awareness pushed through the mist shrouding his mind. Finally, his eyes cleared and focused. The squalid chamber, its browns and grays, proved an odd comfort.

It was only a moment ago that he was back in his family's work yard, pounding furiously on a slab of granite, pounding with a recklessness born from rage and angst. Pounding, arm drawn back until the muscles in his great, bronze shoulders pinched around his spine, then throwing the full weight of his being behind the mallet. Great chunks of granite exploded from the rock. Sparks flew like tiny suns around his hands. The sound of the chisel cutting great wedges of granite shocked his ears, reverberated to his fingers and elbows.

In this sleep reality the stone took shape. It was a tombstone. His father stood behind him, shaking his head, an expression of hopelessness on his face. He said nothing, only shook his head. "Show me!" Dominico beseeched. He could tell that the stonework was crude, the curves and corners unkempt, uneven. It was the work of an amateur, the work of one who had never learned how to read the stone. "Show me, damn it! Show me!" His father walked away, head hanging limp on his crooked shoulders, defeated.

Dominico turned to the stone, afraid to put the blade to it again. Afraid of the stone—afraid of what it was. It was a tombstone. In rough, unfinished letters was "*Signora* Guglielmo." *Madre della Maria Angelina Rossa* was written in pencil in preparation for carving.

"Be like stone," the voice behind him commanded in a brutish accent. Dominico turned to see the German captain. The old, stoic sailor stared back, condemnation in his unnatural gray eyes. Dominico saw the men of steerage behind the captain, kicking and beating the sailor to death, cursing, and spitting on his destroyed body. Deaf to the commotion behind him, the captain stared at Dominico, "be like stone."

Dominico growled in a rage. He lifted the tombstone above his head and threw it over the side of the ship, watching it sink into the gray-green ocean. He could feel the stone sink. He could smell the putrid water, ruined by human feces, urine, and vomit. Sinking—Dominico was sinking into the water, pulled under the waves by an unseen hand clasped around his ankle. He reached out, stretching to the black ship looming great and ugly before him. He reached for...for his father standing high above him, wearing the captain's uniform. His once dark eyes now an eerie gray. Dominico reached for him, but his father did not respond. He only stared at his son as the young man's face disappeared beneath the waves. "Be like stone, *Figlio*."

"Dominico, you were having a nightmare!" It was *Signore* Guglialmo's son, Cologerro. "Are you alright?"

Dominico nodded, he was not yet able to talk. He could still feel the cold ocean engulfing him, pouring into his mouth, into his lungs.

"That could be a bad sign. Nightmares are messages from the dead. You should go see *La Maga*. Maybe she can tell you what it means."

"No." Dominico stated.

"I would do it if I had a nightmare. What was it about?"

"I don't remember," Dominico whispered. "I forgot it as soon as you woke me. There's no sense talking about it." Dominico was aware of the potentially grave import of dreams. Knowing this, he was sure he did not want this fearful dream interpreted. He could not allow himself fear. He had something to accomplish.

"You should try and remember, Dominico. It might be important."

"Enough, Cologerro, enough! I told you I don't remember. Did anything happen last night? Is there any word?"

Cologerro shook his head. His otherwise boyish features had aged since his mother's death. His coal-colored hair was matted and dirty. "No. Yesterday was S. ay. Papa said that they don't do anything on Sunday."

"Four days now!" Dominico pounded his fist on the table.

It had been four days since *Signora* Guglielmo died. Signore Guglielmo watched as she exhaled for the last time. He and Dominico could not move, paralyzed by the impossible thing that had just happened. Only a few days earlier, *Signora*

Guglielmo was the most alive, most powerful presence in steerage. Certainly, she was the strongest spirit Dominico had ever met outside of his own grandfather. Now she was gone. The squalid air had claimed her ghost.

"Dominico," *Signore* Guglielmo moaned, "go get Tomas and Cologerro. Go find them. They should be here." He then fell upon his knees before his beloved. He had to be strong for the boys. There was no mor strength left.

Dominico walked around then looked toward the hatchway that exited steerage. His sorrow, combined with his fear, kept him from running. He was afraid that he would be stopped and not allowed to leave the hold for he did not have the weight of the masses behind him. If he did manage to get out, he was afraid of facing Tomas and Cologerro with this devastating news.

The door was unguarded, abandoned by guards charged with an impossible task. Dominico stepped onto the deck. The cool, brisk air nipped at his cheeks. It was warm when he left Naples, now the winter was upon him. The cool air was refreshing. The breeze across his face reminded him of the hopes that were currently on hold in response to more immediate sorrow.

Dominico looked around. The first thing that caught his eye was the skyline. The buildings off in the distance were so great he thought he could reach out and touch them. Many of them reached ten, fifteen stories, even more. He scanned the hazy shore, his eyes drawing a line into the distance. The city seemed to go on forever. Dominico wondered if the entire country was covered in city. A city that dwarfed anything he had ever seen.

At last, the upper decks of the ship obscured his view. A mass of people gathered on the upper decks cheering and laughing as the great ship was tied to the port. My how these people shined! The women were the color of flowers in their beautiful, flowing dresses and broad brimmed hats. The men were erect and clean, the suits and top hats flawless as they pointed at the various buildings. anticipating the great business they would conduct. The upper decks were cheerful gardens of those whose voyages were comfortable and gleeful. It was an image of intoxication.

On the aft deck the scene was much different, more sober. The mass of émigrés who pushed past armed guards to enjoy their first glance of the new world were now silent and motionless. Occasional sobbing broke the silence as the women cried, tears of joy flowed down their cheeks. Families held onto each other, drawing strength and warmth. Dominico stood alone among them, ragged and worn, the odor of steerage clinging to his tattered clothes. Faces drawn and wrinkled framed wet eyes heavy with fatigue but bright with hope.

They stared at one point. All eyes turned to the giant, greenish statue. The beautiful woman rose from the gray water, her arm bearing a torch held high to the heavens, her eyes set to peer into the distance, wise and unconquerable yet warm and welcoming. *La Statue De Liberta*. For a people familiar with icons and statues of their saints, there was never such a great promise, never such a warm welcome.

Those above, in the pretty dresses and flawless suits laughed, pointed at, and reflected upon the great statue with passing attention and curiosity. For them this really was just another day. It was a quaint little trip, a story to tell their pretty, painted friends, they day they saw the Statue of Liberty. For those of the tattered cloth, however, she was their first and only hope for the future. This was not a moment for celebration, but a solemn moment of reflection, for musing on a home left behind and a dream under the shadow of this wonderful statue and the great looming buildings. It was a time for dreams under a sun that shines only on America.

Dominico had only a moment to admire the great lady. He shuffled through the crowd, pushed through the dense bodies and deep emotions. After two minutes of pushing and prodding through the crowd he found Tomas and Cologerro. He took them by the arms and dragged them through the crowd back to the steerage cabin. They followed with solemn footsteps. There was nothing to explain. Only one thing could have pulled them from that moment.

That was four days earlier. While Dominico mourned with the Guglielmo family the émigrés were moved back into steerage where they were told they would await debarkation. The first- and second-class passengers were to be given preference and were allowed to disembark at a separate port.

Once the ship was emptied of all but the third-class passengers, the captain returned to steerage and informed the émigrés that they would not be allowed to leave until the perpetrator of the crime against his crew was given over to him. A pall of despair replaced the hope in the émigré's eyes. The captain read this change and used it as a weapon. He vowed that he would lock the hold and return the émigrés to Italy where they would be imprisoned if he did not learn the secret of his disappeared crewman. Men, women, and children were pulled from steerage and questioned, but none betrayed their countrymen, even under this horrendous threat.

It was becoming obvious to the émigrés that they would be turned back. They prepared themselves for disappointment. Dead ends were not unfamiliar to the émigrés who had learned well how to deal with adversity. The only variable that they could control was whether to talk to the authorities. This they would never do. They would never submit. Every member of steerage was in some way complicit in the crime. They did not dare come forward with the truth.

Dominico and Cologerro occupied themselves with a game of *mora* while *Signore* Guglielmo tended to his dead wife whose body remained where it lay. It was for him to decide where she was to be buried. He wished he could take her back to Calabria to be buried in the churchyard of her own *paesera*. However, he did not have the money for a return trip. He was at a loss and there was no consoling him.

On what must have been a Monday, the hatch opened, and the captain walked inside followed by three robust and ruddy men in top hats and shiny, silver suits. In their mouths were large, black, obnoxious cigars. Some of the men in the compartment eyed the great, smoking cylinders with jealousy.

Upon stepping into the hold, the ruddy men stopped and lifted their feet from the sticky floor. They eyed their contaminated shoes with disgust. Then they continued to what must have been appointed positions. They stepped and another man followed. He was a tall, imposing, barrel chested man wearing white. A black overcoat reclined over his broad shoulders. His white fedora only enhanced the shadow on his dark, pock marked face. In his white, equine teeth he clenched a long, thin pipe. His red eyes scanned the mass of émigrés with contempt, none of whom so much as moved from their places or even stopped what they were doing. They looked upon him as they would a new tormenter. Only this tormentor, under his shiny clothes, looked like one of them. In fact, to the sorrow of those in the hold, his demeanor was familiar. His was the presence of *Une Padrone*.

He looked around the hold, approaching mostly the men. He asked them questions in Italian. Soon he was standing in front of Dominico. "*Ragazzo*, where are you from?" His voice was rasping, like a plain against knotted wood.

"*Villa De San Giuseppe en Campania, Signore.*"

The man sneered. "You may call me Don Costillo, *ragazzo*. What do you do?"

"I'm a stone carver, Don Costillo." Dominico struggled to keep his eyes from dropping when he spoke.

"You're young to be a craftsman. Why should I believe you?"

"I'm a Rossa, Don Costillo. My family has worked in stone for centuries."

Don Castillo spat on the floor. "Are you alone."

"*Si*, Don Costillo. I'm alone."

The pock marked man lifted Dominico's deft arms with his walking stick. He examined the young man's hands and noticed the calluses there. They were not the calluses of a farmer or a *contadino.* Don Costillo knew those calluses well. Dominico's hands and forearms were those of a man who worked in stone, broad, round, and dry. He pounded his fist into Dominico's chest. Dominico stood, little phased. The Don nodded toward him but nodded in such a way that he communicated disdain for the boy.

After Dominico, he questioned another man, thin and emaciated. He was Rudo Confamiglia, a *Latino*. Don Costillo asked the same questions asked of Dominico. The man was a tenant farmer back in *Latium*. His eyes were pale, and his chest was concave. He traveled alone, having left his daughters in the care of another until he could send for them. Don Costillo did not bother to touch the filthy man but backed away and covered his mouth with silk handkerchief when he heard the old *giornoleri* cough.

With an abrupt turn, his coat fanning behind him, he strode confidently back to the captain and his corpulent entourage. He looked once more toward *Signore* Confamiglia and left the hold. The men followed and closed the chamber door.

The émigrés were unaware of the dealings above decks. Don Costillo and a half dozen businessmen met some customs officials and his dayroom. Don Costillo spat venom at the captain and the customs officials for delaying the release of the steerage passengers. The émigrés were needed and must be released. The captain protested. The representatives of industry retorted with invective. Eventually a mutually agreeable solution was met.

Don Costillo returned with some armed members of the German crew. He pointed a gloved finger toward Rudo Confamiglia then left. Two crewmen approached the old *giornoleri* under cover of two rifles aimed at the mass of émigrés. When he realized his peril, *Signore* Confamiglia tried to make an escape, but it was too late. The big Germans had him under both spindly arms and were dragging him across the slimy floor.

He screamed. He invoked *San Genarro.* He pleaded for the sake of his daughters who would be put out if their ward did not see some money soon. Indeed, without their father they would be turned out onto the streets to make do in any way they could. Would that mean prostitution? It did not matter. Rudo was the scapegoat for the unknown crime. The captain required closure, Don Costillo required laborers. Rudo Confamiglia's body was anemic and riddled with illness. In other words, he was expendable—culled from the herd. Dominico thought back on the day of the crime. He did not remember Rudo participating in the murder. In fact, he was most likely sick, in bed, too weak to move. This was Rudo's condition for almost the entire trip. He was only the first whose dreams were snuffed out by an instant decision, however. Dominico felt that if Rudo Confamiglia were not there, he himself would have been chosen as sacrifice. He could only thank his youth, health, and chance that his journey was allowed to continue. There was a twinge of guilt that carried over his relief that Rudo was the sacrifice.

CHAPTER 2

merica, the land of opportunity where all men, rich and poor are created equal. That some are afforded this equality more readily, however, was not lost on the émigrés as they found themselves assorted by class and status, literally stratified on the ship. Besides the obvious layers of privilege experienced most sharply by the "third class," it was made clear during disembarkation that the higher classes were to be given the utmost courtesy. The first and second-class passengers, now long gone, enjoyed cursory medical examination on board before being released gently into the waiting arms of their smiling loved ones on a lower, Manhattan pier.

Of course, it was assumed that they were healthy, for they were clean and plump and pink in the cheeks. They were a stark contrast to the sallow, emaciated, malodorous passengers in steerage. They were assumed to be honest because they were people of means. Such people were not inclined to take part in baser pursuits, unlike the swarthy, shifty eyed, criminally invested passengers of steerage. The upper tiers, clean and honest, drifted across the platform like flower petals flowing along a gentle stream. Celebration, reunion, the pleasant, awaiting embraces of their clean and honest loved ones in their clean and honest clothes. Oh, what kind of world this would be had the passengers been stratified by the contents of their hearts rather than the contents of their purses and their petticoats.

The third-class, let alone being subjected to a tortuous quarantine and threats of deportation, was forced to undergo more intrusive, more intensive examination. These were the huddled masses, the "wretched refuse" whom America was to adopt with open arms. With open arms they would be adopted so long as they were not too wretched, too sick, too poor, too old, too useless.

The fabled Ellis Island had burned down some years earlier, and though it stood glistening and new in the harbor it would not be opened for another two months. Instead, the émigrés were herded by the score into crowded ferries and taken to Castle Garden where they were to be "processed." Processed…like criminals, like chattel, like meat. The barge office near Castle Garden was the judgement ground where it was determined who was good enough, clean enough, honest enough, young enough, healthy enough, useful enough to enjoy America's embrace. The pathetic rest were without ceremony, nor apology, turned back.

The contradiction, so blatant in this land of equality and opportunity, went unnoticed by Dominico and his fellow travelers. That there were those who could glide happily onto her soil and those who had to be processed was of no consequence nor surprise. Dominico had never read the Declaration of Independence. He had never seen nor heard read Jefferson's words, "endowed by our creator with certain inalienable rights." Perhaps it was by virtue of the process that one became equal. Perhaps one had to earn equality or demonstrate that equality as a birthright. Perhaps one needed to be especially healthy, or especially clean or especially useful to be equal. Having had no experience with equality, or how this equality came to be, he and his fellow voyagers could only accept what was happening to them as a "Process of equality." To them, their first experience with American equality was just another rite of passage, another obstacle to be overcome. It was just like home.

Unlike the floral passengers in second and first-class who disembarked into the arms of their loved ones, the first people encountered by third-class passengers were blue clad marines. These were doctors performing the initial examination to ensure that this wretched refuse was healthy enough. The émigrés were lined up outside a row of partitions inching their way toward ominous curtains.

Dominico witnessed, as if through a fog, as dozens of people with whom he had traveled, were sorted with no regard to family. Ubiquitous crying tortured his heart. Pursuing one's dreams could not be like this. Before him, the Trentina family stepped one by one into the tiny, partitioned rooms. One by one they exited the other side, some baring chalk marks on their breasts, some without. Those with chalk marks were led away to another room. Those without were allowed to continue with their processing. But this was a family. A family that managed to remain intact as it traveled from a village outside of Bari, Apullia, to the Bay of Naples. They stuck with each other through sickness in the fetid womb of the *Halzbad*, nursing each other through fevers, rashes and seasickness. Now they were separated by chalk marks...simple chalk marks. Even the baby, Ignascia, bore the burden of the chalk on her dingy, gray blanket. Mama stroked her infant daughter, papa cried and reached for his children. He could not reach them. They were led away screaming and crying, "Papa, don't let them take me, Papa!" "*Aria*! *Aria*! What is wrong?" The crying never stopped, even among those who were allowed to continue the process. The most basic cornerstone of being an Italian, the family, was rent asunder. Toward the sanctity of the family the marines revealed as much emotion as would be necessary to lance a boil or clean an infection.

As Dominico neared the dreaded curtains his heart pounded more rapidly. He closed his eyes and tried to slow the unnatural, mechanical pounding. He feared that the soldier would interpret his racing heart as an illness and mark his jacket.

Signore Giulieto stepped from behind the partition and fell onto his knees, his hands clasped in prayer beseeching the soldier to remove the mark from his jacket. He cried, he told the marine that his village was gone, burned to the ground to purge an epidemic. He had nothing for which to return, *"Per favore! Per favore!* Have mercy on me! *Per favore!"* There was no mercy to be had. *Signore* Giulieto was carried to the unknown place reserved for those who were too wretched. Dominico's eyes swelled with tears. They were tears motivated by empathy, by sadness and desperation for *Signore* Giulieto. They were also tears motivated by fear for his own fortune.

In what seemed an eternity Dominico, at last, was next. Despite his drive, he would have waited another eternity if it meant avoiding the uncertainty within. Head down, eyes averted he stepped into the partition. The marine indicated that he wanted the green identification card that was clenched in Dominico's fingers. He checked the card then opened Dominico's shirt without so much as an at-your-leave. Not that Dominico expected such respect. Dominico knew men in uniform to be nothing less than brutes.

The examination was much more thorough than it was in Naples. The marine checked his throat, his skin, his heart. As uncomfortable as it was to allow this stranger to scrutinize his body, the worst part of the examination was when the marine, without regard to personal comfort, lifted Dominico's eyelid with a buttonhook and examined the tissues of his eyes. Of all the diseases carried by the huddled masses, trachoma was among the most feared. Trachoma was a painful disease that caused ulcers in the eyes and eventual blindness. It was feared more than the many social diseases that were making their way steadily through New York. Living conditions of steerage were perfect for the transmission for trachoma.

Indeed, the eyes were much abused during the voyage. Dominico remembered all the smoke and salt spray that had invaded his eyes. He remembered the tears withheld when he saw *Signore* Giulieto on his knees.

"Hm," was the only sound uttered by the marine. This was of bad portent. Dominico's eyes must have been red and swollen, and the doctor thought him to be ill! He removed the buttonhook from Dominico's eye and picked up the chalk.

"No!" Dominico cried and stepped back, but it was too late. The marine scrawled an awkward "E" onto Dominico's chest. He was marked. There was to be no reprieve. This was the end of Dominico's journey. If he could only talk to the marine, make him realize that he had made a mistake. If he could tell him his story, how he loves this woman and how he must make something of himself in America to have her. If...

'...Dominico...' his father admonished from the distance of untold miles and untold experiences '...Dominico...you are a Rossa. Be like stone." It was not for a Rossa to beg. It was a Rossa who stood up to Don Alfredo's son. It was a Rossa and a Rossa alone who suffered the consequences of that action without surrender, without one thought to giving up. It was a Rossa, a Rossa man who stood before this marine and would have to face his fate alone in a foreign land with all his hopes and dreams in the balance. Pretending his father's dignity Dominico followed another marine to yet another line where he stood among those who were similarly marked. He wanted to cry with all the others, but he didn't. He was like stone and soon, many of those around him were equally stolid.

As he made his way, he refused to listen to any more of the crying. He had to allow his eyes to dry. They had to be clear when he was examined. If he had to close his heart to the pain and suffering around him, then that is what he would do.

"*Parle Inglese*?" asked another man. This man wore a white coat and a polite smile as he asked the question. He was an older man with thick glasses and a pinkish white face that exuded sincerity as he pushed this practiced Tuscan dialect from his unpracticed mouth.

Dominico shook his head, "*No.*"

The old man smiled and nodded, looked at the paper that hung off center on his clip board, then examined Dominico's eyes. He was gentler than the marine, but he spent considerably more time peering under the young man's lids. He examined every corner of both eyes. He then smiled and patted Dominico on the back, "*Va bene. Va bene,*" he whispered and pointed to the great lines from which "processing" could continue. He gave Dominico a card, then called the next person for examination.

Dominico showed his card to another man in uniform. The man directed him to stand in the shortest of the immense lines that approached the long desks of the front of the hall.

Dominico waited in that line for hours leaning against the posts to rest his sagging legs.

While in line, he struck up a conversation with the man in front of him. He did not recognize the man from the *Halzbad*, so he must have come from another ship. He was Italian from *Lazio*. After Dominico told him where he was from, the man claimed that he once marched with Garibaldi through *Campania*. Dominico pretended to be impressed. He was old enough to know that when some people have nothing of which to be proud, they often make something up. Riding with Garibaldi was the fiction of choice for such men.

"You've never been through this before?"

"No." Dominico admitted.

"You'll do fine. The trick is to answer the questions without giving them any information. Be careful how you answer. Do you have family here?"

"No, but I was told that I would have a job waiting when I got here. I have this card." Dominico reached for the card that was given to him back in Naples.

"Nononononono." The man responded, holding Dominico's hand and looking around the great hall to ensure that no one saw the boy's transgression. "You don't tell these guys up here that you have a job. They'll think you were shipped here illegally, which you probably were. You tell them that you have excellent prospects. Do you have a trade?"

"I'm a stone carver."

"Good, good. You don't tell them that you have a job, and you don't show them this card. And if they ask you, tell them you have friends here with whom you will stay until you get a job."

"I have no friends here."

"Give them the name Frederico and Alma Spotsia. That's my brother and his wife. They've been here for a few years. Give them that name if they ask, but only if they ask. You don't give them any information about you. Oh, and one more thing. Pronounce your name carefully—very carefully."

Dominico gave a quizzical look.

"They have more letters in their alphabet than we do, and they insist on using them. You'd be amazed at the different ways these people have changed Italian names. I've heard of processors who, when confronted by a grand, long Italian name simply wrote 'Smith' on the paper. Those people had to go around with the name Smith for the rest of their lives. And sometimes they just don't know how to spell. D's become T's, C's become S's. There's no telling what they'll do. No, if you like your name, you will pronounce it clearly."

"Thank you," Dominico said as the man was led away. Dominico would never forget this man, though the only name he knew was that of his brother and sister-in-law.

"Ros-sa. Dom-in-ic-o Ros-sa." Dominico was careful to enunciate every syllable. He wanted no mistakes. He was a Rossa, and a Rossa he would remain.

The man behind the desk was clean of face though his hair was a mess. He was stiff yet cordial.

"So," the man behind the desk straightened the papers and placed a copy of the ship's manifest from the *Halzbad* next to another paper with questions and lines on it. "Do you have a job waiting for you?"

Dominico could feel the card burning in his pocket, but he remembered his earlier conversation. He hated the idea of lying, but desired entrance more than anything. The din of crying and the odor of crowded bodies seemed far away, yet it was a reminder of the desperation that propelled him. He had gone through too much to be stopped now. "I have excellent prospects. I am a stone carver." Not a lie, just not all the truth—He wondered what his grandfather would say. Are all moral virtues so tested in America? Are all virtues thus compromised little by little?

"So, you have a trade."

"Yes."

"You look young to be a stone carver."

Dominico said nothing. The man who shrugged and scratched on the paper.

"Do you have family waiting for you?"

"I have friends."

The man nodded and scratched on the paper.

"Have you ever been convicted of a crime?"

"No."

The uncomfortable questioning continued for a few minutes before the man signed the bottom of the paper and smiled. "Welcome to America young man. Good luck to you."

The smile that crossed Dominico's face was the release of his anxiety. All the muscles in his jaw and neck relaxed. The smile, the first he had enjoyed in a long time, felt good against his cheeks. "Thank you. Thank you." The man nodded and called to the next person in line.

In a state of euphoria Dominico glided toward the ferry that would bring him to the Promised Land. There were no more sounds, only a blur of activity around him, of hope and sorrow, of anxiety and angst, of pathos and victory. Dominico Rossa passed every obstacle and was soon to step upon free soil, a free man. Perhaps he even earned his right to be equal, to walk with kings and queens without bowing or kissing anyone's hand. He was soon to be in America. A strange place, indeed.

It was a slow ferry ride to Battery Park. At least it seemed that way to those who wanted nothing more than to touch American soil. The vast, New York cityscape crept closer, bouncing with every wave against the ferry's hull. Dominico heard the hustle and bustle that awaited him. Even the sound of music, faint, ethereal, found its way to his expectant ears. Or perhaps it was just his elated mind that could hear the singing of angels about him. He was sure that it was under some angelic guidance that he found himself here. In his heart he could feel the long journey end. He could feel the tugging of a new beginning, of a calling, of a fulfillment of his dreams. Then there was the irascible jolting born of his ties to *Campania*, to his family, to his history.

The ferry unloaded in Battery Park. The émigrés gathered before the great gates searching desperately for their loved ones. When the gates opened all became a chaos of embracing and clutching. The ever-present tears of sorrow and desperation became tears of joy and relief. Women were lifted off their feet and spun around in great whirls, their dresses flapping and twirling. Babies were kissed and held high overhead in the hands of awaiting fathers. Children clutched their parents' legs. Some children met their fathers for the first time, hiding shyly behind their mother's haunches.

Dominico was alone, surrounded by joyous chaos. He noticed the police peering into the reunited crowd like lions searching for the best prey among a herd of beasts. They circled, spinning their clubs around their wrists ensuring that none of these huddled masses stepped out of line.

The reality of his presence in America was sinking into Dominico's consciousness. There, all around him, were buildings large and small. Carriages clopped and creaked by in a steady stream. Occasionally, a motor car squeezed through the horse drawn buggies eliciting whinnies of protests before disappearing. Dominico had never seen a motor car, not even in Naples. He could no longer see the Statue of Liberty. The great vastness of the city was overwhelming. Here he would sculpt his life in stone that would last forever. Yet here the stone was an unknown, a shape he could not grasp. There was no beginning and no end. The very pulse of the city demanded that he have a place. He had no place. He was alone in the most dynamic place on earth. He had determined the course of his destiny, but now what was he going to do?

CHAPTER 3

…We think it is astonishing that in the midst of such hard times such hordes of a single nationality come to our country and get employment while our own manor born go hungry: and it is still more astonishing, as before stated, that unselfish and manly patriotism is so manifestly lacking in those who are paid to further the welfare and good of our country and the American People.

A.O. Nash, "Italian Immigration and the Irish,"
American Protective Association
Vol. 3, no. 1 (August 1896). Pp. 1253-5

He started the letter to Pratolina. He swore that he would write to her every chance he had. He would tell her of his adventures, keep her updated on his progress. Eventually he would let her know when he was ready to come home and take her for his wife.

Lately, however, his letters were wearisome, an incomprehensible weight. His life was a misery of defeats and setbacks far from the adventure he imagined. As for progress, it seemed he was walking backwards since stepping foot in New York. There was no progress to report, no money to speak of. In the last month or so Dominico found himself further and further from home. Every day the hope of a proud return to his village faded into the tenuous ether that held his dreams.

He sighed and tucked the unfinished correspondence into the box under his bed. Laying his weary body upon the musty, paper-thin mattress, he felt the rusty spring pinch him. The tattered blanket that curled around him smelled stale, as if kept in a damp tomb. Soon he would be forced to place Pratolina's blanket on top of the tattered, moldy remnants, adding insult to his discomfort. That such hallowed fabric should share space with filth was injustice, but the cold had no sympathy for sentiment.

"Hey, Dominico." Gabriello whispered from the bunk above, "you got a cigar?"

"No, go to sleep." Dominico did not feel like conversation, especially with Gabriello who was not very bright. Like most people of Gabriello's intellect, however, he thought himself a genius.

"Damn you, Dominico, why don't you start smoking like everyone else? It'll clear up your lungs from this terrible air."

"Shut up, Gabriello."

"What you mean, shut up? I don't tell you 'Shut up,' when you want to talk. What you mean?"

"I mean you've already asked that question and I've already answered it dozens of times. I want to be left alone. I want to think."

"Oh, you want to think, do you? What you want to think about in this god-awful place. You can't think here. You want to think about that little, dark-haired girl you left in Campania. You keep thinking on her you'll get blue balled. Then what'll happen, you blue balled and all."

"Shut up, I'm sorry I told you."

"The little boy, pining away for his lost love. How romantic..."

"Don't make me shut you up, Gabriello..."

"Don't make me shut you up, Gabriello..." the mocking echo no sooner reached Dominico's ears than he kicked the top of the bunk. He could feel Gabriello physically rise from the mattress and fall back down. Gabriello was laughing, though Dominico knew he had to be sore. He had kicked him hard.

"All right, all right, I'll leave you be." Gabriello conceded.

"Thank you."

Two minutes passed before Gabriello spoke again. "Dominico."

"What," exasperated, Dominico replied. It was no use. Once Gabriello started talking he could not be quieted. Without some wine in him he would talk and talk all night.

"Why'd you say you're not taking up smoking again?"

Dominico closed his eyes and pressed his head into the mattress, the springs creaked underneath. "I told you, Gabriello. I have more important things to spend my money on."

"Oh, like the wedding, I supposed." Gabriello giggled.

"Shut up, Gabriello."

Gabriello was not a bad sort. He was just talkative. He was one of those people whom his grandfather had warned about—the kind that talked constantly and said nothing. Nonno used to say that wise men speak because they have something to say. Fools speak because they have to say something. He claimed that that line came from some Greek philosopher, but Dominico forgot which one. Gabriello was in the fool category according to those standards, yet he was not a bad sort.

In fact, Gabriello was the kind who would give the shirt off his back if it meant helping a friend. He was processed on the same day as Dominico, though he came from a different ship. They met quite abruptly and Gabriello showed himself for the selfless person that he was.

The street outside the Barge office was a bedlam of activity. Families, long separated, came together. Tears mingled with laughter. Older women knelt and wailed, their rosaries aloft, thanking God for safe delivery across the sea. Peddlers mingled among the crowd, selling wares to the luckless greenhorns, intent on Americanizing them with American watches and American top-hats, American shoes. Some offered opportunities to become rich, all they had to do was give their money to an "investor" and the next week they would double what they deposited. To Dominico this seemed a fair exchange, and he certainly would have taken the man up on his offer had he enough money to get through the week.

Before a better deal could be made, one of the many men in blue uniforms approached, waving his club. The "investor" disappeared into the crowd. Such a strange country.

On the end of the pier were three men wearing leather jackets, work-boots and flat top hats. They smoked cigars and smiled through dirty teeth. They held signs that said, "Signore Castillo...*Agenzia Di Collacamento*." Dominico checked the yellowed card in his pocket. The name was the same. This was where he was to go. Even as he started walking, however, he lost sight of the men in leather jackets as hundreds of people with similar cards noticed them. It was not long before these people became a throng, calling and shouting, reaching over each other's heads in the hope of being noticed.

One large man pushed Dominico aside to get through the mob. Dominico, in his frenzy, was not about to be pushed aside. What if they had only so many jobs? He would miss his opportunity. That was not going to happen. He grabbed the man and pulled him backwards, unbalancing him for a moment. The man took offense at this and proceeded to curse at Dominico in some language that the young Italian did not understand.

It was then that Gabriello was squeezed between them, a warm smile on his face. He was a thin, small statured young man, with a beat shaped face. He was about Dominico's age but looked younger because of his size. Before Dominico knew what was happening, this young man embraced him as if they were long-lost friends. The large man grunted, growled something to the two young men, then went ahead to push his way through the crowd. Gabriello only smiled and nodded.

One by one the men and women were separated, given cards and led to wagons on the back of which they were loaded. Soon, all the wagons were filled. Being in the back of the mob, Dominico and Gabriello had to walk behind as they began their trek through the city.

Great buildings towered on either side of them. Dominico could only see slivers of the cold sky hanging like a great, steel curtain behind brownish red concrete. The gray was impenetrable. Dominico thought he would never again see the sun. From the many windows hung curtains. Laundry was drawn across the crowded streets on lines like spider webs. People on stoops drank and spit as the parade of tired, timid émigrés traveled past. For such a giant city everything seemed so crammed together. New York was an endless labyrinth of concrete, clotheslines, alleys and windows. Despite its vastness everything was packed so tightly that Dominico wondered if he could ever fit. He feared he would never find space enough in such a dense crust of the world.

Ahead of the caravan Dominico heard a cacophony of angry voices. They shouted and chanted, often in unison, the same words over and over. It did not matter that he could not understand the language. The voices raged in the universal language of anger and desperation. They were the voices of hundreds of people speaking out in simultaneous rage. Dominico heard only such voices in his dreams. He heard his fellow villagers gathered around the *Latifundo* shouting for justice as they trampled the statuary and fountains into the dusty earth. Then he would wake up and the voices were silenced. He never expected to hear such voices in this place, this greatest of the great cities, in this nation so full of opportunity. Yet the voices awaited him at the end of this long walk.

The caravan turned a corner, and a crowd came into view, lining the streets. This was the source of the angry chorus. Soon Dominico was amid this angry crowd. Furious faces crowded his existence, their teeth clenched, or their mouths wide. Soon, he was close enough that he was able to match the angry faces with the angry voices. The same faces he left in Italy stared at him now in America. They were the faces of hatred and resentment. Men and women, some holding babies in the cold, glared at him as if he'd done something wrong. They were poor, desperate, abused faces, hungry not just for sustenance but for justice. Dominico knew well the faces of poverty. They gathered on both sides of the street and shouted at the parade of émigrés. A chill went through him. The people waved great signs. Words like "dago" and "wop," "scab labor" were painted in red or blue on most of the signs, but Dominico did not yet know what these words meant. He did know that he was the source of their grievance. Somehow, without his knowledge or intent, he had wronged these people.

Men in blue uniforms held the rabid crowd at bay, sometimes striking them to the ground with short, black clubs.

The émigrés were spit upon, menaced with sticks and chains. Rocks were thrown, one cutting into Dominico's forehead. One old man broke through the line of blue uniforms and grabbed a terrified émigré. He shouted in the man's face, "no better'n the niggas! No better..." and he spit in the man's face before being clubbed and pulled away.

This was not what Dominico pictured when he thought of America. 'How could such anger and hatred exist in such a wealthy place?' he thought as he dabbed the blood from his face.

The caravan was led into a gated area. The angry crowd could still be heard, but the rocks and spit could no longer reach them. Dominico stared at the rabid crowd until the gates closed. Something was very wrong. Somehow, he felt guilty, as if he had perpetuated a grave injustice. The sound of the gate closing was, to Dominico, the sound of a prison. Was that where he was? In prison for having committed some unknown crime. When he faced forward, he became aware of Gabriello clinging to him like the frightened children in Battery Park. Gabriello had been clinging to him since they encountered the mob.

"Let go. What are you doing?" Dominico shook the young man loose. He did not even know the man's name.

Gabriello only pointed and stared into the distance. All around them were men in dirty clothes. Their skins were various shades of brown, some almost coal black. Dominico heard of the dark-skinned people of Africa but had never actually seen the race. He was fascinated.

Gabriello, however, was frightened. "I'd heard stories of Black men who steal babies." He trembled.

Dominico smiled, "You're not a baby, are you?"

Gabriello swallowed hard.

"I don't see any babies here. I suppose they are here looking for work, just like us. From the look of their clothes, they work pretty hard." Still, Dominico was ill at ease around such alien faces--hungry alien faces.

"Yeah, pretty hard." Gabriello nodded but would not take his eyes from the Black men.

Once the gates were closed, a man in denim stepped onto a tall pallet and began to address the crowd. Another stood beside him and translated into a southern dialect of Italian that was easy for Dominico to understand.

The crowd was informed that they were all under the employment of Douglas Cannery Inc. They were temporary labor, but if they worked hard, they would be considered for full time employment. Their assignments were on the cards that were handed to them at the pier. The rules were simple. They were to show up for work at six in the morning, a half-hour lunch at one, dinner at seven and then to bed. Board was provided, including a bed, blanket and footlocker. Meals would be provided. They would be paid at the end of their term. Until that time there was no reason to leave the cannery. Judging by the angry crowd outside, that option was unrealistic, anyway.

Now, over a month later, Dominico felt like he always worked for Douglas Cannery. The furious chanting from the angry crowds on the wharf was a continuous din. They shouted epithets through the tall, chain link fence that was his dreary fortress. *Campania* was like a dream, something or someplace he had invented to break away from the rigors of his job.

Billy Boy Sullivan was his supervisor, but he could not understand a word the man said. It was all very well. Mr. Sullivan took special pride in screaming at his "dago" laborers. He derived just as much satisfaction by yelling in the face of his "nigger" laborers. The niggers, as Dominico came to know them, could understand the venomous words that emanated from Sullivan's lippy mouth. They rolled their eyes and looked impertinent. At that they would be kicked and then "docked" a certain amount from their pay for insubordination. Dominico, however, could not understand Sullivan's insults and was thus able to avoid such punitive measures.

The work was not difficult to understand regardless of the language barriers. Since Dominico was broad shouldered, he was assigned to the docks. There he unloaded whatever arrived to be processed in the cannery. "Processed." It was interesting how the same word was applied to Dominico when he entered this nation as was used for the bloody hog carcasses he unloaded from the trucks. Sometimes a load of fish would come in, also to be processed. The smell lingered as only the most meager of washing facilities was provided for hundreds of workers.

Dominico was grateful, however. After all, he had the opportunity to work outside. Never mind that the work was mind numbing, back breaking and insulting to a skilled craftsman. The damp cold of the New York winter pierced his very spine, an experience he never had on even the coldest days in *Campania*. But it was outside. For that, young Dominico was grateful.

Gabriello was not so lucky. He was slight of frame and therefore given a job cleaning the refuse that was left after the products were sufficiently pulverized for the canning process. The scraps he peeled up from the muddy floor, from under the worker's feet, were recycled into the canning process. Gabriello swore he would never again eat canned meat again. It was not long before Gabriello's health started to fail. His eyes were sunken and the bones in his wrists protruded from his parchment thin skin. His skin, once such a glorious bronze, was now the color of the sickly, gray sky. Wherever he went, a persistent and deep cough went with him.

Life in the cannery was drudgery of the worst kind. More filthy conditions could not have been invented for the processing of food. Vermin were often ground into the gears, making the mechanisms fail. More often they were ground into the food and released into the unsuspecting market. Those who worked inside were rarely exposed to what little sun would shine through the New York sky. Everywhere was damp, the floor, the walls, dripping yellow water from the ceiling. Dominico knew that there was not a healthy inch of space in the whole cannery.

And those voices beyond the fence? They were the voices of former employees of Douglas Cannery. Ailing and dying from the putrid conditions in the cannery, rewarded only with wages that barely kept their families fed, they tried to improve conditions. They complained to their bosses. They protested. At every level they were shut down and silenced. Then, they decided they would stop working until pay and conditions were improved. At that point, they were cast to the street.

To Dominico such an idea seemed radical and bold. Imagine if everyone in his *Paesera* refused to work until Don Alfredo treated them well. He would most certainly shoot every one of them. But could he? Indeed, not if everyone acted together. Dominico remembered the secret meeting, the promises. He remembered the assault on his work yard, and the promises broken as his family was destroyed. That the employees of Douglas Cannery possessed more tenacity than his countrymen back home impressed Dominico.

"How are they feeding their families?" Dominico asked one older man who was filling him in on the conflict.

"They're not. And Douglas has it set up with some here who help bring in workers from other places. He has connections in Italy. Those are the guys you fell in with. He uses us until the people are sufficiently hungry that they're begging for their jobs back. Then he'll hire them back for less than he was originally paying them."

"What about us?"

"We get thrown to the street." He said with as much emotion as he would have spent saying the world is spinning.

Dominico learned that people were hired to bring in the Black men from the south to work in the factories. That's where they came from. Many of the Italians came to call them Moolies, among other things. Dominico was warned to beware of the Moolies as they were a violent and untrustworthy race. He had no choice but to believe what he was told. Moolies did not interact with dagos, so he had no first-hand knowledge of the matter. He did, however, know that his father might say, "I guess those people on the other side of the fence, the one's calling us wop and dago, think that we are a violent and untrustworthy race." He put the thought out of his head. There was so much to learn about this country.

And the voices outside the fence lulled, quieter and quieter, in the cold.

"Come on, Dominico! What's on your mind?"

Dominico returned from his musings. Gabriello's pale, sunken face hung upside down from the bed above. He looked like a gray, frowning bat. "What do you want?"

"I've been talking for fifteen minutes, and you haven't even told me to shut up once. Something's on your mind. Out with it."

Dominico turned over, clutching his blanket and making a pillow from the crook of his arm. "Leave me alone, Gabriello. I don't want to talk right now."

A surprising silence lingered, but Dominico never heard the springs of the bed above him creak. Gabriello was still hanging there, waiting.

"Gabriello."

"Yes."

"I think today's my birthday." Dominico was off by two days. He had already turned eighteen years old.

CHAPTER 4

It was a bitter, cold morning when Dominico and Gabriello were cast to the street. The sky, a sickening, dirty gray hung like a shadow between the buildings. Spurs of icy rain bit Dominico's flushed face. The ground was covered with a matted carpet of snow stained a yellowish brown by the city's filth. An angry wind wailed through the buildings, challenging those who cried for warmth.

Dominico's clothes were not fit for the task of protecting him from the biting cold. His shoes were thin and worn, clothing tattered. His only saving grace was the wool blanket given to him by his beloved. He wrapped the blanket around his shoulders and neck and coiled his red, callused hands into its folds.

Gabriello frowned next to Dominico. His clothing was not much better, and his skin was certainly thinner. He was wasted by his toils and by the invisible bacteria that invaded his body. His eyes, sunk into black and swollen sockets were those of a man struggling to sustain his soul.

They were not alone. Hundreds of émigrés walked aimlessly around them. They had done their jobs well. The strike was over. Not only did the work get done, but the strikers were forced to accept unconditional surrender. They returned to the cannery with only a fraction of the pay they were making before going on strike. Somewhere, high in the offices overlooking the cannery, men in clean suites and manicured hands were drinking a round of scotch and nodding with satisfaction as they watched their workers, their flesh, enter the cannery gates.

They walked through the gates like a defeated army. Their heads were bowed, shoulders stooped. Without a sound they walked past the throng of exiting émigrés. Quick, narrow glances betrayed the hatred that the defeated felt for the scabs. After making eye contact a few times, Dominico knew that he was hated, and hated for good reason. He and his fellow countrymen had unwittingly taken food from the mouths of children. They had robbed the strikers of hope and of the certainty of victory. He wondered how much better the lives of this dejected army would have been if they were able to force the suits to give in to their demands.

"So, where do we go from here?" Gabriello whispered against the wind.

"Super told us that *Il Padrone* would have our pay. We go to him. Don Castillo."

"Where's that?"

"I think this way." Dominico held a small, hand scrawled map. "Mulberry and Broome Street."

They walked together. The ice and rain fell against them.

Mulberry Street was a sea of activity. The snow and inclement weather forced much of the businesses inside, but crowds of people still scoured the dirty streets and cluttered sidewalks. Some intrepid entrepreneurs sold their wares on the sidewalks, the only space available to them. Men pushed carts along the muddy road and set them up where they could. Others clustered around burning barrels and warmed their hands, conducting business under the gaslight posts. The brownish buildings rose five or six stories high. Women stood on iron fire escapes, desperately pulling their laundry from the icy rain. They shouted out open windows to their husbands or to their children, giving directions and cursing. Women on the street haggled and shouted with the men in the stores, their arms waving with fury. Horse drawn carriages clomped and sloshed their way along the streets, occasionally splashing an unwary pedestrian.

At first glance the people were unkempt. Ragged clothes hung loose on their backs. Jackets and sweaters and breaches revealed patches and pale fabric where the cloth was thread-bare at the elbows or the knees. Dominico's first feeling for the ragged people of Mulberry Street was disdain. He never expected people to be dirty or tattered in America. The wealth of this country was so ingrained in his mind that even after three months of squalor he still perceived the poor as failures in a land of plenty.

Then Dominico looked at himself. Dirty, tattered clothes wrapped in an unwashed blanket. His feet were pushing against the thin leather of his shoes. Failures, indeed.

Occasionally, however, well-dressed men and women walked by. They were not bothered by the cold as their jackets and top hats were sufficient for the cold. In their gloved hands the men wielded canes, though Dominico did not see a single one of them limp. The women often carried neatly wrapped packages. The well-dressed rarely stayed on the street long. They were walking from one area to the next. Perhaps they were there to visit a tailor of quality or to purchase items only found in Little Italy. Regardless, they stayed only long enough to conduct their business and get out before their clothes were dirtied.

It was the children who carried the bulk of the dirt. They sprang from side streets and alleys, throwing muddy snowballs at each other. Some were barefoot. They frolicked, unconcerned in their condition. Older children, however, appeared more severe, the boys doing their best to look like hardened men. They wore their jackets open, or half buttoned, and their flat hats pulled low over their foreheads. Each boy, even the youngest, stared at Dominico as if he had insulted them in some way.

Dominico said nothing. He was not much older than them and did not feel that it was his place to stare into their eyes.

He wished only to walk by without conflict and find his pay. Gabriello was uninterested in the goings on around him. He had developed a cough and was doing the best he could to keep himself breathing in this hellish air.

Soon, they found their place. *Castillo Imbarcazioni.* "Castillo Shipping" was etched in English and in Italian on the great, glass window. Dominico and Gabriello entered. The room's warmth tingled against their frozen ears and cheeks.

"Signore?" said a Black bearded man. He sat behind an oak desk which was covered with paper.

Uncertainty clear on his face, Dominico stepped forward. "We were told to come here to receive our pay."

"Who told you?" The black bearded man's voice was gruff and accusatory.

"We come from Douglas Cannery. We were told that you held our pay."

"Your names."

Dominico Rossa and Gabriello Bardetti." Dominico said, pointing to his emaciated friend. "I worked on the docks and Gabriello worked with the cleaning crew."

The black bearded man mumbled some as he shuffled papers around his desk in what Dominico perceived to be a senseless circle. He finally found a small, black book. Inside was a list of names. "Hm, hm, hm." The black bearded man pushed his finger into the book, and then tore out a page. He continued to leaf through until he tore out another.

"Here you are. Rossa and...yes...Bardetti." He put a monocle in his eye and turned to a big, clunking machine sitting precariously on the edge of the desk. After punching the machine with his broad fingers, he reached under the table and picked up a metal lockbox from which he pulled some bills and coins and threw them on the table. On top of the bills, he slammed a piece of paper making a loud thump with the flat of his hand. "Sign here. You can sign your name, can't you?"

"*Si*," Dominico said. "How much is our pay?"

"Ten dollars apiece."

Gabriello lifted his weary head while Dominico's jaw dropped. "That's impossible. We were contracted at ten dollars a week. We were there for three months. That should be about hundred and twenty dollars."

The black bearded man's eyes narrowed. "Are you questioning me, *ragazzo*?"

"No *signore*, but there must be a mistake."

"Do I look like a man who makes mistakes?"

"No, *signore*, but..."

The black bearded man grabbed the pieces of paper from his pocket and ripped a tape from the adding machine. "Look... you make ten dollars a week. You owe Douglas Cannery for the room and board for three months. That's fifty dollars. You owe Don Castillo a finder's fee, plus a fee for holding your pay for three months. So, Don Castillo is good enough to charge a flat fifty percent of your total wages. That's sixty dollars. That leaves ten dollars. *Buon Giorno*." The black bearded man turned and knocked on a door behind him. A large man, seemingly cut from the same oak as the desk, strolled through the door.

"Come on, Gabriello." Dominico tugged on the little man's sleeve. "We've been taken, that's all."

The cold scratched their faces like nails. Dominico pulled the blanket across his neck, but Gabriello just stood there. He held the ten dollars between his boney fingers and stared at them. A tear fell from his swollen right eye, then the tears streamed down his face in a torrent. Steam rose from his tears into the frosty air.

"Come, Gabriello. We'll find a place to stay and find work. We'll be fine." Dominico held his friend by the shoulders. "We'll be fine. We'll find work. Look at all the businesses here. We'll find work. Come on."

Gabriello nodded and followed, folding the money and placing it in his pocket.

There was no work to be found. In many areas the moment Dominico opened his mouth he was known to be an outsider, a *Napolitano* who did not fit in with the *Siciliano* on Prince Street or the *Pugliano* on Hester, or *Calabrese* on Mott between Grand and Broome. They were not *paesani*, therefore they were not considered for work. Everywhere they were turned away. Once they were chased from the store by an old woman with a broom.

Even where they did fit in, on Mulberry, south of Kenmore, they were turned away. Only, they were turned away with sadness, appreciative nods and apologies. Some families gave them food. One old man gave Gabriello his own coat. There was simply no work for them in the middle of winter. Come back near spring and things would pick up. Wherever they went they found closed doors.

As for a place to stay, ten dollars bought them a damp room in the back of a tanner shop. There the two young men slept in a drafty, pipe cluttered storage room. Dominico did not sleep, but clutched his blanket close and hoped that tomorrow would find him solace. Gabriello cried until sunrise.

Sunrise could be discerned through the wide, drafty cracks in the walls. Gabriello was the first to rise. Dominico rose when he heard his friend moving.

"Where do you want to look, today?" Dominico smiled. He bit into a piece of fatty, charity sausage.

"Home...I'm going back home." Gabriello groaned, staring at the loose floorboards. "At least when I die in the streets at home someone will recognize me and take me back to my family. Here I'll only be thrown away with the garbage." He looked up and stared into his friend's eyes with as much fortitude as his illness wracked eyes could communicate. "I'm going home, Dominico."

"You can't go home. You just got here. Come on, we'll find work."

"There's no work. There's no mercy here. I'm going home." Gabriello stepped out of the room and into the tanner's workroom. Dominico followed him out.

"Come on, give it a chance. We only just got here." Gabriello had become the only constant in his life. Though he was ill and fatigued and only a fragment of the energetic, charismatic young man he had met at port, he was still a pleasant reassurance that Dominico did not have to go through this experience alone. Now his only source of comfort was abandoning him.

"You give it a chance, Dominico. You're stronger than I am. I'm going home." He stepped out onto the street. The mud was frozen solid and powdered with fresh, white snow. Gentle flakes settled upon Gabriello's jacket as he walked back to Hudson Bay. The clean snow made the city shine. It was beautiful for those who could see it. Gabriello could not see it. "Good-bye, Dominico. I hope you get to marry that *la tua ragazza*."

Dominico chose not to pursue. The plainness of Gabriello's words convinced him that his friend's mind was made. There was no desperation, no anger, no fight. Only a stiff and stolid resignation as Gabriello disappeared around the corner and out of Dominico's life forever. Their friendship only lasted a few months, but for the rest of his life Dominico would wonder what became of Gabriello, his first friend in America.

CHAPTER 5

Cecilia sat next to the grave as Dominico stared, unblinking into the diary. He was consumed by it. As he read, Cecilia noticed his back become straighter, the color returned to his skin. His eyes remained sad, but an inner strength restored their dark color. He was becoming a man again in the pages of a diary closed long ago, in his boyhood.

"What does this mean?" Dominico's eyes dried, the streaks of dirty tears traced dark stripes down his face. "Here she keeps talking about a secret. What is her secret?"

"Dear Dominico." Cecilia straightened her collar. "Your arrival here may very well be fulfilling a dream that she had so many years ago. You will know the secret but know it from her own words as you should have heard it from her own lips."

Dominico turned the brittle page with his bandaged hand and continued reading.

Though the tanner was good enough to allow Dominico to stay in his storage room without pay, the cold and exposure to the elements were exacting a miserable toll. Every day

Dominico walked the cold, wet streets, his shoes soaked with icy, fetid water. In the evening, he made a pallet in the drafty storage room only to wake the next morning, don damp clothes and start the process again.

His desire for work carried him throughout the city. It was not long before he learned of the boundaries in which he was expected to remain. Within a few blocks he was in areas in which the denizens did not know his language and looked upon him as trash. From some neighborhoods he was literally chased by men wielding sticks and throwing epithets.

Christmas was approaching and the city was decorated in greens and reds. Store windows depicted bucolic winter scenes that were alien in this great, concrete canyon. Miniature pine trees and cottages were covered in pure white snow. The windows flickered from candles inside. Rolling hills stretched to touch a clear, star lit sky with one great star in the middle. Some store windows had a functioning train that circled the tiny villages. Little wisps of white smoke drifted from the miniature smokestacks. Such a place as this could only exist in the window of a store in a great, brown, crowded city.

Dominico did not know how many days there were until Christmas. He had long since lost track of monotonous time. That is, he lost track until the day he heard about the strike.

Dominico found himself in front of a bakery hoping for a handout of bread. At the end of the night the bakers would discard loaves of bread that were too old, and Dom learned to harvest this bounty. On this day, an unusually sunny day, two men stood at the doorway. One of them mentioned a strike in Pennsylvania. Some minors had decided that their working conditions were too dangerous considering their compensation. They were refusing to work.

Refusing to work! Dominico asked how far away this Pittsburg was. The men laughed and pointed in a direction. They informed him that he did not want to work in the mines. He would be better off begging for scraps of moldy bread—better off and healthier. But Dominico hungered for work not only for sustenance, but for a sense of being that he had not felt since leaving home. If he could work, if he could make his way, he knew that everything would be okay. He had known that at some point he could save up enough money to join his Pratolina and make her his wife. He decided that he would not stay in America as this was nothing like a home to him. It was more like a lonely purgatory, the penance he was paying for loving the wrong woman, the price he had to pay for the Heaven of her arms. If he could only get ahead, put some money aside, he could leave this purgatory and return to his village a man of respect. It did not matter whether he earned this money from stonework or from digging for coal. He needed to right his path.

That was when the feeling struck him. Vertigo spread through his limbs, starting with his legs. He dropped his bread and reached out for the nearest wall.

"Hey, you alright?" One of the men asked, reaching out to steady him.

"Yes, I'm all right. I've just been walking all day and I'm tired."

"You better sit down here."

"*Grazie*." Dominico sat and weakness overcame him. His peripheral vision blurred, and an immediate weight of fatigue overwhelmed him.

"You don't look so good, Dominico. You better go on to bed and get some rest."

"Yes, rest. That's all I need. I'll be fine in the morning."

He was not fine in the morning. Fatigue had evolved into ague that pulled at and cramped his muscles. His joints became swollen and stiff. Every movement hurt. Every sound pierced through him.

The tanner looked in on him and asked if he was sick.

"I don't know."

"I don't want my family getting sick. If you're sick, you're gonna have to leave here. Go to one of the shelters. They'll take care of you."

"I understand. I think I'll be all right if I just get some rest."

When the fever set in that night, he knew that there would be no rest. He understood and appreciated the tanner's wishes. Dominico had no desire to spread this illness to the tanner's family, but he could not move. He could not sleep, yet he could not lift his head or get out of bed. The fever made him sweat, the frigid air made him chill. Between the heat of his body and the chill of the air he shivered yet burned.

The tanner, however, was insistent. If the boy was sick, he had to go. He would not risk his family. He lifted Dominico from the pallet, helped him gather his belongings then led him to the door. "I hope you get well, Dominico. It's nothing personal." The tanner's eyes showed sympathy, but no remorse for sending the boy into the cold.

At some point Dominico found himself stumbling through the streets of the city, Pratolina's blanket wrapped around him. The icy wind buffeted him while he shuffled on spongy legs. The tanner had mentioned a shelter, but he did not know where it was. From his confusion he could only recall the presence of a church. It was a shaky recollection, or it may have been a delusion, some cruel joke of the mind. Dominico made his way up the street. With every step a jarring pain rushed through his body.

No one offered to help him. His stammering and crooked walk was of no significance on the same city streets as drunkards and prostitutes. Instead, he trudged with only one thought in mind. The church. In the church he would find help. That was what a church was for.

"Young man...young man." The voice was far away.

Dominico opened one swollen eye just enough to see. A tall, older man stood above him. He was wearing black with a white collar. A priest. His was the universal garb of the priest.

Dominico forced both eyes open and strained his ears to hear what the holy man was trying to say. He could not understand him, but his fevered brain could not figure out why.

"Young man...are Ye' all right?"

Dominico shrugged. He could not understand.

"*Italiano*?" The priest asked.

"*Si*." Dominico would have smiled if he had the strength.

The priest stood and shook his head. He continued with the same unrecognizable language. "Young man, ye've come to the wrong place. Do you understand? Uh...*capeesh?*"

Dominico shook his head.

"This is an Irish Church, you see. Irish...uh...*Irlandese*."

Dominico understood the word but could not grasp the meaning.

"Oh, dear...you don't look so good. Come, I'll help you." The old priest took Dominico by the arm and lifted him the best he could. Dominico was sick, but he had lost nothing of his stone-like weight at this point. After leading his patient into a back room, the priest said something to another who left the room. Dominico felt nauseous, but there was nothing in his stomach to satisfy his need to vomit. Instead, he was overcome with dry spasms as his body tried to expel something that did not exist in his body.

It was not long before another priest entered the room. This one was older, but his skin was darker, his cheeks ruddy, his eyes mild but not without strength.

"*Come ti chiamo*?" the priest asked with a smile.

"Dominico Rossa. *Sono un intagliatore di pietre. Hai un lavoro?*

"No, Dominico." The priest turned to the others. "His name is Dominico; he's a stone carver. He asked me if I have work for him."

The group of priests gathered around the young man and shook their heads, sad eyes betrayed their expectations.

"Help me bring him to Saint Joseph's, Father Carmichael."

The tall priest took Dominico under one arm while the kindly priest took Dominico's other. Upon being raised Dominico began to dry-heave once again. He would do this four more times before being carried across the street to Saint Joseph's church—the Italian church.

CHAPTER 6

> …Steerage passengers from a Naples boat show a distressing frequency of low foreheads, open mouths, weak chins, poor features, skew faces, small or knobby crania, and backless heads. Such people lack the power to take rational care of themselves; hence their death-rate in New York is twice the general death-rate…
>
> Edward Alsworth Ross
> "Italians in America,"
> Century Magazine, vol. 87

Dominico's first memory after stumbling into the church, the first real memory unencumbered by the distortions of a fevered mind, was of a room full of sad people. They were people whom he did not know, but he felt for them in their sadness, whatever it was.

He was too weak sustain concerned about much of anything. His muscles were sore, and his head ached. Racked with pain, he turned over, grunting as he moved.

"Mama, he's awake." He heard in the distance.

A hand touched his forehead. "*Lode a Dio*. Blessed Mother Mary has spared this young man."

"Can you hear me?"

Dominico swallowed hard and nodded.

"I'm Rosella Schiaparello. This is my daughter, Giulianna. Do you remember us?"

He shook his head and closed his burning, bloodshot eyes.

"Giulianna, go get him some water. Are you thirsty? Of course you are. Go get him some water. You've been very sick, *Signore* Rossa."

The young woman, Giulianna, held a cup of water to his lips. "Sleep," Dominico said, then closed his eyes.

He awoke again in the same room.

"It's a terrible loss. A terrible loss." A man in the corner of the room said. He was a robust and red man with leathery skin. There was an affect about him that reminded Dominico of his father. He did not look anything like Enrico Rossa, but how he stood, how he looked through the corner of his eyes. Enrico did that when he was thinking.

"Wh...wh...what?" Dominico asked.

The leather faced man turned to Dominico as if he were involved in the conversation all along. "Giuseppe Verdi...he's dead. Died today." Then the man offered a brief smile. "But it looks like you're going to live. It's been touch and go. Rosella!"

The older woman entered the room. It was dark and a gas lamp burned yellow in the corner. When she stood under the yellow gas lamp she did not seem as old, but her eyes lost nothing of their kindness.

"It looks like you are going to be all right. It finally took. Bepe, go get *Signora* Marset. Go now, go get her." A young boy ran from the room.

"Where am I?" barely audible.

"You're here in the Schiaparello home." The leather faced man said. "I'm Dante, this is my wife, Rosella. Giulianna, my daughter, is holding the rag. Bepe, my youngest son has gone to get *Signora* Marset. She treated you. Now she can come back and remove this smelly concoction from the room."

"How?"

"Father Zulo brought you here. You ended up in Saint Joseph's a couple of weeks ago. You've been in and out of a fever since. Didn't think you would live this long, let alone survive."

"*Malochio!*" the course voice of an ancient woman creaked from the door. "Someone very, very bad gave you their evil gaze."

"*Signora* Marset," Dante winced as she spoke, "You're going to take all this stuff away now, huh. You're going to take it away. It stinks up the place worse than ever."

"Quiet you atheist germ! This is the only medicine that would cure the boy!" Marset screeched through her parched lips. Dante winced again, rubbed his eyes, and mumbled as he turned away.

"You don't pay any attention to that vile man. He's an atheist and an anarchist."

"I'm not an anarchist!"

"He's a damned anarchist and an atheist. He doesn't believe in anything. You don't listen to that man. You listen to me. I'm *Signora* Marset, but you can call me *Mama* Marset. I like you. You can call me *Mama*." *Mama* drew the sign of the cross in olive oil on his sweaty forehead. "You'll be just fine, now." She then took a bowl with black, malodorous contents and threw them out the window on the other side of the room. A cat yowled in anger. From the open window a frigid wind blew in, reminding Dominico that it was winter.

"That was your illness I just threw out. The holy oil's been collecting the blackness that touched your soul when you were touched by *il malochio*."

"*Mama mia*." Dante whispered and threw his hands into the air.

"Ah, my son. You're better I see." Another voice. A tall priest entered the room. "You probably don't remember me. I'm Father Giuseppe Rizzulo, but everyone here calls me Father Zulo." He placed his hand upon Dominico's head. "Good temperature. Not clammy. That's good. Many prayers have gone into your recovery, young man."

"OK, everyone out," Rosella called out. "Everyone out but you, of course, Father Zulo and *Signora* Marset. Everyone else out. Leave this boy some time to rest."

It was not long after opening his eyes that Dominico regained the bulk of his strength. He insisted upon sitting at the dinner table with the rest of his adoptive family. It was good being part of a family again. In this case, an extended family. Three families lived under the Schiaparello roof. There was simply very little room in the vast city of New York for Italians. Dante and Rosella Schiaparello belonged to an aid society that some say was founded by Sister Francis Xavier Cabrini herself. They had four children: Dante III the oldest, Gianna the oldest girl, Giulianna the next girl, and Giuseppe, called Bepe, the youngest. Gianna was married to a man named Garibaldi Desouza. They had one baby, Henry. Garibaldi's Mother and three sisters lived with the Schiaparello's. Geraldo Santogiorgio was a friend of Dante. He, his sister Alva, his two children Santo, Gregorio, and Alva's child Franki also lived there.

This was a crowded living arrangement even though the Schiaparello's apartment was larger than the standard. The rooms were divided much like Dominico's little cottage in *Villa De San Giuseppe*. Dante and Rosella had a room of their own. Curtains were set up for Garibaldi, Gianna and the baby. Then another curtain was set up to separate the men from the women and young children. Dominico, after recovering, shared a pallet with the younger Dante, Santo and Gregorio. The four boys were similar in age, ranging from Dante at nineteen and Gregorio at sixteen. Franki and Bepe, not yet in their teens, shared a pallet at their feet. Somehow, Dominico took refuge in the presence of these sleep mates. He despised sleeping with Paulo back in Italy, it was a great comfort having the warmth of bodies next to him in the cold night.

Dominico found that the Schiaparellos were a fine, hardworking family. The women, except for Mama Desouza and Rosella, worked in a textile factory. At night they carried bundles of garments home from the factory and continued their work sewing buttons on shirts and pants. This was called piece work. The more buttons they sewed to garments the more money they made—at least theoretically. The irony was, as the women became more efficient with their sewing and were able to produce more the supervisor lowered the price per piece or increased the requirement. The younger boys were then taught to sew to increase production, but to no avail. The family never made any more money.

Dante was the undeniable head of the household. He was a short, stocky man with years of labor pressed into his skin, and years of bitterness pressed into his heart. He was bitter with the 'capitalists' who forced him from his family for twelve to sixteen hours every day. Even Sunday, the traditional day of rest, was lost as his bosses often 'strongly suggested his presence at the work site'. A skilled tradesman, a carpenter, he made his living hauling and stacking materials to construction sites. In all his years in America, had not set one frame, he had not erected a single dwelling for pay.

All the men worked, and older boys worked. From Dominico's understanding, the household should have been larger had it not been for the premature deaths of the men who worked the factories, the tunnels, the dangerous construction sites. Papa Desouza died from black lung at age forty-five. Garibaldi's brothers all died in industrial accidents, one mauled by a rolling machine, another died while doing construction on the Brooklyn Bridge. Dante's own brother died in a cave-in while building the vast, underground railways of the New York Subway. There was no compensation for these deaths. Every lost body was one less chance at a better life.

"*Signore* Schiaparello," Dominico sat at the table and took his share of the bread and oil, a couple of slices of bologna and some lentils. "I'm ready for work."

"You're ready for work, are you?" Dante stared at the boy through his brow.

"Yes. I've taken advantage of your generosity long enough. I want to earn my keep."

"Are you strong enough?"

"Yes. I'm not what I was, but that's because I've only been running errands. Once I start working in stone again, I'll strengthen up. I just need someone to show me how to find work. Father Zulo said you might be able to put in a good word for me with the construction company."

"For what my word is worth. Tomorrow morning you will come with me if you are ready. I'll see what I can do."

"I really don't know how to repay you for your kindness."

Rosella caressed his hand and nodded with a kind smile. He could feel Giulianna brush against him as she stood to get some bread for the table. Her hip brushed his shoulder.

"There's no need." Dante leaned into the table. He raised his thick finger. "We must all come together if we are to get anywhere in this world. It is us against them, Dominico. Don't you forget it. If they have their way they'll have us in chains, building their damned city for nothing but breadcrumbs. Don't you forget it. There is one thing, however, that I want you to do." Said Dante

"What is it?"

"You will learn English. A man will get nowhere in this country unless he knows the language."

Dominico looked confused.

"Do you wish to be nothing more than the ignorant peasants that crowd this city?"

Dominico shook his head.

Dante said, "then from now on we speak English," but Dominico could not understand.

CHAPTER 7

Dearest Pratolina:

It is with the most heartfelt warmth that I write you today. I was sick for a long time, and that is why I was unable to write. I hope that you have not lost faith in me as I remain faithful and focused on our hopes. But, at last, I have a residence here in New York. Here is my address. I look forward to finally reading your words. Life is so difficult here in America, but word from you will fill me with hope and with pride for what I am here to achieve.

I have been taken in by some good people, Pratolina. Signore Schiaparello has taken me to his work and has helped me get a job. I'm not yet working in stone, but at some point, I'm sure I will be. He is also teaching me to speak in English so I can communicate like an Americano! Things are finally starting to work in my favor. It won't be long until I can put money aside and return for you.

I look forward to hearing from you, my Beautiful Darling.
Love

Dominico

The work was cold. A January frost penetrated the ground, making it like rock. The earth shattered as Dominico struck it with a long, steel pole. Chips of earth sprayed like stone under his deft chisel, only it was not stone, and it was not a work requiring skill. It was work requiring nothing more than muscle.

Signore Schiaparello helped the boy sign with the company he worked for. The foreman eyed the boy, his deep chest, broad shoulders showed through the layers of clothes he wore to stay warm. The foreman knew exactly the job he would assign to this strong-looking dago. Digging ditches through frozen ground was, to the foreman's eye, right up Dominico's alley. Italian labor was considered best for this torturous work as they accepted lower pay and were indefatigable as they pounded all day, their hands swollen, frozen, and cramped by the end of their shift. Some of the workers lost their ears, fingers and toes to the cold. Yet still they toiled and by God that ditch was dug. For Dom this was the most excruciating way to be reintroduced to work. His muscles were still atrophied from illness. Only a month earlier Dom could have wielded the steel rock breaker as if it were an extension of his own arm. Still recovering from idleness, his muscles ached after only a few, weak thrusts. By the end of the workday his arms, shoulders, and back screamed disdain for his labors. *Signora* Schiaparello would have rubbed lineament into his aching sinew, but Dom never complained of his pains. He had to work. There was no sense in people expending unnecessary concern.

"Put your back into it, ye dago bastard." The foreman cackled under his fur hat. "We're not payin' ye to pat the ground, we hired ye to dig a ditch." He continued.

Dominico understood little of what was being said, but *Signore* Schiaparello educated him to the terms "dago" "wop" "guinea." These were the words of the *Americani,* and they were meant to keep the Italian down, make him low. If the boss can make you feel like an animal, then he could treat you like an animal with minimal resistance. This was always the nature of Dante's lessons.

"Only it won't work in the end." *Signore* Schiaparello pounded his fist into the palm of his hand, his jaw jutting out. "If you abuse a human being he will respond like a human. He will be 'humane.' But if you abuse him and treat him like an animal, eventually...eventually he will respond like an animal and tear you to pieces."

Dominico spent a great deal of time listening to this weather-beaten man. He said things that Dominico knew ran through his father's and his grandfather's minds. However, they dared not speak. They dared not use such strong language back in *Campania* even to their own. Yet this man spoke of blood and hatred and violence every day without concern.

"The American businessman is playing a dangerous game with the lives of working men. In treating them like animals they are sowing the seeds of their own destruction. Can you imagine the wrath of a hundred thousand angry animals coming for you? That's the fate of the capitalist. A hundred thousand sets of teeth in their throats—or a hundred million."

The sky was black, and snow fell cold and wet, settling into their clothes as they trudged home at the end of the day.

"It's already started Dom. It's already started. Whenever the people begin to rise up the capitalists bring in the army to put us down. They club us and beat us and kill us, but we keep rising. Eventually all the guns in the world will not be able to stop us."

Dominico nodded, but did not know how to respond. 'Bring in the army?' he mused.

"You'll see, Dominico. There will be a revolution, the working class against the capitalist. I'm sure we will see it in our lifetimes. Then what's going to happen? If the people are made desperate enough, made hungry enough, made angry enough then we will bare our fangs and there won't be a force in the world that could stop us."

The apartment was not as cold as it was outside, but the family still had to gather around the stove to keep warm. The youngest were kept closest to the stove. The men stood at the back of the group.

"How was your first day at work, Dominico?" Giulianna smiled and poured steaming coffee into a cup and handed it to him.

"It went well."

"You're not taking on too much, are you now, Dominico. You were sick for a long time." *Signora* warned.

"No, no. *Sto bene*. It feels good to be working. Perhaps soon I'll be able to go back to working in stone."

"They'll never let you do that." Dante shook his head. "The skilled work is done by the Irish or the Germans."

"Papa, that's not true. Italian stone workers are considered among the best." The younger Dante claimed with a smile.

"Yes, they are. There are some Italians thrown in to make us think we can make it, but we can't. We're playing with a stacked deck."

"Would you like some more coffee, Dominico?" Giulianna smiled again.

"Oh, no thank you. This is fine."

"I'm sorry there's no sugar."

"This is fine."

Giulianna smiled and inverted her eyes. The girl was sixteen. She was pretty, with chestnut brown eyes, and round features. She was not beautiful, like Pratolina, but pretty. Dominico felt flushed.

The first chance he got, Dominico separated from everyone and wrote another letter to Pratolina.

"At least there are no bugs, and the rats are pretty much out of the question." *Signore* Schiaparello said as he sifted the ashes and started the stove the next morning. "When spring comes, we'll be competing with them for food and living space."

"Why are you here, *Signore*?" It took a while for Dominico to build the courage to ask this question. He had heard nothing from his self-appointed mentor but disparagement about this country. Why not return to Italy and make a living there. Instead, he stayed in this land for which he had nothing positive to say.

"I don't know, Dominico." Dante stared up at the gray sky. "There's no place else to be." He did not say another word until reaching the job site.

At the job site, some colored workers were waiting for instruction.

"This isn't good, Dominico. This is never good." Dante pointed at the black and brown faces.

"Why?"

"They come up from the south looking for work. If they come up during the winter that means they are especially desperate. They work for practically nothing."

"Now hear this!" A ruddy foreman stood on a pallet and addressed the waiting workers. "It seems that there's a sudden glut of labor." The foreman said. "Our employer, in his infinite good will has allowed these niggers to work in the ditches so they can feed their families. However, in order to do this the rest of you will have to accept a pay cut of ten cents a day."

"Son of a bitch!" *Signore* Schiaparello shouted. The crowd of workers glowered in a low rumble.

"Anyone who does not like it is welcome to draw his pay and leave." The foreman said in a calm voice. His eyes squinted with a sadistic smile. "Is there anyone who wishes to leave?" He scanned the crowd of workers. There was no response. "I didn't think so. The reassignments are listed on the board. Have a good day."

"Those bastards...those black bastards." People shouted.

"Mulatto...garbage."

Signore Schiaparello shook his head and picked up the iron rod to which his hand was fitted. "Every time. Every time."

"We'll have no trouble from ye, Shopparelli!" the ruddy foreman approached as if sneaking up on his prey. Dominico could only make out a little of what was said.

"Whata you mean?"

"We'll not have ye gettin' the rest of yer dago friends in a tizzy over this. Ye know where all yer dago friends are now, don't you? Ye'll go there too if there's any trouble from ye."

"No trouble comesa from me. You tella you boss, he makes trouble, not me. You tell him."

"Ye know where all yer friends are. Couple're in the ground, too, if I'm not mistakin'. You'll be wise to just keep yer mouth shut." The foreman poked his gloved finger into Dante's chest and glowered, sinister blue eyes flashing against the snow.

When the foreman turned away Dante said, "That son of a bitch doesn't know what trouble is. You see, Dominico. Animals."

The rising sun did nothing to take the edge off the cold. On this day, the sky was a deep, clear blue, unlike any sky Dominico had ever seen before, but the cold was almost intolerable. His gloves were a patchwork of spare cloth Giulianna had spent an evening sewing together. She presented them to him on his second day of work. She stayed up late to finish them in time. Dominico's fingers were numb from the cold, but the cloth gloves offered some protection from being burned by the frozen, metal rock breaker.

"Why don't you watch where the hell you're goin'!"

Dominico turned, a large man glowered over him. Dominico did not know how he offended. "*Scuzi*." He said and went about his business.

"Skyoozy? What the hell is skyoozy? You must be some guinea sonva bitch."

"Ah…" Dominico smiled, "No under…standa." He shrugged.

"No understand, huh. Ignorant guinea son of a bitch." The man shoved Dominico, causing him to fall into a ditch. "Don't walk so good either, huh." The big man laughed.

Dom did not expect to be pushed. He did not know the person standing before him and had no reason to expect a quarrel, let alone a physical confrontation. Despite his ignorance, he was embarrassed to be caught off guard and enraged by the man's caustic laughter. A low growl arose from Dom's throat. His unfeeling grip tightened around the rock breaker.

"Whatcha gonna do, wop? You gonna hit me wi' that pole? I don't think so." The large man lifted his clenched fists like a boxer ready for his first round.

"Dominico..." Dante drifted over to him and helped him to his feet. "This isn't the way."

Dom's teeth were gritted and his jaw set. This man underestimated how much muscle was locked in Dominico's shoulders. His rage compensated for the weakness of his convalescence. At that moment, this young man could have swung that heavy rock breaker as if it were made of cotton.

"If you do it, all your dreams come to an end. There's another way." *Signore* Schiaparello spoke in Italian. The big man did not understand. "If you hit him and break his head they'll kill you. If you want to fight you have to fight at the source. You have to hit their bankrolls."

Dante then faced the large man, still posed in his boxer's stance. "Excusa the boy. He'sa new here. He dona know the rules so good."

"Well, he'd better god-damned well learn. You learn him. You learn him quick." The big man strode away, victorious.

Dante glared at his back.

"This is the land of the free, Dominico. This is the job. We have to put up or our families starve. But we'll have our day, Dominico. We'll have our day.

CHAPTER 8

Dominico's red eyes froze on the fragile pages. The book was tiny in his shaking, battered hands.

November 17, 1900:
Where is Dominico? Where is my dear, sweet Dominico? His ship may well have sunk in the Atlantic for all I've heard. I don't imagine that he's turned his back on me. And I know that he would never turn his back on his own child. If only he knew. If only I could communicate with him, I could tell him of the new life that grows within me, the life that he put there. He's to be a father and he should know, but I don't know where he is. I feel his presence, but I can't reach him. We may very well be staring at the same star even as I write, but still, I cannot reach him. I await his first letter, breathlessly hoping that one arrives soon.

Yes, it must arrive soon, as there are others whom I must tell. So far, my belly is still flat but will not be for very long. I fear for the shame that I will put to my father. I fear Alfredo's reaction. But I revel in the fact that I bare the child of the man I love.

"A child?" Dominico could not close his eyes. "Cecilia, a child? I have a child."

She nodded and smiled, placing her hand on his shoulder.

It was the first warm day in America that Dominico experienced. It began as a conspicuous blue crack in the tattered, gray curtain. A thin, pale ray of light pierced the satin overcast. The blue fracture in the sky expanded until only patches of dingy cloud remained. A new revelation had fallen to the earth, a new covenant with God enjoyed by humanity as the sun peaked through the towers. The sun danced across the buildings, gilding them. Gray and brown and muddy sarcophagi glowed with the light of the Ascension. Windows, long closed, glittered like diamonds in a mosaic of stone and brick.

A shovel in his hands, Dominico pondered the blue. The gray in his soul cracked and disintegrated. Suddenly there was something there that hadn't been there for a long time. Something intangible. Something filled with vitality that made him feel, for the first time since his feet lifted from Campanian soil, that perhaps his dreams could come true. He wiped some grease from his face. The great, shining buildings were pristine, plastered against a perfect, blue sky. Marveling at the unexpected beauty of the city he inhaled—his first real breath in America.

Dante's shining eyes marveled more at Dominico and his reaction to the birth of a brand-new world. "Sometimes," his hand on Dominico's shoulder, "sometimes small miracles do happen."

Without taking his eyes from the sky Dom said, "I thought *Signora* Marset said you were an atheist."

Dante shook his head, "No, I believe in miracles. Miracles I believe in. I've even seen a few…"

"You lazy son's o' bitches! Get yer lazy, dago asses to work before I have you starving in the streets with yer mis'able, little dago children!"

Dominico jerked at the foreman's harsh voice. Dante never twitched. He climbed calmly into the ditch.

"Yes, young Dominico, miracles I believe in…"

"Fuckin' wops."

"…but as for God…if God exists, He has some explaining to do."

Dominico smiled and shook his head as he stabbed at the earth with the shovel. The things this man said, amazing things. "You expect God to explain himself?"

"Let's just say that I have greater expectations of God than I have of that son of a bitch." Dante pointed at the long-necked foreman. "If God's just another boss man, or worse, another *padrone* we're all better off being atheists."

Dante watched the foreman jot something on his clip board.

"But not you, Dominico. Not you. You stay a good Catholic." He smiled. His eyes held a wicked laugh.

The shovel swung and a wave of dirt flew. "Why are you so interested in me staying a Catholic?"

"Giulianna likes going to church with you." Dante did not look up. He focused on his work.

Dominico hesitated only a second then continued shoveling.

"What do you have to say about that?"

"I...well..."

Dante laughed and swatted the back of Dominico's pants with the flat of his spade. Dominico responded by dropping dirt on the older man's shoes.

"Oh, you're a spirited one after all."

Their laughter was interrupted by the foreman's whistle. The men on the work crew gathered around the foreman as the whistle communicated that he had something important to say. The foreman never communicated good news to the laborers, so the whistle was an ill omen.

The foreman stood on a crate of mortar and coughed for attention, a snake-like smile on his face. "Mr. Neal has jus' sent us word that we gotta have this pipe laid by Tuesday. That means that we're askin' volunteers to work on Sunday to finish the ditches. So, all o' yous is volunteers."

A clamor rose from the men.

"Calm down, calm down. It's not like ye've not been asked to work on Sundays before. This project is very important and needs to get done. We're already behin' schedule. Time is money."

"Our time isn't money." Dante said under his breath.

"What was that Shoparelli?"

"Uh...*signore*...I'ma sorry." Dante spoke English well. "Tomorrow is *festa*. Isa very important to us to attenda with our families. We can no work tomorrow."

"Well, in't that sweet." The foreman bared his yellowed teeth behind a sardonic smile. "This festi you talk 'bout's jus' gonna hafta wait. This ditch needs to be dug an it's gonna be dug. Capeesh! Now if you ain't gonna do it then we'll just fin' someone else to do it. Capeesh!"

All the men turned to Dante who scowled but conceded.

"Fine," the foreman clapped. "We'll see ya in the morning. Mr. Neal is feelin' 'specially generous today so he's giving yous the rest of the day off to be with your precious little faaamilies. In't that nice of him?"

Dante looked at his watch. Fifteen extra minutes. "By God, Dominico, miracles do happen just like I told you." Dante eyed the foreman walking away with his thin pursed lips and upturned nose. Then Dante looked at the pump that kept the ditch drained of water so the men could dig. His eyes narrowed.

As was customary, Dominico rinsed his arms in some of the draining water that spouted from the pump. Dante joined him, leaning the spade against the pump. Dominico noticed how close the spade came to the valve switch. Dante stared at the young man and offered a half smile.

"You want to see a miracle happen?" Dante spoke through his teeth.

Dominico eyes went wide, and he smiled as he realized what Dante was about to do.

Dante stood upright, picked up his spade and turned around without a care in the world. The spade's blade struck the valve switch, closing it. Dante and his young friend walked away without looking back. By morning, the ditch would be a flooded and muddy mess.

Festa was wonderful. The festivals held in Dominico's village were nothing compared to the merriment that happened on Mulberry Street that day. The street was alive with commotion. Vendors sold their wares on the sidewalks. The delicious scent of sausage and peppers, garlic and onion and bread were ubiquitous. High tempo music, mandolins and horns, drums and singing set the rhythm and melody of the street. Some men sang opera on the corner—some were even good at it. Most just let their voices fly, their breath smelling of wine, their eyes flashing with delight dancing around their smiling wives. Children ran, giggling through the adult's legs as though through some magic, dancing forest.

Dante and Dominico were just in time for the procession.

"*M'amore!*" shouted Rosella as the Schiaparellos circled around Dante and hugged him. "I thought you had to work today."

"You know, it's the craziest thing. We got there this morning and the whole worksite is flooded. Somehow the pump just let go and that whole lake just drained right into the ditches. Damnedest thing you've ever seen." Dante smiled and winked at Dominico. "Why if we tried to dig ditches we'd have drowned."

Rosella stared at them knowingly. "What did you do?"

Dante's eyes grew wide, and he shrugged, "I don't know what you are talking about. Just one of those things."

"You're lucky they didn't make you dig ditches anyway." She smiled and kissed her husband's leathery cheek.

"By the time we got there they had all their engineers trying to figure out how to fix the problem. They sent us ignorant wops home because we obviously don't know anything about engineering. Do we Dominico?"

Dominico shrugged. "Our aqueducts only lasted two thousand years."

Dante smiled and kissed his wife.

Giulianna sided up to Dominico and tapped him on the shoulder. "I'm glad you could be here. I…I can show you where all the best food is."

Dominico smiled and nodded. "Thank you."

She placed her hand at his elbow, barely touching him at all. "Look, the procession."

Banners crossed over the streets and hung from the fire escapes, waving in the wind. Giant, flowery vines entangled the brownish buildings. Men wearing their best suits strode down the street beating drums and clashing cymbals. Some played horns. Their chests were thick and round, bulging with pride as a stream of Italian flags flapped and clapped behind them. Some bold, older men in black shirts followed, waving banners. Garibaldi's army? Perhaps. At least that is what they claimed. They all marched to the music and the chanting, and the bad opera danced through the buildings.

Dominico and Giulianna strolled along the streets. A vendor was selling *zepolle* from his storefront and Dominico, for the sake of dignity, bought one for his companion.

Dozens of little girls in pink dresses walked along the street throwing confetti into the air.

"The queen of the festival is coming." Giulianna grimaced. "There. There she is...Oh..." Giulianna looked away. There, being pulled behind two nearly white horses sat Ula Castillo, Don Castillo's daughter. "She gets it every year." Giulianna smiled. Dominico shrugged. He expected nothing less.

"No, no, no!" Dante yelled and slapped his hands together. He was talking to a group of friends, most of whom were laughing. "Damned if you don't understand anything, Carlo. Listen to me...there...there's Dom." He grabbed Dom and pulled him into the group. "Young Dominico, he's just a young man and he can tell you. Tell him Dominico...go ahead, tell him." The rest of the group laughed except Carlo who was turning red in the face.

"I...uh...well..."

"You see, he agrees with me. You run along now, and you stay close. You see, when only one or two people control all the wealth where does that leave you and me? All we have is numbers, but numbers is enough to make a change..."

Giulianna pulled Dominico away from her father and continued to walk. Dom looked behind him and noticed *Signora* Schiaparello within eyesight, always within eyesight.

Fireworks went off in the distance. Some men and women walked barefoot down the street with the procession. They were walking backwards with their arms outstretched. Suddenly a cluster of people swarmed around them. Above them an icon of the saint was hovering, held aloft by select men, given the honor of carrying him. It was a task that was more difficult than it sounded. People clustered and grabbed at the saint. They tugged on the fabric of its robe, most pinning money to it, others just trying to touch. The money collected paid for the celebration, and hopefully for the next.

More fireworks. Firecrackers skittered across the ground upsetting the young horses. The older horses remained calm and stepped aside. Dominico had very little money, but he managed to pin a bill to the icon. He did not know if the saint would intervene on his behalf, but he felt that he could use all the help he could get. It was customary for his family to give at these celebrations, and custom was all that most of these people had left. It would have been a betrayal of custom not to give at least a little. As it was, he was ashamed the paltry amount he was able to give. He vowed that with his next pay he would make a larger donation to the church to make up for his transgression.

Behind the icon another band played on a flat cart that was being pulled by two slow donkeys. Dozens of people danced the tarantella. Young and old, their legs moved to the rhythm. They cheered and laughed.

Giulianna's eyes danced with the procession as they neared, her thin lips curled into a pleasant, whimsical smile. Dominico coughed and stuttered, but finally took her hand and led her to the street. They danced for the rest of the celebration. Danced the length of Mulberry.

Dominico smiled and laughed.

That night he wrote a letter to Pratolina. The most longing letter he had written so far.

CHAPTER 9

"What's wrong, Dom?" Dante asked, helping himself to another chunk of bread that he dipped deep into the olio.

Dominico frowned. It was not for him to ruin the evening meal with his sorrows. He hoped that his disappointment did not show, but how could it not? He was nothing but disappointment.

"I'm fine. I guess I'm just tired." He could feel the weight of the families' eyes on him. Concerned eyes...especially concerned were the large, kind eyes of Giulianna.

"Well," Rosella smiled politely. "As hard and as long as you work it's no wonder. It was just a few months ago that we were thinking about having the last rights administered for poor Dom, now you are out every day toiling in the cold and rain."

"The capitalists don't care about illness. They don't care if you die so long as you pull that last shift. Dig that last foot. If you die at the end of the week all the better. It saves them a week's wages." Dante, as usual, now owned the discussion. He often managed to squeeze his politics into most dinner discussions, a habit which the rest of the family found exasperating. This time, however, the divergence was more purposeful. Dante, over the last few months, learned Dominico's inner workings. He liked the boy. He was a good boy, but deep with much on his mind, as if he were reciting the words of a vast poem in his head. He could see that Dominico was uncomfortable as the focus of conversation, a position Dante did not mind at all. So, he stole the spotlight.

Dante knew that his young friend had the heart of a poet rather than the mind of a statesman. Oh, he hoped that Dom would come around. The boy was learning English. He was learning the ins and outs of being an exploited laborer in America, but he seemed slow in picking up on his mentor's brand of radicalism. To Dante, this was an invaluable part of an immigrant's education.

Dom, however, lacked the visceral anger that was the pulse of radicalism. He was not planning on being an American. He was intent upon making enough money to go back to his backward little village and be a man of respect. Dante knew that this was unlikely to happen, but Dom was intent on returning to his home. There could only be one answer to this mystery.

Dominico stayed out of political discussions. Not that he was uninterested. He just felt ill prepared to share the same discourse with a political powerhouse like Dante. Besides, there was so much more on his mind than mere politics. To Dom it was all the same, Italy, America. It was all the same.

Toil in America, toil in Italy. It amounted to the same sweat and fatigue. The only difference was that in America there was more toil to sweat over. For Dom this meant more opportunity to make money. For Dante it was more opportunity to be exploited.

Dante patted Dom's hand, "So, Dom, tell me. Is it a woman?"

Dinner was cleared and the bulk of the family was sitting down to do piecework. Frantic fingers stitched sewed buttons to shirts. Each morning *Signora* had a stack of shirts to deliver to the factory. The standard was raised once again, amounting to just over three cents per shirt, so the family had to work harder to clear the same amount of money.

Normally Dom would help sewing buttons on shirts, but this time Dante wanted to speak to him on the fire escape. There they stood, looking at the stars on this clear night.

Dominico did not want to answer, yet he wanted the truth to be known. Something about Dante's demeanor pulled the truth from him. Dante nodded and stared at the street below.

"Engaged to be married?"

Dominico shrugged. "I don't know. It's complicated."

"It always is."

"I've not heard from her. I've written dozens of letters. Then today you come in with an arm full of mail from the old country. I knew that there would be a letter from her, but there wasn't, and my heart just sank. I don't know anything anymore. This whole trip was for her."

"Well," the older man smiled and frowned at the same time. He had a queer way of doing that. "You know, women are fickle. They want one thing, then another. You've been away for a while. These things happen."

Dominico shook his head. "No. That's not it. There's got to be something else. She wouldn't just change her mind."

"You're young, Dom. You're very young still. You will learn these things."

Once again, his youth was used as an excuse to patronize him. This angered the young man, but part of him knew that Dante spoke from experience. He was older and wiser, more intuitive about the darker corners of life. Dom had to respect that, but he also resented it. When does a man earn the right not to be patronized by his elders? Regardless, he deferred to Dante's authority as the older man put his arm around the boy.

"You know, Dom, Giulianna's a fine girl. She'll be ready for marriage about the time that you are ready. You are the best worker I've ever seen. You'll always be able to support a family. We could arrange for you two to spend some time together. It's obvious that she fancies you and she's right here. She's a good cook and a loyal girl. You could do worse than to marry Giulianna."

Dominico smiled. "I'm honored, *Signore*. Really, but I hope you understand."

Dante nodded. "You have to follow this through. I know."

"Perhaps if I can send her a ticket, I can get her here. Then we can be married. We can always return when I've made enough money. She's the one I want to marry, *Signore* Schiaparello."

"Perhaps you can do that." Dante stared at the street. Don Castillo was down below on a stoop making some illicit deal. It was amazing how one person could pollute a community, Dante thought. "You really love this woman. Tell me, is she the woman of your dreams? Do you dream about her all the time?"

"Yes."

"So, she's the woman of your dreams?"

"Yes."

"Dominico, I'm going to share something with you that I'll never share with anyone in the family."

"Your confidence is safe with me."

"Do you think that *Signora* and I are happy?"

"Oh, yes. You two are very happy."

"Very true, Dominico. Very true. We are happy. Rosella is the woman of my life, and my parents were wise enough to see that and arrange the marriage. But she is not the woman of my dreams."

"*Signore*?"

"No, she is not the woman of my dreams. The woman of my dreams I've not seen for many years now. She's married and gone her separate way. For a long time, I was angry with my parents for not giving me permission to marry her, but it was for the best. You see, she's still the woman of my dreams, but she could never be the woman of my life."

"I don't understand."

"There will be two major loves of your life, Dominico. One is the woman of your dreams. Hopefully, she will come first. She will make you crazy with desire, make you dance in the clouds, but you can never marry her. You can only marry the woman of your life. If you make the mistake of marrying the woman of your dreams then you will destroy her in your heart, and then you will resent her. You will resent her for growing old and getting fat from bearing your children. You will resent her for not living up to your dreams. There's no way any woman can live up to our dreams, so over time she will diminish in your eyes.

"But the woman of your life. She will ground you. She will bare your children, and you will not mind that she is not Helen of Troy because you will realize that she is beautiful in and of herself, not because she's young and tight but because she makes you a man, completes you. She is the woman of your life. This girl in Italy. Perhaps she's the most splendid woman in the world. She's most likely the woman of your dreams. If so, she is never meant to be your wife. We should not marry the women of our dreams. If we are lucky, we marry the woman of our life."

"But I have to try, don't I? Otherwise, how do I know? I have to try."

Dante nodded. "I suppose you do."

The next day was the first in which it was warm enough to work without a shirt. Unfortunately, the company boss did not allow such exhibitionism on public streets. Summer was fast approaching and the work on the bank was going slow. This made the bosses angry and nervous, so all was not well for the laborers. They worked through many a Sunday. For a week straight they worked at night under gaslight.

"We need more help." Dante suggested to the foreman as he was criticized for lack of progress. "We are making more progress than any human being's I've ever seen in fifteen years. You don't have enough workers and that's why the work isn't getting done."

The foreman grunted and walked away.

The next day the laborers were summoned around the foreman who stood on a stack of palettes. A representative from the construction company that hired them stood on the palettes as well. The company rep was well dressed, donning a fedora made of straw. He stared at the ground, his hands in his pockets, and pursed his lips.

"It has become clear that our work force is inadequate for the expectations of the job. For this reason, Mr. Donleavy has suggested doubling the work force."

The laborers looked around at each other.

"Now Mr. Donleavy has looked around and has hired some more workers. However, only so much money has been allocated for labor. Fortunately, Mr. Donleavy has found a number of men who will work at reduced wages which means that instead of cutting your wages by fifty percent they will only be cut by twenty five percent."

The workers shouted and threw their fists in the air in outrage. Under the cursing and the threats those who spoke English translated for their non-English speaking friends. When the non-English speakers learned of how they were being robbed they joined the irate throng.

"Mr. Donleavy will understand if this is a hardship and welcomes anyone who wishes to leave to draw his wages now."

"Mr. Donleavy is a son of a bitch!" an anonymous voice shouted from the crowd.

The representative whispered in the foreman's ear. To which the foreman faced the crowd and with a crooked smile announced that there would be a thirty percent decrease in wages. The crowd became silent.

"Very good. Now get back to work. The new labor will be here any moment."

The labor arrived and Dominico was not surprised to see the black skinned crew picking up their tools from behind a truck and entering the work yard. He recognized some of the faces from the Douglas Cannery. One face stood out. He was a head taller than every man in the work yard and had the broadest shoulders Dominico had ever seen. Forearms and biceps were knotted muscle. This was a man who was hard to forget, recognizable even from a distance. As he walked to his station the giant, black man caught Dominico's eye, recognized him, and turned away.

"I know that guy," Dominico said then turned to Dante. Dante was not there. Dante was talking to another man, an Italian whom Dom had never seen before. He could not hear what they were saying, but Dante nodded and rubbed his chin while the other man waved his arms. When the foreman walked by, Dante and the man separated and continued their labor as if they never stopped.

"What the hell are you doing, Shopparelli!" The foreman called.

"Takina my break." Dante responded, his voice calm as if sharing a basic fact. The policy was always a half hour break for a ten-hour day. Dante worked twelve hours easily if not more.

"You saw the notice. Mr. Donleavy's suspended any breaks 'til we are back on schedule."

Dominico stood there, not knowing what to do. Dante lifted his lunch pail and popped it open. "We need a break. We've a been workin' like dogs. In half hour we'll worka some more."

"You'll work now, Shopparelli, or you'll be blacklisted, so help me god!"

Dante sat on a wall and sipped the steaming soup from his cup. He looked at the foreman, licked his lips and sighed with satisfaction, then winked at the skinny man above him. The rest of the work crew stood watching, black faces to the east and brown faces to the west. Dirty and desperate they stared at Dante as he ate his lunch in open defiance of the foreman.

"Shopparelli, get off my work site! Ya heard me, ya son 'v a bitch, get off my work site!"

"I'll get offa when I'ma done witha m' lunch."

"Then I'll leave too," said another man. It was the same man Dante was talking to earlier. The man threw down his crowbar and sat down next to Dante. Like Dante, he opened his lunch pail. The smell of lentils filled the air.

"Then me." Said another who dropped his shovel and sat down where he was previously standing.

As if in a cloud Dominico dropped his rock breaker and opened his container as he sat beside Dante. He could not believe he was doing this. All he wanted to do was make enough money to get Pratolina to America. This could jeopardize everything.

On the other hand, there was something primal in this, some hidden desire that was welling up inside. This is what he had expected from the villagers in *Villa de San Giuseppe*? If they had stood together against *Il Padrone,* would he even be in America right now? He looked up at the foreman, hoping to present himself as defiant and cocky as Dante. His turning stomach, however, betrayed his attempt to portray calm.

"You're making a mistake Shopparelli. There's a lot more niggas on their way from Alabama who'll be more'n happy ta take your job in a minute."

Dante ignored him and turned to Dominico. "You know whata young Henry said to me today, Dom?"

Dominico shook his head.

Dante took another sip of soup and turned to the man on the other side of him. "Henry, he'sa my grandson. And smart, like his Mama. Well, thisa morning before we leave the house I hear hima crying in bed. So, I go to him, and I ask him what he'sa crying about."

"What the hell is this about ye stupid, dago bastard?" the foreman stepped forward, snarling.

"So, he looks ata me, he hasa those little brown eyes, all red and wet and he says to me, 'grandpa, am I gonna be a slave too when I grow up?' Son of a bitch! He asks me if he's gonna be a slave a when he grows up. He's how old? And he's worrying about stuffa like that. I say, I ain' no slave. I say by the time he grows upa the world will be changed because there'sa so many more of us anda so few o' them."

He turned to Dominico. "You see, when you think about it, we are the onesa with the power. We do the work. We do the building. Why, ifa the oxen, thousands ofa years ago, decided not to till the fields humanity would stilla be running around naked in the forests. I'ma no goddamned ox and I'ma no goddamn slave. All I want to do isa eat my goddamn lunch and that'sa what I'ma gonna do, Mr. Foreman. You can tell Mr. Donleavy that if he doesn'ta like it he cana blacklist all of us, then see if hisa God damned building goes up on time."

"You'll pay for this Shop..."

"Ah, ah ah." Dante waved his finger. "The name is Schiaparello. She...op...a...rell...o. Schiaparello. Make a sure to role the r's as they are supposed to be." Dante demonstrated rolling R's then went on to mock the flat, America "ar." Everyone laughed but the foreman.

They got their lunch without repercussion.

CHAPTER 10

Cecilia reached for the book, took it in her gentle hands, and scanned the page. "Ah, you've found it. I wondered if she'd dare to even write about it."

"Is it true?"

"Yes."

He read the passage again, stunned. This could not be. It was impossible. He turned to Cecilia then hastened his attention to the tiny diary lest the words rearrange themselves on the page and prepare a different meaning.

"Wattahells at boya doin'?" Frettallino shouted and wiped the sweat from his forehead.

Dante dropped the bag of concrete onto the pallet. The pallet groaned from the weight, but Dante seemed unphased. His body was that of a pack animal, used to the excess weight and distortions from his work. He knew that at some point his body would just stop, then he would be out of work. It was his good fortune that his sons were almost old enough to make a living. He would not starve on the fateful day that his body gives out.

When he lifted his head and looked in the direction indicated he smiled. "It looks like no one would give him a job, so he just took one."

There, before them, Dom stood glistening with sweat, his shirt sleeves rolled to the shoulders. In one hand a trowel, in the other a brick. He was building a wall one brick at a time. Next to the brown young man stood a tall Irishman, arms like tree trunks and a barrel chest. He was setting brick as well but struggling to keep up with this galling young man. No sooner would he secure and finish a brick, but Dominico was already finishing his second. It was a race. The workers loved a competition, especially between an Irishman and an Italian. It was not long before the two bricklayers were the center of attention.

Dante and the petty laborers dropped their tasks and sauntered to the scene. The skilled laborers descended from the scaffolds and trellises. Soon a crowd formed around the two men engaged in this unusual contest. The dark, Mediterraneans, newcomers ignorant to the language gathered near Dominico. The Irish and Germans, many first-generation Americans gathered about the Irishman. The Blacks stayed behind, but their work lulled as they peered over heads and shoulders of the crowd to see what was happening.

It was the Irish who started calling out and whistling. "Show that dago bastard, Heaney." "Go, Heaney, you can do it." "Faster Heaney, faster." "I got one dollar on Heaney." Money started changing hands in excited fury. Heaney wiped his hands through his matted, red hair.

"I'll taka someva you money!" one dark haired Italian called out. Dante reached into his pocket and removed his paltry pocket money.

From Dominico's side a cacophony of voices rose. So many languages that one could swear they were speaking in tongues.

"Go, Dominic, Go!" "You got 'im, somanabitch!"

Amidst the yelling and cheering and cursing the wall grew. Brick for brick, mortar for mortar, a wall that was no more than waist high was quickly approaching the shoulders. It was a lopsided wall as the section in front of the young Italian grew taller by at least half again as many bricks. Heaney redoubled his efforts, but there was no catching up. It seemed the faster he worked the young wop would go faster that much more.

For Dominico there were no voices, no shouts, no cursing or epithets. There was only the stone. Be like stone. The rough planes felt good on his hands. The trowel fit readily into his palm. Metal scrapping against stone, shink...shink...shink, became his heartbeat. He never looked at Heaney, never saw anything more than the next brick he was to lay. The wall grew taller before him.

The Black men were the first to get back to work. They had an innate sense of when the boss was coming. The rest of the crew was oblivious in their zeal for shouting, cursing and placing bets.

"All right! All right! Break it up, the lot o' yas! I'll dock a week's wages from every one of ye sonsa bitches. Get back to work!"

The crowd parted as the bossmen approached. Around the bosses were men who were hired by the company specifically for the purpose of breaking up any more labor "troubles" that may arise. When the bossman says there's no time for lunch, there's no time for lunch. These large men held sticks threatening to strike the first person to say otherwise. Within seconds only Heaney, Dom and Dante stood by the wall.

Heaney stared at the wall, at the young man's work, perfectly straight lines, perfect thickness of the mortar. Beautiful.

"What in the hell is goin' on here, Heaney? 'zis another one o' your stunts, Shopparelli?"

Dante shook his head and held out his hands as he took a step back. The wry smile on his face, however, demonstrated that he stepped back to extract himself from the scene, not out of deference.

"Well, Heaney?"

"Sir, I was jes settin' hyea eaten me lunch when this young sprite come over hyea an' start placin' me bricks, sir. I swea ta ye, sir."

"So, what happened."

"Well, Sir, he starts layin' the brick like I say, sir, so's I goes up to 'im an tell 'im to get back with th'other dagos in the ditches, sir. Well, he acts like he don't even hyea me, sir. He jes goes on layin' brick and layin' 'em good. Then he looks at me an' smiles like the divil he does an' I knows he's challengin' me, sir, soes I takes him up in it."

"Looksa like he tooka bettav ya." Dante laughed and pointed at the wall.

"Well, he did have him a head start, sir." Heaney smiled and scratched his head.

"Young man, what makes you think you can just come in here and do skilled work?" The fattest of the bosses chortled.

Dom stood straight, chin up and replied, "*Sono una Rossa*."

"What?"

"Um, *signore*, don'ta minda the boy." Dante interceded. "His English isa not so good asa mine. He saysa he's a Rossa. That's hisa family name. They are stone workers. For him, back in Italy, thisa work is insulting for a man in hisa trade."

"How old are you, boy?"

"I'ma man." Dom stated.

"A man, boy you don't look older than a pimple. I should send both of you home without pay. Because of you, all those miscreants thought they could just take time off and watch the fun. Foreman!"

"Yessir."

"Get the names of everyone who was watching this fiasco and dock them an hour's pay. No, make that two hours."

"*Signore* Dunlevy. We were here no more than fifteen minutes." Dante protested.

"Perhaps you would like to have a day's wages dropped, Shopparello."

"No, *signore*."

"What about the blacks?" the foreman asked.

"Were they participating in this?"

"No, sir. I don't think so sir."

Dunlevy placed his finger under his bushy mustache. "Dock 'em anyway. Tell 'em it's courtesy of Booker fucking Washington." He turned to walk away.

"Uh, Mr. Dunlevy." Heaney spoke.

"What?"

"Uh...I don't mean to tell ye how to run ye business, sir, really I don't, sir, but he's...well...he's pretty good at layin' the brick, sir, and...well, sir...I could use a hand, sir, bein' b'hind schedule an' all, sir."

Dunlevy sized up the arrogant young dago, then looked at the foreman. "How's his work?"

The foreman inspected the wall. "I can't tell where Heaney ends and the wop starts, Mr. Dunlevy."

"I'm not payin' him any more money. If he wants to do skilled work, he can be Heaney's apprentice. And tell the crew they'll work an extra hour to catch up. The niggers, too."

Dominico's small victory energized the laborers, especially those darker skinned Europeans of the Mediterranean and Baltic regions. One of their own made a mark, albeit a small one. He was recognized for skill, for accomplishment rather than criticized for his ignorance or strange customs. Just once the immigrants got to see someone shine through the filth of poverty that covered him. With this small victory their steps were a little quicker, their movements more graceful. By the end of the day, they accomplished a little more than they did the day before. Their work was better quality. Each man left the worksite with the notion that it was possible to make it. It might just be possible to get ahead after all. Every man left the work site smiling, a small glint of hope in their eyes as they shared their own stories about this young man.

Of course, this was lost on the bosses who saw only a despicable and unkempt resource of laborers droning through the menial tasks that no one else would do. At least no one else would do such labor for the pay that they were getting. Instead, the suited nation sat in their offices making decisions, bottom line decisions in the interests of their stockholders. How can we make this work progress faster, cheaper? What can we do without? They were blind to the lesson before their eyes.

It was this concept of doing more with less, of investing capital only in what was absolutely necessary for the completion of the job that contributed to many sorrows among the laboring nation.

Every day, Dunlevy and Associates transported tons of brick or pipe or I-beams. These loads were secured to trucks with rope, chord, and chains. It was not expensive to replace the rope, chord, and chains after so many trips to ensure that the payload was secure. It was cheaper still, however, to keep using the rope, chord, and chains until the visible sign of wear became impossible to ignore.

It was one of these rusted, twisted chains, showing significant wear, which was used to secure over four tons of pipe during transport by crane from a cargo train to the worksite. Dante and a young man called Pico were directing the crane.

Pico was a small ball of energy. Dante once commented that the young man never walked anywhere. He ran or jogged or jumped all over the worksite. Even at the end of the day when all the workmen were exhausted, Pico could be seen skipping home. Pico could not look at a pile that was less than four feet high without jumping over it. If an object was suspended within nine feet off the ground Pico would run, jump into the air and tap it with his palm.

For this reason, Pico was often used to carry messages from one end of the site to the other. A supervisor would hand him a piece of paper Pico would disappear like a gazelle swerving through the pallets and other litter that made such places a veritable maze of activity.

Using Pico to carry messages had other benefits. He was completely illiterate and surely not smart enough to ever learn to read. Pico was also almost totally without guile. When given directions he followed them to the letter and without detour. This was important among the foremen and supervisors who distrusted the swarthy masses before them. Everyone knew that dagos were always scheming to stab someone in the back, steal their money, seduce their women or any number of despicable things. But not Pico. Pico was just too damn stupid.

As the load was descending Dante and Pico pushed on one end to slowly nudge it parallel to the ditch in which the pipe was to be laid. One side of the pipe touched ground gently, just as usual, only this time some defect in the chain was placed under excessive stress. Pico felt a sharp ping under his hand, and somehow, his dull mind sent an instant message to his lightning-fast body that there was danger. Pico's springy legs reacted just as the chain snapped and four tons of pipe crashed to the ground. Pico pushed Dante into the ditch, then jumped for his life.

Dominico heard the resounding toll of the pipe breaking free. He knew that Dante was working with the crane. He dropped his awl and trowel and scampered down the scaffolding, Heaney close behind. By the time he approached the jumbled pile of pipe there was a crowd gathered in the ditch.

"Dominico, come quick. It's Dante."

Dominico pushed through the crowd. In the ditch lay Dante, half buried in mud, a huge pipe wedged into the ground on top of him.

"What happened? *Signore*, are you all right?"

"*Cavolo no! No sto bene!* I think this pipe took my god damned legs off?"

Dominico and a group of men grabbed the pipe and pushed it, but it would not budge. It was too heavy and buried too far.

"Can you move your legs?"

"No, all I feel is pain."

A greater crowd gathered. The supervisor approached. "What the hell? Oh, my God! Ya'll right Shoparelli?"

Dante screamed in response.

"Mizzo, go see if the crane op'rator can lift this pipe." The supervisor directed. "We need more help in here."

Men tried prying with rock breakers and pipes, others dug at the mud to no avail. The mud was thick but would not resist the bars and shovels enough to gain leverage against the pipe. With all the manpower pushing on the pipe it gave nary an inch of motion.

The crane operator informed the supervisor that he would have to get another chain. Blood was starting to appear on the mud at Dante's waist.

Desperately Dominico pressed his broad shoulders into the pipe. He growled as he pressed with every muscle, his legs shaking with the strain.

"That's it, it's moving!" Dante howled.

"Can ya get your legs out?" The supervisor called down.

"I can't move!" Dante moaned.

Dominico pushed while others pulled and pried.

"Hold on, man. Le's see 'f we kin push tagetha."

Dominico opened his bloodshot eyes. There, in front of him was the tall, broad shouldered Black man. His coal black skin glistened with sweat. He had stripped his shirt and balled it over his right shoulder. The man's torso was that of a statue cut into obsidian with sharp perfect lines, a statue of an African god. He braced his great shoulder under the pipe.

"On a counta three." He said.

"*Contando fino a tre*." Dominico shouted to the Italians. The order was repeated in a number of languages.

"*Uno...Due...Tre*!"

The Black man did not know the language but understood the count. After "*tre*" his face twisted. The mighty, round muscles knotted under his ebony skin. He and Dominico pressed and growled, "Keep goin'...I feel it move...Keep goin'!" The pipe gave an inch. Others wedged blocks under the pipe to keep it from falling, but the blocks sank into the mud.

"Agin..on three!" the broad-shouldered man called.

"*Uno...Due...Tre*!"

Dominico's broad, bronze back ached under strain and fatigue. The man before him bowed his head, arched his shoulders and growled like a lion, a mighty black lion pushing against the world.

"Keep a goin', Dominico...It'sa comin' It'sa comin!" One worker called. They shoved more blocks and wedges under the pipe, and soon they stopped sinking.

The pipe surrendered to the determined force of the men, but not easily.

"Hold it! Hold it!" Two men grabbed Dante by the arms and pulled. Dante screamed as the men lunged backwards, landing in the mud. He was clear. Dominico and the Black man counted three and everyone let go, allowing the pipe to crash to ground with defiance. Mud splashed high from the force, covering many of the workers. They did not notice, as they were intent up on helping their workmate.

The Black man sat on the pipe as Dominico raced to help Dante. He was expecting to see him lying in a pool of muddy blood, two stumps for legs. In fact, Dante's legs were still attached, though his left leg seeped a significant amount of blood from a large gash ripped from his thigh.

One of the men pulled Dante's worn-out leather boot from his foot. "Dante! Dante! Move your toes, Dante!"

"He moved them. He moved them!" about a dozen men cried in unison.

"Well, let's go, get him to the dispensary." The supervisor spat. "I need a crew here to clean this up." He shouted.

Dante clasped Dominico's hand and nodded to him. "I'll be all right. You go home and tell *Signora* that I'll be late, but I'm all right."

"I'd rather go with you."

"I'd rather *Signora* knows that I'm all right. You go."

Dominico hugged Dante as his hero was carried away. He watched the men place Dante on a truck to transport him to the dispensary.

When the truck was out of sight he turned to where he left the Black man sitting on the pipe, but he was no longer there. Dominico scanned the work. Being about a foot taller than anyone else made him easy to locate. He spotted the giant's broad back glistening like obsidian. Without ritual, he was returning to his own race to pick up his shovel and return to work.

"Hey!" Dominico called and ran over to the clustered Black workers. The brown workers stared at him. When he got close enough, he reached out and got the man's attention. "*Grazie*. Ah…um…thanka you." He held out his hand. "My name isa Dominico Rossa. I'ma from Campania."

The great man looked down at the young Italian, unsure of how to respond. He looked around at his own, then at the Italians who stared from a distance. Then at the young man holding his hand out. His eyes showed concern, but his broad mouth pulled back in a sincere toothy smile. "I'm Madison Rice. Uh…I'm from Montgomery. Montgomery, Alabama." His giant hand engulfed Dominico's.

"You are a gooda friend. *Signore* Rice."

Madison continued to smile, but his eyes narrowed with anger. "You know damn well they ain't never gonna let us be friends. It ain't never gonna happen, you bein' what you are and me bein'…what I am."

"I donna think they hava say, ussa bein' friends."

Madison smile was reduced to a smirk. "We cain't never be friends no matter how hard we try, cause we both have to feed our families. When the time comes, and it'll come, an' you an' me is fightin' for the same job for we can feed our kids a little better, you an' me cain't be friends then. You see, we cain't be friends never. They won't let it happen."

Dominico was prepared to argue with Madison. His mind scanned a repository of Dante's speeches and lectures for a response that included solidarity, unity, commonality of purpose…

"Hey! Hey!" Someone shouted from the chaotic pile of pipes. "Where's Pico? He was here with Dante. Where is he?"

Dominico, Madison, and the rest of the workers, white, brown, and black, looked around, calling his name. He did not respond. Pico could not have left the site. There was only one other explanation.

They looked at the pile of pipes. Nothing could be alive under there.

CHAPTER 11

Probably no reasonable, intelligent, and honest person in the United States regrets the death of the eleven Sicilian prisoners on the New Orleans jail. Whether they were members of the law-defying Mafia or not, they belonged apparently to the lowest criminal classes, and on general principles deserved, and no doubt expected, to meet a violent death.

They were charged with complicity in the assassination of the Chief of Police…After a trial by jury one was found not guilty, and no verdict was rendered regarding the others…

The excitement attending the action of the jury was calculated to bring about the conviction of the accused at a subsequent trial, but, without waiting for the law to vindicate itself, an armed mob, led by respectable citizens, broke into the jail and deliberately murdered the alleged assassins.

From "The New Orleans Outbreak
Leslie's Weekly
March 28, 1891

"We must treat each man on his worth and merits as a man. We must see that each is given a square deal, because he is entitled to no more and should receive no less."

Theodore Roosevelt, 1903

"Well, perhaps now we'll see some change." Frazilli said. He did not know where to look. The mood of the city was solemn, a great pall descended upon a normally vibrant, noisy world. Flags were lowered to half-mast. Great construction machines were silent and still, like dead insects. Worksites were abandoned to the enormity of the tragedy.

"Don't be a fool, Frank." Dante grunted as he scraped tar from the bottom of his dilapidated shoes. His left leg, still weak and sore, throbbed with pain, causing him to grimace as he turned his foot. "Things never change. At least not from the top."

Dom did not know where to look. His mind wandered back to *Villa de San Giuseppe*. It was a lifetime ago when that rider, his steed frothing from exertion, announced the death of King Umberto, assassinated by an anarchist. There, in the dust of a ruined village in a ruined province, Enrico Rossa, the head of a ruined family, saw in this act no portent of change.

Now, here in this vital land, surrounded by towers and fortunes and the tapestries of greatness, the coffin was sealed on another national leader. President McKinley, shot by an anarchist days before gave up his ghost. Yet Dominico's adoptive father in this world offered a similar prognosis.

"This man, Roosevelt, he seems to be a good man. He says he's going to change things. He says he's going to make

America an even greater nation. He says he's going to help the poor, working man get ahead." One man said with hope.

"He's not like the kings and the *padrone* back in the homeland. He's going to do it because he's got to be re-elected in a short time. He can't lie like the kings." Another nodded and peered at his friends for support.

"That's just exactly the reason he has to lie." Dante spit. "Not only does he have to lie he'll have to convince all the people he made promises to that he's doing what he said he would do, just to keep his job. But make no mistakes. That man, Roosevelt," Dante's finger shook in the air, "he's no friend of the working man. He's no friend of the foreigner and he's no friend of *Italiani*. No, hear me all of you, there'll be no change until we fight for change. No man of power has ever, by himself, done anything for the working man. He requires pressure from down below, from us. Until we all stick together, we'll continue to live in swill, families cramped in fire traps toiling for drabs of money that the wealthy deign to give us. Just enough to keep us alive. Just enough to get us to raise their buildings, build their bridges, their subways, hell, their entire cities. Like cattle they drive us, and when we can't lift another brick or drive another rivet, they let us die where we drop."

Dante was drawing a crowd. For a while it seemed that the only sound in the city was Dante's growling voice. He grew louder as the crowd became larger so those in the back did not have to struggle to hear.

"You can take your Theodore Roosevelt if you want him. He's no good to me. Why I had friends in New Orleans when those Italians were lynched, helpless and unarmed in a prison cell. The courts found no reason to indict, but they held them anyway. Held them until a crowd of drunken southerners dragged them into a back alley, stood them against a wall, and blew them away. What did your friend, Roosevelt, have to say about that? What? Do you know? He said it was a good thing! That's what he said. It was a good thing! I guess the less *Italiani* the better. Or maybe he thought that it would help keep us in our place. Either way, do you think that you are going to get mercy from this man?

"This country was built by slaves. Now it is being built by the displaced and desperate. For that they fear and hate us. They think that theirs is the fate of the Romans who became fat and lazy while barbarians built their palaces and served in their armies until finally invading and laying waste to the Eternal City itself. They see us as an invasion of barbarians...

"...No! Even worse, they see us as an infestation. They think we are going to infest their country with disease. They think we are going to infest them with our religion, our politics."

"That's right, Dante!" Members of the crowd called.

"Tell them the truth, Dante!"

To Dominico's knowledge Dante never physically prepared a speech on paper. He did, however, have a talent for speechifying at the spur of the moment, rendering orations that would have been the envy of William Jennings Bryan himself.

Envy, that is, if his orations were in English. Dante, though fluent in English, lacked the ability to translate his rhetorical fire in this barbaric tongue.

"They are afraid that we will thin their precious Anglo blood. Of course, to do that we would have to seduce their women!"

An uproar of laughter echoed through the city streets. "Casanova! Don Giovanni!" some called out.

"They fear us," Dante continued, allowing the laughter to die down, "like they fear diseased vermin. But unlike diseased vermin they keep bringing us over to do their dirty work. Why?"

"Why, Dante, tell us why?"

"I'll tell you why. Because they've gotten soft, that's why. The real men went west to tame the wilderness. There's no one left on the east man enough to build their towers or their bridges or tunnels. They need the hot blood of the Mediterranean to do this work."

"That's right, Dante!"

"He speaks the truth!"

Dante appealed to their manhood, an aspect of Italian life that was most under attack, kept under the yoke of economic exploitation. The men in the crowd embraced this confirmation of their masculinity as if driven by instinct.

Dominico was always amazed at how quickly Dante's fury spread like a great flame through a gathering crowd. The power that Dante yielded awed Dom and instilled in him great fear. To wield so much power, so much control over the hearts of so many people was almost...godlike. But Dante was not a God. So, what was he? A demon? No. No. He was just a man. A man full of such boiling anger that he burned all with whom he came in contact. He was a man who could not only express his rage but do so in such a way as to awaken the sleeping fury of those around him. The fuel for this flame was dry and heavy, just waiting for that one spark to ignite a conflagration.

Dante was that spark, his words the flame. Dominico, awed by his mentor's fire, could not help but fear him a little, and fear for him a great deal. Even in his short life, Dominico had learned that it was not uncommon for a good man to be consumed in his own fire, becoming angry at the world and resentful of all that was in it. Such a man could not see through the flame, could not distinguish that which was to be cleansed by the fire from that which was to be destroyed. Dominico also realized that there was great danger from outside as well. The elite, knowing that the fuel was dry and heavy, could not allow such a flame to rise. It must be extinguished. Extinguished at all costs.

"And let me tell you what's more." Dante's voice resonated throughout the city. "Let me tell you what's more. Do you think when this bank is built that a single one of us will be allowed inside? Are your meager savings going to find their way in there?" He thrust his finger at the rising steel and brickwork that would become a bank.

"No, Dante! No!"

"That's right. We can build their city so long as we stay out of it. They give us a hovel, overcrowded rat traps, and so long as we know our place we will be tolerated. But as soon as we stand up like men we'll be knocked down. Knocked down like the coal miners in Colorado, under machine guns..."

"What's going on here, Shoparelli?" The foreman approached. Dante speaking in Italian made the foreman uncomfortable. "Mr. Dunlevy tol' yas t' all go home. We'll not have any business on the day our President dies. Go home an' do whatever it is you people do when someone dies...sacafice a lamb or somethin'."

Dante glared at the foreman. "Mista Foreman! My name is Schiaparello! Dante Simon Schiaparello! I ama the son of a master carpenter. I learneda the trade from him when you werea still suckin' froma you momma's tit."

The foreman stepped forward, clenching his fists, "That's enough out of you, you guinea bastard! You'll not talk 'bout my mother!"

"I'm talkin' 'bouta you! I'm sure you momma's a nice a person. I'm sure she would no approve a the way you treat us. But you are American. Born here in America. You hava no skills, you hava no trade, you hava no history, buta you hava positiona where you cana tella those of us who hava those things what to do. You cana push us 'round an' make usa feel bad. Does thata makea you feel good?"

"Shut up or I'll kill you, you sonva bitch!" the foreman lunged, but half a dozen burly Italians, including Dominico, stepped between him and his intended target.

Dante nodded, peering between the shoulders of the men in front of him. "You a probly will, Mr. Foreman, buta not today. Not today! Perhapsa you'll wait until I'ma helpless in a prison cell, so there'sa no chance you gettin' hurt, buta you won't do it today."

Dom glared at the foreman.

"Go home, Dante! There's nothin' for ya here. You're finished here. I'll see ta that."

"I never evena started here. Not once in the years I've been here has my hand helda the tools ofa my trade to make a my livin'. Not once. I was a finished before I even arrived in this land."

"Then go back where ya came from, Shoparelli! Go back all o' yas...all o'yas. We kin git along without yas."

"Who'll build your bridges and dig your tunnels?" An unidentified voice shouted. "Who'll do all your dirty work?"

"There's not enough Polls or Czechs in the world for this city!" the crowd laughed. The foreman retreated.

"Who'll make love to your women!" another voice, gruff and strong. An uproar of laughter.

The foreman glared over his shoulder at Dante before turning the corner.

Dante turned to the crowd and pointed at the retreating foreman. "Do you expect that man to change regardless of who's president."

An October wind caressed the dirty crowd gathered in the evening. Off in the distance the din of footsteps along the road, a clanking of chains. Things were going to get bad. Dante turned to Dom and smiled. It was a grim, half smile as if gripping defiance in his teeth.

"You all right, Dom?" Dante asked. "You can go home. My wife would be unhappy with me if you got hurt. You'd be doing me a favor."

Dominico was doing the best he could to hide his fear. He did not know how successful he was. He shook his head then turned toward the road and the approaching footsteps. His spit stuck in his throat, heart pounding. 'This is it,' he thought. This was what he was hoping for in Italy, in his work yard while his family was being destroyed under the wide-eyed gaze of the villagers. Unity! This was unity. Now he needed the courage to make it work.

The conflict started shortly after President McKinley died from his wound. The foreman never forgot his mistreatment Dante's hands and was spoiling for a fight. Humiliation was fine for ignorant wops, but for an American born man, an insult required an answer—a violent answer. He chided and insulted Dante, pushing him and kicking him for the smallest reasons, practically begging the smart mouthed wop to swing at him. If he could just make Dante swing things would be much easier. But Dante wouldn't play into the foreman's trap. Dante only smiled and shook his head. Ironically, the more he accepted the foreman's insults, the more solid he became, the less empowered the foreman felt.

"You thata scared of a little 'talian peasant?" Dante taunted as he found himself the immediate 'volunteer' for every dirty or dangerous job on the worksite.

The project was coming along. What was once an ugly iron skeleton was taking shape as the great bank made of stone crept skyward. Dominico never worked this high off the ground before and was exhilarated scaling the rusted and creaking scaffolding. He and Heaney worked together most of the time, and though the Irishman was never short of Dago jokes he really liked the young wop. The two became unusual friends, and Dom did not mind laughing at the jokes.

It was from this position on the scaffolding, about four stories high, that Dominico witnessed the incident that was to ignite an explosion of resentment and bring the bank project to a screeching halt.

Dominico was an apprentice, so no longer worked with Dante who was classified as unskilled. However, they both made it a point to keep an eye on each other. Dante knew that his speech making was putting him in a dangerous position. Dominico, virtually an adopted son, was also in danger by virtue of his ties to Dante.

While sealing a facing Dominico looked below at his father figure who was working beneath the scaffolding at the other end of the building. Nothing was out of the ordinary. When Dante stood and waved, Dominico smiled and responded in kind.

From the corner of his eye, Dom noticed the foreman slinking along the third story scaffold directly above Dante. At first this did not seem unusual as the foreman always patrolled the work site, but something made Dominico stop and observe the crafty boss. The foreman looked down, an eagle sizing up its prey. Dante cleared some lumber below, unaware that he was being observed. Then the wrench fell. A large pipe wrench rested at the foreman's feet. With a slight shift of his foot the iron tool dropped headfirst, its handle spiraling behind. It was too late for Dominico to respond, the warning trapped in his throat.

The wrench did not hit Dante as intended. Instead, it struck old "Stu" Sztubinski clean in the middle of his skull. Dominico would never forget the sickening sound that reverberated around the brick canyon—the sound of a melon crushed under a great weight. The old Pole dropped to his knees then fell backward into a disturbing, twisted mass.

Dominico was halfway down the scaffold before the old man fell. When he reached Dante's side he gulped as he looked into the vacant stare of a dead man a halo of black fluid growing around his crushed head. The unskilled help was not vouched the "added expense" for helmets, so the heavy tool plunged at least three inches into the old man's skull.

"Y'all right, Shoparelli?" Dark fluid seeped from the old man's head and washed over the foreman's muddy boots where it pooled at his feet.

Dante's jaw hung open for a moment, then set firm, the muscles under his ears bulging as he bit down hard. He glared at his foe, hatred darkening his eyes. "I'ma all right. It'sa Stu. He's dead."

The foreman looked at the ground, frowning. "I keep tellin' them guys not ta leave their tools lyin' 'round. I knew somethin' like this's gonna happen."

"You're a liar." The words flew from Dominico's mouth, as if from their own conscience.

"What'd you say, boy!"

"Dom?" Dante turned to him.

"You're a godadamned liar!" The words came louder. He spoke to Dante in Italian. "He did it. I saw him. He waited for you to step under him then kicked the wrench off the scaffold. I saw him. He was trying to kill you."

"What's that dago sonvabitch sayin', Shoparello? What's he sayin'?"

"Nothing." Dante turned to the foreman. "He's asayin nothing. He'sa just upset."

Dominico glared at the foreman but took Dante's lead and said no more.

"It was an accident, at's what it was. It could happen t' anyone."

Dante's eyes were slit. He and Dominico picked the old Pole up and placed him on a piece of drop cloth. "Yeah, an accident. There'sa many *accidents* in thisa place." Two others covered the old man's body with a tarp.

Sztubinski's wife was left destitute even though Dante, Dominico and a number of other people informed Mr. Dunlevy of his foreman's actions. Sztubinski also had a son. His only son. He was thirty and born an idiot, the result of lead poisoning in the womb. With the mind of a six-year-old he became a burden of the state. The Widow Sztubinski was not so lucky. Dante made the case that the company should compensate her for her loss. Surely, she would starve to death. Her arthritic fingers could no longer manipulate piecework. She was helpless, dependent upon her husband's ability to work. There would be no compensation.

When Dante found out that the foreman was suspended for a week for causing the death of a fellow worker, he flew into a fit of rage. He expressed this rage by climbing a scaffold and yelling epithets at Dunlevy and his men who arrived to examine the worksite. He accused them of complicity, of slavery, of treating his workers as no more than meat. A crowd of workers dropped their tools and wheelbarrows to gather around and listen to Dante speak. He vowed that this building would never be built.

Dante pointed his thick, calloused finger at Dunlevy, "So help me God...this bank will never go up! So help me God not another finger will be lifted until that good woman is taken care of."

From that moment the workers, most of them immigrants, Italian, Czech, Pole, Albanian, and Greek refused to move from the worksite. They interfered, sometimes violently, in any attempt to resume construction. Sometimes Black laborers were assigned to begin work, but they were outnumbered and could not be coerced into approaching the pipe and chain wielding men on the work site.

Some members of the group thought that they should start tearing down the building. Many of them even started to dismantle the building with sledgehammers. Dominico remembered his father throwing the sledgehammer at Don Alfredo's son. He felt this was a bad omen. Dante talked the workers out of this rash action. He reminded them that it was their intention to get some money for Stu's widow. Destroying the building would eliminate their only chance for negotiation.

Now they stood, poised for battle. Hands gripped around whatever weapons could be found: chains, hammers, sledges, boards, pipes. If it could be gripped in the palm it could be used as a weapon.

"There they are!" There was no other sound but footsteps.

From a side street the first of the enemy approached. Pale faced men dragged chains and held knives. The procession weaving into the alley was a great snake that would not end.

The streetlights cast harsh shadows on their faces, highlighting their thin, determined eyes.

"Keep still," Dante urged. "Keep still."

Dominico's heart stopped beating. Directly in front of him a tall, grim man held a board with six long nails driven through the business end. Dominico tightened his grip on a long crowbar.

There was a brief pause. The two armies glared at each other, sized each other up. Which side would start this rumble? Which side would make the first move? Who would draw the first blood?

Dante held his hands out from his sides, palms facing his men. He knew the politics of strike breaking. He knew that the police were right around the corner waiting to clean up the mess. He knew that no matter who started this fight his group was going to take the blame. If he could ensure that the workers were in the right there would, at the very least, be room for righteous indignation. High in the darkened windows people were watching, working people who were wondering just who the good guys were. Dante wanted them to have empathy for his small, tattered army.

With a shout, the strike breakers raised their weapons and charged the strikers like a mighty wave crashing against rocks. At first the only sound was the striking of bodies, the clashing of chains and crowbars, sledges and ax handles. Knives and shovel blades flashed under the arc lights. Then the sound of hard objects against flesh, snapping bones, crushed heads.

This was followed by the screams of those who fell, trampled underfoot.

To spectators, and there were many in the surrounding buildings, it was a scene of some surreal battle from the dark ages when two phalanxes crashed together in a screaming cluster of spinning metal, clutching hands and spraying blood. Man fell upon man until the mass of ferocious bodies became one chaotic entity, falling in upon itself, imploding with hatred.

Dominico found himself fighting blind, swinging and pounding and punching any pale face that he could see. Anonymous hands grabbed at his throat, pulled at his hair and clothing. He tried to keep his feet firmly on the ground. Be like stone, be like a rock, give no ground. Beneath the weight of his crowbar a skull thumped, a forearm snapped. Something red sprayed across his face. Something hard struck him in the eye, causing him to step backward two steps. Be like stone. A snarling face swinging an axe handle, a sharp pain in the ribs under his left arm. The hook of the crowbar ripped the snarling face. Heads and hands and arms forced him, pushed him. Who was there? Another pain in the shin, a ripping sound over his right shoulder. Swinging and striking, cracking. His instincts pushed him to rum. His heart cried out, 'No! be like stone!'

All around a sea of bodies pressed him. He had never felt more alone. The screams intensified. Above the screams the sound of sirens, hard shoes pounding the pavement, men shouting. It was almost over, just like Dante said.

Dominico found himself falling backward, a crushing pain in his back, fluid running down the backs of his legs. Above him a man waved a pipe high over his head like a banner. Dominico rolled, his back burning, the pipe clanged on the ground. The man was dragged away, someone's arm around his throat. Dominico jumped to his feet, swinging and striking...screaming, a burning pain wrapped around his waist, then again from the back of his neck to his chest he was spun around. A square shouldered man with a chain spinning over his head whipped the chain toward him. Deep burning as the chain bit into his left arm, across his back, a ripping sound, the sound of the old *contadino*'s flesh surrendering to the whip. The crowbar fell from his hand. The chain spiraled around his neck. Dominico jerked forward, looked into the sinister eyes of the man. Those eyes seethed with hatred then eyes widened in pain. Dominico struggled for air, but none could pass the tight grip of the chain. The dull thud of a skull cracking, both men fell to the ground. A man in a blue uniform, held a black stick stood above them. Dominico was lifted by the hair and placed in the back of a truck. The door screamed shut.

CHAPTER 12

"**Y**ou're a fool, Dante. Call your dogs off. Can't you see it makes no sense?"

Don Castillo pounded on the bars with the palms of his hands. Dante, inside the cell, said nothing. What was there to say? This prison was a zoo in which the people were in cages and the predators were pacing outside. There was no freedom for Dante or for those who were struggling to make a good life for themselves and their families. The American businessman held the job, the power of life and death. It was the boss man who, like the capricious gods of old, determined if one lived or died. When Italians were not under the thumbs of their bosses, they found themselves under the gaze of the Don.

The Don, *Il Padrone*, controlled the street corners and the store fronts. Every vendor from wine makers to rag men paid their tribute to *Il Padrone*. In exchange the vendors were "protected." Protected from whom? Why, protected from *Il Padrone*, of course. The Don was always there, always willing to loan a little money to help, as the serpent was willing to help

Eve in the Garden. He was the self-professed cornerstone of the Italian community. Most people in the community saw him for what he really was—a parasite, living off the natural vitality of a hardworking people.

The parasite was especially noxious, however, when *Il Padrone* was in the employ of the Boss Man.

"It makes no sense, I say." Heavy palms thudding against iron. "Look at you! You're a caged animal and for what? And the people who followed you—look at them. What about them? They have families, too."

The 'rioters' were all hauled off to jail, most groaning in pain from their injuries. Others were dragged to their cells railing against the injustice, their faces pressed against the bars, arms flailing for free air. They were all charged with trespassing, disturbing the peace and assault. Cells were emptied to make room for this dirty army of malcontents. Cramped and dingy, there was little room for them, but the jailor was creative in his accommodations. Not a single striker was left without a cell to house him. The strike breakers, however, were sent home with a warning. After all, a jail could only hold so many miscreants.

Dante turned to Dominico and offered a weak smile. 'Incarceration is not for the boy,' he thought. Jail was hard on them both, but for Dominico the strain created a metaphysical affect. He still stood tall, looking everyone in the eye. He never voiced a word of complaint or a whimper of discomfort despite the gaping wound that was ripped across his back from his left shoulder to his right hip. Dante tried to control the bleeding, but there was no medical care for the prisoners. The boy bore his injuries and imprisonment with seeming indifference, but his eyes betrayed the content of his heart. It was not defeat. No. It was more visceral, more carnal. It was the look of a man who was punched in the stomach. He may still have the anger, may still have the desire to overcome, but without air, his fight was over.

Dante knew that there was more to the uncertainty in this young man's eyes. Dominico was the reflection of the rest of the strikers, once so ready to fight, now desperate for what little autonomy that could be found on the other side of the bars. In the back of Dominico's mind was the irreconcilable fear that his journey was over. Here was a foreigner, an unwelcome guest in an alien land, sitting in jail for taking part in a riot. Never mind that he knew his cause was just, it was not his land, it was not his home. Perhaps foreigners had no right to expect just treatment. Why should America, the home of Americans, wish to extend their freedoms to Italians? Why should Americans have mercy for foreigners who strike and riot in their streets? Why shouldn't America send such rabble away and content itself with more docile and amenable workers?

This was the crux.

The overarching fear of being sent away stabbed at Dominico's resolve. Where would he go? It was only luck, or perhaps divine intervention that brought him into the home of the Schiaparello's. Would he be so lucky if he shipped off to work on the ranches of Argentina or the plantations of Brazil? Certainly, such fortune only happens once in a lifetime.

And what about Pratolina?

Dominico did not want to think about her. He could not bear the thought of losing her. America was his only hope. No stories ever reached his town of Italians becoming rich in Argentina. It was America that held the key to the future. America that would unite him with Pratolina—America that would fulfill his dreams. Perhaps he should have left well enough alone.

Dante saw similar doubts in the eyes of all the prisoners. He wondered if it was fair to use his anger to arouse them to action when the probable consequences were so dire. Which was the lesser evil? Should they accept their status quietly, relenting to the abuse and exploitation in the hopes of someday breaking free, or should they rail against injustice and stand up for what was right...and lose all they ever hoped? Dante remained quiet in the face of Don Castillo.

Within a few days Dunlevy offered freedom to any who chose to return to work—for less pay, of course. The courts did not want to deal with this, and Dunlevy felt he could take advantage of his workers incarceration to lower their wages. Dante sat without saying a word. Dominico sat next to him waiting for a response. Everyone was waiting. There was none. Dante just sat and stared at the wall. He was a leader of men now. He led by example. He led by his silence. Soon their indecision turned to resolve. Who would be the first to turn a back on his compatriots? Like Dante, they all sat like statues and stared at Dunlevy.

The great concern of the prisoners, however, was their families. Arrangements were made with a few messages sent back and forth among the few visitors they were allowed, mostly priest and social workers. Families donated food and arranged to help pay rent. A community of Italians from all regions came together for the greater good. But how long could this last? What would be the ultimate price paid by households without men to head them? Would the children be forced into the streets to beg and steal, or, even worse, forced into factory labor where they could be mutilated and killed in the gears of heartless machines.

This was their stand. They had nothing but a vision for which they were fighting. Their families would be taken care of, at least for the time being. Each of the strikers clung to tenacious hope, the hope that some miracle might happen...

...Before winter set it.

"You're all being replaced," Don Castillo said. "You all need jobs. Soon there won't be any jobs for any of you.

"Dante, you are a reasonable man. Be reasonable."

After days of silence, Dante turned to Dunlevy and spoke. "They are free to do what they will." He waved his hand indicating the dirty inmates. He stared directly at Dunlevy, then at Don Castillo. His gaze was accusatory, and this was not lost on the Don. Dante continued in Italian, directing his comments to *Il Padrone,* "As for being reasonable, I think it is reasonable that human beings should expect to be treated as human beings, not chattel. I think it is reasonable to expect that our employers pay us for the work that we do rather than squeeze us for every little bit of work and pay us just enough to keep us from starving to death. I think it is reasonable to expect our employers to take responsibility for their actions, especially when those actions lead to someone getting hurt or killed. I am a reasonable man, Don Castillo, but I don't get treated as a reasonable man. I get treated like an ox on a yoke."

Mr. Dunlevy tapped Don Castillo. "What is he saying? Can't he speak in English?"

Don Castillo ignored Dunlevy.

"You're wasting your inflammatory speeches on me, Schiaparello. Here's the bottom line." The Don's voice became that of an asp. He continued in Italian. "I stand to lose a lot of money if this project doesn't get finished on time. You are going to send these men back to work or you'll never have a safe day in your short life."

"What are you saying?" Mr. Dunlevy was growing uncomfortable. He was intentionally isolated from the conversation, and therefore could not control what was being said.

Dante stood and glared at the haughty, pock marked Don in his expensive suit. "You listen to me you worthless *contadino*! You can't threaten me. I don't get scared. I left the motherland to get away from scum like you. You remember *Il Padrone* when you and your family were starving, huddled in your grass hut."

Don Castillo bristled.

"That's right, that's right. I know what you are. I know your background. It's written in your hands. You can't get the dirt of the earth off your hands. You're nothing but a peasant. You can wear all the fancy clothes you want. You can polish the lint off your top hat, but you can't get the soil off your hands or the scars off your face. You come to America a peasant, but because you sink your teeth into your own people and suck them dry you become *Il Padrone*. The very thing you despised. I know you. I've seen a dozen men like you.

"And you dare to threaten me. Perhaps I'll have to look over my shoulder for the rest of my life. I'll do that with or without you. Perhaps even I'll be killed. But when the time comes, I'll rest well. This prison cell is my peace of mind, Castillo. Where's your peace of mind?"

"I demand to know what he is saying!" Dunlevy pounded the tip of his walking stick on the floor.

Dante's eyes flashed from Dunlevy to Don Castillo. "Perhaps I should start speaking English. Maybe the Boss Man would be interested to know of your less than humble background. How do you think he would look at you then, Castillo? Do you think he'd still be willing to do business with a peasant?

"You see, you really don't scare me. I must have something to lose that is of value, and I don't really have that. Even my life isn't of value in this country. And you wouldn't dare to threaten my family...not mine of all people's."

Dominico had never heard anyone speak to *une padrone* like that. Dante's eyes were those of a raptor, wild and caged. Dominico could not sort his feelings enough to know whether he was exhilarated or scared.

Behind Dante's vitriol, however, was the reality of passing time. It was autumn when the strike started. Winter came sooner than expected that year. The grey walls of the prison became wet and cold, damping spirits and destroying bodies.

It was the older men who gave in first. Their bones ached and their lungs filled with fluid. Dante had to defer to their diminishing health and suggested that they make whatever arrangements they could with Dunlevy.

Then word of hardship faced by the families entered the prison and saturated their hearts. Their communities were too hard pressed to help. Winter diminished the demand for work. There was not enough piecework even to sustain their wives and children. For many, donated bread was all they had to eat.

The strike was over. What began as a matter of principle was crushed by the pressures of reality. Those who fought for the right were forced to yield to the ambivalent forces of nature.

Winter was Dunlevy's ally. He never went hungry. His family was the benefactor of great feasts, a warm house and clean air. His great wealth was shelter from the icy wind and snow. All he had to do was wait for the starving masses to beg his forgiveness. And they did.

Before each ragged man, aching from the cold, Dunlevy made his concessions. Charges would be dropped, but the men would return to work at once, accepting a reduction in pay and work more hours to make up for the extra labor and lost time.

In the end Dante and Dominico sat alone in their cell. The last of the strikers returned to work. Dante never approached Dunlevy and received no less than expected. As the instigator and the leader of the strike he was tried and convicted. He would remain in jail until his time was served. From then on, he would be blacklisted. No one would hire a rabble rouser like him.

Dante did, however, convince loyal Dominico to ask for release. Dominico, despite his own failing health, was ready to stand beside Dante until Hell touched the Heavens. To be close to a man with such resolve, a man who was not afraid to stand and fight was well worth his time between cold rock and iron. Dante, however, had other plans. Someone had to take care of the family. Dante's eldest son had taken his family to Pittsburg with the promise of steady work. There was no one left Dante could trust more than Dominico. Both men choked back their tears when the final decision was made. Dominico would return to Mulberry Street, leaving Dante behind in his cell.

"Is this the way it works, Dante?" Dominico asked.

Dante nodded.

"It's not right. It's not right."

Dante stared at the floor and nodded. Then he kissed Dominico on both cheeks and wished him well.

When Dominico left the prison Giulianna was waiting for him at the bottom of the stairs. She threw a heavy coat over him as protection from the icy wind. She had stitched the coat together herself from rags and patches of cloth.

CHAPTER 13

Dearest Pratolina:

Every day I miss you more and more. I work hard, but it seems that the harder I work the more I get set back. Things are not as I thought in America. Greed is the guiding principle here. But I guess we are all greedy. Americans are greedy for the dollar, but am I any less greedy for wanting you? Perhaps not. Yet the two seem to be tied together. Without wealth I cannot have you. So, to satisfy my desire I must make enough money. However, to make money in America, I must sacrifice the principles as taught to me by my father. I'm a Rossa. The Rossa name stands for something. You fell in love with a Rossa. Would I sacrifice your love if I were to sacrifice who I am for the sake of your love? Do you understand the impossibility of my situation? Then I have the added burden of knowing nothing about what is going on with you. I've written as much as I could, yet I've not heard from you in over a year. It's been such a long year away from you. Longer still without word as to your wellbeing. My life of labor and toil has no meaning without you or the knowledge of your security and love. My life in America has become intolerable. I've worked hard. Worked hard at my job, worked hard after my shift to make extra money in the community, worked hard on Sundays and holidays, still wealth eludes me. However, I have saved enough to purchase a ticket to bring you to me. It is a second-class ticket so you will not suffer the deprivations that I endured. The village would never see us together unless I were a man of means, but America sees no such boundaries. Here we can be together. I recognize the sacrifice that I am asking you

> to make. With me in America you will not have access to the
> kinds of comforts that you are used to. At least not yet, but
> we can be together. In our last discussions you expressed that
> that is more important to you than anything else. It is with
> great excitement that I give this gift to you, this ticket. In two
> months, we will be together, and all my labors will not have
> been in vain.
>
> I love you
>
> Dominico

It was midnight before Dominico returned to the apartment. He was working for *Signore* Pristone repairing the loading stage at his warehouse. His body shook with the impact of the winter nights. His hands shook, bereft of all feeling, for he could not work with the thick gloves Giulianna made for him. His illness of the year before made him especially vulnerable to the effects of the cold, but he had to work. He had to support Dante's family.

Dante's family? Were they really Dante's family, or were they, in fact, his own family, an adoptive family? The Schiaparellos were the only family he had in this country. America was still alien to him, but with a family he could thrive. He knew where he stood. He knew who he was so long as there was a family. Now he had standing with that family. The responsibility of taking care of the family in Dante's absence was heavy, but warm, like the patchwork coat he wore in the cold. Filial responsibility fitted Dominico, warming his resolve despite the chill in his blood.

To satisfy Dante's wishes he worked harder and longer at the worksite. The bank climbing out of the frozen ground like a stone goliath. He showed his skill beyond bricklaying. At one point he helped with erecting the columns on the marble stairs that he built. The seams of each step were so tight that one would be hard pressed to fit a piece of paper between the slabs. With his deft hands he evened out the "flaws" he noticed in the stone carving that decorated the mighty building.

It was not long before established stone workers took notice of his craft. 'Very talented for such a young man.' They all whispered. Heaney even realized that when it came to stone and brick, he was far out classed by this young dago.

Still, Dominico worked at unskilled wages. His nationality as well as his participation in the strike defined his worth regardless of skill. For this reason, Dominico did what Heaney called "husslin'." He spent what free time he had wandering the streets looking for jobs, creating work for himself as he had done in Naples. He convinced *Signore* Ciccolini that concrete around his dress shop would allow him to sell his wares outside without getting mud on the cloth. He convinced the owner of his building, Mr. Chisolm, that the courtyard needed work. This became his most valued skill in America. It was even more valuable than his trade. Husslin' was the American way of doing things. Someone who could not hustle would get nowhere. Dante, as brilliant as he was, as full of passion as he was, had no skill in husslin'.

All this husslin', however, was taking its toll on the young man. He slept no more than three or four hours a night. Some days he worked straight through, foregoing sleep altogether. Large bags developed under his eyes, marring what was otherwise developing into a rugged, handsome face. Coffee was the staple of his diet, especially after he discovered the effects of sugar on the normally bitter taste. It was not long before his behavior became erratic, drifting between bouts of depression with sudden bursts of uncontrollable energy. He became absent minded, one day leaving his tools at the worksite where they could easily have been stolen had he not run back in the middle of the night to retrieve them. These tools were more than just instruments of work. They were gifts from the community. People pitched in as much as they could so he could buy the tools he needed. Some donated old and worn tools and Signore Palma made Dominico a box to carry them out of pieces of scrap wood. To lose such tools would have been more than a personal loss. It would have been an affront to the community.

Even on the nights he did not have work lined up, he could not get to sleep. He paced the narrow confines of the apartment and thought about Pratolina. Where was she? How was she? Why hadn't she contacted him? Each night without word from her seemed to double his anxiety or to reinforce his depression.

Giulianna beseeched him to slow down, to stop working so hard. Tears often came to her eyes as she pleaded with him.

Despite her emotional pleas, Dominico shrugged and went on his way. His income, a few cents here, a couple of dollars there was the life blood of the family. There was nothing more to say. He promised Dante. He promised Pratolina.

Seeing that her entreaties were falling on deaf ears the distraught young woman confronted her mother. She insisted that Signora, as matriarch of the family, make Dominico stop, force him to slow down. Giulianna's eyes were swollen, wet and red as she tried to emphasize how important Dominico's wellbeing was to her.

That evening Dominico was donning the patchwork coat, preparing for that evening's labors when Rosella stood, hands on hips, in front of the door. Her eyes were stern, her legs solid. She shook her head and pointed to the palette where Dominico used to sleep.

"You're done, today, Dominico. Look at you! You can barely button your coat. Go lay down and get some sleep."

"I'm sorry, *Signora*. I have this job to do, but when I'm done…I'll sleep."

"Now, Dominico!"

"I promised *Signore* Degliamo that I would be there."

"I know him. I'll explain it to him. You will lie down and get some sleep. Tomorrow is Sunday and no one will wake you."

"Tomorrow, I have work at the Santilli's."

"Not any more you don't. Tomorrow, you sleep. There are other men in this apartment. They can take up some of the slack for a while. You need to rest."

"But *Signore* asked me to look after the family. The other men...they have their own families to look after."

"*Signore* does not expect you to kill yourself to do it. Remember last year. You almost died last year you were so sick. Do you want to go through the same thing again? I'm not going to do it. You get sick again, I'm putting you on the street. Now get undressed, your clothes are damp as it is...get undressed and go to sleep. Giulianna has warmed a blanket for you, and she will hang your clothes to dry. Monday you can get back to work and I will not bother you again."

Dominico glanced at her.

Rosella smiled, "until the next time. Get over there and go to sleep." She kicked him lightly in the rump. His sense of duty and honor demanded that he meet his obligations. His mind and his body, however, were shutting down. There was no more energy left to move him. Arguing with *Signora* sapped him of his will to defy fatigue. He allowed himself to stop just long enough for his body to regain control of his will. His long-distance run was over—at least for the day.

Dominico smiled sheepishly. His eyelids were narrow and swollen. His legs shook with the effort of keeping his body standing. With nothing more to say, he accepted the warm blanket from Giulianna and wrapped it around him. When he fell onto the pallet, he was already asleep. His body hungered for the lumpy mattress.

Sunday afternoon the families gathered for their usual meal, the one meal during the week when everyone had enough to eat. After the meal Dominico stayed at the table. The women stood to clear the table, but Dominico asked Rosella to sit for a moment. He realized as he drifted from sleep to wakefulness that morning, that *Signora* was making decisions without knowing the whole truth. He knew that the time had come to reveal at least a part of his secret thoughts to the people who had taken on the role of family in his life.

"*Signora*, I appreciate your concern for me, but there's more to it than just making money to support you."

"Yes?"

"*Si*. There's a woman...back in Italy..."

Giulianna stopped short, caught a quick glance from her mother. She did not realize that she stopped breathing until her head became light and her lungs demanded to be filled.

"Her name is Pr...Maria Angelina. She is my fiancée. My hope was to make enough money to go back to Italy and marry her, but that does not seem probable."

Dominico eyed the tablecloth. He left a stain in front of him which he tried to rub off with his thumb and forefinger.

"I saved enough to buy her a ticket to come here. I would like to have your permission to invite her to stay here with me until we are married. If not, I can understand. I can make other arrangements, but it would be easier..."

Giulianna shook. "Giulianna," Rosella said, "go into my room and straighten the bed, please." Without looking back the distraught girl ran for the other room.

"Dominico, I don't recall ever seeing any correspondence from this woman."

"No...I have not heard from her. That is true."

"Is this a traditional betrothal?"

Dominico stared at her for a moment. A flash of shame crossed his face. "No."

"I see," Rosella sighed.

"We are in love. The only way for us to be together..."

"Was to come here and make your fortune. But it is not working that way."

"No."

"And you haven't heard from her."

"No."

"Is it possible that she's married another? You know how things work in the old country."

"I've thought about that."

"I mean, it's been over a year. A year is a long time for a young woman."

Dominico nodded but could not look at Rosella. "I've thought of that. I really have. But I don't believe she's married another. She promised she would not. I don't believe it."

"Time tends to weaken the threads of promises, Dominico."

Dominico nodded.

"Besides," Rosella leaned closer and whispered, "Dante and I were hoping that you would consider marriage to Giulianna."

"I know."

"She's a good girl, Dominico. Loyal. A good cook. You could do worse than Giulianna. And she's right here."

"Yes, she's a good girl, *Signore*, but not the woman I love. And I've made a promise. Regardless of how long ago, I've made a promise. I must see my end through, no matter what the result."

Rosella touched his hand, "You sound so much like Dante. Of course, you must keep your promise. This woman...Maria Angelina...she's welcome here. We'll prepare for her arrival."

"*Molto Grazie.*"

"But Dominico."

"Yes."

"You must prepare for her not arriving."

He mailed the letter, with the tickets, to *Pratolina* not knowing that it was the last such letter he would ever write.

CHAPTER 14

"Why doncha just go home. The gate's closed. There' s no one left. Just go home."

The policeman was more than patient. At least he was more patient than other lawmen Dom experienced in the last few months. Perhaps it was the look of hopelessness and dejection on the young man's face. Perhaps it was the new suit, shave and haircut, over a week's wages worth of sculpting that turned Dominico into the model of a gentleman. Or maybe it was the bunch of flowers hanging limp from Dominico's large hands, wilting in the dusky air. Whatever it was, the sun was long since lost behind the mighty buildings before the officer approached him.

Dom stared at the black club hanging from the policeman's wrist. He was almost afraid to speak lest his foreign ancestry be betrayed in his accent, but the words had to come out. "She...she wasa supposta be ona this ship."

"I know, young man." The policeman smiled and patted Dominico on the shoulder, "You go home now."

"We were supposta be married."

"It happens. Go home to your family, young man. Go home and have a good meal. Maybe drink some wine or somethin'. You can't hang 'round here. Someone might come 'long who's not so understandin'."

Dominico nodded and rose. The policeman's hand was surprisingly gentle on his shoulder. 'Perhaps they're not all bad,' Dominico thought. 'Perhaps they don't all want to crack the skull of some work-weary dago just trying to get a little more out of life.' For so long the police were nothing more in Dominico's mind than the automatons of the state. Not this one. This one was human. Dom could imagine this uniformed man sitting with his family, wearing his t-shirt, kissing his wife.

The flowers, *il prataline*, fell to the ground, and there they lay until their petals were scattered by the ocean breeze.

Dom walked away from the pier. The red sun bled through the buildings.

The Schiaparellos eyed the door as Dom entered—alone. The silence was uncomfortable, heavy. He did not want to talk about it. He did not want to talk about anything, but he felt responsible for an explanation.

"I...she..." there was really nothing to say. It was obvious. Dom was alone.

Alone he walked to the fire escape. He did not cry, but he did not open his eyes. Be like stone.

The fire escape was a small garden. With the first dew of spring Dante planted herbs and spices, tomatoes and cabbage, anything that would fit in the limited space. In Dante's absence, Rosella was the gardener. Dom was surrounded by the first green shoots of the Schiaparello harvest.

"Dominico?"

Giulianna stood by the window. *Signora* stood in the background watching.

"I know you probably don't want to talk, so you just listen."

Dominico looked down at the dark street.

"I don't know what happened, but I'm sorry that she's not here. I think she would have made you happy and...you... your happiness is important to me. I want you to be happy, Dom. I really do."

"I should go back. Something's wrong. She would have been on that ship if something did not happen."

"Many things happen, Dom. It's been a long time since you saw her last. Maybe you won't like what you'll find when you go back. But if going back is what will make you happy, then perhaps you should go back. I know that we don't want that. I...know that...that *I* don't want that. But I guess you will do what you feel you have to."

Again, he nodded, his mouth a wide frown.

"But, Dom, I want to ask you something. Do you think... do you think that you might just be able to find happiness here? Do you think that maybe we can make you happy? That, maybe...I...I...might be able to make you happy?"

Silence.

"I'd like to try, Dom, if you'll let me."

The world turns erratically. Nothing is ever where it belongs when the world comes around again. There's always something missing, or something in the way that was not there at first. If only the world would stop spinning so. If only the world could slow down so someone could get their feet planted and their course straight. Dominico remembered how difficult it was to make his feet do what he wanted them to do on the *Halzbad*. The world always swayed like a ship tossed on the ocean.

Here, in this land, so full of pitfalls, so replete with traps ready to snare the common man one had to fight to gain any kind of even footing. Yet, one could fight, fight bloody against a ferocious resistance, against an enemy with almost limitless resources. One could stand up to tyranny and know that his brothers, his compatriots, his countrymen were behind him. One could stand up and know that he was not standing alone for he could feel the shoulder of the men beside him. One could feel heat from all who would limp away, bloody and beaten, but still fighting.

In Italy there was no more fight. There was nothing left for a man in the old world. Perhaps there never was. As much as Dominico wanted to go back and find his love, there was a hopelessness to the thought of breathing Campanian air again with nothing but a new suit to show for his labors. His pride would have to be surrendered. All that he fought for, bled for, fevered for, all his labors and struggles would be lost, only to return to the old work yard where no work would take place. Returning home allowed him nothing more than to watch his noble family die in ignominy. Returning home meant raising his children in a land where being a Rossa was once a thing of pride, but no more. Maybe he would marry the Patrillo girl and try in futility to create a legacy with a dead heritage.

And what of the Rossa family? He came to America to make money so he could claim a woman as his own, like a prize, a prize he desired more than anything. But he also came to America to help his family pay their debts and earn back their respectability.

The Rossa work yard was still. No work was being done. Hortensia's dowry was too small for her station. Paulo and Anna were still too young to be of much help. The only thing maintaining the Rossa's, the only hope of betrothal for Hortensia, was the money that Dominico sent home every month. As meager as it was, American money was welcome in the old country. What would become of the Rossa family should Dominico return home—return home a failure, no less.

No, Dominico would not return to Italy. At least not yet.

"Dom?" Giulianna touched his hand. "I know that you don't love me. I know I'm not the one you want. But maybe...maybe someday. I'll try very hard...I'll...I...I just hope you'll stay." Tears streamed from her eyes. Her voice cracked. "Maybe you can build a future here. Maybe...someday...you might just...be able to build a future...with me." Then she ran into the house covering her face. Her mother waited to embrace her.

Dominico stared at the street. For a girl to speak so to a man...this was a strange country, with a strange effect on those who came here.

A gentle rain fell on the party as they waited in front of the prison. At last, Dante was to be released. Despite the rain, the family waited in front of the imposing fortress. The prison was located outside of city limits, too far to walk, so Signore Petrocello carried the family in his wagon. The canvas covered wagon provided meager shelter from the rain, however.

"Maybe they're not going to let him out," said little Bepe, still too young to understand the import of this moment, but old enough to know that he missed his Papa and wanted him home. "Maybe he did something bad, and they are going to make him stay."

"He didn't do anything bad. He's been a model prisoner." *Signora* responded. She was impatient. "It's more likely they enjoy watching us stand in the rain."

The door opened and someone stepped out. The family took a breath and jumped forward only to be disappointed. Again, the door opened, again, the same breath followed by the same disappointment.

"Look, Momma, there he is." Gianna jumped.

Signora stood, but this time did not take that excited breath. "That's not him. That can't be him."

"It's him, Nanna, it's him." Shouted little Henry.

Dominico nodded and smiled. "It is him."

Giulianna smiled and jumped next to Dominico. "It is him, Momma. It is him."

From the door the man spied his family and waved, making his way in haste down the stairs.

"My god, he's so thin." *Signora* said. Her smile glistening from tears, she jumped forward, running to the gate. "He's too thin. He's too thin."

Soon husband and wife were caught in an embrace. Tears mingled on their clothes as they swayed back and forth, holding each other tighter, tighter only to clasp tighter. Around them the younger children gathered, pulling at Papa's pant leg, jumping up and down excitedly.

Giulianna's hand closed tightly in Dominico's palm. She used the back of his wrist to wipe the tears from her eyes and the rain from her face. This was all right with Dom.

Finally, Dante and Signora ended their embrace and walked to the wagon. "*Signore* Petrocello, I thank you for helping my family, and it is good to see you, old friend." Dante shook his hand.

"Wouldn't have missed it. Imagine the state letting a dangerous man like you out of prison where you can roam the streets freely."

"You're too thin. You're too thin." Signora continued, tugging at the clothes that hung loose from his shoulders and hips. "Didn't they feed you? Did not you eat, you're so thin. Are you sick?"

Dante laughed. "I'm all right, Darling. I'm okay. I ate just fine, but they serve Irish food in prison. You know Irish food isn't fuel enough for Italian blood."

Signora looked at him sternly. "Well, there's plenty of food back home and you better eat it all or you'll deal with the back of my spoon."

Laughter as they helped the children onto the back of the rag cart.

"She means it, too," Dante said to Dom. He noticed Giulianna holding Dom's hand but said nothing.

"I know it." Dominico smiled. "I've had to let my pants out twice since you've been away."

"Who's had to let your pants out?" Giulianna pinched Dominico.

"It looks good on you. You all look good. You did well, my friend. Thank you. Thank you for taking care of the family while I was gone. I knew you would come through for me."

"I would have had it no other way." Dominico smiled with pride. They embraced, kissing each other on the cheek.

"Rosella, let me speak to Dominico, man to man for a moment."

"But only for a moment. You've been away from your wife for too long."

Rosella caught up with the wagon. Dante and Dominico followed behind, tipping their heads and hunching their shoulders to rain.

"How did they treat you, Dante?" Dom asked.

"I've been treated worse. I've been treated better. It's all old news now anyway. There're more important things that we need to discuss. I was able to read. I was able to read a lot, and I made a lot of connections. I talked to a lot of people in the same boat as we are—good people. I talked to anarchists and socialists and communists and others who've all been put in prison because of what they believe. They've been put in prison, but this is a country that says we can believe whatever we want to believe. But something that I learned that I should have thought about before."

"Yes?"

"There's so many of us. And there's more coming every day. More and more are coming every day. The thing is that this is a country that runs on votes. Soon there'll be enough Italians in this country that we can start electing our own to office. We can start seeing change coming. Maybe my grandchildren will see Italian senators or representatives. Maybe someday even an Italian president. But there'll be no progress unless we all stick together and vote."

"Vote?"

"Yes, Dominico. We must vote. I got in touch with a man who is on a voting drive. He may want to run for office. He wants to get as many Italians to apply for citizenship as he can. In a couple of years there's going to be another election. Italians must vote during these elections, and we must vote in mass."

Dominico nodded and scratched his chin. He had just started feeling like an adult, but such a hat was ill fitted.

"Dominico, you must apply for citizenship."

"Citizenship. I don't know...I..."

"You must become an American. You must do it for all of us."

"I was really planning on going back."

"When? When are you going back? And why? Not to rub salt in your wounds, Dom, but it seems that your only reason for returning to that godforsaken sand is gone."

Dominico felt the sting of that comment, but did not respond. It was the truth, and Dominico learned to take the pain of truth in silence.

"You and Giulianna, eventually you will be married, are you really going to take her back to your village? Are you going to raise your children, my grandchildren, there? I don't think so. Face it, Dominico, you are in America to stay. You might as well become an American."

The walls shook with screaming and pounding. There was a crash and a loud thud over their heads. The extended Schiaparello family sat down for their first meal together, their first meal with Dante at the head of the table in a long time. The happiness of the moment yielded, unfortunately, to the violent argument that exploded from the apartment upstairs. Dante and his family tried to ignore it. The goings on of families was no one's business. The tempo of the discord increased, however, and all who heard it became agitated and uncomfortable.

This was no typical quarrel. It was an out and out fight between two people who once vowed to love each other until death they did part. Pietro and Fiorella Monblanco and their three children lived in the apartment overhead. They were married almost ten years, most of it happily. Signore Monblanco had a stable job in a textile factory until the merger. He went to work one morning to find the gates locked and men on the factory grounds boarding the windows. There was no explanation, no warning. He was working one day and unemployed the next.

Since then, he struggled to find work that came close to his monthly wages in the mill, but having worked there for nine years, that was close to impossible. Employers did not pay unskilled labor based on experience. Unable to make ends meet he had to secure a loan from Don Castillo to pay his rent. When he was unable to pay back the loan two of the Don's henchmen reinforced the importance of making good on his obligations. They did this by kicking him in the ribs so many times that he had to spend a month in bed. Don Castillo's boys then came to his apartment and took everything, furniture, cooking utensils, everything. They even garnered, by force, the pay that *Signora* Monblanco was making from piecework.

Once he was able to secure work it was too late. His debts had grown to be so exorbitant that there was no way he could catch up. Washing windows would not pay the bills, nor feed his family. Like many men of the time, *Signore*

Monblanco's only surcease was found at the bottom of a bottle. This did nothing to cancel his debts, nor did it ease his pain with anything more than a temporary numbness. Drinking was, however, what ruined men did. He could find comfort in a room full of men whose lives were also in ruin, men who gave up on ever getting ahead. There was some comfort in a room full of men becoming numb to the world, numb even to the fact that the bar was owned by none other than Don Castillo.

During the last few months, the arguing became intense. *Signora* Monblanco tolerated the nights he spent in the bar. She tolerated the nights he stumbled into bed and the mornings treating his drinking illness. When he started to bring his drinking home, however, that was more than she was willing to accept. The arguing began.

When they argued, *Signore* Monblanco would just storm out of the apartment and return to the bar. This was acceptable to his wife. But some nights he became obstinate. It was his home, and he was the man of the home, and he was going to do as he damned well pleased. He was not going to be the henpecked cuckolded husband! She objected violently to being accused of cuckoldry. He responded by calling her *una puttana*.

"I'm a *puttana*!" she screeched. "If I'm a *puttana* maybe there'd be food on the table!"

Then the world exploded into a cacophony of screaming and yelling and children crying.

The sound of crashing was a new phenomenon, however. This could not continue for long before...no one wanted to think about the possible consequences. It just had to stop. Dante tried to talk to *Signore* Monblanco, and Rosella spent hours during the day consoling his wife, but each night the conflicts got worse until nothing existed in the building except the epithets, accusations and profanity.

On this night, however, the yelling came to an abrupt halt after a resounding cracking then crashing. Dante, Dom and Garibaldi jumped and rushed to the door, followed by the corpulent Geraldo. That was when the screaming started. Not the usual screaming of anger, but that of pain. Pain mixed with crying and pleading.

When Dom and Dante pushed through the brittle door, they saw *Signore* Monblanco standing over his prostrate wife pointing a finger in her face and waving his fist in the air. *Signora* Monblanco lay quivering and crying among scattered shards of broken dishes. The left side of her face was swollen and already turning a sickening yellow and blue. Dante, Dom and Garibaldi grabbed *Signore* Monblanco and pinned him to the opposite wall. He was not a big man, but his rage possessed his sinew with considerable strength.

Rosella and Giulianna entered the room before Geraldo, who had to take a break on the stairs. They ran to the sobbing woman now lying face down in the broken dishes.

"Get her out of here," said Dante to Rosella. "She'll stay with you tonight downstairs. Dom and I will stay with Pietro."

He was still struggling, but his rage turned to despair. Tears flowed from his eyes and his legs, no longer strong enough to carry the weight of his emotion, buckled underneath him. Dante sat on the floor with Pietro who was now sobbing into Dante's chest.

"Where are the children?" Giulianna asked. "I'll find the children."

"They've taken everything from me, Dante. It's all gone." Pietro cried, "How can a man come home and face his wife when he's been emasculated?"

"I know, Pietro. It'll be all right." Dante stroked the man's thinning hair.

"Where's Fiorella, Dante? Where's my wife?"

"She's downstairs with Rosella."

"I want my wife, Dante. Go get my wife and bring her here." He pleaded.

"Not right now, Pietro. Let her stay with Rosella tonight until everything calms down."

"She's a good wife, Dante. A damn good wife."

"I know, Pietro. You shouldn't be hitting her."

As if having his worst fears confirmed, Pietro whimpered and buried his face in Dante's chest. "She's a good wife."

Dominico put a pot of coffee on the stove. He remembered the first time he'd seen *Signore et Signora* Monblanco. They were so happy. What happened? What could happen to a man that he could forget or neglect his duties as a husband?

"I have no power over my life anymore, Dante." Pietro cried as Dante walked him to the kitchen table. "I can't find work. I can't support my family. Now I don't even have control over my own soul, Dante."

Dante only nodded but said nothing.

"I used to be a good man, Dante."

"You're still a good man, Pietro."

"No," he shook his head, "No, no more. I'm not even a man anymore. Where did my manhood go, Dante? Where did it go? How can a man lose his manhood?"

This story was not a rarity in Little Italy. Dante saw this narrative play before his eyes too many times before.

Dante looked up at Dom who approached with a cup of coffee. Pietro's head lay in his arms on the table as he sobbed beyond consolation. "This is why you need to become an American. Our people are tearing themselves apart. Hopeless men are taking their anger and powerlessness out on their families. This is why you must become an American. This is why you must vote."

CHAPTER 15

Signore Patrillo:

It has become increasingly clear that my stay in America will be much longer than I had planned. For this reason, it would be unfair of me to ask you and your lovely daughter to wait any longer for her to wed. As I am not in the position to provide for her in a manner befitting her station, I must do the honorable thing and decline my betrothal to Signorina Patrillo. As this is of great disappointment to me, I hope you will honor your word given five years ago as I will honor mine. Enclosed is the value of the dowry, paid in American dollars. For your patience I have enclosed an additional fifty percent. It is my desire that this does honor to my family and justice to yours. May our long-standing friendship last forever, untarnished.

My best regards to you and to yours
Dominico Rossa 1905

"I don't know what happened," Dominico knelt before the rail in front of the tiny, recessed chapel. "Somehow it all looks so different from how I imagined it five years ago."

His dreams were simple, pure, yet so fully confounded by life's winding maze. Innumerable crossroads took him far from his intended destination. With every day in this labyrinth another door closed behind him. He had to accept the fact that he was too far to turn back but was too lost to ever find his way. Pratolina was a lost dream, another unrealized hope. Now that she was lost to him, he surrendered to his fate. As much as he tried to navigate through his life, he found that, without a map he could do nothing more than stumble along.

It was painful to let her go, painful to let go of this dream that sustained him through so much hardship. A gnawing regret settled into his heart—a parasitic could-have-been. Occasionally, this germ would awaken and pollute his mind with thoughts of a life that could never be. It filled him with the sorrow of an unrealized dream. Even later, as his own beautiful children slept peacefully next to him his mind would wander into old dreams.

This, however, was the way of *il Mezzogiorno*. Letting go. Letting go of hopes and dreams that can only come true in a world of hopes and dreams. In the real world there was no room for such luxury. The best one could hope for was to get by, to handle disappointment in silence with stoicism—to be like stone. A man created a family and provided for that family. A man took care of his responsibilities. A man let go of the rest. If he was lucky, his family would be healthy and fed. If he was lucky his responsibilities would not torment him—if he was lucky.

As pathetic as this sounded, such was the mindset of the denizens of southern Italy. Ironically, this dispiriting realism ensured the survival of those who emigrated to foreign shores and faced not streets of gold, but rather the realities of the ghetto, exploitation, and the ubiquitous *Padrone*. Letting go of dreams and pushing on despite grim reality was the strength of the Italian immigrant.

There was something about this dream, however, that Dominico could not let go. So strong was it that, on the day he was to be wed, he found himself praying not to Saint Joseph as was expected, but to the very corporeal Pratolina.

"I know that it is you who is supposed to be here. I should be seeing you step into the church in your white gown. Somehow you are lost. I know not how." He closed his eyes. Be like stone.

"She's a good woman, Pratolina. You would approve of her. You would like her. She's strong and warm, devoted to me completely." Perhaps, he thought, even more devoted than Pratolina herself. Pratolina had never written, never contacted him. Dominico remembered standing alone at the pier, the loneliness, defeat, humiliation. In his mind's eye she was there, standing under that tree, her bare feet in the grass, wildflowers in her hair. She was there, striding gracefully down the gangway of some ship, compelling the entire country with her beauty as she walked through its gateway. In his mind's eye, the clarity of what could have been, the even harsher reality of what never was.

"She's not as beautiful as you, but...pretty. Yes, she's pretty. She has bright eyes that smile when she talks. Her eyes make her pretty." Hers was a comeliness that one had to get to know, as it was not immediately obvious.

His hands tightened around the unused rosary hanging impotently in his fingers. "Yes, she's a good woman, a strong woman, a loyal woman. She'll be a good wife...yes, a great wife." Making the sign of the cross he stood, straightened his tuxedo. He met Heaney, his best man, at the door before entering the church.

In fact, Giulianna was beautiful. She was the most beautiful woman he ever saw. At least for that moment, that one shining moment when the music started to play, and Dante turned the corner with his daughter nervously clutching his arm. She was beautiful. Her smile radiant, a soft light painted by the stained glass danced across her as she stepped down the aisle, one foot after the other, step by step, the gown was once worn by her mother and her grandmother dragging its long train behind her in a flawless white fan.

She stood beside him, and they knelt before the priest. It was then that Dominico realized that Giulanna had always been beside him, since the first time he saw her. Half crazed with fever he looked up and she was there with a cold rag. When he was sore and stiff from too many hours of labor, she was there beside him. Torn and battered by strike breakers and street fights, she was there beside him, tending to his wounds.

She was there, beside him in ways that Pratolina never was. Beside him now, kneeling before the alter of marriage was her rightful place, a position well earned through love and fidelity.

It was a tender kiss that sealed their fate together. A kiss that Dominico's mother would only hear about in a letter, a kiss his father would never see. A resounding cheer shook the church as they opened the doors to the city that seemed so much cleaner, so much happier. Under a shower of rice, they kissed again, then again. A gentle wind caught her veil and carried it away.

"Dominico...Dominico..."

"Yes, *Signore* Mezzella, thank you for coming. It's good of you to be here, but when are you going to play for us?" *Signore* Mezzella was famous for his mandolin.

"Soon, soon. I wanted to give you this." He handed Dominico an envelope. "It's a little extra I had laying around. You take it and buy your wife something nice with it."

"*Signore* Mezzella, you've already given..."

"No, no, no...this is for you to squander. All that money you get will go to pay for the wedding or rent and food and what have you. This money you spend on your wife. You get her something nice, something just for her. You get her something nice because women like to have nice things once in a while. And you take my advice. You always put a little something aside so you can buy your wife something nice every once in a while, something frivolous. You do this and you will always have a happy marriage."

Dominico smiled and kissed the old man, "*Grazie*, Signore Mezzella."

Giulianna strode up to the two men. She radiated happiness. A broad, white smile stretched without surcease during the entire reception. "What are you too conspiring?"

"I've been giving the boy here a little wedding night advice." *Signore* Mezzella's chubby fist tapped Dominico on the chest. Dominico laughed and tried not to blush.

His bride blushed, "You are a rascal, *Signore* Mezzella."

"Dominico, Giulianna," Dante called to them as he approached.

Their smiles faded. Don Castillo limped next to Dante, his arms outstretched.

"Ah, the newlyweds." *Il Padrone* smiled, his teeth crooked between pock marked lips. "It's so good to see two people so happy. I'm honored to be here."

Dominico swallowed hard, "It's an honor to have you, Don Castillo."

"Now you take care of this fine woman. I've known her for a long time, and she's always been a good girl." He cupped her cheek in his calloused palms. '*Contadino*,' Dom thought. Dante once called the Don *contadino*. It appeared that all was forgiven. "Here, you take this. It is a gift, a personal gift from me to you."

The envelope, handed to Dominico rather than stuffed into Giulliana's *bursa,* looked heavy and thick. Dominico put his palm up, "I...I couldn't, Don Castillo."

"I'll have it no other way. Newlyweds need money. You will need money. Maybe you can start a bank account for your son when he comes to us. Whatever you want, you take it."

"Thank you, Don Castillo." Giulianna bowed and accepted the envelope.

The Don gazed upon Dominico through the corner of his eye. "I've met you before."

"We've met only briefly a couple of times, Don Castillo. It was of little significance for you to remember." Dom remembered seeing him on the ship, then again from behind jail bars. Don Castillo tended to be where bad things happened.

Il Padrone nodded under his hat and reached into his coat pocket. "This is my card. If you ever need anything, you need anything at all, you come see me."

"Thank you, Don Castillo." He had no such intention.

"Dante, it's a great reception for these beautiful young people. You give my complements to *Signora* for me."

"I'll do that, Don Castillo."

As the Don left Dominico scowled, "Why did we invite him?"

"Castillo has a standing invitation everywhere. Don't let it ruin the day." Dante's eyes, from slits became wide and happy. "Dance, dance, dance! Go on! This is your day!" Signore Mezzella started playing the mandolin. Heaney tried to get his feet to move to Italian folk rhythms. He was awkward, but his good humor and laughing desire to be a part of the fun made him a hit. His tendency to infuse his Irish stepping into the Italian dance was given a good-natured applause.

The reception was held in the courtyard of their building. All in the building were invited as were many people in the community, mostly Campanian's. Throughout Mulberry Street the Tarantella and other upbeat folk songs echoed among the buildings. Everyone knew that two people were joined. People danced and laughed. Food was brought from all corners, candies and pastries abounded as women cooked for days in preparation. There was no such thing as a small wedding in Little Italy

Dominico danced and laughed with his new wife, pelted with sugared almonds, called *confetti*, for good luck. The older women forced plates full of food on him, begging him to taste this and that until his stomach ached from spiced antipasto, calamari, polenta and baccala, lasagna, multicolored cookies and pastries, all washed down with rich, red wine. For days before the wedding the winds wafted of cooking and baking in preparation for the wedding. Every household contributed food.

Between dancing, Dominico walked among the crowd and thanked all for their contributions in making his wedding a special occasion. Weddings were not just a family affair, but a community *festa*. Everyone pitched in to make it successful. Carpenters erected a stage. Women cooked and sewed and prepared curtains and adornments. Throughout the day people stuffed money into the bride's *bursa* to defray the exorbitant costs of the wedding. Without the community a couple without means could never be married in the appropriate manner. Traditions had to be followed. Folkways had to be ensured.

One could not take the chance of *maloccio* at one's own wedding. This would be the worst luck, resulting in disaster. The happiness and fecundity of this marriage was dependent upon the good cheer spread during the celebration. This insurance was expensive.

Soon, the time came for the new couple to retire to their chamber for their first wedding night. Even this they could not do alone or without fanfare. Dante made the announcement and resounding laughter, and raucous cheering filled the air. Wine was spilled and a coterie of gleeful guests followed Dominico and Giulianna to an apartment that was prepared for this evening. Once again, the *confetti* flew to the point that the newlyweds had to cover their eyes for protection.

When they entered the bedroom, they found that the bed was carefully prepared, draped in white, lit with scented candles. Bags of *confetti* hung from the bedposts. Salt was sprinkled around the room for good luck.

One by one the guests entered the room, hugging and kissing the newlyweds, slapping Dominico on the back. Dominico ignored the physical discomfort this caused. The damage from being struck by a chain years before never fully healed, leaving a numb strip along his back. Now was not the time for past injuries, and the burden of planning for the future was to be put off for tomorrow. Now was the time for the present, a wonderful, joyous present. To him this line of congratulators went on forever.

The last person to leave was *Signora* Rossa. Traditionally, Dominico's mother should have made the final preparations. If anyone could stand in for his mother, however, it was the Schiaparello matriarch, the woman who nursed him back to health, and tended to his needs for the years he was in America. She straightened the bed nostalgically then kissed Dominico, holding him in a trembling embrace. One of her tears fell against his neck. Then she turned to her daughter, straightened the young woman's hair and smoothed her dress. Smiling, she kissed her daughter. Her cheek rest against Giulianna's, imparting the wetness of her joy.

When the door closed, they were alone. An awkward silence passed as they looked at the bed, then at each other. Holding hands was the only contact they had experienced with each other, and even that was not done alone. Now they were cast into this roll, this final, true ceremony of their joining, their becoming one. How to continue? Up to this point every move was scripted, followed according to hundreds of years of tradition. Every detail was prescribed. Even Dominico's previous experience could not prepare him for this. Once he was guided solely by passion, unfettered by tradition. With nothing binding this passion, however, it escaped him. He had learned his lesson. The rules had to be followed, and they were. Every detail was rehearsed, and his every step was given guidance by those who knew. However, facing his new bride at the matrimonial bed was never rehearsed. At this point what were the rules?

He kissed her on the forehead. She looked at him, her eyes shining with joy. She touched him, awkwardly at first. His body was solid, straight and strong. Her hands danced on his broad shoulders, his thick neck. He kissed her on the cheek. His arms were round and firm, tight against the fabric of the tuxedo. He kissed her mouth, his lips warm and soft. He kissed her mouth again, lingering, tasting her. She pressed against him, she felt small but safe pressed against him. His coat slid from his shoulders.

Slowly, haltingly, they got to know each other that night. The wedding gown lay across the bed and Dominico touched her soft belly, her sturdy shoulders, her round hips. She was not statuesque, not tawny and proud, but rather warm, inviting. They lay down together, her hands gliding down his back. His body was not that of a classical hero, flawless and sculpted. He was scarred and weathered and calloused. She accepted his body.

The music and dancing and laughter continued in the background.

She really was beautiful.

Dominico wondered why it took him so long to notice.

It was dark, well around midnight. Dominico held Giulianna against him, their limbs entangled, their bodies warm and satisfied.

"Listen Giulianna." Dominico looked around. Only one candle remained, a pathetic looking clump of melted paraffin capped by an obstinate dot of a flame.

"What is it? I don't hear anything."

"Neither do I." The music stopped.

A creaking echoed faintly on the stairs.

"Oh, no!"

Before they could prepare themselves, the door burst open and what seemed like a dozen men clambered into the room. Dante, the first into the room, handed Dominico a bottle of wine. The men then lifted the bed with the two newlyweds and started for the door. They had to tilt the bed slightly to pass the door jamb, and Giulianna clung tightly to her husband, screaming, pleading with her father to make them stop. Instead, he led the men with an old Italian marching song, using a bottle of wine for a baton.

The room was chosen because it was on the second story, and the stairwell was relatively wide. Slowly the procession made its way down the stairs. There was no escape. Dominico and Giulianna rushed to cover themselves with fragments of clothes that remained on the bed and on their person. When the outer door opened, the cool night air brushed over them. They were outside, the men singing and laughing as they set the marriage bed down in the middle of the intersection of Mulberry and Spring.

From the windows and fire escapes more *confetti* fell among shouts of "*Molto familio*" "*Buon fortuna*" "*Bella, Bella*" and "*Signore et Signore Rossa*." Young children ran to the bed and gave the blushing bride flowers and candy. Dominico drank from the bottle of wine, then handed the bottle to his wife. They smiled and blushed, waving to the good people of their community.

The sound of the cheering was so great that it drowned out the muffled report of a pistol in the distance. The joyous shouting was the last sound Don Castillo heard as he bled to death at the door of his own office.

CHAPTER 16

"**S**he told Alfredo during a fight." Cecilia said.

"A fight?" Foreboding showed on Dominico's face. He tried to imagine what his Pratolina went through—what she went through alone. She was betrothed to the son of the most powerful man in the *paesera*, yet pregnant with another man's child. Only cruelty and ostracism could have awaited her. Most of the rules of *il Mezzogiorno,* a sinful yet unforgiving country, were unwritten. They were set in hard stone of tradition, rigid in their application. The life of a woman without virtue was nothing. A woman known to be without virtue was shunned, a woman without a country. Dominico shuddered to think that he did this to her. He should have resisted. He should have lived according to the rules of the land. He should have...been like stone.

"Alfredo proposed formally. On his knees and everything." Cecilia's smile was that of an adult recalling a mischievous childhood. "Pratolina said 'no.' To think someone could actually say no to Alfredo Belan. Well, he went into a rage—as was his right. To have been denied as he was, was a betrayal of his entire family.

The pain in Dom's hand, slow, dull throbbing intensified as he unconsciously clenched his fingers. "What did he do?"

"He was angry. He insisted that she was going to marry him. He told her she did not have a choice. And he was right. She still refused. He grabbed her and threw her onto his bed. He tried to take…advantage…of her."

His wounded hand was incapable of making a fist, yet still he clenched his fingers as beyond what they were capable.

"Funny thing is if she had just submitted to him, if she'd given in, she would have been fine. She could have claimed the baby was his, married him and her life would have been spent behind the walls of the *latifundi*. She would have had all the luxury in the world, at least for a little while. The droughts destroyed most of what was left of luxury here. Then the war took the rest. But she would have done better than anyone here."

"But she didn't…submit?"

"No," Cecilia looked at the distant village. The sun was high, and the village was almost without shadow. "She did not submit. She never submitted. Never!" Dom found himself lifted by the pride in her voice.

"Instead, she told him about the baby. She told him because it was the only way to break the betrothal. Personal dishonor."

"My god! What did he do to her? Did he hurt her?" He could have done anything and been justified. He could have gotten away with murder.

Her eyes became sad. "He beat her. He threw her to the floor and kicked her. He kicked at her stomach, trying to break her womb. He just kicked her over and over, trying to kill the baby..."

"But he did not...He did not kill the baby!" A different kind of desperation echoed in his throat.

"No. Pratolina curled up. He beat her badly, but she protected her womb, protected the baby." Cecilia clutched Dominico's arm and with tenderness looked him in the eyes. "A girl, Dominico. A beautiful, little girl."

Dominico fell exhausted to her breast. She stroked his hair and neck to comfort him as the tears fell from his eyes. There was no more stone left to him. All that was left was the chaos of raw emotion, like a relentless tide battering the sea walls until they, with reluctance, shatter and are consumed. There was no more stone to hold back this sea of emotion.

"Where is she? Can you take me to her?"

Anna wiped his tears. "She's close. I can take you to her."

"And that's why this election is so important. There's never been an election so important. It's time to put someone at the reins of power who is a real voice of the working man... Eugene Debs..."

The hall was full. Men were sitting at the front of the stage. Some were standing shoulder to shoulder against the walls. Dominico had never seen nor even imagined such a meeting. The hall was speckled with white faces, black faces, brown faces. Dialects from all over the world resonated against the walls, Romance, Germanic, Gaelic, Slavic, Alabaman. The air wafted with the aroma of greens, calamari, cabbage. The room was a firmament of cultures, an explosive collision of worlds. Yet all eyes were fixed on one place, all voices cheered as one, all dreams were bound together, interdependent. For the first time Dominico experienced the kind of unity that happens when different people realize they share the same desire. No matter dialect, no matter the food eaten, all men and women wanted merely to get by as best they could, to live their lives free of unreasonable burden, happy and hopeful that tomorrow would be just a little better than the day before. Parents wanted to raise their children in a world that was clean and safe and full of love.

Total unity. Even women were present, standing with the men, mixing their sopranos and altos with the tenor and bass that usually dominated politics.

One of the honored guests was a woman. Seated next to "Big Bill" Haywood was an elderly woman referred to as Mother Jones. The speaker was Joseph Ettor, representing the Industrial Workers of the World, a true union of working people.

Weeks before, Dante was approached by a man representing "Big Bill" Haywood, an important union organizer. To show his sincerity the man negotiated a carpentry job for Dante. A job in his trade. That was all Dante ever wanted, a chance to ply his trade, a trade that he had mastered in Italy, but never so much as practiced in the United States. He wanted a chance to build a better world for his children, build it with his hands and his skill. All he wanted was to be a man as he was taught to be a man. Instead, he became a spur in the side of his bosses and blacklisted from the trade he loved.

Now, because of the efforts of this union Dante would work with wood, hammer in hand and a smile on his face. The old, comfortable calluses were coming back, and Dante got a glimpse of what happiness could be. In return Dante pledged loyalty to the IWW. This was his ray of hope, just one step in the road to fulfilling his dream, living up to the expectations of his culture and his manhood.

Dante was desperate to share this find with his young friend who proved so loyal. Now, however, his friend was not so young. Dominico was a twenty-six-year-old man who long since earned the title of manhood. He had borne the countless battles of the common man. He stood firm in the face of adversity and more often than not, he lost. Now this wonderful entity that promised hope for the working man finally arose, but Dom was not allowed near.

It was decided that Dominico should not attend meetings while he was still working toward citizenship. It was imperative that Dominico and as many immigrants as possible receive their citizenship before the upcoming elections in 1908. Paramount was the candidacy of Eugene V. Debs, hero of the working man now running for president against no less than William Howard Taft, Roosevelt's hand-picked candidate and William Jennings Bryan, the aging idealist and his aging ideals. Also of significance were the many such voices that were running for lower offices.

Dominico took his oath just that morning. His very first act as an American was a meeting of socialists and anarchists in the shadow of Eugene V. Debs.

"So," Dante laughed and shook Joseph Ettor's hand, "We've come to the crossroads. Dominico, there's going to be a new revolution in this country. Maybe a revolution without violence—a president who really is the voice of the people."

Dominico smiled, shaking Ettor's hand as well.

"It is good to see a new face." Ettor returned the smile.

"And Dominico, here, is now *un'americano*." Dante kissed Dom's cheek and laughed. "He'll be voting in the next election."

"Well, I hope we've helped you make up your mind who to vote for."

Dom smiled and nodded, "I'll vote for *Signore* Debs. But if you will excuse me, I'm sure Dante has much to discuss with you." He stepped away from the group as delicately as he could. He was uncomfortable among the higher ranks of men. Even these men who proclaimed equality and dismissed hierarchy as a capitalist lie and an excuse to step on the working man. Regardless of ideology, the difference between them and the "average" man was distinguishable. Dom had not resolved the contradiction of a man proclaiming equality endeavoring to one of the most powerful positions in the world hierarchy. Dom attributed his inability to explain this contradiction to his own ignorance of political matters.

He always preferred the less visible corners of the room. He was very conscious of his foreignness, his awkwardness. He had been in America for almost nine years. He had a certificate that said he was an American. Still, he did not quite feel like an American. Perhaps that would come with time. For now, he did not like being in a position where his ignorance could bring embarrassment to himself and, more importantly, to Dante.

Dante, however, danced well on that stage, beaming with pride to be associated with such important people. Dante found himself on the stump more often, railing against the oppressors and riling the enraged masses with his fire and anger. He was rising through the ranks of this new and powerful union. It was a source of stress to Dom to think his own ignorance might negatively impact this powerhouse of a man.

So, he strolled to the comfortable side of Heaney, whom he jokingly referred to as an honorary Italian. After all, Heaney did dance the Tarantella at his wedding. Next to Heaney was the large Black man, Madison Rice.

"Do you still think we can never be friends, Madison?" Dominico slapped his friend on his broad shoulder.

"I…I…" Madison shook his head. He was speechless.

Dom rapped him firmly on his muscled back.

"I never thought this could happen. I never thought I'd see the day. Lands alive I never thought I'd see the day."

"He does fill you with hope and possibility, that Mr. Debs. I think he might just be president."

Madison offered a crooked, white smile. "He'll never be president, but he does fill you with hope."

"I don't know why he wouldn't be president. There are more working men than anything. He's the only one speaking for us."

"Yes," Madison nodded and rubbed his hands. "But it's like no 'merican wants to be a working man. So, when time's to vote we pretend we rich, or that we might be tomorrow, and we vote like we rich."

"Not me," Heaney puffed up.

Dominico shook his head.

"Dominico! Dominico Rossa!"

"Here! I'ma over here!"

A man named Emilio Guazziano pushed his way through the crowd as fast as he could. By the time he reached Dominico he was out of breath. He grabbed his knees to regain composure.

"Dominico…it's…it's time. It's happening," he said in Italian.

"Giulianna?"

"*Si*. It's time."

Dominico grabbed him by the shoulders and lifted him. "No, it's not," he shouted. "It's too early."

Heaney and Madison grabbed Dominico's arms and freed the frightened Emilio.

"I don't know," Emilio continued. "*Signora e Maga* sent me. They said it was time. It's happening now."

Dominico ran. Without inhibition he grabbed Dante's arm and pulled him from his august company. "She's having the baby now!" He then broke into a dead run with Dante, Emilio, Heaney, and Madison following behind.

'Something's wrong,' Dominico thought. 'It's too soon. She could not be having the baby now. Something is terribly wrong again.'

'Again,' he thought, 'Please, God, not again. I've not been religious, but she has. Don't take another one of my children.'

Dominico's first child was still born, a silent victim to the toxic environment in which they lived. Giulianna went into labor early, just as she had now. 'There must be something wrong.'

The baby inside of her was very active. Much more active than the first. Dom took boundless joy in feeling the little child inside of her kick and stretch. The first child barely moved. All was going along smoothly this time, but such did not guarantee a healthy birth. Dominico could not wait to have children. He could not bear to lose another.

Desperation twisted his face as he climbed the stairs. He was met by five or six men from the building. They stopped him at the door.

"What's going on? What's wrong? What's wrong?"

"It's OK, Dom! Dom, it's all right! Everything is going to be fine, just calm down." One of the men spoke in soothing tones.

Heaney and Dante caught up with him and helped calm him down. Madison, had run with Heaney up to the boundaries of Little Italy, stopping before crossing Canal Street. He watched Heaney and Dante cross and called forth his best wishes to his unexpected friend.

"Sometimes it's earlier than expected, that's all." Dante smiled with as much good cheer as he could muster. He swallowed his own fear. That was his little girl in that room. He knew the dire consequences of a troubled birth, especially for the poor. "Let the women take care of this. They know what they are doing."

Dominico stopped trying to push through the web of arms holding him in place. He sat on the stairs with his head in his hands pulling at his thick, black hair. He could hear yelling in the room above his head.

"Is that her?"

"Yes. *Maga 's* up there and *Signora* and my wife and a couple of other midwives from the building are helping." Pietro said. Pietro had become a dedicated friend of the Schiaparellos and the Rossas after they helped him become sober.

"Dominico, everything is going to be all right."

"We'll just wait here until it is over."

"Just relax, Dominico. It could be a long night." Pietro handed him a thermos full of steaming coffee. Another brought a bottle of wine.

"You want to come into my apartment, Dominico? The night's going to get cool."

Dominico shook his head. "I need the air. I want to hear what is going on."

Giulianna's screams grabbed at Dom's heart and sinew pulling his body rigid. He shook his head trying to remember the old prayers. He could no longer remember which saint to pray to. He was convinced that all was not going as it should. His ears were pricked for every sound that might have been out of place. The men gathered around him and comforted him the best they could. They told him stories of their own children coming into the world. They conspicuously avoided stories of their own tragedies, concentrating only on tales with happy endings. Then another scream and Dom pulled at his hair.

The sun was breaking through the patch of horizon between the buildings, and the screams were regular, almost constant. Giulianna would groan then scream, then draw desperately for air, then groan again. Dominico paced the street, pulling at his hair. The men of the building stayed with him. Dante drifted up and down the stairs for updates and coffee. It was almost time. Dom had heard that the baby could come any time.

Dominico sat in the street as the stores began to open and the merchants with their wagons started their travels through Little Italy. Dom peered into the window overhead. Occasionally, he saw a shape pass by. Then he stared at the street.

Then the screaming and groaning stopped. For an interminable second all was silent. Most of the men who had been waiting with Dominico had to go to work. Only Dante and Heaney remained.

"What's going...?"

"Just wait." Dante raised his hand.

No sooner did Dante intervene than the crying started... the wonderful crying...baby crying, a strong, incessant trumpet blast. Dominico wanted to rush up the stairs, but Dante bade him wait until one of the women told them it was all right for them to come up.

It was not long before *Maga* came to the door and motioned them to enter. She was tired and her clothes were bloody, her gray hair disheveled. But the beauty of her toothless smile warmed Dominico.

"It's a boy, Dominico. A beautiful, healthy boy. *Molto fortunato*." She said as they walked up the stairs.

Dominico's legs were almost too weak to climb the stairs.

"Giulianna? What about her?"

"She's lost a lot of blood, but she's young and strong. We made sure there will be no infection. She'll be fine. Come. Come see your son."

When Dominico entered the room, his vision was shrouded with tears. There was his beautiful wife, fatigued but glowing. At her breast was the tiniest baby he had ever seen. Such a tiny baby. He was beautiful, his little hands reaching for his new world, a world he could not even see yet.

Dominico kissed Giulianna on the forehead. "Thank you." He whispered, his throat tight with joy.

She clasped his arm and kissed his hand. "Meet your son, Dominico."

"Dominico," Dom sighed. "Little Dom Rossa." He gently stroked the baby's head.

"OK. Out." *Maga* croaked. "Everyone out. The baby must eat." She pushed Dante backward through the door then tugged at Dominico. "Out, out, out!"

As Dom stepped out the door it closed behind him. Then the door opened again, but only a few inches.

"Dominico," *Maga* whispered, her voice crackling, but mysterious and deep.

"Yes." Dominico became suddenly concerned.

"You'll see her again, you know. You will see her again."

"Giulianna?" what was Maga saying?

"No. You know of whom I speak. You will see her again, but not how you expect."

"I...don't understand."

"You will see her again." The door closed.

CHAPTER 17

"I tell you, darling, it's the most beautiful place I've ever seen."

Giulianna stroked her husband's thick hair while he lay on her soft bosom.

"It would be a great place for Little Dom to grow up. There's room for him to play and explore. Hills and mountains, cool, clean air. And now, little Enrico. He can grow up away from this dirty, brown city. He can have the full benefit of growing up in a place that does not stink of rot and coal."

Their new baby, Enrico, lay on the bed between them in serene sleep, bathed in their combined warmth. He was born while Dominico was away, another early baby that would become Giulianna's hallmark. Little Dom rested in a crib Dante built on the other side of the small apartment. He clutched a stuffed bear brought to him by his adored father, after returning from his time away.

"It does sound wonderful, Dom. It sounds nice, but…"

"Everywhere you look you see green mountains and the people there are beautiful. They're from all over the world.

And I would work in my trade there. I won't have to lay brick anymore. I can cut and sculpt the stone, the granite that the cutters break from the mountains themselves. I can do what I've always been trained to do, what I've always wanted to do."

Dominico was talking about Barre, Vermont. This was the town he visited during the most recent strike in New York. Thousands of workers in the city refused to return to their jobs, demanding more pay, better conditions. Organized by the IWW, some workers with special skills were sent abroad to work and send money back to the union. The union used that money to help feed the families that were most burdened by the strike. The confrontation between labor and capitalist was ruthless, neither side wishing to compromise, neither side giving in. Scab labor was viciously turned away from the factory doors by hordes of angry strikers. The owners, meanwhile, did their best to bide their time until winter would end the strike and force the malcontents back to the factories.

But they were losing money. Factory production dwindled to a trickle. Not enough was being produced to satisfy the demand. Prices could not be raised to compensate for the shortage, as buyers rejected the higher costs. The owners, in their top story office suites realized that waiting for winter might ruin them. This strike was much better organized, planned to inflict the most damage before the year's first frost. Indeed, this was not a reactionary strike in which the laborers, frustrated and exhausted, just walked off the job without thinking about the consequences. This strike was proactive, and the industrialists were coming to realize that they would have to change tactics if they were to defeat this implacable foe.

Dominico, after his talents as a stone carver were discovered by the union, was sent to Barre to work with another in his profession. In return, he sent his pay back to the union. His family, including his pregnant wife, was among the first to receive care and provision.

For Dom, this was a chance to get away from the city, a stone fortress he viewed as a prison. It was a chance to see what more there was to America than the brown of city life. As much as he did not want to be away from his family, he was seeing things in terms of the greater good, he was seeing this fight as a way of making things better for his children.

Strangely, though he continued to have difficulty seeing himself as American. He had equal difficulty seeing his children as Italian. They at least were American, even if he was not. They would enjoy the fruits of this land that were held so far from his own reach.

The train ride to Vermont was unlike anything he expected. America was a beautiful country. He saw pictures in books of the rolling mountains and the vast plains, and the mighty Rockies. He was not convinced, however, that these were anything more than a fiction used to lure unsuspecting immigrants to this country to work for slave wages in the vein hope of owning a house by a cool mountain stream. For all he knew the pictures of the Rockies could were taken in his very own Italy, to the north.

Looking through the thin, dirty train windows, however, Dom realized that the natural beauty of his adoptive country was no exaggeration. Tall, straight pines swayed for miles, painting the distant mountains in sap green. The brighter greens of the maple and elm, the broad oaks only highlighted the darker, richer green of the tall, straight pines. So many trees! Dom had never seen many trees.

Interspersed among the trees one might see giant chunks of granite as if deposited there by some reckless god. Then a white steeple, made by man, but no less a part of the landscape, would stand among the pines marking the presence of a town. The towns seemed to blend into the countryside, the apple orchards, the grape arbors, the dusty roads on which bales of hay were carried to the far country.

There was something more to America. There was something more than the factories and the mills, the docks, and storefronts. There was something majestic about America once one left the stifling, smoky cities and traveled her back roads. This was the magic of America. This was where every single person in the city wanted to be. It was the America of the white steeple and the green pines that was the American dream—A dream that was often swallowed by the exigencies of life in the cities, a dream one could revisit every so often on a simple train ride into the country. This dream served as the life blood of all who toiled in the factories and mills, under dark brown man-made clouds. Every man who toiled in the cities did so with an image of a little white house on a green piece of land in the back of his mind.

When he arrived in Vermont he was greeted by a white-haired man with a thick, curling mustache. His name was *Signore* Augustino Villeppe. He was a Carraran stone carver who offered to take Dominico in for the duration of the strike. Dominico, in the meantime, was to take note of the goings on in Barre. The town was as close to perfection as he had ever seen, however, it was not without problems. The capitalist reach was long and firm. The stone carvers there were in the midst of a battle for their very lives. Many of their number were becoming sick from the new pneumatic tools with which they were expected to ply their trade. The tools made it easier and faster to cut the stone and were thus more efficient. However, they created a great deal of dust, inhaled by the cutters, resting in their lungs where it would eventually kill them. The value of human life, however, was not worth as much as a product brought to market faster and cheaper. So, some dagos die, their lungs torn to shreds by tiny silicate particles. There were always more dagos.

While in the Villeppe home, Dominico had an opportunity to prove his handiwork. *Signore* Villeppe smiled as Dominico struck an image into the granite. The young man had good skills—great skills, even. He had a sharp eye. Nevertheless, *Signore* Villeppe suggested that the young man's skills were raw and untrained. Before Dominico could protest and invoke his family name, the old man took the tools from his hand and demonstrated his own methods.

The two men shared techniques, *Signore* Villeppe discovering that he could learn as much from this young man as he could teach. The Villeppe family, like the Rossa's, was an old stone carving family. As such they handed down their trade from generation to generation. The same techniques were learned, relearned and refined. Rarely did novel techniques find their way into the family trade. In the old country, novelty was a trespass to be resisted as an infectious transference of a hereditary defect.

In America, however, there was no such barrier. Often old families found themselves working side by side. Old skills were challenged by American time frames and emphasis on efficiency rather than quality. *Signore* Villeppe told the story of how we once with little markers all over his body. He was filmed by a scientist who marked and graphed his every move. Later the scientist made suggestions about how he could reduce the number of movements he made and get the same job done in almost half the time. The scientist's suggestions made no sense, but *Signore* Villeppe, under the direction from his employer, did what he was asked. At least he did it for about a week. He slowed down his efforts then returned to his age-old methods once his boss had forgotten all about the scientist. *Signore* Villeppe laughed when he told every story.

Before Dom returned to New York *Signore* Villeppe hugged him and informed him that he would always have a place in Barre and a job working in stone.

Returning to New York, that long train ride through the country with which he had fallen in love, was a journey of mixed feelings. Dominico closed his eyes and drifted into sleep. He remembered the light cooing of his brand-new baby as he heard it through the telephone lines. After two weeks of dreaming about Little Enrico he would finally get the chance to hold him in his arms and play with his little feet. There was joy in seeing his family, rejoicing in Guilianna's always happy eyes, peeling Little Dom off his leg where he liked to clutch his father's pants and ride his foot. Even the apartment, so small with its wet, sagging walls, ancient and acrid smells, was at least a place of comfort, a place where love was found.

All Dominico could dream about, however, even his most lucid daydreams, was scooping his family up and taking them to Barre. Albeit, that town was a utopia only in his mind, it was a healthier place to live than Little Italy where they drank polluted water, lived in rat-infested fire traps, and sucked in fetid air. Barre was a haven from a place where the city streets devoured kids who saw crime as their only chance of escape. Little Dom and Enrico could grow and learn to respect their father and their family traditions, the family trade, rather than gain the street view of their hard-working father as a fool toiling interminably for a reward he will never receive. His greatest fear was that his boys would be lured into the world of street thugs and gangs stealing and extorting for the neighborhood *padrone*, their eyes gray and cold, their smiles sinister, teeth razor sharp. Such children could not respect their fathers for they saw the pursuit of money not as a means of taking care of the family or building respectability, but as a sign of manhood in itself, a sign of pride—sinful pride.

"We could live in Barre. We could live a good life." Dom smiled and kissed his wife between her breasts large with nourishment.

Giullianna giggled. "But Dominico, our family is here. We'll be leaving everyone we know."

Dominico almost responded that he had already experienced such separation. A new life was possible. There were new people to meet. The family would always be there. He realized, however, that talking to her about the trials of emigration was useless unless he was speaking to her heart. He had left everyone he knew with the hope of building a better life. He remembered the tightening chords of *Villa De San Giuseppe* pulling on him harder and harder with every step he made closer to Naples. Every minute he had to convince himself not to turn back. Then the *Halsbad* closed its hatches and sailed from the port. The chords to his village snapped painfully like sinew stretched too far. The ties were severed by the momentum of the ship, and he was free-floating in a morass of nowhereness.

A man who no longer had a home, no longer had connections to a place was truly an individual, truly, and painfully free. Such a man was cauterized from forming any such bonds again. Dominico felt the pain of separation now and again, his old village as it existed in his mind took on a pleasant aspect that did not match the realities of that dusty, ancient corpse of home. Dom often had to remind himself of the truth he left behind. Despite the occasional nostalgia, Dominico never felt the pull of his connections there, even as he was planning on returning for Pratolina, his actual ties to the old *paesera* were gone forever.

Giulianna, on the other hand, having made the voyage at her mother's breast, never experienced separation from her home. She never had to break those chords. Being tied to a place was a part of the Italian character that only the direst of circumstances could sever.

Dominico did not know if he was ready to pull his wife away from her home. He did not know how such a move would affect the health of the children, especially the new baby. He would have been in his rights to do so, being the man of the family. His wife, however, the mother of his children, held significant sway in his heart. He loved her. To pull her away from all she had ever known before she was ready would hurt her. Dominico could not stand to see his wife hurt.

"Can't we try to make our living here? Shouldn't we do what Father Tomas suggested and make our home a kingdom of God? After all, you are doing well. We are putting money away. Things will get better. People are always coming to you when they have work."

"Laying brick and mortar. Any fool can do that. I'm tired of it."

"But it's providing a living. It's putting food on the table. Pretty soon we can get a better apartment."

"This will never be a kingdom of God."

"We can make it that way. We can make a better life here, can't we? Shouldn't we try? Let's at least try?"

Dominico lay back on the pillow and covered his face with his bulky forearms. This was the indicator that he wanted to be left to his own thoughts. Normally, Giulianna did not intrude on this attempt to make his own space, but she was feeling insecure about the conversation.

"You and Father have been fighting so hard for so long. You fight to make this a better place." She knew that she should not have pressed the issue, but her sense of security was jolted. She needed reassurance.

"We'll stay." Dominico whispered, but his breath was full of exasperation. His voice carried the inflection of a dream ending. 'Perhaps when Enrico is a little older.' He thought.

"*Signore* Falcone is desperate to get rid of his store house. Make him an offer. You can do your work from there and have room for all the supplies you need. Maybe you and father can do something together."

"We'll see."

"You have a good reputation here. You'll do well to start your own business where you don't have to worry about strikes or bosses."

"I'll go talk to *Signore* Falcone."

There was more Giulianna wanted to say, but she knew that her husband was becoming frustrated with her intrusions. The baby would be stirring soon. It was best that she not make her husband angry before the baby awoke. She was convinced that babies knew when their parents were upset, even when they were too good to show it.

CHAPTER 18

Nearly all of a hundred coffins lay in a long row upon the pier, awaiting removal or identification of the charred bodies they contained. Forty human forms so burned, blackened and distorted that they cannot be recognized, lay covered by white canvas in plain pine coffins apart from those less horribly mangled. Unless they are identified by the trinkets and jewelry found on their blackened limbs they will fill a single grave of unknown dead.

A signet ring, found clinging to a shred of flesh on a little girl's finger, made identification possible, where all other means would have failed. A man, who had stood in line six hours, wandered aimlessly among the bodies seeking his missing daughters, until with a groan he identified a heap of charred clothing as their garments. He collapsed and sought to kill himself, but the police prevented him, and he continued to search for his wife, also missing.

A pale girl bent over a mis-shapen mass long and doubtingly, and then with a final effort she grasped a hand which protruded from beneath the canvas, and with a shriek collapsed. The blackened mass, she sobbed, had been her sweetheart, to whom she had become engaged the night before the disaster. A ring on his finger told her of his identity. She asked if the dead man had had a watch. They brought it to her; she opened it and gazed at her own portrait.

Twenty Sicilian women became hysterical upon recognizing their kin in the pine coffins. A man whose face was marked by a sear of flame, found his brother among the dead. The two had worked side by side pouring water upon the fire. A cutter identified his dead sweetheart by their engagement ring and her purse. It contained her week's wages, $3.

From: The Triangle Shirtwaist Fire
Los Angeles Times
March 27, 1911

"Ya gotta understand Mr. Rossa, I'd like to hire ya, but I don't want no trouble." The foreman said, shaking his head as he walked through the construction site.

"I really needa the job." Dominico walked next to him, but respectfully behind about half a step. "I'ma the besta there is. You aska Heaney. I'ma good worker. I'lla worka hard afor you." The air was brisk, but the sky was clear. A good day for working.

"I talked ta Heaney. He said you're a good man, but you're a socialist. Everyone knows you're a socialist. And your father-in-law, he's a troublemaker. No one'll hire him anymore. Geeze you'd think he'd get the point an' stop runnin' his mouth, but he just keeps on goin' and goin'."

Dominico shook his head. "I have a family. I hava to feed the children. I may be a socialist, but I'm a harda worker. I justa wanna what's right. Just like you. You have a family?"

"Yeah, I have a family, but I don't go makin' trouble ever' time you turn aroun'. It's like that, see. You keep your mouth shut you do fine. I started in the trenches just like you, see. Now look at me. I'm in charge of a crew here. I'm respected."

Dominico nodded, 'and you'll be nothing more than that,' he thought, but kept his mouth shut as suggested.

"Look, Dom. Heaney says you're a good man, and I know Heaney's a good guy an all, but my hands are tied. My boss finds out I hired you, he thinks there's a chance of Schiaparello come sniffin' round here, it'll be my ass. I got a family, too. I'm sorry. There's nothin' I can do."

Dom's jaw set firmly, his teeth grinding. He watched the foreman walk away. "Be like stone," he whispered through his teeth.

In the distance he saw Heaney finishing a façade on the new subway extension. He looked around then approached his old friend, tapping him briskly on the shoulder.

Heaney turned sharply then smiled when he saw Dom. "Hey, ye dago sonva bitch. You get the job. I really talked ye up."

Dom shook his head.

"I'll be damned. That bastard tol' me..." he shook his trowel in the direction of the foreman. "Sonva bitch. I shoulda knowed he'd never give ye a chance."

"It'sa all the speeches Dante'sa been makin.' Everyone's a scared o' him, so they're a scared o' me."

"You're still hustlin' pretty good, though, ain'tcha?"

"I get a little a bit here an' there. Not enough...not enough."

Dom tried his hand at business upon returning from Barre. He took over the rent from *Signore* Falcone, who was distraught to have to close the doors on the store that took him a lifetime to build. But the time came for him to move on. He had other opportunities elsewhere that he wanted to pursue. This was not true, of course. Dom suspected that the reality was much more sinister. *Signore* Falcone never told Dominico why he had to close shop, and out of respect, Dom never asked.

The real story was that *Signore* Falcone was forced, like most of the businessmen in the neighborhood, to pay protection to Don Coste, the new *padrone*. Because of this, he was able to stay afloat, but nothing more. Then, in an attempt to expand his business, he became indebted to Giacomo Leone, an area loan shark. Legitimate banks would not approve a loan, so Leone was his only hope. Unfortunately, his ambitious plan fell through leaving the middle-aged store owner buried in debt to the most dangerous elements. He could do nothing else but leave New York forever, as he would never be able to pay.

When Dominico took over the store he unwittingly inherited *Signore* Falcone's protection 'contract.' Shortly after opening the doors to Rossa Stone Works two kids, no older than sixteen, entered his shop. He finished moving bags of mortar from a pallet, then brushed the dust from his arms. At first, he thought the young men were looking for a job. Their faces were carved by long poverty, lean, almost bony. Their clothes, however, were neatly pressed and expensive. This indicated that they were not in need of employment, much to Dom's satisfaction as he hated turning people away, but he had no work for anyone at this point.

"Hey, Rossa!" one of the kids shouted, sucking on a cigarette.

Dom turned and stared at the boys, "That would be *Signore* Rossa." The young were becoming disrespectful, even disdainful of their elders, especially those elders who came by boat.

"I say Rossa. We're here to pick up the protection."

Dom shook his head curiously, "protection from what?"

"You know, don't play stupid, Rossa. Old man Falcone must have told you. We're here for the protection. One hundred dollars, fifty for last month, fifty for this month. Give it over or there's gonna be trouble."

"I don't need protection. Everyone here likes me." Dom granted a wolfish smile. He had already decided what to do while lifting a fifty-pound bag of mortar, pretending to strain against its weight.

"Not everyone likes you, Rossa. For instance, I don't like you. Now pay the protection or there's gonna be trouble."

Dominico ignored the speaker and turned to the other boy. "Don't I know you?" Dominico stared at the larger of the boys, a smooth faced thug with hard, unforgiving eyes. "Yes, I know you. You're the Prizella boy. I knew you when you were no taller than my knee. I did some work for your father. You remember? What was it? I fixed his wagon back when I was hustling for work. That's it, his wagon. Your father, he's a good man."

"My father is an idiot. Now all he does is sit upstairs and drink his wine. Still in the same old rat hole I was born..." he never got the rest of his words out. A fifty-pound bag of mortar pounded into his chest, knocking the wind out of him and crushing him to the floor. He was shocked that such a heavy object could be thrown with such little effort across the room. When he looked up, Dominico was holding the other boy under the collar, raising him off the floor and yelling at him. Then Dominico threw the rough faced boy like a rag doll on top of him, knocking the wind out of his lungs yet again.

"Now you get out! Get out! I'll not pay your protection. Your fathers would be ashamed of you. Parasites! Now go!"

That was the beginning of the end of Dominico's short-lived business venture. Soon rocks were thrown through his windows, supplies were stolen. Even a fire was started that would have destroyed the shop as well as the apartments above, but Dom happened to be walking home from a meeting late that night and saw the embryonic flame glowing faintly through the edges of the boarded windows.

It was not long before he was sleeping in the shop, guarding it, refusing to give up all he had strived for to pay blackmail to another two-bit *Padrone*. Every night he found himself fending off intruders or chasing down kids intent on damaging his property. The constant combat took its toll of sleepless nights, and days spent hustling for work from people who were afraid to do business with a man who defied Don Coste. After considerable urging from Giulianna, worried about his dissipating health, he gave up the shop rather than pay the demanded protection to parasites that draw blood from their own people.

He tried to find a front outside of Little Italy where he wouldn't have to worry about protection. Outside of Little Italy, however, there was a different kind of protection racket. The rents were exorbitant in most places, far out of reach for immigrants. In areas where the rents were more reasonable, the landlords refused to rent to immigrants born in under the Mediterranean sun. Dominico's first attempt at entrepreneurship was over.

His debts, however, were not. He had borrowed money from local lenders, wisely avoiding the loan sharks. There was much promise in Dominico, whom everyone knew to be true to his word and indefatigable in his labors. No one had a problem loaning him money. He spent the next two years trying desperately to pay off the loans and make ends meet by hustling jobs where he could. To his shame Giulianna had to find work in the textile mills. She found a position as a cutter at the Triangle Shirtwaist factory and supplemented the family income with piecework.

For a while the children, Little Dom and Enrico, stayed with *Nonna* Rosella while Dom and Giulianna tried to make their way. Rosella, however, soon had to find work as well. Dante was blacklisted after helping organize a women's walk out in the textile industry in 1909. Ironically, it was to the textile industry that she had to turn to support her family. Giulianna was able to secure her mother a job as a seamstress at Triangle Shirtwaist. Even little Enrico, no longer so little, found a job at a foundry, dangerous work for a child so young. He would never learn his grandfather's trade of carpentry.

That the money Dominico was making was not enough to support his family was a source of great pain to him. To have Giulianna working rather than taking care of the children was more than he could bear. He had to find a way to bring her home where she could be a mother and a wife. Working in the mills, inhaling cotton fibers, bent over some machine was not what he wanted for her. He defined himself and the health of his marriage based upon simple terms. It was his job to provide for the family, it was his wife's job to raise the children and take care of the home. He was a man because, no matter what it took, he was able to provide for a stable, traditional family structure. In this case, neither he nor his wife could satisfy their traditional roles.

"It's just not enough." He stared at the ground and scratched the back of his head.

"I know what ye mean, my friend. When's Dante's revolution supposed to…what in the hell is that?"

"What?"

"Over there. Look. Smoke." Heaney pointed east.

Dominico turned and saw a great serpent of black smoke coil into the sky. His jaw fell as he tried to get his bearings.

"Isn't that near your neighborhood?" Heaney asked, but Dominico was already running toward the smoke.

The fire was not on Mulberry Street, but close by. The smoke settled into the street, choking and burning the eyes of the merchants and shoppers. People were running like unbridled horses in a storm. The women ran to their homes to secure their few possessions and their children. The men ran toward the fire to see if there was something they could do to save their homes from eventual conflagration. Well, they knew the devastating consequences should the fire find its way to Mulberry's fire traps.

Dominico stopped a dress maker who had just moved his merchandise from the street. "What is going on? Where's the fire?"

"The Triangle Shirtwaist is on fire." The dressmaker cried. "They say it just went up all of a sudden. Boom, like a flash." He waved his arms in a great circle.

"Giulianna!" Dom ran furiously around the corner before the dress maker could lock his door.

When Dominico reached Washington Square the Triangle Shirtwaist factory stood ablaze like a giant candle wick. One flame, streaming from the windows, engulfed the great building. Dom's legs would not work. He stood before this towering Hell agape, the furnace heat pushing him backward. From numerous windows women jumped to their deaths, only the flames on their dresses surviving the fall. Dom smelled, for the first time, burnt, human flesh. The odor that invaded his nostrils was unmistakable—death, hellish death!

Dominico did not hear the fire trucks that whipped past him. He could not hear the men screaming for buckets to try to douse the flames. He did not hear the women screaming as they were engulfed in flame, nor did he hear the bodies strike the ground with sickening crunching sounds. He simply ran to the burning building, grabbed a bucket, and flung the water into the huge fire where it evaporated before even touching the flames. Run, get another bucket, throw it on the flames... another bucket, the heat burned his face, singed hair, hot soot beneath his eyelids. The only thing coming from his mouth... Giulianna, God, Giulianna. It was not long before he was part of a well-organized line steadily dropping buckets of water on the flames. They were like ants trying to put out a campfire before it engulfed the entire forest. The fireman pumped, their arms like furious pistons, to maintain a stream of water. Others worked desperately to keep the fire from spreading to other buildings.

Dante appeared from the smoke, running around the building pulling bodies, some of them still burning, to a place away from the fire. He checked them for any signs of life, finding few. With every victim he found, he stared into their faces, praying that he did not see his wife or his daughter among the dead. They had to be alive. They had to have found a way out. They were smart women. They could have gotten out. They must have gotten out.

One woman, burned unrecognizable, was wearing a dress like one Rosella owned. It could not be! The wind evacuated his lungs. Then he sighed, relieved. The woman was wearing a charm that he knew his wife did not own. Again, he ran to the building and grabbed another mound of charred flesh, dragged her away from the flames, checked her for life, for familiarity...*Signora* Destatella! She was the woman down the hall who took glory in baking pies. No signs of life, her burned eye sockets open, black, and empty.

Dominico threw more buckets of water. The firemen pumped water in impotent streams into the colossal flames. Smoke belched into the air, onto the streets, a great, toxic blanket. His lungs burned as he threw more water on the fire. He ran, collapsed, picked himself up and dragged another bucket to the flames. Dante dragged more bodies.

"DOMINICO!"

In the distance beyond the sirens, the screaming, the audible dying, he heard his name. A shrill voice fought its own weakness and fatigue, pierced the smoky carpet, and penetrated his ears pulling all the sounds of hell with it.

"DOMInico!" The voice became weak.

He turned. The horrid sounds of the moment blared suddenly in his mind, as if a door in perdition was thrust open.

"I'M HERE!" He stumbled through the smoke.

Before he could understand what was happening, he held her in his arms. She was caked with soot, her clothing singed black and falling from her like dead skin, hair burned almost off. She was unrecognizable. There was no mistaking how she felt in his arms, however. It was Giulianna. They held each other and cried into each other's dirty necks, the building burning behind them. The sounds of panic drifted away once again.

The coffins were set in rows on the pier. People were lined for miles, guided by police and firemen to the coffins one by one. Some bodies were burned beyond the ability to recognize them as human. They were set aside at the far end of the pier with the hope that someone might recognize a locket or a charred and tarnished wedding ring. Occasionally, a family member would stare into a coffin, rub his or her eyes and just stare, then fall, legs losing all vitality, chest unable to pull in air from sobbing. Policemen would carry them away. Others would seal the coffin and write the name of the identified deceased on the cover. Another with a clip board would search a list and place a check next to a name.

Despite the air of composure and authority surrounding the police and clip-board holders, there was nothing impersonal about the looks in their eyes. Most of the bodies were young women or understood to be young women in some cases where the sex was indistinguishable. Most of the bodies were among the reviled Jews and Italians who were spurned by the Anglo majority in America. But one cannot look upon a burned corpse with emotional impunity. It was as if once the skin is burned off and the nationality no longer recognizable, the corpse in death takes on the aspect of humanity that it could only struggle and hope for in life.

Dominico and Giulianna stood in line with Dante, holding him as they approached the pier. Rosella was nowhere to be found. She never returned home. She was not admitted into any of the hospitals. Dante sat in a chair in his empty home and stared out the window, part of him expecting his wife to walk through the door, the rational part of him knowing that that would never happen...never again. Now he stood in line, his daughter kissed him and hugged him every step closer to the pier. She wore a hat to hide what was left of her hair, blisters still marred her face, neck and hands.

"So, you say the doors were locked." Dante's voice was a whisper, but somehow loud with anger and hatred.

"Papa don't worry about that right now. You have to take care of yourself right now."

"I want to know."

"There's time for that later, Papa."

"God damn it!" Dante yelled. "I want to know. I want to know how those sons of bitches killed my wife! I want to know!"

Giulianna glanced at her husband who nodded once quickly. Dom knew that people dealt with the death of a loved one differently. Dante, he was afraid, was going to deal with this through rage.

"The doors were locked, Papa." Giulianna sighed. "They were locked from the outside so the workers couldn't sneak off while they were on the clock."

Dante nodded and growled through his teeth. "Locked in. They couldn't get out. Trapped."

Tears streamed down Giulianna's burned face, prompting Dominico to take her and hold her. He was gentle with her. The blisters and burns prominent on her skin were scarlet and sensitive to the touch.

Giulianna escaped death by the merest coincidence. She was trying to enroll Little Dom in school for the next year. Dominico insisted that his children were going to school and learning to read and write better than he could. He wanted them to learn how to be successful in America, and the only way for that to happen was to receive an American education. Giulianna begged him to let her teach them at home. She had been to the American schools where the Italians were assigned. They were overcrowded, dark and hostile. The teachers were the least qualified for their jobs and the schoolmasters were cruel in their punishments. None of the teachers or schoolmasters were Italian and very few of them had any tolerance for Italian ways. Dominico insisted that only through school could his children get a chance at a better life. Giulianna was not convinced, but she relented. Dominico made very few demands on her with regard to the children's upbringing, but when he did, he was stalwart.

Little Dom was enrolled in Public School 23. This was one of the better schools available to immigrants, and Giulianna would accept nothing less for her little boy. Consequently, Giulianna arrived late for work. She was trying to convince the supervisor to let her in to work the rest of her shift. He refused despite her pleas. She offered to work extra hours. She offered to accept half pay. His only response was, "rules is rules, Missy."

Then the fire started. Cotton fibers that filled the air were sparked and ignited like gas fumes. The flames engulfed Giulianna so quickly that she did not think she could reach the door. Flight was automatic, however, an animal drive to survive. Her first thoughts were of her children and the possibility of their being raised by another woman. Little Dom might barely remember his mother, but Enrico would never know her. Her next thought was of the new life that she suspected was growing inside of her. Dominico did not know yet, as it was still too soon, but she was certain that she was pregnant, and equally certain that she was going to have a girl this time.

Once she was safe from the flames, she filled her lungs with cool air. Her next thoughts turned to her mother who was working inside. She had to get her mother out! She raced for the door from which she had entered, but a great yellow flame barred her way. In desperation, she ran around the building looking for a way in. She had to get her mother out. It was she who begged the supervisor to give her mother a position. Guilt and remorse filled her heart as smoke-filled air was pulled into her lungs. She had to find a way to get her mother out. She never got the chance. Just as she thought she saw a way in, she was grabbed from behind by a police officer who dragged her to the other side of the street and forced her sit where he placed her.

Now they stood in a morbid line of mourners. Each prepared to identify the bodies of their loved ones for the sake of giving them a proper burial. Each prayed that they be spared the torment of seeing their loved ones burned and mutilated. Each held out hope that there was some mistake, and their loved ones would come walking around the corner with smiles on their faces and stories much like Giulianna's. Each man, woman and child who stood in that serpentine line was lost in hopelessness.

Dante was ushered onto the pier, a police officer offered gentle encouragement as he approached the first of the coffins. Dominico held Giulianna away from the pine boxes. It was decided that if Rosella was in one of those boxes, Giulianna did not need to experience the shock of looking upon her. It was bad enough that after her experience at the factory she could conceptualize what happened to her mother.

Dante made his way from box to box. Every splintery lid that lay before him was a door to panic and horror. He expected to see his wife under each. Then the lid would be raised, and he would gasp, convinced that the remains revealed were those of his beloved wife. Then reason would return and despite the revulsion he could study the remains. Dante had to study some of the remains more intentionally than others, for their features were similar to Rosella's. Twenty, thirty boxes he peered into, gasping before each of them. The mutilated remains were a hellish museum display. None held her remains, but they were the remains of someone, someone who was loved, missed, mourned. He turned to a police officer and shook his head.

The officer frowned and led Dante to the coffins which were set aside. Some of these remains were fished out of the embers with hooks. Many boxes were later found to contain parts from numerous bodies that were mixed together. Perhaps they were clutching each other as the fires ate them, holding each other in that last, desperate grasp of human intimacy before death. When Dante was led to these boxes Giulianna buried her face in her husband's chest. This was more than she could bear, even from a distance. The thought of her mother...

Dante took his time at each box. There was no way to identify the remains by looking at them. He had to study each one as the canvas was pulled back. The rings on their fingers, the jewelry around their necks. Wedding rings were the first thing looked for. From coffin to coffin he searched, finding nothing. Then he stopped. He stared into the box, his face distorted with pain and rage. The police officer stood next to him as he reached into the box, sorting through the charcoal flesh and bone. With a slight pull Dante freed something from the box, but Dominico could not tell what it was.

Dante's screams echoed through the city as he cursed God and all those responsible, shaking his fist in the air. Dominico could not tell if he was threatening the lofty penthouses and upper offices of the industrialist robber barons or if his father-in-law was trying to intimidate the very fortress of Heaven. The police officer tried to move Dante from the pier but found that he was not big enough for the job, at least not without clubbing the man out of his insanity and into unconsciousness. With all the news men around, however, this course of action was not advisable. Two other officers accompanied Dominico to lead his father-in-law away as he cursed and fought and spat on the ground.

Dante did not collapse until they reached Giulianna. He gazed into her scared and sorrowful eyes...how much she looked like her mother...he fell, sobbing, at her feet.

Part IV

Ritorno

CHAPTER 1

Cecilia led this weary soldier along the dusty roads through the hills. Dominico stared into the fallow fields. This was the growing season. The fields should have been a carpet of green buds struggling to the sky, but everywhere was brown. Even the neat rows that were the trademark of the fields being prepared for sowing were nothing but trampled and tangled ground.

Were things this bad before he left his comfortable little village so many years ago? He was not lost to nostalgia. The poverty and oppression under Don Alfredo's tyrannical hand was the dominant characteristic of *La Villa de San Giuseppe*. He remembered the fear and seeming spinelessness of the people in this village. Their unwillingness to stand up for themselves sickened him. Their cowardice shamed him. In hindsight, he realized that from the beginning he always wanted to run away. He wondered, at that point, if he would have stayed in *Villa de San Giuseppe* regardless of meeting *Pratolina.* Would he have left anyway? Would he have crossed the ocean even if not to win the hand of the woman he loved? He shrugged this question off as unanswerable. Memories do not share their alternatives.

It was bad in the village, he remembered, but not this bad. Or was it? Perhaps his memories were playing tricks on him. His travails in America encouraged warm, often fantastical dreams of his Campanian homeland. What was indelibly impressed upon his mind at one time, a part of his consciousness, soon seemed vague and intangible. As much as his home appeared to have changed, there was no way to know how much his own memories were distorted by time. He knew the fondness he felt for his village reflected more the warmth of the family he left behind and the innate closeness all Italians felt for their native soil. It did not, however, resemble the reality of a lost culture, a lost way of life. Living in Campania was like watching an old, dear relative die. It may have been time, but that did not assuage the pain.

Still, somehow, it was not quite as bad as this.

As they rounded a little bend in the road Dominico slowed his pace. There was the wall that surrounded the *latifundi*, Don Alfredo's estate. Up ahead was the tree, the sacred place where he first saw the love of his life. In his mind's eye she still stood there, bronze and barefoot under the tree. Light green grass caressed her feet, wildflowers rested gracefully in her long, black hair. She watched him as he approached. A sly, half smile passed her lips. Then she was gone.

The tree was different, larger, branching further out, but somehow less inviting than it was when she stood under it. The leaves were dry and sparse. Broad, cracked roots splintered the dry ground on the very spot where Pratolina's feet once blessed soft grass.

Past the tree Dominico let go of Cecilia's hand. He ran to the corner of the wall, stroking it with his good hand.

He turned to her. "My father and I built this drain." A nostalgic smile crossed his face. On his knees he examined the work. Cecilia did not approach.

Finally, he stood, staring at the drain.

"It's still here. Not a stone out of place."

Dom's hand ached. He smiled as he massaged it. It was only an hour earlier that those hands trembled from the merciless reverberations of pneumatic cutters in *Signore* Villeppe's work shed in Barre, Vermont. In the last three years Dom moved his family to the small, vibrant Vermont town and resumed his trade. He reveled in the dull ache that charged his muscles. Every night Giulianna would press her strong fingers into the tight muscles of his hands and arms and back. He would regale his wife and family with stories about how the stone was taking shape, how it seemed the granite melted away before the machines. Of course, talk about the technical details of stone carving was of little interest to the rest of the family, but all smiled with the exuberance that Dom displayed as his mouth mimicked the noises made by the machines.

Despite the greater ease brought to his trade by the new machines, Dom still made it a point to do some of the work with the familiar hand tools of his youth. This was a fancy *Signore* Villeppe indulged for he lived vicariously through his newest carver's passion for the ancient ways when man shaped stone by the force of his arm and the edge of his blade. He heard stories about those out west who tamed wild mustangs by hand. *Signore* Villeppe imagined that that would be quite a sight, but it would be nothing compared to a stone carver, a master at his trade, taming stone itself, the very flesh of the earth. Stone carvers could make the stone rise into the sky as spires of great cathedrals. They could take a shapeless mass and liberate the Virgin Mary from its core. There was nothing greater to *Signore* Villeppe than to work the stone or to watch another master craftsman at his trade.

And Dominico Rossa was a master craftsman. When he met the young man years before Dom showed much promise as a stone carver. He was clumsy and unsure of the tools at first, having spent so many years away from his trade, but still, the genius was there. Most importantly, the joy was there, the passion was there. At the end of the day, when the rest of the carvers were going home, Dominico Rossa wanted to complete one more curve, one more letter, one more indulgence. *Signore* Villeppe had to force him to rest and eat.

When Dom returned to Barre three years ago Signore Villeppe, true to his word, brought him on to work in his shed. Dom approached his work with relish. It was not long before the rust was fallen from his joints and the uncertainty from his nerves. He was finishing works that matched the best of Villeppe's eldest carvers.

Inch by inch Dom pressed his fingers into his flesh. He was a poor proxy for Giulianna's deft touch, but it was the best he could do. She stayed home with the kids and prepared a great dinner for her father's long-awaited visit. Dom traveled to Montpellier to pick Dante up at the train station. There he sat, waiting for the northbound from New York to arrive, pondering the last time he had seen his father-in-law and his good friend.

Shortly after the Triangle Shirtwaist fire claimed the beautiful Rosella Schiaparello, tearing the heart out of the family, Dom convinced his wife to travel to Barre and start a new life among the Green Mountains. Giulianna agreed at once, much to Dominico's surprise. She could no longer remain in New York. Everywhere she turned was a reminder of how her mother died. She blamed the city as if it were a great, hungry monster that devoured the poor, especially the darker skinned poor.

They tried to convince Dante to join them, but he refused. He claimed that there were things that he had to do in the city. Unlike Giulianna, he did not blame the city. He blamed those who controlled the city, and he would not rest until he brought as much discomfort to those responsible for his wife's death as he could. He was convinced, as were many others, that the revolution was going to take place, and it was going to erupt in New York City. He wanted more than anything to be a part of that great conflagration of the oppressed as they toppled the mighty capitalists by the flames of their rage. Hell, he wanted to hold the torch.

It was painful to say goodbye. As much as Dominico sympathized with Dante, he never saw himself as part of something great. He was not sure that a revolution of the proletariat was such a great idea. Nor was he convinced that any action done out of anger and hate could have a positive outcome. He would remain a part of the fight, and if the revolution did come, he would be supportive, but his priority was his family. For his family he had to pick up the pieces of tragedy and continue with his life.

He had to find honorable work that would support his children and keep his wife at home where she could be a mother rather than a laborer. That is what he found in Barre. The Villeppe's were good enough to board his family when the Rossa's first arrived. Dominico paid little for rent and returned the favor by doing miscellaneous repairs to the Villeppe home. Soon he moved his family into a comfortable apartment in town. After a couple of years Dom was able to afford a small house outside of town.

It was a tiny, humble house that needed painting and considerable repairs, but it faced the Green Mountains and had a small yard where Little Dom and the rest of the children could play. Little Dom's school was on the way to Shed Row where Big Dom worked. Every morning Dominico walked his boy to school and kissed him goodbye before going to work. When he returned home in the evening the house was warm with children's laughter and the smell of Giulianna's cooking. It was the Rossa home, the first in the New World, and it was with immense pride that Dominico would bring his father-in-law through the front door.

A shrill whistle split the warm, summer air. It was the northbound carrying Dante. Pounding and clattering the train approached, becoming an all-consuming thunder until screeching to a steamy halt. People stood and peered into the windows. Those who recognized their loved ones waved and jumped and followed the window until the train stopped. Then they hugged and kissed their loved ones as they stepped down from the train.

Dominico stood, staring into the windows, but could not find Dante. As people streamed through the doors, he surveyed them all, men, women, children, yet there was no sign of his father-in-law. Perhaps he missed the train. Or perhaps something happened. Dom searched every face stepped from the train and fretted for his friend's safety.

Dante became a more militant dissident since the fire. He accused not just the owners of the Triangle Shirtwaist factory, but all industrialists of murder. At one point Dante managed to confront none other than J.P. Morgan himself as he was walking from a hotel lobby. He pushed his way through a crowd, got as close as he could to the very symbol of American wealth and threw a piece of Rosella's burned and bloody dress at him. Morgan recoiled with disgust, waving his jeweled walking stick at this insolent interloper. His entourage grabbed Dante and struggled to drag him away, but Dante would not be cowed. The resulting conflict was mentioned in the New York Times but received considerable attention in the socialist and communist press as well as anarchist pamphlets. There a grainy picture was run of Dante shaking his fists at Morgan as the elegantly clad man gripped the burned rags of Rosella's dress and waved his walking stick in violent indignation.

Dante's verbal assaults, his loathing and his ability to translate his hatred to the masses and inspire action, made him one of the most feared and hated men in the city. Wherever he went rage followed. Wherever he went he encouraged the working masses to surface their own submerged rage and desperation. Some socialists, communists as well as fervent capitalists saw Dante as the embodiment of the coming revolution. For some this was a quality to admire. In the capitalists it was a quality to be feared.

Such a man could not be allowed to continue, but all efforts to silence him failed--in fact backfired. Dante was imprisoned when a demonstration he organized became a riot. During the confusion a woman, an innocent bystander was shot, most likely by a police officer. Witnesses on both sides of the demonstration agreed that the death was accidental, but Dante was held responsible. Had he not organized the demonstration, the woman would not have been "accidentally" shot. Dante was arrested and tried for murder. However, the public outrage was such that it was obvious that though Dante was a dangerous man while free, he was more dangerous still as an imprisoned martyr. The decision was made to drop the charges. He was set free with a stern warning that the next time he would face trial. This only increased his fire and renewed his vigor for justice.

The man Dom finally spied walking toward him, however, was far from the epochal figure, the embodiment of a coming revolution. Dante was gaunt and old. He strained against the weight of his duffle bag. His shoulders sloped and his once robust figure was more of a twisted wire. His hair had grayed. His face was thin and covered in course, gray stubble. Dom realized that while he was looking for Dante, he had seen him but had not recognized his old friend. He approached with embarrassment.

"Dante, *m'amico*," he smiled and kissed his friend on both cheeks. "You look good."

Dante smiled cynically and handed his bag to Dom. "You shouldn't start lying just to be polite. I'm a mess and I know it."

Dom turned his head and walked to the bus that would take them to Barre.

"But you, my young friend. You look good. You look strong and healthy and happy. It is good to see you so."

"Look," Dom placed the bag on the back of the bus and showed Dante the palms of his hands. "The old calluses have come back." He rubbed them with his fingers.

"Like old friends." Dante laughed, but there was something missing in his laughter.

"It's good to be working in my trade." Dom helped his friend onto the bus.

"How are the conditions? Are they treating you well?"

"*Signore* Villeppe insists that we wear face masks. He keeps the doors and windows open as much as he can, but the winters are long here and when the sheds are closed the dust gets very bad. *Signore* Villeppe tries, but other sheds are not so good. There've been many deaths. Especially the older men. Their lungs just get crusted with granite and they die. Silicosis."

Dante shook his head.

"Even *Signore* Villeppe is starting to suffer. He doesn't think I notice, but I see him stifling a cough. He should stop carving, but he loves it as much as I do, so he keeps doing it."

"And Giulianna?"

"She's doing well. You should see the new baby. She's the most beautiful. A tiny thing, all pink and active. More active than the boys were. Perhaps being born in good air makes a difference. She's the happiest of all the children so far."

"How does my daughter feel about your work?"

"She says nothing about my work, but I know it bothers her. She washes the masks I wear every day and insists that I change them when they get dirty. She even tried to get me to stuff cotton up my nose, but it made me sneeze and made my eyes water all day."

"She's a good wife, then," Dante nodded.

"She's a good wife. She keeps the whole family happy."

"And well fed, I see." Dante slapped Dom's belly once flat as a tombstone but now showing a nascent rounding.

"*Si*, and well fed." Both men laughed

When Dante walked through the door he was hugged by many arms. Giulianna wrapped her arms around his shoulders and kissed him while Little Dom held him at the waste. Enrico held onto a leg. Young Gina clasped the other leg, but only because Dom and Enrico were doing it. She had never met her grandfather.

When the kissing and hugging was satisfied Dante looked down at Little Dom. "Well, Dom. You are becoming a man. You are what, fifteen, sixteen?" Little Dom blushed. "I'm only nine, Grandpa." He giggled.

"Nine! No! You are so big and strong, like your pappa! And Enrico, you've started school, no?"

"Ever'one calls me Henry, Ganpa."

"Well, Henry is a fine name. Henry it is, then. And who is this little gem here." Dante cupped Gina's rosy cheeks.

She smiled and turned away, clasping tightly to Giulianna's leg.

"Go ahead and introduce yourself to Grandpa." Giulianna stroked her soft hair.

The little girl blushed and shook her head, clutching more forcefully to Giulianna's leg.

"This is Gina. She's our biggest girl. Aren't you Gina?" Dom smiled and hugged his beloved daughter. "She's a little shy, but she'll warm up to you."

"And who is this." Dante tiptoed to the small bassinette where a smiling, pink baby kicked and swatted at tiny stuffed dolls hanging over her head.

"This is Saralina. You want to go see Grandpa, Saralina." Dom picked up the baby and handed her to Dante. She clutched his long nose and gleefully swatted his stubbly face.

"You have a beautiful family, Dom, Giulianna. You've done well."

"Little Dom. You show Grandpa around the house." The young man took his grandfather by the hand and showed him the house, starting with the boys' room.

Dante was not there for a family visit, however. He had business to discuss—union business. His life was shorn of sentiment though, if he were so inclined, he could have ingratiated himself with luxury in the lap of Dom's enchanting family. Dante dared not indulge himself, however. The world was a brutal place. Somewhere a corporate executive plotted the misery of the common man, plotted the death of a common man's wife or children. Dante would not rest long enough to give that hidden man succor. Every heartbeat, every minute he worked to end capitalism the less likely another man's wife might die in some rat-pit factory. Even the thought of sleeping became, for Dante, a gross waste of time.

After the children went to bed Dante, *Signore* Villeppe and Dom sat on the front porch of the Villeppe house and discussed matters.

"So, here's how it's going to work." Dante drummed his fist into palm as he spoke. The strike is going to start next week. The fifteenth at the morning horn."

"If the owners don't give up before then." Dom stated.

"They won't. They never do." Dante responded. *Signore* Villeppe shook his head and coughed lightly. Dom threw a concerned look in his direction. A look ignored by the old man. Coughing in Barre was an ill omen.

"So, you'll need us to take on the children and infirm if this strike drags into the winter." Villeppe scratched his stubbly chin.

Dante nodded. "We have enough food put aside to get us into December, but not much beyond that. I'm sure the owners know that. We've got to secure the families." It was sickening to Dante how a man's strength, his family, could be transformed into a weakness by the capitalist demons.

Signore Villeppe stood and smiled through his fatigue. "The Union's always been able to count on me."

Dom agreed, adding, "Giulianna can organize the women to can some extra food to send to New York and supplement your stocks. Our home is always open, as small as it is."

"What do you think are the chances of winning this one?" Signore Villeppe asked.

Dante frowned, seemed almost menacing in the eyes. "You never can tell. Each time we get closer and closer. We've made a lot of gains and still our people suffer."

"They give us just enough." Dom added.

"Just enough," Dante confirmed, almost growling, "But change is in the air. You can't hold back a flash flood."

Dante stared into the distance for the first drops of rain.

CHAPTER 2

Dear, Dominico

    My dear brother. It has been so many years since I've seen you. I was just a child when you left for America. I was much too young to realize the seriousness of that day. I'm a man now, Dominico, and, but for the pictures you've sent recently of your beautiful family my man's eyes have never seen you. Perhaps now I never will. The fighting has become intense in the north. I've decided to join the army before they come and take me. I'm hoping that such bravery, if one could call it that, will put me in a better position in the ranks. I see this as an opportunity to fulfill my obligation to the family just as you have, by sending money home to Papa. The war has only served to make things worse in the south. The family would benefit from one less mouth to feed and one more source of pay. As you know, Papa hasn't been doing well. There's no work, and since Nonno died his passion for the stone hasn't been the same. I'm afraid I've been something of a disappointment having never picked up your talent.

    Keep me in your thoughts, Dominico. With some luck I will return unharmed, though I've not seen many who've done so. Perhaps, God willing, I will join you in America when this is over. There's nothing keeping me here.

Paulo Rossa

5 Marzo 1917

Dominico held his wife close as they climbed the jail stairs. He straightened his tie and shifted the package under his arm. Upon entering the stark, gray building the guards took the package from his hands and opened it, examined the contents then returned it.

"Who are you here to see?" the blue clad officer behind the desk asked.

"Dante Schiaparello." Dom replied.

The guard was silent as he opened the clanking cage that led into the cell block. He passed a piece of paper to another officer who led Dom and Giulianna down a corridor that was dark despite the row of lights along the damp ceiling. Dom remembered the time he spent in prison so long ago. He recalled the fear that consumed him, the fear of being sent back to Italy, alone, indigent, a failure. He thought about how he felt trapped, not so much by the bars but by the fact that his life was no longer in his hands. His life was in the hands of a state that was indifferent to its ends.

As they approached a cell near the end of a corridor another guard banged on the bars, "Schiaparello, ya got comp'ny!"

Giulianna restrained a gasp as she looked upon her father. He was once so robust, bronze, tall, and hard. The man sitting in the cell could barely pass for Dante Schiaparello and all he had become. Here was an emaciated, sad looking man holding his gray and pasty head in bony hands. Indeed, the only aspect of the Dante of old was his eyes. When he looked up his eyes retained the pride and fire that was his hallmark. Those raptor eyes never lost their edge, their sharpness, despite the degradation of his body. But they were sad eyes all the same. Sad and wet.

"Dom," he smiled, wiping the moisture from his lids. "You are looking well. And Giulianna. Always so beautiful. Don't say the same for me, please. I've seen a mirror. I know the truth. I'm afraid I've lost all patience for lies, even polite ones."

Dom forced a smile. "I...uh...Giulianna and some of the women made you a package." Dom handed the package to Giulianna to present to her father.

"It's bread and *biscotti* and some other stuff thrown in." Giulianna smiled, but tears rolled from her eyes in defiance of her will. "Signora MacDonald made some of those biscuits you liked last time you came for a visit."

"The Widow MacDonald," Dante smiled. The Widow MacDonald spent considerable energy trying to convince Dante to court her. She was disappointed, but held out hope whenever he would visit Barre. "How is she?"

Giulianna's tears burst as she fell upon the bars and clutched at her father. He held her while she sobbed. A guard approached and cautioned that they were not to reach past the bars. Dominico peeled her from Dante and held her to his chest.

"The children," Dante wiped desperately at the tears falling from his own eyes, his mouth twisted into a forceful frown. "They are well, no?"

"The children are fine. They are staying with *Signora* Villeppe. Little Dom has been a big help to them since *Signore* Villeppe got the illness." Dom tapped his chest to indicate the illness in *Signore* Villeppe's lungs, silicosis.

"I'm glad you didn't bring them. I don't want them to see me like this. They are too young to understand. But I'm glad you are here. I need to see my family before..."

Giulianna bit into her lip to restrain more sobbing. She owed it to her father to make him as comfortable as he could be, and he could not be at ease with her crying.

"I can't believe they found you guilty." Dom shook his head.

"You've been in the country long enough to know better. The deck was stacked."

"But all you did was speak the truth. That is your right." Giulianna added, choosing righteous anger to replace her sadness.

"Not any more it isn't. Not if you speak out against this travesty of a war Wilson's gotten us into. I spoke out. I spoke out against the draft. I spoke about the revolution in Russia. There's perhaps some young fellow who is refusing to fight right now because I stood right out there in front of the recruiting office and denounced the lot of them, Wilson, Creel, the whole lot of them. Maybe there's another young man out there who will learn about Trotsky and make the movement a little stronger. You should have seen me, Dom. You would have been proud."

"I'm sure I would have been." Dom smiled.

"For what it's worth." Giulianna scowled.

"You know, Dom, I always expected to die for the things I said. I resolved myself to it. I even resolved myself to spend a significant portion of my life in prison. You know there's an American author named Thoreau who said, 'under a government which imprisons any unjustly, the true place for the just man is in prison.' I thought that was about right. I always wanted to be the just man and resolved that I would pay the price. But I didn't expect this. I must admit, it smacks of good old fashioned American pragmatism. By deporting me they can shut me up and they don't even have to feed me. It's really practical."

"Where will you go, Papa?" Giulianna cried. "Will you go back to your village? There's still family there, no?"

"Bah! I don't know. It doesn't really matter anymore. I guess I'll save up some money and make my way to Brazil or Argentina." Dante smiled, a mischievous glint in his eye. "I thought that I might go to Russia and take part in the revolution. Maybe I'll even make my way back here once this carnage is over."

Giulianna stroked his bony hands stretched from his cell.

"You know, I've been in this country for over three quarters of my life. For almost that whole time I've fought against the injustices that abound in this land. I've never stopped shaking my fist in the face of power. I never stopped being angry at the exploitation and abuse of the working man that I've seen for almost forty-five years. I've been beaten, spit upon, imprisoned, starved and insulted in every way. But you know something..."

He stared up at Dom and Giulianna, his eyes wet and sharp.

"I never once thought about leaving." He wiped his shaking fingers across his eyes. "Never once did I ever consider leaving. Even when Rosella died...I..."

Dante gasped for breath in a vain attempt to control the sobbing that was welling up from inside his heart.

"I'm an American, damn it...I'm an American...and there's something to be said about that. This is my country. I've given my flesh and soul for this country...to make it...better."

Dante could no longer talk. He placed his head in his hands as Giulianna wrapped her arms around him through the bars.

The guard came and reminded her that she could not reach through the bars.

That's the way it was. The nation was at war. President Wilson, once too proud to fight, was now ready to make the world safe for democracy—by fighting. It seemed, however, that the rest of the country was not anxious to join his campaign. Dominico wondered what would happen if war was announced, but nobody would go and fight, a general strike against war. That's when the draft was instituted. Now Dom knew the answer. They will come get you. That's what they'll do.

Dom was now thirty-five and exempt from the draft, for the time being, at least. But he watched his friends and co-workers, and their sons register. Many of them were called and sent to France where they were trained and where they waited to be cannon fodder.

He was disgusted by this, the folly of sending men, some of whom were not even born in America, to a foreign land to fight for foreign interests. His opposition to the war was steadfast, as was true of his political circle. Unlike the rest of this circle, however, Dom remained silent. Something was spinning in his mind when he watched parents separated from their children, wives from their husbands. Sons and brothers and fathers donned their uniforms and left their homes for war. He wanted to scream, 'don't do it!' 'It's a scam!' 'You're putting yourself in harm's way for nothing!' He wanted to be like Dante and defy the rule of an unjust law and a short-sighted policy.

But there was something else that he could not understand. There was something that kept him silent while Eugene Debs was imprisoned. When the Socialist Party was virtually dismantled from the top down in the interests of national security Dom attended fewer and fewer meetings. He was not proud of this. He knew that soon all voices against war would be silenced, leaving a voice only to those who believed in the righteousness of the war. It would not be long before those who were ambivalent would be convinced that there was nothing more necessary than fighting and dying for their country in the face of the Huns. Yet something gnawed at his mind...

It started biting one night at Lacey's, the local tavern. Dom had come to enjoy going to the tavern a couple times a week. He took pride in the fact that this was not an Italian bar, or a Scottish pub, but a place for workingmen of all nationalities to come and show their scars. He did not take part in the political debates, preferring to talk quietly with those who were of like mind. As the Great War in Europe dragged on, as people who had come from Europe reported on their family members who were actively involved in the horrors of the battlefield, it was becoming increasingly difficult not to speak out.

Then the revolution in Russia erupted like a volcano. As a known socialist, Dom was expected to be a loud celebrant of the great victory that was won—and part of him was. But he was also cautious. He considered himself a working man, a man of stone. He was never comfortable with the ethereal, abstract ramblings of ideology. Acting against an injustice he could see, and experience was his only motivating politics. For Dom that was socialism, or rather that was his kind of socialism. Polemics were for people like Dante or even *Signore* Villeppe in his own, quiet and rational way. These were the men who wrote the banners. Dom was the man who carried them.

Then the first young men were called for the draft. His neighbors and their children were expected to report to the military to do their part for their country. Dom was not sure how sending men thousands of miles away, to die on foreign battlefields on another continent was "serving one's country." That was just another abstract principle with which he was not comfortable. His fellow socialists railed against the impressments of working men for the purpose of doing the work of slaughter in a wealthy man's war. Communists lauded the soldiers of the revolution and recommended that if men were to fight, they should fight to overthrow the capitalists. Anarchists detailed the inherent injustice of governments that send men to war against their will.

Dominico quietly agreed with these criticisms, but when he went to Lacey's and had to face neighbors touched directly by the war, somehow socialist discourse seemed out of place. Yet he could not avoid his own history in the face of his neighbors. They knew that Dom would never have to face the war. He was too old for the draft and his children were too young.

"I say let's let 'em fight. Let's get this business over with and get on with our lives. Whatta ya say, Rossa?" Ralph MacDonough slapped him on the back and leaned his gaping, mocking smile a little too close to Dom's face.

Dom shrugged and slid over enough to get the man's breath out of his nostrils.

"You're a pacifist, aint cha?"

"I dona think war isa the answer. Only a more war canna come from this." Dom practically whispered.

"Well, it's a little late for pacifism now, ain' it? Now we're in it and we should see it through. People like you should keep your mouths shut and let people like me an' my boys get through this." A chorus of responses followed Macdonough's words, some in agreement, some in ridicule.

"I don' know. I'm a workina man a justa like you. What I know? But I don'..." Dom paused to think, "...maybe ifa politicians can shut upa the *pacifiste* by justa goin' to war anyway, maybe we'lla have a more wars."

There was silence in the tavern, which was to Dom's satisfaction. He really wanted nothing more but to share a drink with his friends from the shed. He did not want a political argument.

"Ah," called a man from the bar. "What does he have to say about it? He's not even a real 'merican..."

Dominico stopped going to Lacey's.

"Papa?" Little Dom whispered from his place at the dinner table. He had been quiet for days, his brow furrowed with the weight of inconsolable thoughts. He was like that, Dom knew. He was coming to the age in which he could rationalize and try to understand the abstract realities of the world. This caused him great trouble, but he took his understanding very seriously. When he spoke of such matters it was because he could not rationalize it himself.

"What is it, son?"

"Is Grandpa a traitor?"

The activity of the dinner table stopped but for Saralina who was still too young to understand the import of what was asked.

"Why would you ask that, Domino?" Giulianna was appalled.

"Mackey said that the Huns kill babies. He says that they want to take over the world. He said that his father says that anyone who won't pick up a gun and go fight is a traitor. He said that his father says that anyone who speaks against it is helping the Huns."

"Dom wiped his mouth and frowned. First, Domino, if you are not a dago, then Germans are not Huns. You remember the rule."

"I know, Papa, but that's what Mackey said."

A thought rushed through Dom that put some pieces into place. His son was not really asking about Dante, he was asking about...

"Your Grandfather is not a traitor," Dom patted his son's hand. "Your Grandfather has done a lot for his country. he's a good American and he's always been very brave."

"So why did they send him away?"

"Well, Domino, sometimes America doesn't recognize its greatest until..." Dom stopped and thought about the measure of his words.

"Until when, Papa?"

"Until it's too late."

"Why is that, Papa?"

"I don't know. I've never known why people should have to fight for what's right. It should be understood."

"Is the war right, Papa?"

"War is never right, Domino."

Little Dom was about to respond but was cut off by his mother. "That's enough war talk at the table."

"The boy's just curious, *Signora.*" *Signore* Villeppe said. "He sees all the propaganda. He wants to know the truth."

"He can be curious after dinner," Giulianna suggested. "The meal will not be ruined with talk about politics." The kitchen and the table were Giulianna's domain and her rule was absolute. Long ago she wearied of her hard work becoming the setting for political frenzy. Convinced that one could not enjoy a meal while talking about politics, she ended such discourse when it started. Her hard work was not for mere sustenance but was to be tasted. Besides, she reasoned that the excitement of political debate was bad for digestion. At one point she threatened to go on strike if such conversation continued—an ironic twist that ended political debate at the dinner table.

Dominico smiled and winked at his son, then at his wife.

"Tell Papa what you learned in school today." She instructed her son.

Signore Villeppe led Domino out to the porch where his father waited on a wicker chair, smoking a cigar and drinking a cup of wine. Little Dom was excited. The porch was where the men gathered to talk. He was never allowed onto the porch when the men were talking. He was always told that he could come out when he was older. Well, Little Dom knew that he was growing up. He was tall and straight and strong, the fastest runner in his class. He wanted desperately to be a part of the manly discussions held every night, imagining that he would have so much to say, so much to add. Someday, he thought.

That day had come, only he did not know what to say.

"Domino, come and sit down by Papa. You are getting so big, you know that. You are twelve now, no?"

"Yes Papa."

"What do you think, *Signore* Villeppe? Do you think he's old enough?"

Signore Villeppe smiled and coughed. "Perhaps. I don't know."

"I'm old enough, Papa. I'm old enough."

Dom smiled and patted his boy's head, stroking the soft, thick hair. "I think there are things that you need to learn. I don't think it's fair that you have to learn them so soon, but you will be working soon, perhaps, if this war lasts long enough, you might have to register for the draft." Dom frowned at this thought. It was then that he realized what it was that had eluded him for so many months.

"I don't mind, Papa. I don't mind so much."

"I mind, Domino. I want you to stay in school as long as you can. The sheds are no place for you." He looked over at *Signore* Villeppe who, even at this moment, was succumbing to the silicates implanted in his lungs like microscopic arrowheads. "I wanted to teach you the family trade, but in America it's different. It's not like the old country. It's better that you stay in school. Do you understand?"

Domino nodded. He really hated being in school. He hated sitting at the desks doing boring work, reading what he was told to read, being told what he needed to know with little regard for what he wanted to know. For his whole life, his father said that no one gets anywhere in America without an education.

"Son, I'm against the war, like your grandpa was. It's not a popular way to think. Many of your friends, their fathers believe in this war, and they are going to say things."

"Do they ever say things to you, Little Dom?" *Signore* Villeppe asked.

"They say stuff about pacifists being cowards. They don't know that you are one of them, though."

"Do you think that pacifists are cowards, Domino?" Dom asked, his mind spinning behind his normally calm eyes.

"I don't know, Papa. I don't think you are a coward, but the H...the Germans are doing such bad things. And my teacher says that the Austrians are trying to take over Italy and that we Italians should support our families who are fighting in the war."

"Like your Uncle Paolo, whom you've never met." Dom smiled.

"Yes, like Uncle Paolo. But then you say that the war is bad."

"Domino, back in the old country nations have been fighting for centuries. You know that from school."

"Yes."

"Then when one war is done there's another one waiting." *Signore* Villeppe added.

"But the reason I don't approve of this war is because there are only a small number of people who will benefit when it is all done. The poor will fight it, and the rich will profit from it."

"So, you will not go and fight, Papa?"

Dominico lowered his head.

"Mama said you don't have to go because you are too old. So, you'll stay here, right Papa?"

"I don't know. If the government needs more people they'll change the requirements. I don't know."

"But if you are against the war, how can you go and fight?"

Dom rubbed his head. "I don't know how to answer you right now, Domino. There are some things that are hard to understand until you get older. It's not that simple."

"But in the meantime, young man," *Signore* Villeppe jumped into the conversation once he realized that Dominico's mind was somewhere else. "You don't listen to anyone who talks about being a coward. Why, when your father first came to this country young men like you were already bent and mutilated from working in the factories. Your father and your grandfather fought hard to change that and they still fight. You've seen the scar on your father's back?"

"Yes," Domino never tired of hearing this story.

"You know how he got it, don't you. He was fighting so that the working man could..."

Dom heard no more of the conversation.

"Dom, are you coming in?" Giulianna opened the door and whispered. The children were asleep, it was late, and Dom had to work in the morning.

"I'll be in." He said as he stared at the stars. The smell of pine was exceptionally strong and compelling, and the sky was clear and moonless.

Things were coming into focus. The war...the war...such a slaughter after four years of fighting and millions of lives lost. Neither side was able to gain an inch of ground. How long would it last? A year? Five years? Ten years? And when it ended, when would the next war start?

Since Wilson declared war back in April, Dom heard many things about what it means to be an American, to fight for freedom and justice. He did not believe this war was an example of that. He knew that it was just another European conflict that the United States was best avoiding. In the few times that he expressed this he felt the sting of epithets, "communist," "traitor," "coward" and, worst of all, "un-American." None of these terms were unfamiliar to Dom. Instead of recoiling upon their utterance, he was used to wearing them like a cloak. This time, however, there was something different.

He had children. Children for whom he would be best to stay home. Children who needed their father.

Yes, he had children, specifically one boy who was coming into manhood. Certainly, his boy would be called should this war continue another five years. He heard about boys not much older than Domino conscripted and fitted for rifles in Europe. Would America be much different if its back was to the wall? He could not imagine that France or England would capitulate to Germany with or without Russia. Now that America was involved, the war could last another five years. Then his boy might be sent off to die in some foreign land. Could Dom watch his son, dressed in green, rifle in hand, sent off to the front? He fought back the nightmare images of his boy killed in France, alone, calling for his father. The image would not leave him, would not let him sleep.

The war had to be stopped, but speaking out would surely deny his children a father should he be arrested or deported. After four years of slaughter, mere protest would not bring this war to an end.

The war had to be stopped by men willing to fight and die to do so. Dom realized that he could not send his son to die in a meaningless war, but...

"Giulianna..." He whispered as he finished the last of his wine for the evening.

His wife stood in the doorway, her arms stiff and shaking.

"You're going, aren't you?" she said.

CHAPTER 3

Dominico did not share in the complaints fostered by his fellow soldiers. He was never one to complain. In fact, until that moment, Dominico felt he had little to complain about. Army life was not difficult. Indeed, it vouched certain benefits which only a man of his background could appreciate. It was stable, predictable, with steady work and clear rules—qualities that his life up to that point was lacking.

Those around him, however, did little more than complain, carouse and play cards for money. They did this from the start, from the moment they were sorted, prodded and processed for military service before being shipped overseas. Dominico was no stranger to being processed. He was amused by the fact that this was the easiest "processing" he had ever endured. Once it was determined that he had no ailments his acceptance by the military was assured. The fact that he could read was considered nothing more than miracle for a man who spoke broken English. This was the most welcome he had ever experienced in America outside of the Italian ghettos. One man even commented that Dominico was a credit to his race.

He wondered at the nature of society which was less stringent about whom it sent off to foreign lands to kill and die than it was of those whom it brought in from other lands to work and build.

The daunting and fatiguing training regimen that awaited him as he arrived in France was only that, daunting and fatiguing, nothing more. Again, Dominico was no stranger to fatigue. At least on the training fields of France Dominico knew what was going to fatigue him ahead of time. He knew the obstacles that awaited him and even the time he would face them. More importantly, he knew when he would no longer have to face, he knew when he could rest. At nine in the morning he ate, then again at noon, then again at five. Between those times he ran and jumped and pulled and fired his rifle at targets. Then he slept only to wake before the sun and start the process again. For his troubles he was guaranteed regular pay, most of which went home to his family.

What was there to complain about?

Sergeant Mallory was the only unknown variable during the day. He had taken a dislike to Dominico from the moment he introduced himself to the trainees. The sergeant spent some time excoriating the raw men without provocation, his eye always on Dominico. He then approached select men and asked them where they were from. He eventually made his way to Dominico.

"Ya look a little old fa me ta call ya 'boy.' I don' 'spose I should askya how old ya'ar."

Dominico said nothing.

"Whea ya from?"

"Barre, Vermonta, Sergeant." Dominico rolled his r's as was typical of every Italian dialect. The sergeant leaned in close, a sneer across his face. Dominico could smell tobacco on the man's breath.

"Whea you say you from?" Sergeant Mallory squinted, his teeth grinding.

"Barre, Sergeant."

"You lyin' to me, Mista?" Sergeant Mallory screamed.

"No, Sergeant."

"You must be lyin' to me, cause you don' soun' like no Vermonter I ever known. When I ask you whea you from you tell me whea you from, y'understan."

"Yes, Sergeant."

"Now whea ya from?!"

"Villa de San Giuseppe, Campania, Italia, Sergeant.'

"Whoee, Mista, you said that mighty fast. Betcha know Eyetalian real good, dontcha? Too badja can't speak English worth a damn, though. Ain it?"

Dominico was silent.

"Looks like what we have hea is one o' them Dago sonsabitches don't know how to speak proper 'merican. Ain't that right?"

Dominico remained silent.

"What's yo name, Mista?"

"Dominico Rossa, Sergeant."

"Well, Domini Roza, I'm gonna learn you 'merican 'fore I sen you off to fight. By the livin' God that made you you're gonna learn ta speak English. I don' wanna hea anotha funny sounding 'r' or another 'uh' at th' end o your words or nothin' ya got me?"

"Yesa, Sergeant." Dominico did not realize his mistake until it was too late.

The sergeant grabbed him, threw him to the ground and held him demanding push-ups. Sergeant Mallory watched as this dago strained his arms to complete every push-up demanded. Dominico's arms, hardened by years of stonework did not fatigue easily. The sergeant had stopped counting, instead ordering "again...again..." It did not matter to Mallory how long it took. This wop's arms would give out eventually. They did. Dominico pushed as hard as he could, his shoulders shaking with the strain, but there was no more strength left to give. He fell face down into the dirt.

"Git up, you lousy 'scuse for a soldier! Fucking waste o' matter swhatchu are. I need soldiers and those petticoat wearin' sonsabitches send me a broke down dago who'll no doubt catcha bullet not ten minutes into the fightin'. Well, I ain't puttin' my life on the line with no European nigga. I may be forced ta sit in the muck witcha, but I ain't takin' no shit off ya, y'understan' me?" Sergeant Mallory grabbed Dominico by the collar and lifted him to his feet.

"I asked you a question. Didju undastan' me?"
"Y...Yesss, Sergeant."

When the squad was dismissed Dominico brushed himself off, looked at the rest of the men and smiled. Most strolled away from him, snarling as they turned their heads. Some remained behind to talk to him. "Man," one said, "I don't know if I coulda taken that." "I'da knocked his god damned head in," said another.

"Eh," Dominico smiled through his teeth, "he's justa 'nother foreman. I'va worked for worsa." And he was not exaggerating by much. Sergeant Mallory could make him do push-ups until his arms fell off, but he could not fire him, and he could not dock his pay. Dominico felt he was in a much better position than he had ever been with a crew supervisor.

The only task Dominico found daunting enough to complain about was running. There was a great deal of running in the military, and it seemed that he did more than anybody. He was a thirty-five-year-old man, among the oldest in his company, and he was not used to running. On top of that, his years in the sheds breathing particles of silica had taken a toll on his lungs. He did not realize how much he had been affected until his first run when it felt as if someone were sticking nails into his chest. He thought about Signore Villeppe who had to give up working in the sheds because his breathing was so strained. There was a man who worked the last thirty years in the sheds. Dominico had only breathed the particulates for less than ten and already he was beginning to realize the terrible damage done to his body.

It did not take long for Sergeant Mallory to ascertain the difficulty that Dominico had with running. He took advantage of this weakness. Every time he heard Dominico's accent creep into his speech, heard him "talk dago," Sergeant Mallory made him run twice around the field. Dominico became light-headed, his legs cramped, and his lungs felt as if someone reached through his ribs and squeezed a great handful of tissue between angry fingers. But he never stopped running. He would complete his circuit and limp to the sergeant, stand up as straight as he could and look him in the eye. Sergeant Mallory would ask him to repeat what he said, and Dominico, through gasps of air, would make the necessary corrections.

He would then limp off to three men who became his friends, Roberto "Bob" Giancarlo, George SanAntonio, and Howard Lefkowitz. They would give him water and curse the Sergeant. Bob suggested putting a bullet through ol' Mallory's head the first chance he got, but Dominico waved him down.

"Thatsa not how a we do things." He would say. He never complained, even to his friends. Instead, he did as Signore Villeppe suggested. Signore Villeppe suggested that Dom become a voice for in the steady chorus of war. That he share his understanding of justice with fellow soldiers. Since he was in the trenches with them, they would listen more earnestly than if he were just another agitator who never left his own neighborhood. So, he spoke to his friends, quietly at first as was his wont, but soon he spoke comfortably, with more confidence than he ever had in speaking with others. He spoke to his friends about the reasons for the war—the real reasons, money, power, bank loans that must be paid. He spoke of the burden of the poor putting their lives on the line for the rich. Especially potent was the reminder that each of them could die, leaving their families destitute, while those who would profit kept their children safe at home.

George would argue, Bob listened politely but said nothing. Howard, on the other hand, ate up what Dominico had to say, agreeing wholeheartedly. Dominico never complained. He simply did what he was told and spoke what he believed to be the truth whenever he got the chance.

His three friends, Bob, George, and Howard were an unlikely trio. Bob was the son of an Italian immigrant, a shoemaker from Abruzzi. He was the oldest outside of Dominico. He was also the most cynical about humanity. Almost every day he recounted how his old man would work and smile upon his Anglo clients as if they were not looking down on him. His father would try to explain that that was his way. He was good to people and people were, more often than not, good to him. Bob did not believe that. He saw the ugliness that existed in everyone and was disgusted that his father could not see the truth that was right before his eyes.

As a boy, Bob made every excuse he could to avoid his home with his insufferable father. Instead, he spent his time in the streets with a group of young men who formed a gang called Le Tigri—The Tigers. The Tigers were, according to Bob, in charge of everything. At the rate they were going, and as tough as they were, it would not have been long before the Third Street Tigers had their fingers in "everyone's pie." Then the police shut them down, arrested the lot of them. Bob found himself locked up and beaten, lying on a cold, concrete floor waiting for bail, but bail never came. His father came. His father had to sell his shoe store, but he took his son home.

His father worked out of a wood carriage for the rest of his life, and Bob blamed the world and all of humanity. So, when he witnessed Sergeant Mallory abusing Dominico, he was among the first to pat him on the back and suggest that the old man not take any guff from that crusted son of a bitch.

George was of a more uplifting nature. His family was Portuguese and made a living selling produce. George was the oldest son at twenty-one years old and was set up to take over the family business. First, however, he had to do his duty for his country. His father always preached that George was an American, that America was his country, the greatest of all countries. It was in America that George's family secured a decent living, owned their own business when once they were nothing more than dirt farmers on a rocky patch of land in the Azores. George would do his duty and fight for his country, then come home and let his father retire. The young man had a great head for numbers and a passion for growing things. Behind the barracks he was cultivating seeds that he found in a field during one R and R. Tiny, fragile stems fought their way through the soil and stood proudly in their pots. George bragged daily about their growth, as if they were his children.

Howard was the youngest. He lied about his age, and the army in its zeal to get recruits, never checked. It would not have been hard to check. Howard did not look a minute over fourteen, though he confided in his friends that he was really sixteen. He said that he was running away from his father, a drunken bastard with a mean streak and a leather strap he kept wound up in his pocket. Howard was the only child, an accident as his father never missed an opportunity to remind him. He was also, according to his father, his mother's murderer. His mother, a sweet and beautiful woman, died giving birth to Howard. The infant was raised by his aunt until she died from pneumonia when Howard was just eight years old. He spent the next half of his life being beaten by his father. One day he fought back. A thin, wiry boy, he was surprisingly strong. He pulled the strap from his father's hand and struck him repeatedly with all the rage of a lifetime of abuse and neglect. However, his father was a large man, every bit as powerful as he looked. It was not long before he had the better of his smaller attacker. With one punch he dropped the boy to the floor, then picked up a piece of broken table and pounded him with a relentless assault. Howard curled into a ball. At one point his father lost his footing, providing an opening for his battered son to escape. He bolted for the door, his father in a rage giving chase, waving the bloody piece of a broken table over his head. Howard ran into the recruitment center because it was the first open door he could find to get away from his father. Volunteering for service made that status permanent. It was a move he did not regret. He would never go back home. In fact, he planned to stay in France, find himself a beautiful French girl, marry her and have a dozen children, all of whom he would love unconditionally, never letting a day pass without showing them this adoration.

For Howard, Dominico was not just a friend, but a father figure. He loved Dominico more than any other person on earth. At first, he did not want to have anything to do with this older man whom the sergeant obviously had it in for. It was not in his best interest to bring unwanted attention to himself by associating with a man who was marked by the one in charge. This wariness was dispelled one night while the rest of the barracks was playing cards or throwing dice. Dominico stood with a group of friends and showed them little pictures. They were his children and Dominico smiled and puffed out his chest as he talked about how smart little Dom was, how creative Gina was, how skillful Henry was. He loved his children, and Howard loved him for it. From that moment, where Dominico went, Howard was not far behind.

The one thing that they all complained about, Dominico included, was the waiting. They did calisthenics and obstacle courses and work details until they could no longer stand it. They were not anxious to go into combat. Combat was this fearful monster waiting over the next hill. It loomed over them, a distant but certain menace and constant source of angst. On a few occasions Dominico and his friends had work detail around a local hospital. They saw the wounded soldiers brought in from the front. They were mounds of blood and burned flesh borne on stretchers, destroyed in indescribable ways. Some were no longer whole in body, missing limbs, pieces of the faces. The most pitiable, however, were those no longer whole in spirit. Every man, regardless of condition, had a lost look in their eyes. Some, however, were more than lost. They were empty as if their eyes were the dusty windows of an abandoned home.

Dominico, Bob, George, and Howard looked at each other, whole in every way. What would they look like after the experience of war? There was no way to know who, if any of them, would walk away. They all understood that facing combat was best put off as long as possible. With luck, the war would end before Americans were required to fight.

As the weeks wore on with this monster always just out of view, however, the men began to crave the opportunity to face this beast at last. The fear worked its way into their souls and became a fever. Once the fever broke, they wanted only to face their fears and get it over with. Anything was better than the mundane routines of army life. 'Let's get to the god damned front and get this war over with so we can all go home,' one man shouted. Most of them felt the same way. They waited enough, trained enough, dug enough ditches. It was time to see some action.

Besides, many of the townspeople who had hailed them as heroes when they first arrived now scorned them as hangers on. "When is your General Pershing going to do his job?" Americans were gaining a reputation as make-believe soldiers running around like children in their father's uniforms. The sideways glances and often the outright annoyance of the townspeople was wearing on the Americans. They had come to fight, with greater or less enthusiasm. Like it or not, it was time to fight.

Eventually, a few Americans were sent into combat and had proven themselves at last. Dominico was in attendance when Colonel Macarthur received the Croix de Guerre for his exploits. 'It won't be long now,' Dominico thought, not without apprehension. 'If I can just get through it, I'll go home to you, Giulianna. That's all I want to do. Maybe this was a great mistake on my part.'

In the meantime, Dominico volunteered for every work detail he could. It was his way to make the days go by and fill his time with meaning. After a lifetime of work, he could not tolerate spending his leisure playing cards or looking at the dirty pictures the men passed around. He was too old to enjoy the revels of the young in France, but too young to rest his energetic body. He felt that he had to do something. It was this attitude that got Dominico noticed by the Master Sergeant who put in a request that he be promoted to corporal.

CHAPTER 4

June 6, 1918

To My Darling Wife and Children:

I wish that I was man of words like your father that I might begin to express how things are here. I have written this letter in my mind for the last few days. One of the men in my platoon is a poet and he seems to be able to describe it well, but my use of English is still too poor to be of much help. I do not want you to worry about me, but I do not want to be dishonest with you or to fill you with false hope. You are a strong woman who has seen the worst of what people can do to each other. Imagine the kind of anger during the worst of our struggles in New York. Now imagine what would have happened if both sides had the ability to deliver total destruction to thousands of people all at once. If you imagine New York in ruins, the great buildings collapsed, the streets still and littered with dead people and horses, trees burnt and black. That's the best I can do to describe what I see every day.

Since coming to the front, we are told that we are conducting ourselves well. The French seem to like us now that we've joined the slaughter. I'm glad they think so highly of us. To me it seems like we're stumbling through the dark. Last week the fighting was very bad. We drove the Germans out of a village, but it did not take long for them to return. Again and again, we fought them back. Again and again, they returned. Then they stopped coming. When we were relieved, we were called heroes. Some of the younger guys appear to believe that. Not me. I just followed my orders and shot where they told me to shoot and prayed whenever I had the chance. San Giuseppe preserved me for you again. Unfortunately, he was not looking after Howard Lefkowitz. He was the youngest of the friends I told you about. He was the one who was listening to me the most. He probably would have joined the movement when the war is over. He was just trying to get away from his father when he joined.

Thank you for the rosary. I've used it more in the last few months than I have in my life. I've never been a man of religion, but perhaps that will change now. I'm sure your father would not approve.

I'm sure you read these letters first before reading them to the children. Let Little Dom read the letters. He's old enough now. He may find himself being the man of the house before long. Tell the children I love them and think of them every day.

Love Dominico

"Rossa! Rossa! Ammo boxes! I need those goddamned ammo boxes by the livery, now!"

"Yes, Sergeant." Dom replied masking the wariness in his voice. On each broad shoulder rested an ammo box. His legs were weak from fatigue and lack of food, so the weight of the boxes pressed on him as he limped to the livery, or rather what was once a livery. All that remained was the jagged fragments of a stone wall littered with charred splinters that was once a sturdy shelter. Men were clearing the area of debris, repairing the walls, trenches, and bunkers. Some were building rudimentary shelters from the spring rains. Bob propped sandbags into place around his station.

Dom stared at the remains of the wall. It was not long ago that he was building such walls. He could not help but appraise the work. It was well built, probably two-hundred years old. Napoleon's armies may have crossed over this mortar. Surviving war after war it finally fell, defeated. Dom stood and examined what was left, a great stone dragon cut to pieces, drying in the wind.

Four privates black with soot followed, laden with ammunition. The four privates were part of Dom's detail. His assignment was to ensure that each installation was as well supplied as the circumstances allowed. After two days of German counterattacks on their position they were tired and fearful. They carried their fatigue and discouragement with the ammunition, and their knees buckled from the combined weight. Could they withstand another attack? Would they retreat? Which would be preferable? Or would they hold their ground and be slaughtered? If Lieutenant Horste had his way, the latter would happen. He was intent on holding this position and would not be swayed regardless of the costs. The men saw things differently, however, preferring dishonor to death.

Glory was made for warriors like Lt. Horste, but was a course fit on the backs of farmers and laborers.

The five men placed the last of the ammunition boxes on a makeshift pallet raised above the mud. The machine gun was braced in a stone alcove that was once a storage bin for tools of some kind. "That'sa the last of it, Sergeant." Dom informed Sergeant Miller. Miller sucked air between his teeth, his heavy eyes set on the distance.

"Doesn't seema like enough, does it, Sergeant?" Dom whispered.

"Depends on them, Corporal." Miller jutted his broad chin toward the east. The countryside was stripped from where the Germans pushed forward trying to dislodge the wary Americans from Cantigny Village, as if a great glacier had ground its way up to the village walls and defensive trenches, crushing everything in its path. "Depends on them. Maybe they've had 'nough. Maybe we need to whoop on 'em one more time. Whoop on 'em good an' sound an' they'll leave us be." Miller spoke through his teeth, a habit that made Dom a little uncomfortable, though he did not know why.

Dom surveyed the installations with his untrained eye. He knew how much ammo was in each station. 'It doesn't seem enough,' he thought, but kept it to himself. Dom would never have engaged Sergeant Mallory in conversation so openly, but Miller was a man of a different breed. He was a taskmaster who never bided complaining or shirking one's duties. He took to Dom, his new corporal for just this reason. Dom never complained, regardless of the assignment. When Miller gave this dago a dirty detail it was done and never needed another look. Dom worked hard. He would never win any medals. He was not especially brave, or bold, but he followed orders even under the worst of conditions and regardless of his fear. Miller felt he could ask for nothing more from one who was not a career soldier.

Dom may not have been a career soldier, but by this point, he was well broken into battle. The entrenched 1st division lived through almost a month of German bombardment. The German/Dutchmen dropped gas into the allied trenches forcing the men to live close to their masks and lay as close to the rims as possible without exposing themselves to enemy fire. Then the bombs dropped, tearing through the trenches without mercy. Sergeant Miller smiled and said, "the Jerry's sure were tryin' to soften us up." He was sure it wouldn't work. Dom was not so confident.

That's when Howard Lefkowitz was killed. A caught thumb—that's what killed him. His right thumb got caught on his rifle strap during a gas attack. The delay, only a second or two, kept him from putting his mask on in time. Panic caused him to gasp, sucking in the poison that disintegrated his lungs. He died convulsively, spewing bloody froth as Dom held him.

When the time came, however, the Americans returned brutality with brutality. French flame throwers burned the entrenched Germans to cinders while American rifles and bayonets disemboweled those who tried to escape the flame.

Some Germans tried to surrender, only to be cut down, their hands still in the air. After the battle, this nauseated Dom. Not only was he sickened by the hellish disregard for human life, but mostly, in the moment of bestial struggle for survival, he was indifferent about the slaughter of surrendered Germans. Dom vomited whenever he thought about his sin of the heart. Thinking about this moment would make him nauseous for the rest of his life.

"Help Corporal Hallerine with the sandbags then take your detail and get some sleep." Miller's eyes never strayed from the distant trees. 'Right now,' he thought, 'that dago's work ethic is more a hindrance than a help.' Miller knew that the men were at the end of their rope. They were weary and frazzled by a month of battle rewarded by two days of counterattacks from the seasoned German army. They fretted over the next attack, wondering if they would survive long enough for reinforcements. The only thing Miller could do to keep these men together was work them, run them to the end of their wits so they were too busy to think about their impending deaths, until they were too tired to care. He created work details out of thin air to keep the men busy. But Corporal Rossa worked so assiduously that it was difficult to find more work to do. Miller remembered many of the stories about lazy, ignorant, and untrustworthy Italians who'd cut you as soon as look at you, but this wop was not of that ilk. A fine representative of his race, like a hard-working nigger or a sober Irishman, thought Sergeant Miller. Sergeant Miller never considered himself a racist.

Dominico, after finishing with Hallerine, took a moment to speak with Bob. He was the last of Dom's friends. George died from an accidental explosion in an armory shortly before the division was dispatched to the Somme. He did not survive long enough to see battle. Bob was shaken the most by Howard's death, the horror of it. Better to be instantly blown to pieces than to suffocate on your own blood and bile. The men knew how they wanted to die if the time came. They wanted to die quickly, so they would not have to make the decision to be brave through the pain.

"When's it gonna end, Dom? When's it gonna end?"

Dom shook his head.

"We've got the Goddamned village. Why don't they leave us be?" Bob shook.

"You gonna be all right." Dom put his hands on Bob's trembling shoulders.

"They're supposed to leave us be, ain't they? That's how it's supposed to be. We meet, we fight, one side wins, the other side leaves. Ain't that right? Ain't that right? None of this bombing and gassing and keep comin' after us when we've already won."

Dom sighed.

"I used to be a tough guy, Dom. I used to be the toughest kid on the block." Bob shook his head, closed his eyes, and cried into his hands.

Dom held back the tears, swallowed hard, and held his friend.

"All right everyone! Stations!" Sergeant Miller's harsh voice crackled through the air like a static charge over the percussion of shells and the shower of rocks and wood.

"Here they come, boys! Let's show 'em what for!" He strutted from position to position calling the men on, motivating them.

Dominico ran from his sleeping space under a collapsed eve to his station next to the machine gun set up in the fountain. The air was alive with fire and soot and deafening sound. With a leap he cleared the sandbags and rolled heavily into the drained fountain. The pain in his shoulder would go unnoticed until later. As soon as he slid next to the machine gun the scream of bullets pinged and cracked all around them. The enemy was within range, but still the American guns were quiet. Dom checked the ribbon for the machine gun and listened for orders. To his left a bomb exploded through the windows of a ruined building. The great building fell to the ground gracefully, like a sinking ship. Above the shelling and the collapse of the building he heard Sergeant Miller shout, "By God we'll show 'em Hun son's a bitches what it's like to face some pissed off and hungry 'mericans! We'll show 'em what their pansy ass European in-breeding is worth! We'll..."

Then the shelling stopped, and so did Sergeant Miller. His eyelids narrowed, pupils pierced through the dust and smoke. "All right boys, this is it."

Bullets clattered like metallic rain. They bit the walls and shattered what was left of the fountain statuary, filling the air with pieces of stone and mortar that stung the soldiers' faces like a swarm of bees. Dom pressed his helmet to his head and kept as low as he could. The machine gunner, Griswold, ducked his head behind the wall.

"Ready!" Sergeant Miller shouted. Bullets scattered around him as if awed by his presence.

Most of the men in the fountain set their rifles over the sandbags. Many of the bags streamed sand and shriveled.

"Aim!" Miller shouted. He turned to look up at Lieutenant Horste whose station was high in a silo, binoculars in hand. The men brought their rifles to their shoulders and peered over the rim of the sandbags. Sergeant Griswold swung the machine gun, causing Dom to reposition himself. One soldier, private Swelton, was thrown backward, his face devastated by a well-placed bullet.

Dom could only wait for orders. He could not see the approaching column from his place behind the fortification. His job was to keep the ribbon running into the machine gun. That was the only thing keeping him alive, it was the only focus of his attention.

Sergeant Miller faced forward, teeth clenched, "Fire!"

The explosion of sound that barked from the cacophony of rifles and the rhythmic thumping of the machine guns was now familiar to Dom—almost a relief. He mindlessly tended the ribbon as it flowed through the machine gun. Empty shells fell around him, but he could not feel them. All he knew was the shooting and Sergeant Miller shouting and cursing the oncoming German army. "Com'on you sons 'a bitches, com'on. Get a little closer'n we'll run it down your throats you Jerry bastards..."

It was not long before the machine gun needed to be re-loaded. Dom reacted in a fury, set the ribbon, gave a thumbs up and the thudding returned. Men fell around him, but they were just a part of the scene. Thumping, hammering, pounding, the gunner's arms and shoulders a blur of vibration. The ribbon unwound, a swirling serpent striking its prey. Then...

...nothing...

"Shit!" Griswold shouted. The rhythmic thumping stopped, leaving the random blasts of the rifles.

"Jam! Jam!" Dom helped Griswold dismount the machine gun, ignoring his exposure to the enemy. The job needed to be done.

Dom pulled back the firing pin with all his might while Griswold dislodged the ribbon. Having dislodged the misfired shell, Dom reloaded the machine gun while Griswold remounted it. Griswold was bleeding, but his movement was smooth. That the ribbon continued its snaking movement at the command of the metered thudding assured Dom that Griswold's wound was not serious. Dom simply prepped the next box—the last box of machine gun ammunition in this station.

The thumping stopped again, and Dom reloaded. "Rossa, pick up your rifle!" Sergeant Miller shouted. Once that last ribbon was spent the machine gun was nothing more than a useless icon. Dom picked up his rifle and joined the men at the sandbags.

This was his first real glimpse of the battle. German soldiers materialized wraithlike from the smoke and dust. He tried hard to aim well before firing, but everything happened so fast. He knew from training that he was not supposed to blink when he pulled the trigger, but that was a skill he had never mastered. The burning sulfur and grit pricked at his eyeballs like needles. His eyes were next to useless. He fired, reloaded, fired again.

After a while, the wraiths appeared from the mist more slowly. The rattling of bullets came at longer and longer intervals. The smoke and dust began to settle.

"Hold! Hold! Hold! God damn it, hold!" Sergeant Miller's voice echoed. The firing stopped. The sergeant looked around until he received the "all clear" signal. He smiled, gritted his teeth. 'Another one down,' he thought.

Sergeant Miller stood and touched the gunner's shoulder. "Git that looked at, Griswold." He said. The gunner noticed that his left arm was soaked and sticky with blood. "Yes, Sergeant."

Dom stood, aching, and looked around. The livery was gone. Completely gone. 'Bob was stationed in the livery,' Dom thought. 'He must have made it out,' he tried to convince himself. Then he realized, if Bob got out of that livery, he would have had to face German soldiers in hand-to-hand combat. The livery was at the very front of the battle, the fountain was further back. Dom saw the soldiers clad in German blue, some laying only feet away from the fountain. He continued to look around, hoping to see Bob lift himself from the settling yellow dust. The silo was ablaze and crumbling. He did not know the fate of Lieutenant Horste. Then Dom looked at the machine gun. Only two shells left on the last ribbon.

"You too, corporal." Miller said.

"Scusa me, Sergeant."

"Your neck, corporal. Doesn't look so bad, but I don't want it getting' infected. Might use a couple stitches, even."

The dull pain in his left shoulder was awakened by the Sergeant's words though the injury was a faded memory. Dom turned to look. His shirt over his right shoulder was torn, the surrounding fabric a dirty, reddish brown. "Yes, Sergeant."

When the olive-green clad soldiers marched in from the west the men of Cantigny Village breathed a collective sigh. Relief had arrived.

Dom was given the detail of digging graves. The bodies were collected and respectfully laid in lines south of the village. And such lines. Black blankets and ponchos stretched like a rough road into the distance. Beneath were mounds of flesh that were once talking, breathing, dreaming humanity. One could examine the disjointed mounds and surmise the history of he who lay beneath. Some covers formed neatly the expected limbs, torso and head of those who died whole, others formed a misshapen mass of whatever could be found.

Bob was under one of those covers, but Dom had long since lost track of where his buddy lay.

He had to look, however, for he took it upon himself to dig Bob's grave first. He believed that he and his detail would spend the rest of the war digging graves. The least he could do for his fallen friend was to dig the best grave he could, the cleanest, least hastily dug, before his limbs grew weary from this macabre labor.

After the American graves were complete the German graves were dug. There seemed no end to the digging. Like any detail, however, it did come to an end. A company priest led the men in prayer and blessed the disembodied souls of the dead, be they American or German. Their belongings were presented to Lt. Horste who was responsible for sending them in the right direction, east or west.

"They looka justa like ours, Sergeant." Dom mentioned.

"Excuse me, Corporal?" Miller looked at him.

"Excepta for the language, they're personal belongings looka justa like ours."

Sergeant Miller saw the assorted letters, photographs, Bibles, and other baubles upon which some soldier had placed inexplicable value. Both piles, the American and German, were almost identical.

"Ya might not wanna keep goin' with these thoughts, Corporal. You won't get outa this sane if you get out of it at all. Right now, it doesn't matter who or what they are. They are the enemy, and it is our job to kill 'em. An' that's not gonna change for all the knowin' an' understandin' 'em."

Dom did not react, only stared at the new Lieutenant, his uniform crisp and pressed. He strolled confidently and unnaturally clean across the cratered courtyard to greet Lieutenant Horste who stood on the stairs. Horste was dirty and burnt, having survived the destruction of the silo. The two men saluted, shook hands then disappeared into one of the towns few structurally sound buildings.

"How's that neck, Corporal?"

"It'sa good, Sergeant. Dona hurta bit." Dom lied.

Sergeant Miller nodded and watched the officers disappear.

"Sergeant? Whatta you think? Did a we…whoop them up a good enough?"

Miller vouched Dom a, toothy smile. "Yeah, Corporal. We whooped 'em up. Least we tired 'em out real good. I don' 'spect to see Jerry come out here now we have fresh troops."

"Sergeant, look." Dom pointed. Behind the column of American soldiers was a wave of ragged men and women. Villagers were returning to the ruins of their homes. They drifted off one by one to different piles of brick and stone and sifted through the debris. They pushed aside rafters and stones, picked up miscellaneous items. None of them cried. It looked like they wanted to, but none of them did.

Sergeant Miller made a career of noticing only those things that made him a better soldier and ignoring those things that made him more human. Part of him resented Corporal Rossa for making him notice that to which he wished to remain blind. "I see 'em, Rossa. I seen the same thing in the Philippines. I seen the same thing in Haiti. I seen it. What can I say about it?"

"You know whata they doin'."

"They're rebuildin'." 'God damn him,' Miller thought.

"I seen thisa, too." Dom admired the villagers. "In Italy... and New York."

CHAPTER 5

Patrolling Cantigny village was becoming routine. It was some time since the Germans tried to dislodge the combined French/American fortifications around the city. Typically, patrols were easy, but Sergeant Miller still demanded full diligence as if an attack could suddenly appear like a great wave over the horizon. Of course, he was right, but the chemistry of human complacency is a difficult thing to master.

Dominico walked along, reminding himself that an attack could happen any minute, that he might be the split-second factor that contributed to victory or defeat. These were the words of the Lieutenant Horste almost for rote. Dom found them difficult to believe, but he figured that it would be better to believe than not. He walked behind the Sergeant's position and to the left. The rest of the platoon stretched in between. With deliberation, they swung around the established perimeter of the village scrutinizing anything that was out of place. As of the last few days they encountered nothing more than an old farmer pursuing a lost goat. The farmer was desperate to find the animal as it was his last female and his family's only consistent source of nourishment. Dominico and Private Salient volunteered to help the farmer. Most days were quiet, however, though the sound of shelling rumbled constantly over the distant mountains to the southeast. The shelling had become no more to the soldiers than the moan of distant thunder.

This was to be the last of the circuit around the village. The sun was going down. Once they returned, the night patrol would take over. Dominico's platoon would have some down time. Dom was already planning his next letter home.

"Sergeant!" someone called, "Over here! Quick!"

Sergeant Miller gave the signal to halt the line then ran to the soldier who called out.

The soldier was squatting, pulling at something that Dom could not see through the dried, burnt brush. Then he saw the shoulder of a man, followed by a grizzled arm. Dom frowned. Most of his patrols involved finding bodies that were overlooked after the battle. Some were buried in bomb craters only to be exposed by the spring rains. Just when he thought he had buried the last, another would appear as if by some grotesque magic. But it had been a few days since they found a body. Dom hoped to have seen his last. His heart sank as he saw this corpse pulled from the ground.

The sergeant helped the soldier lift the blackened mass. That was when Dom noticed the corpse take a step. The emaciated man's wrists were exposed, black and bony, not quite skeletal. Surely this was the wrist of a corpse, but

Dominico could swear that that corpse took a step in a vain attempt to stand. It could have been the random movements that resulted as Sergeant Miller and the soldier tried to move him. Dom squinted, peered closer, and noticed the man's head. It was bereft of hair and covered in dirt and scabs. His neck was visible, and one could count the well outlined vertebrae, but Dome noticed the stringy muscles strain against the weight of the head. The head defied gravity and lifted on its own.

'My God,' Dom gasped, 'he's alive!'

"Rossa! Med kit!" Sergeant Miller called.

Dom grabbed the med kit from his pack and raced toward them. Sergeant Miller unscrewed his canteen and dribbled water into the man's parched mouth. When Dom was close enough, he noticed the man's sunken cheeks, his skull trying to push through the thin skin on his face. He was weak and dirty, smelling of feces, putrid sweat, pus, and rot. His eyes were red, unfocussed but open. A relieved smile stretched across his face, splitting cracks into his dry lips. The water restored some vitality to his deadened body, or perhaps it was a response to being rescued, the hope of survival.

"Cut the rest of that sleeve away, I don't like the looks of that arm. I smell rot." Sergeant Miller directed.

Dom cut the sleeve off. The man's uniform was black, unrecognizable, but certainly not American.

"Shit. What is this guy? He could very well be a Jerry." Hessen, the first soldier stated.

"That's no Hun uniform." Miller replied.

Dominico washed the soot and dirt from the blackened arm. The man's fingers were uncharacteristically bloated. There, on the man's forearm was a large gash that looked as if it were turned inside out, covered with a greenish brown and yellow scab. The tissue around the scab was coal black as was his swollen hand and fingers. The smell was that of rotten meat.

Dom looked at the sergeant and shook his head. "Nothina we can do a for that arm. Perhapsa the Doc."

Sergeant Miller looked down at the man. Consciousness was bringing a dull shine to his eyes.

"Can you talk?" Miller asked. The man mumbled a reply.

"What was that?" Hessen asked. "I couldn't make that out."

Miller signaled him to be quiet.

"Francais? Anglais?" He asked in sophomoric French.

Once again, the man mumbled something incomprehensible and shook his head.

"He said he hasn'ta eaten ina three daysa, Sergeant." Dom explained.

"You understand him?"

"Yes, Sergeant. He's Italian."

Miller nodded, signaling that Dom should continue.

"*Calabraise*?" Dom asked.

"*Si*." The man nodded and offered a weak smile.

"Ask him if he can walk?"

"He can'ta walk, Sergeant."

"All right, Rossa, you and Hessen get him to the village to the Doc. We'll complete the patrol and meet up with you later."

"Yes, Sergeant." Dom and Hessen picked him up and carried him basket style to the village.

"Well, Corporal, looks like you'll have to break the news to him." Doc smiled sadly at Dom who was now the de facto interpreter for the Italian soldier. The soldier had been separated from his unit, though Dom suspected his separation was not accidental. For days this soldier, named Gilberto Priccone, stumbled through the countryside, skirting German and Austrian patrols before losing time. He could not remember when he reached the allied lines, or exactly when he lost consciousness. He remembered only the pain in his arm and now the pain was gone. The rest fell on Dom.

"Gilberto. You know, the arm must come off." Dom could think of no other way to put it. How does one gently tell someone they are about to be dismembered?

It took a moment for the magnitude of Dom's statement to sink in. Gilberto studied the words, 'your arm' 'come off.' It was unimaginable. He did not know what this American was talking about. Then understanding punched him in the stomach. A cold heat rushed over him.

"No!" Gilberto tried to shout but lacked the energy to panic in the manner that the moment called for. 'These bastards are going to cut my arm off!' "It doesn't hurt anymore! It's going to be fine!"

Dom frowned and shook his head. "It's dead, Gilberto. That's why it doesn't hurt. If it doesn't come off, you'll be dead, too." He was calm, rational, but not detached. He knew instinctively what Gilberto needed. It was what he would need himself under the same circumstances.

Doc placed a bottle of cognac in Gilberto's shaking hand.

"Really, corporal. As weak as he is, I don't know if he'll survive the amputation. There's only so much I can give him for the pain. I don't know how much you want to tell him, but he'll have to be strapped down."

"It's going to hurt, Gilberto." Dom said in the same even, sympathetic voice. "Do you have family?"

"*Si*. I have three children. Please don't do this."

"You'll be seeing them soon, Gilberto, but we must take that arm off if you want to see them again. Do you want to see them?"

The soldier looked disconsolate. "*Si*."

"Then drink. We need to strap you down."

Perhaps it was the easy tone of Dom's voice that made Gilberto realize that there was nothing further to say. The arm was no longer his. It must come off. It would come off. He did not have the strength to fight, even through argument. If he concentrated and thought back far enough, he knew he would lose the arm as soon as the infection set in, and the fevers seized him. When the pain was gone, however, he thought he would be all right. He thought he would not lose it.

"You drink with me?" Gilberto swallowed the cognac. Dominico, without hesitation, followed with a swig of his own.

"Easy on that, Corporal. I'm gonna need you sober."

"Yes, sir."

"These straps will keep him only so still. You'll have to hold him."

Dom swallowed hard. "Yes, sir." He was not counting on being present for the amputation. He had seen men's limbs blown off, but in his mind, there was something especially barbaric in seeing a man's arm sawn off.

Doc injected a yellow fluid into the man's arm. "This will help, but not much. I just can't spare what he's going to need. I'll go as fast as I can. My guess is he'll pass out before I'm done." Doc prepared the saw. "Keep him looking way, Corporal. I don't want him to see the saw. I don't want him to see it coming."

"Gilberto, you want to look over there, out that window."

"Dominico?"

"Yes."

"In my left pocket is where you can write my family. Write to them after the operation. Let them know if..."

"I will. But you'll be fine."

"Corporal, put your hands there and there. When I start, you're going to put all your weight on him. This won't take long."

Doc stretched out Gilberto's arm, placed the blade just below the arm pit. "Okay...now..." he said gently.

Dom put his weight on Gilberto. For a moment it seemed he would crush his frail frame. Gilberto never screamed. The pain pushed the wind from his lungs. He strained, his yellowed teeth clenched, eyes wide, bloody, then relaxed, unconscious. A second later Dom heard the thud of the arm hitting the floor.

"You did well, Corporal. I have it from here." Doc smiled past his sad eyes and applied disinfectant to the wound.

"Will he...?"

"If this stub gets infected, no? Otherwise, the next couple of days will tell."

Dom nodded, reached into Gilberto's left pocket where he found a small leather purse. He left the building that was serving as a hospital, rounded the corner out of sight from everyone, and vomited.

"Rossa."

"Yes, Sergeant." Dom popped his head up from the wall where he and three other men were trying to re-establish flowing water to the village.

"Give your detail to Corporal Burns. Captain wants to see you."

"Sergeant?"

Sergeant Miller smiled. "Maybe he found out 'bout your politics, Rossa."

"Sergeant?" Dom's expression became more desperate. His politics was never something that brought him comfort in the face of those in authority.

"Relax, Corporal. I think it's good news."

Dom stood outside the door of the café. It was the last intact building in the village and was, therefore, the officer's quarters. A sergeant opened the door and allowed Dom inside. Captain Fellows sat behind a large, mahogany desk. Lieutenant Hofstgaard stood to his left.

Dom saluted.

"Yes, Corporal, at ease."

Dom stood at ease.

"How'd you like to go to Italy, Corporal?" Captain Fellows smiled. He was an amiable man with an easy-going demeanor.

"Sir?"

"Lieutenant Hofstgaard is being reassigned to help bring an American company to the front in Italy. Doctor Jessup reported that you were a great help with our Italian guest."

"I'ma familiar witha the Calabraise dialecta, sir."

"Good. Good." Captain Fellows leaned back in his chair, almost lost balance, but quickly sat forward again.

Lt. Hofstgaard stepped forward. He was like a statue of the ideal soldier; his uniform was impeccable, hair perfect, even the ubiquitous dust of the village seemed to settle on him with military precision. "Corporal, we'll be working directly with Italian forces. I'll need to have someone directly under me who knows Italian. Right now, that's you."

"Yes, sir, but..."

"It's a sergeant's position, corporal. The paperwork for promotion has been completed."

"Thank you, sir, but..."

"Yes, corporal."

"I'ma not really familiar witha the northern dialectsa, sir."

"Explain."

"Well, I'm a Campanian. The Italian soldier wasa Calabraise. I learned the Calabrian dialecta in New Yorka where many of a the people I knew were froma the south."

"How different are the dialects, corporal?" Captain Fellows asked.

"I don'ta know, sir." Dom shrugged.

"Well, it can't be that different, Corporal. You're our man for now."

"We'll be leaving tomorrow. O600." The lieutenant stated with a flat, informative tone.

"Yes, sir." Dominico stood at attention again.

"Dismissed, Sergeant."

Dom saluted then marched from the office wondering what he was in for.

CHAPTER 6

"**Y**ou ready for this, Sergeant?" Lt. Hofstgaard's face was like stone as he peered through the binoculars.

Dom said nothing. In the past few weeks he realized that most of the lieutenant's questions were meaningless noise directed here and there for some purpose known only to him. Nor did he care to know the reasons for these questions. He wanted only to do his job and to go home to his family. Anything added to that, even idle interrogation, was extra baggage.

'How could anyone be ready for this?' Dom thought. He stared at the scene before him. 'No,' he thought, 'I'm not ready, but that doesn't amount to anything.' Lt. Hofstgaard was going to dive headlong into battle and Dom, despite all reason, was going to dive in with him. It was not about survival. In a world of bombs and gas and machine guns survival was not necessarily assured to the fittest. It was a matter of what needed to be done. Dom did what was required. For as long as he could remember, he always did what needed to be done.

What needed to be done was unquestioned, but at the same time, questionable. Before the war Dom asked himself if it was right to stay out of this war when others were fighting and dying. Coming into combat, however, answered that question a thousand times. It is right to be against the wanton destruction of humanity. It is right to be against dismemberment. It is right to be against mustard gas and artillery. It is right to be against one man killing another, another whom one does not even know, another against whom one has no quarrel. It is right to be against Armageddon. It is right to be against this.

His bones crashed against each other with every crushing concussion of the great cannon. Fourteen hundred of them sustained a constant bombardment of the enemy roiling the atmosphere with thunder. Thunder—man playing God, creating the thunder that brings terror to young children, and there was Dom, standing there, speechless.

'It wasn't long ago,' Dom thought, 'that I was on the receiving end of bombardment.' With every blast and recoil the images of his lost friends flashed in his mind like tiny explosions. There was George blown apart before he even experienced battle. Howard, asphyxiating on his own blood after a gas attack. Bob, dying in Cantigny, America's first great victory of the war. Satan composed a hellish symphony. The cannon were the rhythm and Dom's dismembered friends and screaming comrades the ghoulish melody. 'It's right to be against this.'

With his mind lost in the artillery and the macabre, the slap of reality was neither a comfort nor bane. Reality was no less an inferno than the nightmares of his fugue. Blood and death splashed around his body, danced around his mind, and wrapped around his soul. There were no safe places. The ugly world of his senses materialized into his reality as gracefully as it dematerialized. Before him, a great and proud rock protruded from the mist. It jutted from the muddy, scarred ground like a stalwart guardian. Mount Grappa, the defiant ground of the Austrian invasion force. All around a fiery garden of explosions bloomed, the blossoms burst, flowering yellow and orange and black, then wilting into a compost of dirt and smoke and flesh.

Another offensive was about to open under Mount Grappa's shade, an attempt to disperse the entrenched Austrians and to liberate the proud Italian people. Only the Italian people were not so proud anymore. Waves of Italians, especially those of Dom's own *Mezzogiorno*, looked at themselves fighting for a land they never considered their own and decided it was time to go home. Even those of the north could no longer see the difference between an Italian King who would willingly send his people to slaughter and an invading Austrian King who would willingly do the same. The meaninglessness of mass destruction turned their tattered boots homeward, their legs relieved of the weight of abandoned ammunition.

Initially, American forces were intended as a moral boost. Italian moral was the identified enemy. American Soldiers spent days parading around the roads and towns of

Northern Italy making an embarrassing show of themselves. Crowds cheered and women wept. It appeared to do the trick. However, Dom knew that appearances were of no more value than new paint on an old, rotten house. It was Dom's job to talk to the non-com Italians and report on the morale. He did so with discomfort. The men sneered when the subject of war came up. They recalled how they too were lauded in brand new, fancy uniforms like prize chickens. It turned out that the fancy uniforms made them perfect targets for Austrian guns. It was not long before they discovered that battle was not worth the pageantry. They predicted that soon the Americans would learn the horrible truth of glory. It was right to be against this.

"Ah, well, Sergeant." Lieutenant Hofstgaard tried to explain during one parade. "We're not doing this just for the Italians. The Austrians are watching. What do you think our presence is doing to them?"

Once again, Dominico did not answer.

Soon the parades were over. Fifty-one Italian divisions plus units from the United States, Britain, France and Czechoslovakia were prepared to converge on Mount Grappa where seventy-three Austrian divisions were entrenched and waiting. Lt. Hofstgaard led one of the American units. Dom was his liaison to an Italian company to which the unit was attached.

An Italian soldier entered the bunker, handed Dominico a sweaty piece of paper, then left. Dom read the note, the ink smeared and jagged. The hand that wrote it must have shaken. He could barely make out the script, but, regardless, knew what it said. He looked up at the lieutenant and offered an uncertain nod. Lieutenant Hofstgaard nodded with confidence, a sick confidence that Dom despised.

"Alpha's our rendezvous?"

"Alpha, sir."

"Well, Rossa, let's drive them to the sea!" the lieutenant smiled.

Another ridiculous comment, Dom thought. The sea was in the opposite direction.

Soon, the familiar chills of battle engulfed him. He ran alongside the lieutenant, the unit running behind, heads down, shrapnel and debris stinging them like bees from the heart of every explosion.

"Down! Down!" the unit dropped in the mist of gunpowder, the crush of bombs.

"Go! Go! Go!" up the unit lifted their faces from the mud and ran again, only there weren't as many footsteps.

Thunderclaps and screaming followed the unit from shell crater to shell crater until they reached Alpha. A great heap of rifles and men fell on top of each other as they dove blindly into the trench that would be their temporary shelter. Alpha was an abandoned Austrian trench (originally dug by Italians), muddy and neglected, but a welcome haven from bullets. When the men composed themselves and looked around, however, the

Italian unit, which was expected to be first at Alpha, was not there.

"All right, sound off!" Sergeant Hall shouted above the thunder. The lieutenant unpacked the binoculars and did his best to peer through the collapsed slits of the bunker. Dom stood by him.

Sergeant Hall approached. "Sir, Santiago, Jordan, Patch, Nelson, and Lebins have not reported, sir. I saw Jordan go down. I don't know about the rest."

Lt. Hofstgaard grimaced. "Patch and Nelson went down. Thank you, Sergeant. Carry on."

"Sir, we can't stay here very long." Sergeant Hall stated.

"Sergeant?"

"The trench, sir. It's carved from rock. Anything fired into this trench will ricochet and tear hell out of everyone." Hall's warning was punctuated by a scream.

"Nothing we can do about it. Tell everyone to stay low. Belly down if necessary. We're waiting for Lt. Rispaldi and his men. Machine guns there and there, Sergeant. Thank you."

"Yes, sir."

"Where the hell are they?" the lieutenant shook his head. His hands shook, eyes narrowed beneath his sooty brow.

"I got 'em, sir. They're coming...there." Dom shouted.

"Son of a bitch!" Hofstgaard let his binoculars hang limply from his neck. "Give 'em cover, boys!" Fire at will!" Men jumped with their rifles to the rim. "Sergeant! Where them goddam machine guns?"

The biting rattle of the machine guns answered his inquiry.

"Worst damn timing! Rossa, where are they?"

"Sir, looksa like they're in a shell crater. There, you see some a lying ina the mud."

"Get 'em movin', Sergeant!"

"Yes, sir."

Without thinking, Dom jumped from the bunker and ran back to the shell craters. Much of what Dom did in combat was without thought. Had Dom thought about leaving the bunker he may not have done it. Dom sprinted and lunged for the crater, the Italian soldiers lay scattered around him, clutching their rifles close to their chests."

"Lt. Rispaldi?" Dom called. Men pointed.

"Here! Here!"

"Lt. Hofstgaard is providing cover. We must go now!" Dom then took a deep breath and ran from the crater. When he jumped back into the trench, he was nearly smothered by Rispaldi's men crashing down on top of him.

Rispaldi extricated himself from the tangle of men and barked orders. Men scattered and took positions on the rim.

"Lt. Rispaldi, *per favore*...my lieutenant needs to know your status."

Rispaldi followed Dom into the bunker where Lt. Hofstgaard sat like Napoleon on a rotted ammo crate. He stood, saluted, and then shook Rispaldi's hand. "What is the status of your unit, Lieutenant?"

Dom translated, then waited on Rispaldi's reply.

"Sir, he's down thirty percent."

"We'll take the next run to Beta. That's when the fighting's going to get thick. Tell him he can set up his machine guns there and there and give us cover."

Once again, an exchange, Dom's face turned white.

"No machine guns, sir. His gunners didn't make it."

"What?"

Dom did not answer.

A ricochet screamed through the trench. Men dropped into the mud, faces down, hands behind their heads.

"OK. He'll take two of ours. There and there. We're behind schedule. Let's go!" Lt. Hofstgaard saluted then left the bunker.

Dom translated then followed. The explosions were coming more heavily. The field seemed to be boiling with dirt and rock. The dash to Beta was a miracle, nothing less, for those who made the next trench. Great waves of men crawling from the ground could only be seen in blurry glimpses between explosions.

"Sergeant Rossa!" Hofstgaard brushed himself off and coughed through the smoke. Blood trickled from his scalp. "Where the hell's my men?"

Dom gasped and looked around. He could not see through his left eye. Grains of dirt and rock scratched against his cornea every time he blinked. He forced it open and dumped the water from his canteen over the eye, but blinking was excruciating. He decided to keep his eye closed for the time being. Through his good eye he could see that over half of the unit was unaccounted for, including Sergeant Hall.

"That's it, sir. No more!"

"God dammit. OK…OK…get ready to cover for Rispaldi!"

"Sir?"

Dom blinked furiously. The vision returned with hesitation, blurred and distorted, looking through a shot glass then the piercing pain blinded him again. With his good eye he glanced around.

"I said get ready to cover Rispaldi."

Dom shuddered when he heard only one machine gun rapport from the trench.

"Sir, yes sir." Dom hesitated.

"Damn it, Rossa, I need you on that rim. I need everyone we can get."

Dom took his rifle from his back and found a place on the rim. When he looked over, he got his first close glimpse of the competition. He could see their troubled eyes. Both sides fired furious volleys. Both sides shed blood like rain. The men on either side of him fell as he fired blindly into the enemy position. He knew that he was going to die. There was no other possible outcome. Suddenly, a hand clasped his collar, and he was pulled from behind. The cacophony above him was a hell scream, a rush of sound blasting, whipping, a gurgling hell scream. For an instant he was sliced with rock and enveloped in heat. In blind desperation he clawed his way to the bunker. Someone had thrown him to the bottom of the trench. Someone, he knew not who, saved his life.

"Jesus Christ!" Lt. Hofstgaard shouted as he lifted himself from the debris that was once the bunker. "What the hell was that?"

Dom sat frozen on the ground, his left eye blinking out on him. He could glimpse a dark red streak fly across his field of vision twice. Lt. Hofstgaard clutched at his thigh and the streak stopped.

"We gotta get the machine guns set up, Rossa! We gotta get Rispaldi here!"

Dom closed his left eye again, stepped out of the ruined bunker and...froze.

"Rossa! Rossa!" the lieutenant's barking was lost in some internal distance.

Frozen.

"What the hell? God dammit, we need those guns on the ledge."

Frozen.

"Move your ass, Rossa!"

A red streak.

Dom turned and faced the lieutenant. He shook his head. "No, sir."

"Whatta you mean 'no?' Don't tell me you're following the footsteps of your god damned countrymen. I gave a god damned order!"

Without saying any more Dom pulled a handkerchief from his pocket and stuffed it into the open wound in the lieutenant's thigh. The red streaks stopped, but the cloth soon soaked dark, crimson. The femoral artery was severed.

"I gotta get you a back." Dom whispered as if to himself.

"What the hell are you talking about?"

Dom picked Lt. Hofstgaard up and threw him over his shoulder. He did not really like Lt. Hofstgaard. It just needed to be done.

"Sergeant, put me the fuck down!" the lieutenant protested and struggled.

He struggled until they left the bunker. The trench was littered with bodies...

...No...

...body parts...

...dismembered bodies...

...not one of them was left intact.

CHAPTER 7

"You're Italian, aren't you, sergeant?"

Dom nodded.

The nurse's smile was genuine as she changed his bandage. "You have family in Italy?"

Again, Dom nodded.

"Where is your family?" She felt that it was important to get the soldiers talking. She did not know why. Her experience with combat wounded imbued her with this insight.

"Downa south. Campania. Villa de San Giuseppe."

The nurse nodded and sighed. 'This soldier will be OK,' she thought. "When was the last time you've been home?"

Dom did not want to think about it. A lifetime? An eternity? Had he ever really lived in Italy? That life seemed disconnected from his reality. Mamma, Papa, Anna, Hortensia, Paulo. Were they real people, more tangible than the phantasms of his memory? He found it hard to believe. His family, for almost half of his life an entity he always knew he could not live without, yet to be without them for so long. He now had his own family, the family he created. He had his own life independent of the decaying town of San Giuseppe. He did not want to think about how long it had been. His youth in Italy was so far away, temporally disjoined from who he was at this moment.

"Oh, this is looking good. You'll heal up fine." The nurse tried to reassure him.

There was something about her smile that sickened him. He gritted his teeth, almost grunting, tensing the muscles of his hand as hard as he could. It took great concentration, but he was able to move his fingers almost an inch. It was more mobility than the doctor said he would have.

Mount Grappa rose before him, crying, the smoke burned his eyes. In his mind the bombshells drowned out the corporeal nurse saying, "You should go see your family when you are signed out..."

There's only one way to move with a man laying across your shoulders—run. Dom climbed from the trench he knew as Rendezvous B and ran, mindless of the bombs and bullets that could not be avoided anyway. His zigzag path through the obstacle course of bomb craters and bodies may have offered him some protections, but God or even blind luck, would have to do the rest. Lt. Hofstgaard would surely bleed to death if not brought to a medic. That Dom was willing to take such a chance was not what he would call a decision. A man could not let another man die, even a man like Hofstgaard. The irony would find its way to Dom's mind much later. A man could kill under the right circumstances, but to let a man die, that was another thing. So, Dom ran and hoped for the best.

Often, he could not avoid the bomb craters or see the trenches through the sulfurous mist. His left eye was useless, making it impossible to judge the distances he had to run. When he fell into the relative safety of the holes, he took the opportunity to tighten the Lieutenant's tourniquet and check his bandage. Lt. Hofstgaard was still conscious, but weak. His body became a dead weight across the shoulders. Dom could not afford shelter for long. 'Don't think, just run.' He ran.

'It won't be far,' Dom thought. He could see the flashes of the machine gun nests and artillery just ahead. 'One more rush.' He tried to convince himself. "One more dash, lieutenant." There was no response.

He lifted the lieutenant over his shoulders and climbed from the crater.

In fact, the installations were closer than he thought. Just a short twenty paces to safety. He would get Lt. Hofstgaard taken care of, then, surely the battle would be over. It was obvious that the Austrians were not willing to let go of Mount Grappa. Just ten more paces. The only question remained, how determined were the allies to take it from them?

Five more paces...

He personally did not feel any determination to take the rock and call it his own.

One more...

Dom was lifted from his feet. His body enveloped in smoke and soot, pelted with stinging, burning rock and slicing metal. Lt. Hofstgaard flew from his shoulders as if ascending bodily into heaven.

Dom flailed in his descent, his eyes braced closed against the grit. His hands grasped for anything that might slow him, stabilize him. He gripped a metal protrusion that seemed to fall into his hand, clasping his fingers tightly. His body slowed and rested, but the searing pain tearing through his right hand and the smell of burned flesh struck his addled senses at the same time. He tried to open his hand but was unable to do so. It burned, but he could not move it, like having his hand held forcibly to a hot stove. Someone wrapped their arms under his and jerked him. He felt his hand, like fabric, rip from whatever he was holding.

When he could finally open his eyes, his hand was a bloodied mess. His skin sizzled black on the muzzle of a machine gun.

'Be like stone,' he heard his father say.

Doctor Shelton was a veterinarian. Of course, he did not want any of the soldiers at the field hospital to know that. They had enough troubles without worrying about their wounds being tended by a Nebraska horse doctor. In fact, Dr. Shelton was a very capable physician. Once under the skin, blood was blood, sinew was sinew. Organs performed as they were supposed to, or they did not. It did not matter their shape and size.

So, Dr. Shelton felt secure when he told Dom that he would never use his hand again.

"See, sergeant, basically the heat of the gun cooked your hand. Your muscle is bad enough, but the tendons...well, the tendons are just shrunk tight like banjo strings. They're just... well...cooked. That's all. I'm sorry." And he really was sorry, especially when he heard that Dom was a stone carver.

'It's a shame,' he thought.

Yes, Dr. Shelton was a competent physician. But there is something that some human beings have that horses do not. Will. So, a week later, when he checked the hand for infection, Dom had a surprise for him.

"Doc, you see this." Dom smiled, his eyes betraying the fatigue he tried so hard to hide.

"What's the matter?" Dr. Shelton reached for Dom's chart.

Dom squinted, his teeth clenched, and by God, he opened his fingers a good half inch.

"That's great, Sergeant. Do it again."

Dom did it, but not without difficulty and pain.

"Do you have any feeling in the palm?"

Dom shook his head.

"Fingers?"

"No."

"Sometimes there's a phantom pain."

Dom shook his head. The realities of his life did not allow for phantoms. What pain he had was in the back of the hand and his wrist. He could not feel the pads of his palm or fingers at all.

"Damnedest thing I ever saw. There's no way you should be able to move that hand. No physical way." Dr. Shelton curled his fingers under his chin. "How'd you do it?"

"I forced it open…ona the floor."

Dr. Shelton stared at him, his mouth hung open. "On the floor?"

Dom nodded.

"That must've hurt." Dr. Shelton knew he was understating the obvious.

"Lika hell."

"Do you think you can keep doing it?"

"I did ita once, I can a keepa doin' it." It was that simple. It needed to be done, so Dom did it.

"Well, sergeant, you keep doing what you're doing. But don't overdo it. Those tendons can't be very strong. You snap one you'll know what for. Once this infection clears, I'm sending you home. You're no good in combat with that hand, working fingers or no."

Dom nodded. There was nothing more to say on that subject. "Doc. Did you a getta the address I ask afore."

"The Lieutenant's. Yes. I'm sorry about your friend. There was nothing that could be done to save him. Between the loss of blood and the shrapnel wounds…"

"He was a no really my friend." Dom reached for the pencil with his good hand. "I guess I shoulda write to hisa family, though."

"Of course." Dr. Shelton nodded. "Would you like a nurse to help you?"

Dom shook his head.

Dr. Shelton handed Dom the address and walked away. The great room was lined with beds, white linen stained spotty with red and black. There was so much work to do. He thought about the young lieutenant that Dom was said to have carried. Riddled with shrapnel, his body torn to shreds. Indeed, had the lieutenant not hung over Rossa's shoulders, all that metal would have found its way into the sergeant's back, tearing him to pieces. In trying to save Hofstgaard, it turned out that the lieutenant saved him.

Like stone was the way Dr. Shelton described Sergeant Dominico Rossa to the psychiatrist who was making his rounds through the hospital. The psychiatrist did not consider this a good thing. Repressed feelings of guilt were certainly digging into Sergeant Rossa's mind. Dr. Shelton did not know about such things. "All I can say is he's like stone."

CHAPTER 8

om's feet ached as he reached the crossroads. They had carried him so far under such a heavy burden.

The train dropped him in Naples. From there a smiling man in an old truck called out, *"L'americano! L'americano!"* and asked him where he was going.

"Villa de San Giuseppe." Dom responded.

"I taka you. I taka you. Get in. Get in."

Dom shook his head. "I'll walk. I want to walk." It was only after the smiling man drove away that Dom realized that that brief conversation was entirely in English.

So, Dom walked, as it seemed he had always walked... slowly, painfully, with much on his mind and much in his heart. When he last walked this road, the sun mostly on his back, he was alone with nothing in his heart but the hope for the future and the love that propelled him. Now, as he walked into the sun, he carried naught but the past, his battles, his pains, his unrealized dreams. 'When did this road change?' He could not remember the moment of transition. The crossroads were not clear to him.

By nightfall he found the old inn, his first stop on his trip to America. At least, he found the remains. The owner had closed its doors long ago. Perhaps the traffic to America ceased, taking with it all of his best customers. There was no longer any place to go in the *Mezzogiorno*, therefore there was no need for inns. Or perhaps the advent of the motor car ended the inn. A day's walk was only a brief trip in a motor car. He tried to imagine a motor car bouncing violently down this horse rutted road.

The inn was now a grayed and dilapidated shell of a building. The rafter's sagged and the roof crumbled. All the windows were broken and the doors missing from the hinges. Hardy grasses and ivies wrapped around the walls were the only structures holding the crust together.

Regardless, Dom found his old room, the floor pocked with gaping holes, the walls more yellow than he remembered. A yellow and torn mattress, perhaps the first mattress he ever slept on, was folded against the wall.

He exercised his hand against a support beam exposed by a crumpled wall. The beam creaked, but did not yield to the pressure, providing the necessary support for the daily ordeal. Dom did not scream, however badly he wanted to. He knew that there was nobody around for many miles, but still, he could not bring himself to scream through the intolerable pain. If only he could convince himself to scream.

He awoke early, his back a single knot of discomfort—the price he paid for sleeping on the floor. The mattress was fragile and infested with mold and insects. A step shattered under him as he left the ruins to continue his journey. His hand throbbed with the sudden jolt. Dom turned and examined the old inn. A disintegrating shell. Had he never come this way it would have remained as it was, at least in his mind. Or would it? Do one's memories become gray and dry, if given enough time? Do one's experiences disintegrate?

Once he reached the crossroads he rested his feet. His canteen was empty, but it was not a hot day, and he knew that he would be home soon. He tried to think about his family. What would they be like? How had they aged? He could only see the family of his youth and the yellowed pages of countless letters. How had he let time go by for so long without coming back? He should have come home when Nonno got sick, or when Anna got married, but there was always something in America demanding his attention: his work, his family, the movement. More than the fates conspired to keep him away. America itself consumed him, ate away at his time, at his youth.

The village became visible as he rounded the last curve. It had a very unfamiliar sameness to it. The stillness, the quiet, the history, its nature had not changed. As he approached, this nature became more acute to his senses. All the old buildings were still there, paint and stucco pealing and chipping, exposing the stonework. The road, parched and powdery, passed through the square where the old *contadino* was whipped to death. The church appeared smaller, paler, but not changed.

Time, for the most part, skipped over Villa de San Giuseppe. Still, there was something.

Dom passed through the town. Some of the faces of the old people were vaguely familiar. They looked at him and smiled, but not with familiarity. These were the same sweet smiles reserved for American soldiers all over the country. Nobody recognized him. There were no representatives of Dom's generation in the town. Children played. Boys pretended to make war, while the girls pretended to raise boys who would grow up and make war. Old women worked at their chores. Old men putted around the same old places and talked and challenged and argued and laughed with each other. Some busied themselves around their shops and stores doing work that lost its meaning long before Dom left for America.

He turned from town and headed for his old home. This road was the most familiar and yet the most changed. Yet Dom could not understand the nature of the change he perceived. It was nothing he saw. The road looked the same as it did when he walked with his father, Paolo proudly leading that stubborn donkey, so many years ago. It was something he felt. A dust devil kicked up spirals of sand and whipped down the length of the road to the work yard. Dom followed. 'I don't belong,' he thought.

Soon, the work yard was within sight. Dom slowed his pace. 'What if I don't belong? Can I still call this home?' But when he noticed someone in the yard cutting wood all thoughts left his mind. His pulse raced as his pace quickened. He tried to identify the person. There was something about him that reminded Dom of his father, but the posture was all wrong, awkward, surreal. As he came closer, he realized that it was a younger man than his father. The clearer he could see the man, however, the stranger the figure's posture seemed.

Dom reached for the gate, but it was no longer there. Rusty hinges marked the place where it once rested. Just as well, for Dom reached with his bad hand. At the sound of footsteps, the young man turned his head. Dom strained to recognize him.

"Paulo?" Dom frowned.

"Dominico!" the young man smiled and laughed. With a hop he twisted his body to face his brother. There was something wrong with his leg.

Dom dropped his bag and ran to embrace his brother. He caught Paulo in his arms and lifted him, surprised that he almost knocked him over even though he could only lift with one arm.

"How are you? How are you, Dominico?"

"I'm well. It's good to be home." It was so long since Dom last smiled that it felt awkward on his face.

"Mama! Mama! Come quick!" Paulo shouted.

"How are you, Paulo?" Dom kissed him. "You look good. The war didn't get you?"

Paulo smiled wildly. "It got part of me." He grinned. He lifted the cuff of his pants. From under the fabric a wood dowel stuck into an old shoe was revealed.

"What?"

"Left it in the alps." Paulo continued to smile. "It still doesn't keep Papa from sending me out to cut wood."

Dom laughed. He remembered it would take significantly more than a missing limb to excuse someone from his chores. "Where is everyone?" Looking around, looking away, he thought, 'my God! My brother's lost a leg!'

Just as Dom asked, Mama opened the front door. She stared at the American soldier briefly then shrieked, tears bursting from her eyes. She lunged for him, embraced him, and cried deep, heaving sobs of joy. "Thank God, thank God!" she repeated. She refused to let go.

Upon the sound of Mama's shriek, another woman ran from the cottage. A toddler clung to her leg. Her swelling abdomen announced that she would soon be visited by a new baby. Her face was round and full, hair tied back securely, but her eyes were lean, solid, and intelligent.

"Anna?" years of black tarnish were falling from his soul. "There's my favorite!" Dom shouted. He wanted to clasp her, pick her up and sling her around like he used to, but he was mindful of her condition. She, on the other hand, gripped him around the neck and pulled him to her level.

"You are so tall, now. What is it about America that makes men tall?" Mama said.

"It's been such a long time. So long, Dominico, so long." Anna's voice was breaking with emotion. It was at this point that Dom broke down. Tears streamed free from his eyes.

His mother hugged him from behind and the tears became torrents. His brother's hand pressed his shoulder.

"And...who is this?" Dom squatted on his stiff legs and wiped the tears from his eyes. He smiled warmly at the little boy clinging to Anna's leg. "Is this little Renaldo, my little nephew?"

The little boy pressed his cheek against Anna's leg. He stared at Dom with wide eyes and not a little trepidation.

"Hey, little fellow. Here...here... I have something for you." From his pocket Dom removed a shiny whistle. He blew it, the metal cylinder tooted. Dom held it out to Renaldo, but the little boy stepped back. Dom tooted again and held it out with a smile.

"It's all right, Renaldo. This is Uncle Dominico." Anna nudged.

The little boy looked at his mother, then at Dom and reached his chubby, clumsy hands for the whistle. He stood behind his mother shaking the cylinder, listening to the chain clink and tinkle.

Dom laughed and strained to stand. His body felt like a useless, rusty hinge where a gate no longer rested.

"*Dio*! Dominico! Your hand!" Mama gasped, covering her mouth.

Dom smiled and looked at the bandages. They were stained yellow and brown. The sores must have broken again. "It's nothing, Mama. Just a burn. Where's Papa?"

"Where's Papa?" Mama scolded. "You come in and see Papa and I'll rewrap that hand. We have some gauze left over from when Paulo came home." Mama took him by the good hand and led him into the house.

Enrico Rossa sat up in bed. His eyes were downcast, his belly round, skin pale. Dominico barely recognized him. Dom knew that the old back injury was bothering him, but he did not know the extent.

"Papa!" Dom withheld the shock upon seeing his father in such a state and stepped into the room as if it were just another day, as his father would want him to do. Be like stone. "How are you, old man?"

"Well, I'll be damned. The prodigal has returned. I was wondering what all the fuss was about?" Papa's eyes brightened. His smile seemed to take a breath of strength. He pushed against the mattress with his arms to lift himself.

"You move and I'll hit you with pan!" Mama shouted over Dom's shoulder. "Right on the head I will. You watch me!"

Papa relaxed his arms and Mama stuffed pillows behind him. "Fool! Every time he feels a little better, he gets out and hurts himself again. Not this time."

"What happened?"

"They've needed people out in the fields. Most of the young *contadini* are off at the front. It's hard for the women."

"So, he goes out and starts pushing plows!"

"Isn't the money I send you enough?"

"The money's helped a lot, Dominico." Mama unwrapped his hand. She never flinched when she saw his palm bereft of skin, oozing with yellow fluid. Years of taking care of war wounds had hardened her. At first it was the boys returning from the front. Then it was tending Paulo, her own son. Now another one of her beautiful boys was disfigured by war. She would tend to his bandages. "American money goes a long way here."

"But you can't eat it." Papa responded. "Much of our food is going north and very little outside goods come out this far. Everyone does their part for the village."

"Except you. You've done enough for this damned place."

Dominico knew that his mother did not use profanity. When she said "damned" it was because she really believed that Villa de San Giuseppe was, indeed, damned.

CHAPTER 9

om settled easily into his old place at the dinner table. Sitting there, at the right side of his father's place was a strange comfort to him, as if had been sitting there for the last eighteen years. There was a natural belonging at the dinner table, a juxtaposition of time, history, and experience. He looked around the cottage. How little it had changed, still possessed of a dilapidated warmth, a comforting reassurance that everything was as it was, as it should be.

His eyes scanned from the stained walls and the drooping roof, the chairs worn from age and the chipped and faded table. The ever-present aroma of his mother's cooking filled the air just as it had in his youth, a moist, strong smell full of spices and sauces and other sources of pleasure. He looked at the faces of those around him. The family had changed. Mamma changed the least. She was fatter, her face rounder, but not marred with wrinkles like those carved into *le contadine* who labored in the fields. Her warmth never changed, nor did her smile, though her eyes held a certain combativeness that supplemented her natural strength. She could hold a grown man in place with a single gaze now. Dom never remembered her having that power before.

She never needed it before Dom went to America. Now she needed to hold Enrico in place, to take care of him. Before Dom left it was his unspoken job to take care of his father. He remembered that moment, years before, when he realized that he, in fact, took care of his father. He was looking at the world through a father's eyes, now. Dom was almost as old as his father was at the time he emigrated. Now Dom sat at the family table carrying the weight of filial responsibility, the malignant scars of toil and combat, his eyes heavy with the perpetual hope, pride and worry of fatherhood. He saw himself lifting, pushing, doing all the things that his young body bore easily, the things his father's shattered spine could no longer handle. At the time he did not believe that his father could no longer do the heavy lifting. He just thought it was his own task, a responsibility bequeathed by his father as a reward for hard work.

Enrico changed the most. He'd spent most of this last year in bed, his back injury knocking him down repeatedly. His body hung loosely from his shoulders. The old scar from Don Alfredo's bully's stretched purple across his forehead from the right temple. But for the scar his face was similar to *Nonno's* before Dom left, thin, like parchment, but backed by a different spirit, a defeated spirit. Enrico knew that no matter how many times he struggled to his feet now, it would never be permanent. He would be knocked down again, or, even worse, he would fall down. Falling down—that would be the end of him. A man can regain his feet after being knocked down. Indeed, there was something about a man that he must regain his feet. It was in his nerves. But falling down—could a man recover from falling down? One could read that question in his father's eyes.

Paulo, once a happy boy, was now a happy young man. Even his missing leg did not diminish him. Nor did it keep him off his feet—so to speak. He took every opportunity to laugh. "I survived the war, Dominico! The rest is easy. I lost my leg, but I still have my life, and I still have most of my mind. I'm never going to war again, Dominico, not even in my mind. I refuse." He walked on his prosthesis as though every step were a triumph of freedom.

Anna was weary, but not without energy. She was sparing with her energy, miserly keeping a reserve. The reserve she kept was for her little boy, and for the baby who was soon to come into the world. With her little boy, Renaldo, she was a fountain of joy and exuberance, but when he was napping so too did Anna rest her emotions. This was the result of recent emotional turmoil. At age twenty-three she was already a widow. Her husband died honorably engaged in combat with the Austrians. His body never came home. She could not hide the sadness from her deep eyes, but she could keep it from her voice. Anna knew that her new baby could hear her voice. She would never allow sadness to enter the lives of her children— her poor husband's children.

Hortensia married Raphaelo despite the paltry dowry. He became a man of importance in *Napoli* when the war began. Dom never understood why, nor could Hortensia explain what it was her husband did. He spent many weeks in Rome, during which time she would come home to help *Mama*. She was still without children, and without hope of ever having children at her age.

Ironically, it was with Hortensia that Dominico most related at this point. He could not explain why. Maybe it was the clear-eyed way she saw the world. It was the kind of clarity Dante evoked, the kind of clarity Dominico always aspired to.

She was away for the day helping the older women with the laundry. She came in for dinner and saw her prodigal brother for the first time. Dominico turned when he heard the door moan open. There was his sister, haggard from work, her hair coming loose from the kerchief meant to hold it in place. She was still lean, but solidly so, not the soft, gentle curve of youthful womanhood. In fact, she held the aura of a matron despite her childless state. Her eyes still played with rich, dark intelligence.

"Just when I was getting used to the peace and quiet around here." She said, unable to hold in her laughter just as she was unable to hold back her tears. She embraced him, throwing her full weight into his broad chest.

There they were, the family, all gathered around the table. The family, the love, devoted to each other in the face of years of separation. Dom thought about his own family back in America. His eyes became wet, but he knew this was not the time for shedding tears—not at the dinner table. Instead, he laughed and pulled from his pocket a tattered leather pocketbook. Inside were pictures of his family. Four war-torn and faded photographs of Giulianna, Dominico, Enrico and Regina, and a yellow, water-stained drawing Saralina, his youngest, whom he did not have time or money to photograph before he left.

"This is the rest of the family. The family in America." Dom smiled. "You'll meet them soon, I hope. I'll pay to bring them here when I get back."

Mama and the sisters admired the pictures. Papa called from the bedroom. "I hear you've been working in stone, son. Has America been good for you."

Dom smiled. Without hesitation he said, "America has been good. And it's been bad. But I guess it's been more good than bad. There's not a lot of room for mistakes in America. Giulianna has been getting my paychecks and working selling war bonds. If there's enough money saved, I hope to buy my own shed. I don't know if I'll be able to carve with this hand anymore." He looked at the white bandages. He realized that this was the first time admitting, even to himself, that his brief time working in stone was over. He stared at his hand. His mother did an excellent job wrapping it. He looked at Paulo's leg. For a moment he allowed his mind to lament, 'why couldn't it be my leg? Why did it have to be my hand?' But such thinking was foolishness, selfishness. 'It could have been your life, you ungrateful son of a bitch.'

"You'll do what you have to do." Mama said. "You're like your father."

"Maybe I'll come with you." Paulo smiled. "I've always wanted to go to America. I want to meet Mary Pickford?"

"I'm sure you will, Paulo," Hortensia laughed, "then they'll ship you right back."

Dom laughed. Hortensia was not far from wrong. "You'll all come. I'll make room for you all."

They all smiled, but there was a silence between their words.

The pallet was not much different from his memories. It still felt the same underneath him, but Paulo's weight was greater than it was almost twenty years earlier. It changed the feel, but not enough to take away from the realization that he was home again.

He and Paulo talked until well into the morning. They talked about the family, their work, eighteen years of successes and failures. Conspicuously, they never spoke of the war. They spoke until their speech slurred with the drunkenness of fatigue. Dominico's lids fell shortly after Paulo fell asleep. His mind entertained dreams of Pratolina...

...his uniform lay folded neatly on the grass beside him. Crimson stained the olive drab folds, but not the cool, bright green of the grass that swayed under a warm breeze. The blades brushed shyly against the soiled uniform with no more prejudice than it did the gray blanket.

"Do you remember this place, Dominico?" Pratolina purred as she stretched out on the blanket.

"Yes." He said. His hand lay gently against her thigh. He stared into the distant mountains, tall, stony. He could see the flash of artillery but could not hear the explosions. He was safe, far away from the fight.

"It's been so long, my darling. You've been away so long." She whispered into his neck. "What kept you from me for so long?" Her small breast brushed against his arm. He squeezed her thigh.

"Things are complicated in America." He said. "Some people get swallowed. Others are spit out."

"You got swallowed?" Her hair was so dark, so perfect.

Dom smiled. "Chewed and swallowed."

"Well, you're here now. You've come back to me. Hold me. Hold me tightly!"

Dom put his arm around her. She fell to him, then stopped, her eyes startled. They looked down at her thighs. There, the hand that only moments before rested gently on her thigh was now wrapped in bloody cotton. A crimson trickle traced its way down her golden skin.

Mortified, Dom apologized. He tried to clean her, to wipe the blasphemy, the disfigurement that was once his hand away from her.

"It's OK, Dom." She said in English. "It's OK." She pulled his chin up and looked into his eyes. But her eyes were different, darker, tired, less pretty. They were Giulianna's eyes.

"I love you." Dom said.

"I love you, too. I've always loved you, Dominico…"

"…Dominico." He stirred to the sound of a distant voice. Hortensia's voice.

The mountains faded into a mist and the confines of the Rossa home, dark and warm, came into view.

"Dominico." Hortensia's voice was urgent.

"What's wrong?" he whispered, mindful of Paulo who lay next to him. Dom always marveled at how soundly his younger brother slept. An attribute that was not a casualty of war. Dom tried to remember his last good night's sleep.

"I'd like to talk to you, away from the family." She said.

When he stepped from the cottage and saw his sister sitting in the moonlight, her expression frightened him. She looked at the distant moon as if wishing she were there. Hortensia never had a problem speaking her mind. She was often considered harsh for this characteristic, a trait that would have been lauded in a man. Dom always admired her openness, even when it angered him. What could be so pressing on her mind that she would travel to the moon to avoid saying it?

"This couldn't wait until morning?" he smiled, trying to break the ice.

"You are going to look for someone tomorrow. It's important that I talk to you now. Mama won't let you out of her sight before breakfast. Then you will spend the day looking for her."

"I..." Dom was paralyzed with disbelief. Was his sister a prophet? "Is something wrong? Papa? Mama? Tell me. What is it?"

"Maria Angelina."

It took a moment for the shock of this name coming from Hortensia's mouth to register in Dom's brain. When it did, he whispered, "Pratolina."

"The girl you went to America for."

He had only ever thought of her as Pratolina.

"I told you I knew about her. I never told anyone. I knew you wouldn't want anyone to know."

Dom shook his head. With his good hand he lowered himself onto the step next to his sister. "I wanted everyone to know. It just wasn't prudent."

"No, I don't suppose it was."

"Do you know where she is? I was going to look for her, but didn't know where to begin. The *latifundi* is a ruin."

Dom looked into his sister's sad eyes. Her eyes were never sad. Angry, sometimes, but never sad. "What is wrong with her? Does she need anything? Maybe I can help."

Hortensia shook her head, then silenced him with her fingers.

"She's dead, Dominico."

Dom was silent. His expression never changed. 'Dead.' The thought of it was too unrealistic, like thinking about the sun going out or the stars falling from the sky.

"I'm sorry, Dominico. I thought you should know before you went looking for her. I thought you should know from family. I'm sure you cared for her, loved her, very much."

"She can't be dead. You must be mistaken. She was younger than me. She was healthy. She can't be dead. You are wrong." Dom shook, a cold fever enveloped him. He was angry with his sister for making such a cruel statement. Dead! Ridiculous! Pratolina was alive.

"No," Hortensia was gentle, but stern. "She left the village shortly after you left for America. I thought she'd gone to be with you. I thought that until I heard about your plans to marry Giulianna. Then she came back a few years ago. She and her young sister. She lived above *Signore* Scalponni, the dressmaker. You remember *Signore* Scalponni, the one with the candy. She lived over his shop. She sewed for him. Then the fevers came." She sobbed, responding to her brother's tears. "I'm sorry, Dom. I'm terribly sorry. I didn't know her well. She helped make some of my dresses. The very dress I'm wearing, in fact. I knew about the two of you, but I never thought it proper, especially since you were married."

Dom leaned forward and buried his face in his hands. Tears flowed between his fingers, soaking the bandages. He pressed his fingers into his eyes to staunch the flow, but it was useless. The tears fell in streams and the sobs were uncontrollable. Hortensia rubbed his back, her hand making that strange sensation where the chains had left their scar so many years ago.

"I should have told you when it happened. I honestly never thought you would come back."

Dom held his hand up and tried to stand on weak, trembling legs.

"Where...where do I ...pay respects?"

CHAPTER 10

The early morning sun had not yet pierced the horizon. It gave notice of its impending arrival by painting the sky a misty blue fading off into a receding darkness in the west. The still, night air was beginning to stir, its gentle stretch in expectation of the coming day. Dom walked up the hill and entertained pleasant thoughts that his sister was mistaken. It was another Maria Angelina, or it was a different name entirely. His Pratolina was alive and well. Her broad, white smile behind supple lips, that honey sweet skin still graced the earth. Dom wondered what she looked like. Surely, she had aged. He was certain that she had aged well. Perhaps some wrinkles, a little extra weight around the hip. One thing was certain. She still lived. Yes, this was not a day for death. This was a day to breathe life with one you loved, to awaken memories...to...

Dom was not quite sure what he would do when he found her. Things were different now. He was not seventeen. He was married. He loved his wife. He had all those scars. His eyes were clear, unclouded by dreams, far seeing but never far from cold reality. Yes, all those scars, and no doubt, she had them, too.

No, things could not be the same, but they could be... something. He could only know by finding her, by looking into her eyes. He hoped that, upon seeing her, some of the clouds would return to his vision and he would know the happiness of childhood.

Such pleasant musings were short lived. The name on the tombstone was clear before his eyes. She was dead, and now a woman whom he had never met was taking him to see his daughter. A daughter he never even knew he had.

"The stone was nice, wasn't it?" Cecilia smiled.

"It was nice."

"It was donated by the church. Pratolina did a lot for the church. She sewed the vestments. She even helped with the books. Her father was a bookkeeper, you know."

"I know."

"She was very giving with her time."

Dom nodded. His mind was far away.

"So, the church bought the stone and commissioned the best stone carver in Campania to do the work."

Dom stopped. His boots scuffed the sandy road causing small swirls of dust around his feet. Cecilia's smile grew and she nodded.

"My father carved the stone?"

"Your father carved the stone."

Dom was sure this was significant at a deep level. There was a message in this only he could not imagine what it was. He started walking again, the back of his battered hand against his head, his brow furrowed.

Thoughts of his father carving the tombstone for his son's lover sank into him. He heard his father say, "be like stone." Be like stone. Stand firm, heavy on the earth forever—nothing can move you. Stand against the elements that pound you, seek to fell you, topple you. Stone is forever.

Could he have known? Could he have intuited that it was her spirit that guided the rise and fall of his hammer, the dance of his blade against the stone? Dom shook his head. This was too much.

"Let's stop and rest here a moment." Dom held out his bad hand and she stopped.

He was not tired. Rather, he was weighed down with history and emotion and the nearing end of a long journey. There seemed to be so many roads ahead of him. So many directions to turn. So much on his shoulders, over his soul.

"We'll stop in the shade of the old ruins. Come." He led her to a crumbling wall.

Cecilia followed. They walked across the field to the old Roman ruins that Papa would point to during their walks together. The last vestiges of the Roman Empire—stone. She sat on the wall, expecting Dom to sit with her. To her surprise, he walked through the ruins as if searching for something.

Most of the stones of what was once an imposing building lay scattered on the ground. The stones that remained, at least. Most of the stones were long since carted off to build other dwellings. Even his father despoiled the ruins when the necessity for material called for it. The result, the purpose of this building, the story behind it, was lost in the darkness of a neglected history.

Here were the insets that once held handsome statues carved by the ancients. The statues were carried away long ago by looters, perhaps the original Vandals from whom the word was coined. Indeed, no statues stood in this place for many hundreds of years. Even their broken pedestals were crumbling into dust and ground into fragments.

Dom was well versed in what few examples of stone carving remained. His father pointed them all out. Some were concealed in the contortions of the old building. Ancient, faded faces peered through the thick mist of time. Their features were worn down, their expressions indistinguishable. Here and there distorted bodies, some human, some equine, one canine, melted into the stone from which it was called forth. There, on the vine covered floor was once a mosaic, most of its tile lifted and lost. Cacti and weeds pushed through the cracks.

There was a time when these figures whispered to him. He thought he knew their secret. He was wrong. They were nothing more than the faint murmurings of ghosts.

Only now the phantoms screamed at him, and their secret was carved into his mind. Stone is not forever.

Stone is cracked and crushed and carved by the elements, by human hands, until it becomes an ethereal dust. Stone disappears, yields to those forces that will not yield to its tenaciousness or indifference. Stone is not forever. It is just another element. Like all elements, it has a fiery birth, a solid vitality, and a slow, wearing death. And in between...yes...in between...

The world that had pressed on his shoulders for so long lifted, relieving him of burden.

"I'm ready to go," he whispered, catching Cecilia off guard.

They walked in silence through the town. Dust swept across their feet. Cecilia, who seemed at first to prompt Dom's steps now struggled to keep up with his pace.

"She'll be at the tailor shop." Anna pointed. "Signore Scalponni has very little business, since the war, but he always finds work for Pratolina's daughter...for your daughter."

"What is her name?"

"Francesca Rossa."

"Rossa?" Once again Dom stopped short, almost tripping over himself. This woman had a discomforting way of throwing information of unexpected weight.

"Mastradelfiori is her middle name. You and I are the only ones who know her real name. She knows, of course, but she has never told anyone."

Dom smiled with pride. His gait never slowed as they approached the tailor's shop. He was nervous, apprehensive, but not hesitant. He wanted more than anything to see his daughter, but did she want to see him? How would she respond? He did not allow himself the time to think about it, like jumping from a trench into enemy fire. With one motion he jerked open the door.

"*L'Americano!*" *Signore* Scalponni smiled and reached for Dominico. Dom never looked at *Signore* Scalponni as the tailor placed two kisses on his cheek. "It's good to have you here." He said in broken English.

"*Sono uno paesano. Mi chiamo Dominico Rossa, Signore.*"

The old man stepped back and stared at the tall, American soldier.

"Dominico? Dominico Rossa?" He hugged Dom with a tight embrace. "I did not know you were back..."

Dom paid no attention.

There, on the far side of the shop a young woman stood separating fabrics.

'Pratolina?' Dom thought. It was her, the very image of his lost love. The same black hair hung over a honeygold face. Her dark eyes were soft and bright. It was as she looked on the day he left for America.

What could he say to her? How does one begin such a conversation?

Cecilia broke the silence.

"Francesca," she placed a gentle hand on the girl's back and turned her to face Dom, "this is your father."

The young woman lifted her head. At that point Dom could see beyond the ephemeral features she shared with his Pratolina. Something was different when she looked into his eyes. He could see part of himself in her, far away, intangible. She was her mother's daughter, but she was his offspring.

Dainty fingers twisted in the fabric.

She looked away, looked through the fabric.

"Mama said you would come."

"I've come."

Her eyes snapped forward, stared into his. "Are you going to take me home?"

He reached for her, and she fell into his arms.

"Yes, I'll take you home. I'll take you to America."

Finito

ACHNOWLEDGEMENTS

This book is a work of historical fiction. All major and minor characters described are fictional, though many of the stories shared are variations of real-life stories that I have had the good fortune to be exposed to throughout my life. The list of dynamic storytellers in my family, especially those of the beautiful Italian tradition, who inspired great characters like Dominico and Enrico, Dante and Sara, even Madison Rice and Heaney, are too many to mention. Most prominent among them is my father, Joseph Andoscia, who nurtured my love of stories and history. His personal story spanned one-hundred and six years, from the end of World War I into the third decade of the twenty-first century. May we all live to tell such wonderful stories!

I endeavored to be as historically accurate as possible. Descriptions of specific historical events such as the Triangle Shirtwaist Fire, the Battle of Cantigny, the Battle of Mount Grappa, are all drawn from primary sources. More generalized events, like the labor strikes, riots, and sabotage are also drawn from primary sources, but do not reference a singular event.

Like any fiction author, I did exercise some poetic license. For instance, Dante's description of Theodore Roosevelt's response to the lynching of Italian suspects in New Orleans is accurate based on the president's own correspondence. However, it is unlikely a man of Dante's station would be privy to such information at that time. The rally with "Big Jim" Haywood, Mother Jones, and Joseph Ettor is pulled from an actual event, but it did not take place in New York at that time...at least not to the best of my knowledge.

To get the history right, I drew from many sources. My most common starting points were *La Storia: Five Centuries of the Italian American Experience* by Jerre Mangione and Ben Morreale and *A Concise History of Italy* by Christopher Duggan. My go-to sources related to Italian culture, traditions, and mindset were *Italian American Folklore* by Frances M. Malpezzi and William M. Clements and *The Italians: A Full-Length Portrait Featuring Their Manners and Morals* by Luigi Barzini. The racism and bigotry experienced by the turn of the century Italian immigrants could not have been elaborated without Salvatore J. LaGumina's *WOP! A Documentary History of Anti-Italian Discrimination*. The primary sources that opened chapters 3, 6, and 11 in Part III were drawn from this source. The illustrated history, *Land of the Free: A Journey to the American Dream* by David Sean Paludeine, with its wealth of photographs, was very helpful in establishing a realistic setting for the novel.

I learned a great deal from doing the research for this book, but a prized discovery for me was the history of Barre, Vermont. From the start, Dominico Rossa was imagined as a stone carver, a trade for which I had exactly zero prior knowledge. I stumbled upon Barre in my research. Mari Tomasi's novel *Like Lesser Gods*, set in Barre, helped me add some flesh to Dominico's plot.